Kathryn Freeman started her w
but soon realised trying to decip
for her. In 2011, backed by he
pharmaceutical science to begin life as a self-employed writer.

She lives with a husband who asks every Valentine's Day whether
he has to bother buying a card again this year (yes, he does) so the
romance in her life is all in her head.

www.kathrynfreeman.co.uk

X x.com/KathrynFreeman1
f facebook.com/kathrynfreeman

Also by Kathryn Freeman

BOOKED FOR SUMMER

KATHRYN FREEMAN

One More Chapter
a division of HarperCollins*Publishers*
1 London Bridge Street
London SE1 9GF
www.harpercollins.co.uk
HarperCollins*Publishers*
Macken House, 39/40 Mayor Street Upper,
Dublin 1, D01 C9W8, Ireland

This paperback edition 2025
First published in Great Britain in ebook format
by HarperCollins*Publishers* 2025
1

A catalogue record of this book is available from the British Library

ISBN: 978-0-00-872925-7

Printed and bound in the UK using 100% Renewable Electricity
by CPI Group (UK) Ltd

Chapter One

Jade's toes, currently slotted into a pair of sparkly flip-flops, curled with excitement as the train pulled into the station. Okay, maybe a teeny bit of her still wished she was heading to a tropical island because, duh, what sane, sun-worshipping, book-obsessed person wouldn't want to spend three months in a place where they could read steamy romances on perfect white sandy beaches? This Nantucket place though, the one she'd never heard of a few months ago … well it certainly wasn't Twickenham. In the guidebook she'd devoured on the plane to Boston, she'd seen pictures of sandy beaches, though they did look a bit windswept. Also, marinas with long wooden pontoons, lighthouses and deep blue waters dotted with white sailing boats. Nantucket had a small-town vibe, so the book said, but with a heavy dose of glamour, taste and style.

She'd had a little snigger to herself when she'd read that. In her twenty-five years on the planet, she'd managed Devon, Margate and a week in Spain. A *culturally sophisticated* island in the Atlantic off Cape Cod was not a place she'd ever expected to find herself. Especially one that she'd read wasn't the playground of millionaires, but of *billionaires*.

God knows what they'd make of her.

The Cape Flyer – even the name of the train she'd taken from Boston to Hyannis sounded posh – finally drew into the station. Butterflies flapped in her belly as she stuffed her Kindle into her bag. She didn't even mind that she'd left the devilishly handsome billionaire in a state of tortured agony as he watched the woman he'd fallen for walk away from him. Daft sod hadn't told her how he felt. Thankfully, there were still another few chapters left for him to come to his senses, but for now, Jade was more focused on her own story. Her own new chapter.

The train came to a halt and she leapt out of her seat, clean forgetting the half-eaten bag of gummy bears on her lap, which cartwheeled into the air, landing on the lap of the woman across the aisle who let out a disdainful sigh.

'You seem in a rush to get off,' her fellow passenger remarked as she brushed the poor buggers onto the floor. 'Where are you headed?'

Jade's happy buzz was too great to be dimmed by the condescending look. 'Nantucket.'

The woman's eyes flicked from Jade's flip-flops up to her white shorts and then further, to the pink T-shirt straining over her boobs, before landing on her face and giving her a tight-lipped smile. 'It's not a usual holiday destination for someone … like you.'

She let the insult roll off her. It didn't mean it didn't niggle, didn't rub at old scars. 'Oh, I'm not on holiday. I'm going to manage a bookstore over the summer. Little Bay Book Shack. Isn't that the cutest name? I originally applied to run one in the Maldives, but this sounds way cooler, don't you think?'

The woman frowned, studying Jade. 'You don't look like a bookstore manager.'

'Oh, I'm not one, not yet.' Jade pushed a smile on her face. 'I'm a publishing assistant.' It was the title she'd told her parents when she'd got the job, hoping they'd be impressed, at least more impressed than they had been with her waitressing job. Sadly, while she loved the idea of working with books, so far all *publishing assistant* had turned out to be was a posh name for the office dogsbody.

Brushing off the depressing thought – she was here to make new, positive memories – Jade reached up to grab her backpack from the overhead rack. Damn, it was wedged, and God knows what on because five-foot-two flip-flop wearers had no hope of seeing up there. Taking hold of the strap, she gave it a determined tug. 'Buggeration.' The backpack flew out of her hand and fell onto the floor. She bent to pick it up, giving the keyring she'd secured on the zip an absent-minded stroke.

'Stop staring, Roger,' the woman hissed to the man next to her. 'It's not like you've never seen breasts before.'

You'd be taken more seriously if you wore less revealing clothes.

Jade shook off the memory of her sister's words. She liked looking sexy. It made her feel confident, even when inside she was bricking it. Like now, because even though she'd not stepped foot on it yet, she knew Nantucket was a million miles away from what she was used to.

And way too sophisticated for a girl in shorts, flip-flops and a Kindle packed with steamy billionaire romances.

'I suspect he's staring at my good-luck charm,' Jade supplied, waving the keyring and letting Roger off the hook. 'I bought it years ago because I kept being told I was a bookworm, so I figured a bookworm should have a worm. But then someone told me that what I thought was a cute fury worm was actually a caterpillar. Worms and caterpillars are pretty similar, though, don't you think?'

She didn't get an answer, just an excruciatingly polite smile. Still, at least her boobs were no longer under discussion.

Stepping into the aisle she shuffled along to the end of the carriage. When she spotted her neon pink suitcase she went to reach for it but a male arm got there first.

'Don't want a lovely little thing like you straining yourself, honey. I'll carry it off for you.'

Jade turned to find Roger giving her a broad wink. Over the top of his bald head, the woman he'd been sitting with was staring daggers at them.

'Tell me, Roger, the woman you're travelling with, is she your wife?'

He gave her a puzzled frown. 'Yes.'

'And you've been married for how long?'

'Thirty years.' He shrugged, his shirt pulling over his paunch. 'Give or take.'

'So why are you helping me, someone you don't know and will never meet again, over the person you share your life with?'

His face reddened and he opened his mouth, then closed it again, much like a trout.

'Bye Roger, and Roger's wife,' she added, peering round him.

Ignoring their nonplussed looks, she gave them both a little wave before lugging her case off the train.

Shame he'd been fixated on her boobs, because the thing was frigging heavy, but women had to stick together. Even sour-faced ones.

Once out of the station, she opened Google Maps on her phone and set off to the harbour, dragging her case behind her along the red brick path until she reached the wharf. And, wow, it was a pretty harbour: fishing boats jostling alongside sailing boats. Inhaling a lungful of fresh sea air, she set down her case and reread the email containing instructions for her pick-up.

Ignore the ferry sign, head instead for the Haven Resort water-taxi pontoon.

Apparently The Little Bay Book Shack was next door to a five-star resort, and she was hitching a ride on their boat.

Trundling her case behind her, she made her way along the waterfront, stopping at the wooden pontoons to look for a sign. She paused at a gleaming white motor yacht and gave a silent high-five when she read the name written in elegant font across the side. Holy cow. Now that's what she called a boat transfer. It looked like it should have been moored at Monaco, waiting for an elegant film star in a floaty silk dress and uber chic shades, or a guy in a cream linen suit and Ray-Ban's.

Not a travel-worn office minion in flip-flops.

But you're not a minion now, not for the next three months. With a grin, she picked up her case and hopped on board. Jade Taylor, formerly of Twickenham, was heading to work on a frigging thirty-metre yacht.

'Hello?' She tapped on the smoked glass door.

It slid open, and as she craned her neck to look up at the man on the other side, her jaw almost fell to the floor. That guy in the linen suit and Ray-Bans? He was right *there*. The suit was pale blue not cream, and the shades were slipped into the top pocket of the jacket, but the whole image screamed hot, sexy film star. Jet-black hair, square jaw, steel-grey eyes, cheekbones that would make a model sigh. There was an edge to his looks – dark stubble, a scar that bisected his right eyebrow – that stopped him from looking too pretty, too perfect.

And left him looking instead like the hottest man she'd ever come across.

'Er, hi, I'm Jade.' Cool eyes stared back at her. Feeling self-conscious, she rubbed her sweaty palms on the shorts she'd slopped clam chowder soup down during yesterday's mad dash tour of Boston. 'Are you waiting for the transfer, too?'

His eyebrows scrunched together. 'Sorry?'

'The transfer to Haven Resort. Oh, wait, are you the driver?' He didn't look like a typical taxi driver, but this was a *water* taxi.

A humming, awkward silence met her question, interrupted only by the gentle lap of water.

'You're waiting for a transfer to Haven Resort?' he said finally.

Her belly fluttered. He even had a film star voice, all deep and gravelly with an American drawl. Still, he wasn't exactly friendly. 'That's why I'm on the boat. And I presume you're on it because you drive it.'

One of his dark brows arched upwards. 'I own it.'

'Oh.' She knew a lot of taxi drivers owned their own cars, but this was another league. 'But you drive it as well?'

He slid his hands into his pockets. 'I sail her, yes.'

Sail, not drive, got it. Though the lack of an actual sail surely made him wrong, not her. She glanced around at the jetty. 'Are we waiting for anyone else?'

His gaze swept her up and down. 'You're expecting me to take you to the Haven Resort?'

Was there an emphasis on *you*, or had she imagined it? She straightened her back. 'That is where I'm heading, yes.' Fumbling around in her bag, she pulled out her phone. 'My instructions say to head to the Haven Resort dock and catch the waiting water taxi.'

'The Haven dock is the next one over.'

She frowned. 'But it says Haven on the side of this boat.'

He sighed and rested his hand against the door frame. It tightened the white shirt across his chest, giving her a tantalising glimpse of tanned skin and dark chest hair. '*Ocean Haven*. It's the name of my boat.'

'Oh.' Shit. Embarrassed now, she started to giggle, which was a habit she really wished she could break. 'That's a bit of a coincidence.' Those eyes levelled with hers. Stormy grey, mysterious looking, they provided no clue as to what he was thinking. 'So, I guess I'll just hop off your boat and...' She motioned towards a less impressive-looking boat moored up on the next pontoon. 'Skedaddle onto that one.'

His gaze stayed on hers for another few humming beats before finally following the direction of her hand. 'He appears to be waiting for you.'

And now she saw a weathered-looking man dressed in a white shirt and black shorts, standing at the front, looking over at them. 'So he does.'

She gave her new driver/sailor/taxi a wave and went to pick up her case, but Mr Film Star let out a muffled curse and took it from her, stepping easily off the boat and onto the wooden pontoon. Then he turned and held out his hand to her. As she settled her hand into his, her tongue glued itself to the roof of her mouth. Warm, calloused, strong, his touch sent sparks racing across her skin and when his gaze collided with hers, something hot and achy pulsed between them. Was he ... was he *attracted* to her? Did he feel this, too? But in a flash his hand was gone, and with it the moment.

Pulse still racing, she watched him stride ahead of her to the next jetty and hand her case over to the guy on the boat.

'Um, thank you for carrying my case,' she said when she finally caught up. He nodded, his gaze coming to rest on her rucksack, and the keyring. 'Do you think he looks like a caterpillar, or a worm?'

He stared at her blankly. 'Does it matter?'

'It does to him.' The man's eyes flew open, and she liked that she'd caught him off balance. Evened her up a bit.

'Worms are brown, he ... *it* is green.' He shook his head, as if he couldn't believe he was having the conversation. 'Enjoy your stay, Jade.'

Her stomach swooped at the sound of her name in that deep

drawl. A second later he was gone, those long legs striding back towards his boat.

'Welcome, Miss.' Her new driver – she was sticking to that. They used a wheel, didn't they? – gave her a wide smile. 'You're going to Haven Resort, yes?'

'Um, well, not exactly.' Seeing as he seemed friendly, she added in a whisper, 'I'm actually going to work in the bookstore next door.'

'Ah, you're Flo's girl.' He gave her a conspiratorial wink. 'Don't tell anyone but we have an arrangement. I let her shop use the resort water taxi, and she sorts the wife out with books whenever she wants one. So maybe we'll see more of each other. I'm George, the wife is Emma.'

She held out her hand to shake his. 'Pleased to meet you, George. And I look forward to talking books with your Emma.'

He chuckled. 'Careful, don't go being too friendly or she'll never leave your shop. So, have you been to Nantucket before?'

'Nope, it's my first time.'

'Ah, well it's an odd mix of quaint and sophisticated but there's something for everyone. And the scenery is spectacular.'

Involuntarily, her gaze tracked the tall, lean, dark-haired figure as he climbed back onto his motor yacht. 'I can imagine.'

Liam resisted the impulse to stop and … what? Stare? Walk back to continue a conversation about worms, for Christ's sake. But God, the desire to turn around, to have those enormous blue eyes rest on him a little bit longer … it was almost overwhelming. He was used to female attention – amazing what a bit of money could do – but he wasn't used to enjoying it. Craving more of it.

And he knew where she was heading. The same place he was.

The smart side of his brain told him he didn't need the

distraction, and there was no way the blonde Brit with the curvy figure crammed into a bubble-gum-pink top and tiny shorts, would be anything but a distraction.

The side of his brain connected to his dick told him a distraction was exactly what he needed while he tried to juggle expanding the Haven Resort empire, managing the Nantucket resort (thanks to the resignation of his resort manager) and finally completing the purchase of the neighbouring wharf from a highly eccentric seventy-year-old he'd been trying to pin down for over a year. And who'd just wriggled out of yet another meeting.

If you'd not been so rude, that curvy blonde bombshell of a distraction could be with you now, in your boat. Looking up at you from under her lids with those big eyes.

He shook away the image and cast off the mooring lines. Sliding open the doors on the main deck, he walked forward through the salon to the bridge. Unable to help himself, he turned to watch the Haven transfer set off. A blonde figure, dressed in bright pink, sat on the aft deck, face turned towards him. No, face turned towards his boat. She couldn't possibly see him through the tinted glass.

Enough. He yanked his phone out of his pocket and dialled Jeremy, guest-services manager at Nantucket and, whether he wanted it or not, now his right-hand man. 'I'm on my way.'

'Sorry, who is this?'

Liam scowled down at the phone. 'You know damn well who.'

'Well, okay, I might know because I might have you saved in my contact list under Big Bad Boss Man, but a few pleasantries wouldn't go amiss.'

God, the man was frustrating. If he wasn't such an organised pain in the ass adored by customers and staff alike, and if he hadn't made himself indispensable since the resort had opened, and Liam wasn't already one key member of staff down, he might suggest Jeremy find another resort owner to piss off. 'I'm warning you I'm on my way, rather than turning up unannounced, how much *pleasanter* do you want me to be?'

Jeremy let out a pained-sounding sigh. 'I suppose in your world that was a kindness. Okay boss, see you soon. We'll get the red carpet out for you.'

Liam ended the call, well aware the man was being sarcastic. Neither Jeremy nor Leroy, the restaurant manager and Jeremy's fiancé, tried to kiss his butt, which Liam had a grudging respect for. But he was the boss, something he'd worked fucking hard to achieve, and he figured he was owed some respect.

Speaking of respect, or lack of it, he punched in the number for Flo.

'Ah, Mr Haven, I thought you might call.'

He forced a calm into his voice that he wasn't feeling. 'You didn't bring me the signed contract.'

'I know, but I checked my horoscope and today wasn't a good one for signing deals.'

Give him strength. 'Tomorrow, then?'

A pause, then a tinkle of laughter. 'You're an Aries, aren't you? Blunt, assertive, can be seen as aggressive. Often quick-tempered and impatient.'

'It's not my birth date that's making me impatient.' He exhaled, pinching the bridge of his nose. 'This is the fourth time you've said you'll sign and haven't. Do you want to sell or not?'

Flo owned the wharf next to the land he'd bought five years ago and had turned into a thriving resort. He wanted the wharf for many reasons, not least because it was where the water taxi and his own yacht were docked.

'I don't want to sell.' She paused, then let out a gentle sigh. 'But I'm not getting any younger, and my children need the proceeds.'

'Well, next time you cancel, the offer gets reduced.' He paused, decided to drive the point home. 'You know it's not worth what I'm paying to anyone else.'

She humphed. 'I've got old and lazy. With the right person in charge, the shop and the wharf could be a viable asset.'

'You're using prime real-estate land to sell books.'

'To sell beautiful books that guests in your swanky resort happily part with their money to enjoy. I hope you'll remember that when you take it over.'

'When it's mine, I'll do what I want with it.' He was a lot of things, but he wasn't a liar. Still, he couldn't bring himself to say he'd be bulldozing Little Bay Book Shack (it was every bit as kitschy as it sounded). 'But as I've already told you, I'll honour any commitments you've made.'

'I suppose that's the most I can hope for.' Her voice sounded resigned, and he was glad. Whimsical bookstores had no place in the hard reality that was life.

'I'm here for a few days.' He decided not to tell her he was stuck for a while until he hired a new manager. 'I expect to receive a signed contract from you.'

Shoving his phone back into his pocket, he gave the bow a kick with the thruster to pull away from the berth. Then he headed in the direction of Nantucket, and the Haven Resort – one of three under his name, though this was the flagship resort. The first, the largest, and the one that had given him the most satisfaction.

He'd been fourteen when he'd vowed to turn Haven into a name that was respected, not sniggered at or dismissed. With his recent acquisition of the waterfront next to the Nantucket resort, and the wharf nearly in his grasp, he was well on the way to keeping that promise.

On that positive note, he pushed the throttle in, relishing the shift in power, the list of the boat as it cut through the waves. This was why he travelled by sea, not air. Nothing beat the feeling of freedom that sailing solo could give him.

Maybe tonight he'd look out for the blonde. It was unusual to see a young woman travelling here alone. Most of the guests were couples or families, who came to get away from city life and relax in the beauty of the island. Whatever it was that drew her, was her business. But if he locked eyes with her again, and if hers held the same spark of arousal they had when he'd taken her hand, he might forget his no-guest rule and see if she was willing to mix that business with pleasure.

Chapter Two

Jade was in love. Seriously, she didn't think the sight of Ryan Gosling emerging naked from the sea would make her swoon any more than her first view of Little Bay Book Shack.

The view coming into Nantucket had been jaw-dropping enough – long stretches of sandy beach, large, grey-wood houses and a gorgeous, stubby white lighthouse with a black top perched at the harbour entrance. But this, the wooden shack sitting proudly on the wharf ahead of her, white Georgian windows and grey tiled roof to match the soft grey wooden slats. Wow, just wow. A mix of quaint and elegant, of historic yet endearingly cute, the sight snatched the breath from her lungs. The entire waterfront rocked a row of similar-looking grey wooden buildings set on a red brick walkway, interspersed with olde worlde lampposts and dozens of flowerpots that burst with colours; pink, white, purple, yellow. All set against a backdrop of glinting blue sea.

It was so tasteful, so pretty. So vibrant. So different to anything she'd ever seen.

George expertly manoeuvred the boat alongside the jetty and jumped off, securing it before giving a hand to the other customers – a pair of newlyweds who'd kept looking at each other instead of the awesome views, and a couple in their fifties dressed in what her gran would call 'posh' clothes; loose flowing trousers for the woman, chinos and a blazer for the guy. Once they were all happily on their way, two porters from the resort wheeling their luggage, George turned back to Jade.

'Do you want some help with your case, honey?'

She looked at the short distance to the bookstore and laughed. 'I reckon I can manage.'

'Well, I'll leave you to it, then. Be sure to look out for me and the wife. Nantucket's a small island, we're bound to bump into each other.'

He took her hand and helped her off the boat. She didn't miss the way his gaze kept firmly above her shoulders. Good on him, and lucky Emma.

Heaving in a lungful of fresh, salty air she started to walk along the small wooden pontoon. The wheels of her case made a clickety-clack noise as they bumped over the planks, sounding loud over the backdrop of waves lapping gently against the jetty.

With every step she took towards the shop, excitement pushed up against the nerves. When she finally came to a halt in front of her home for the next three months, her heart was thumping against her ribs.

Shack didn't seem the right word. It was more an upmarket, two-storey cabin. Roses wound around the trellis to the right of the front door which was painted in a shade of subtle off-white she suspected she'd find on a Farrow & Ball colour chart and matched the window frames. A peek in through the lattice-style window drew a gasp from her. Driftwood shelves, quirky and asymmetrical, burst with books in a way that would have any book lover swooning, their eye-catching covers a dramatic splash of colour against the whitewashed walls. Nestled in the bay-fronted window and in the colour of the Atlantic Ocean she'd just crossed, was a comfy sofa, perfect for a quiet read while glancing out at the cloudless blue sky.

Heart beating furiously, Jade peered behind the plant pot, found the key safe and punched in the numbers, her fingers shaking so much it took her several attempts. Finally, she had the key in her sweaty palm and unlocked the door. She was about to skip inside – this was definitely a skip moment – when her phone rang.

'Flo,' she answered giddily when she saw who it was. 'I've just got here and it's amazing. No, what's a better word than amazing, because amazing is what I say to a really good pizza.'

The husky laugh of her employer echoed back. 'Have you found the key okay?'

'Yes and I'm just about to go inside. God, I can't believe I'll be working here for three months. It's like I'm dreaming – and if I am, please don't wake me up.' A beat of silence, followed by Flo clearing her throat, and then … nothing. 'Hello, Flo, are you still there?'

'Yes, sorry honey. It's a bad line,' Flo replied finally, 'there is something we need to discuss, but I'll do that in person when I see you. Meanwhile, I'll give you a few days to settle in. Daisy, who you're replacing, said she'll pop in sometime today to give you a quick rundown before she flies home.'

'Hiya!' Jade looked round with a start, only to see a pretty brunette walking towards her, waving. One she recognised from a photo.

'I think that's Daisy now,' she told Flo.

'Fabulous. I'll call you again soon. Enjoy!'

She barely had a chance to end the call before Daisy ran over and hugged her as if she was a long-lost friend, not a stranger who was taking over her job. 'Welcome to Nantucket. I'm Daisy.' She laughed. 'Maybe I should have said that before I practically mauled you. It's just I'm so happy to see a fellow book lover.

You're going to have *the* best time here. I'm sad to be leaving, but I missed my family and friends, so I'm also mega excited to see them again.' She laughed. 'Well, for about five minutes until they start to annoy me!'

Jade was used to being the talkative one, but it was clear Daisy had her beaten. 'I know what you mean. I'm going to miss my family, too.' She thought of her parents, of their reaction to her coming out here. *Are you sure you're not biting off more than you can chew?* Of her sister, Lauren, who was a registrar in emergency medicine and, if their parents' reaction to *that* was anything to go by, could apparently walk on water, too. Not that she wasn't in awe of everything Lauren had done. She just didn't need it rammed down her throat all the time. 'But right now, I'm glad of the break from them.'

'Come on, then, let's get you settled.' Daisy grabbed Jade's case and headed towards the rickety looking stairs at the back. 'First, I'll show you upstairs where you'll be living, then we can go through the shop.'

By the time Daisy had finished the tour an hour later, Jade felt like she'd been dragged through a tornado. It wasn't the flat, it took all of five minutes to show her the open-plan studio with a small bathroom and kitchenette. Nope, it was the bookstore and what she was expected to do that had left her dazed.

'I think that's everything,' Daisy concluded, stepping away from the computer. 'But don't worry, the pace here is slow so you'll have plenty of time to get used to things. Customers come in waves and they're never in a rush. Most are on vacation and out for a browse, though I hear it gets crazy busy with tourists on the island in the summer so you might find it harder work than I did.'

Jade ran her eyes over the rows and rows of shelves lined with books of every shade and colour, set against the neutral walls and bleached wood floor. Then skipped to the deep blue sofa, and next to it a glass-topped coffee table made from pebbles and shells.

'It looks like the perfect place for choosing a book.' Perfect. The word bounced around her head. How was she supposed to make an impression, to leave a legacy, when the shop already looked so much better than anything she could have conjured up?

Daisy laughed. 'Don't worry, you'll have loads of time to enjoy it. The shop's opening hours are 9 a.m. till 5 p.m. but Flo always said to take an hour for lunch and if you have to go out during the day, to do a workshop or whatever, you can always pop the *Back Later* sign up. Oh, and it closes Sunday and Monday, so you get two full days off.' She gave Jade a nudge. 'Just make sure you keep the blog up to date so I can try and live vicariously through you while I'm back in the concrete jungle of New York.'

'Will do.' Nervous butterflies buzzed in her belly. She'd never written a blog, never run a workshop, never sold anything, unless food and drink counted from her stint as a waitress. Never even lived by herself, away from home. It was too late for doubts now, though. Somehow she'd managed to convince Flo she could do this. Now all she had to do was convince herself. 'Any advice for what to do when I'm not working?'

'Oh, you know, all the usual: chill on the beach, eat a lobster roll, take a boat trip to Martha's Vineyard.' Daisy winked. 'Have a holiday fling.'

Jade thought of how her last two relationships had ended. 'I think I'll give that last one a miss. I'm off men for a while.'

'Well, if you change your mind, Nantucket is renowned for being a playground for the rich and powerful. And you've got one right on your doorstep.' She fanned herself. 'The guy who owns the resort next door is seriously hot.'

Jade gaped at the slim, very attractive brunette, who she'd put at mid-thirties. 'You've slept with him?'

'Sadly, no, but I know someone, who knows someone, who has. Apparently, the woman came over on a short-term contract as a fitness instructor last year. She ended up having the hottest sex of her life one night with a guy she later found out was the resort owner. She'd wanted a repeat but was told by staff he'd already left the island so it never happened.'

'Have you actually met him?'

Daisy let out a dreamy-sounding sigh. 'Oh, yes. I fluttered my eyelashes in his direction a time or two, but he didn't take the hint.'

Privately, Jade wondered if the hotness of the guy was purely down to the fact he was loaded.

Daisy's phone bleeped. She glanced down at it and swore. 'I have to go. I'm heading back by plane and my lift is here to take me to the airport.' She gave Jade a final hug. 'Enjoy Nantucket. And remember, I'm only a phone call away if you need anything.'

As she watched Daisy make her way along the waterfront, Jade felt a pang of sadness. It would have been good to spend longer with her. To have a friend out here. Someone who actually knew how to run a frigging bookstore. Her stomach lurched and she turned to face the sea, letting the breeze flutter across her face, the clean air filter up her nostrils.

One step at a time. For the next three months, this wasn't just her work, it was her home. Surrounded by books, and with a beautiful island to explore, her adventure was about to begin.

Liam stood up from the desk and stretched out his legs. Fuck, he'd been sitting for too long. He wasn't an office man, he was a guy who liked to be on the move, *doing* rather than reading. And doing *alone*, he added irritably as a knock on the door disturbed him mid-pace. A second later, his visitor burst in. Dressed in a white shirt decorated with pink flamingos, paired with pink pants, he was … eye-catching.

'Most people knock, then wait to be asked in.'

Jeremy shrugged, the rebuke rolling off him like water off a flamingo's back. 'I thought we established that I'm not most people. That's why you hired me.'

Liam had recruited the guest-services manager five years ago when he'd built his first hotel on the island, later expanding it to become Haven Resort, Nantucket. Most times, they tolerated each other. Other times, the man deliberately, or so it seemed, found the right buttons to press. Ashley, the resort manager, had acted as a well-needed buffer between them but until he found a replacement for her, they were stuck trying to rub along together without incurring too many dents. 'What's gone wrong now?'

Jeremy frowned. 'Don't you mean how can you help me?'

'You don't need my help.' There was a reason he'd asked the man to act as deputy manager. 'If you've come to see me, it's to give me bad news.'

'Well, that kind of depends on your definition of bad. For some, bad would mean something serious, like a fire, or an outbreak of salmonella. For others—'

'Just tell me.' He'd had a brutal few days in Cape Cod, trying to buy land from a man in his late sixties who seemed to enjoy giving him the run-around. Liam half suspected he was being dangled on a string for the sheer entertainment of it. After that debacle, he'd travelled straight to Nantucket for a meeting that had been cancelled. Since then, he'd been stuck in this office for – he glanced at his watch – over four hours, making calls that should have been made last week, and scrolling through endless emails. He felt punch drunk with tiredness, his temper on a knife edge.

'Leroy said the delivery he's been waiting on still hasn't arrived, so we're running with very abridged menus tonight.'

Their rich guests only had a choice of five main courses instead of ten. 'And?'

'And the couple in the presidential suite say the shower isn't working. Of course, they have two, but—'

'The price they're paying, everything should be in full working order.' He worked in the service industry. Liam understood why his customers expected what they'd paid for, just as he understood why they'd get some bad reviews as a result of tonight's so-called limited menu. But when you'd lived in a room with a shared bathroom down the hallway and existed off canned soup from food banks because your grandma had lost one of her regular cleaning jobs, it was hard to feel too much sympathy. 'Give them my room. I'll sleep in the boat.' He had a perfectly good house on Martha's Vineyard, was having another one built on Nantucket, but he often preferred to spend the night on his yacht. There was something soothing about being on water. The gentle sway helped him sleep, something he'd had a problem with since boarding school.

'Right.' Jeremy shifted on his feet. 'Now, don't take this the wrong way. You are, of course, a joy to work with, but is there any update on a replacement for Ashley?'

'I'm working on it.'

Jeremy cleared his throat. 'You know there are rumours circulating about why she left.'

'I don't pay you to listen to rumours.'

'No, but if you told *me* why she left, I could quash the rumours and then you wouldn't be paying half your staff to listen to them.'

'It's nobody's business.' Hotel gossip was vicious – Liam knew from bitter experience. 'Anything else?' He sounded too blunt, but he needed to get out of these four walls and into a shower. Follow that with an unwinding drink at the bar, and then sleep for twelve hours.

Yeah, as if he'd ever managed more than four.

As always, Jeremy ignored his bad mood. 'That's all I have to ruin your day with for the moment. I'm sure I can find something more for tomorrow. Enjoy your evening, boss.'

After moving his suitcase onto the boat – he'd not had time to unpack so at least that made giving up his suite easy – Liam took a shower, dried off and looked longingly at the king-sized bed. His body wanted to collapse onto the mattress, but he knew his mind would refuse to rest with it. With a sigh, he dragged on a pair of shorts and a T-shirt and slipped on some flip-flops. The sun was setting as he headed towards the resort, painting the sky in vivid hues of pink and orange. This was his favourite time of the day on the island, the light more mellow, the hustle and bustle of the tourist crowds temporarily lulled as people disappeared back to their hotels for a shower before heading out to eat.

At the bar by the beach he spotted Leroy, Jeremy's partner, and the man responsible for the resort's three bars and restaurants. As if he sensed him, Leroy looked up from where he was talking with a group of guests and nodded in Liam's direction. He was almost the total opposite to his fiancé; rich brown skin to Jeremy's freckled white, dark hair to Jeremy's ginger. Also, quieter and more serious, which probably explained why Liam felt more comfortable dealing with him.

'Usual?' Leroy asked, slipping behind the bar.

Liam nodded. They often conversed like this, a single word, a look, a movement of the head.

Raising the glass – a double Macallan 18, neat – in salute, Liam wandered off towards the beach. Discarding his flip-flops, he walked into the sea and savoured the first sip of the smooth and slightly sweet whisky. Also ridiculously expensive, but that's why he'd first chosen it. When you didn't have money but were trying to bluff obscenely rich people into investing in you, drinking ludicrously expensive whisky was as important as wearing a Tom Ford suit and custom-made shirt. Six years later, and he'd developed a taste for the damn stuff.

An exclamation of surprise to his left caused him to turn, and that's when he saw her. The sexy blonde from the boat. She'd sunk into one of the sprawling sofas set on the sand and from the way she was frantically wiping at her sundress, she'd managed to spill her drink down herself.

Instinctively he set off towards her. He wished he could say it was the gentleman in him, wanting to help, but he knew himself better than that. This instinct was primal. Jade had oozed sex, and his body had suddenly decided sleep could wait.

'Jade. We meet again.'

She jerked around, her expression shifting from surprise to embarrassment to something that looked like the same crackling sexual awareness he was experiencing. 'Oh, it's you. Kicked anyone else off your boat recently?'

He felt a flash of shame. His grandma would slap him if she knew how rude he'd been. 'I apologise for earlier. You caught me at a bad moment.' He indicated towards the now empty cocktail glass in her hand. 'Can I buy you another?'

She nibbled on her bottom lip, which did not help his straining libido one little bit. 'That would be great, thanks. Unless you're doing it to watch me throw another cocktail down my dress, because let me tell you, once is definitely enough.'

I'm doing it because you fascinate me. And turn me on. He reached to take the glass and as his fingers curled round hers, his gaze wandered to the V of her dress. Immediately lust shot through him, every cell in his body now wide awake and primed to go. Inhaling, he breathed in the scent of coconut, of something floral, mixed with the sweet smell of cranberry juice. 'Sea Breeze?'

'It is a bit windy, sure, but it was more a case of misjudging how squashy these sofas are.' She winked and he found himself smiling back. Fuck, she was an almost irresistible combination of sex bomb and funny. 'How did you guess what I was drinking?'

'I recognise the smell.' He inhaled again, shifting ever so slightly so his body touched hers, feeling another pulse of heavy arousal at the quick intake of her breath. 'I'll bring a towel, to mop the rest of it off.' Stepping back, he looked down at where her dress now clung to the luscious curve of her tits and swallowed, hard. The things he could suddenly so vividly imagine doing to clean her up, had no business being spoken out loud.

Chapter Three

The moment the yacht owner with the film-star looks and come to bed eyes turned and headed for the bar, Jade collapsed back onto the sofa. Holy fuck. *He'd remembered her name. And he'd offered to buy her a drink.* She wasn't so stupid that she couldn't read a come-on when she saw it. Sure, he had her down as easy, but the fact was, she, Jade Taylor, had attracted the attention of a seriously hot-looking guy who owned a seriously expensive-looking boat.

'Not so trashy, after all,' she murmured to herself, wishing Paul (second from last boyfriend) was here to witness it.

She'd meant what she'd told Daisy, she was off men, but that didn't have to mean she couldn't have a bit of fun flirting with a totally unsuitable guy. As long as the guy made her feel better about herself, not worse. That was her new rule. It should have been a frigging rule from day one, but somehow she'd missed making it and ended up with men who put her down, made her feel stupid or cheap.

She'd like to bet Mr Yacht had a whole playbook of ways to make her feel better. It didn't take much imagination to picture those smoky grey eyes locked on hers as he ran his long, tanned fingers up her legs, before deftly trailing them between her thighs…

'One Nantucket Sea Breeze.'

Flushing at her very unladylike thoughts, she accepted the mouth-watering red drink, clinking with ice, topped with a wedge of lime.

'And one towel.' He handed over a white tea cloth, and as his gaze captured hers her belly swooped.

'To pat me dry?'

A pair of steel-grey eyes seared hers. 'Are you asking me?'

Frigging hell. Why was the thought of him doing that, smoothing the towel over her body, making her feel even wetter? And she'd like to bet he wouldn't actually do it smoothly. She sensed he would be … rough. Deliciously, just the right side of dirty, rough.

He let out a low groan. 'Jade?'

Crap. She shook off the fantasy, tugged the towel out of his hand and made a mental note to ease off the steamy books for a while. 'Sorry, thanks.'

Hooded eyes watched her carefully as she ran the towel over her damp dress. What was he thinking? Did he want to be the one holding the towel as much as she wanted him to? Maybe abandoning the towel and licking her clean with his tongue…

Suddenly her blood felt too hot, her pulse too fast.

No, no, no. She was here to work, to be taken seriously, for God's sake. Not fall into bed with the first guy she saw. Even though he was unbelievably hot.

'I'll give more than a penny for them.' When she jerked her head up to give him a puzzled look, a small smile crossed his face. 'Your thoughts.'

She felt a blush scorch her cheeks. 'Er, definitely not worth the money. You'd be better investing it in one of those games at the arcade, you know, where the penny falls onto the level below and eventually, if you're lucky, when you've pushed a dozen of the damn things into the slot, you might get a couple back.' When he continued to stare at her, she felt the blush deepen. 'Maybe you don't have them over here. They're called Penny Falls, or Coin Pusher, or—' *Shut up Jade!!!* 'Anyway. Now you can see why you totally overvalued my thoughts.'

'Quarters.' His eyes continued to assess her, like he was trying to work her out. 'We have them over here and feed them with quarters.'

'Ah, okay, good. I'm glad we cleared that up.'

'It was probably a safer topic of conversation.' The knowing look he gave her sent prickles racing across her skin and she had to force herself to remember to breathe.

'Yes.' She cleared her throat and poked around in her brain for something to say that wouldn't send her thoughts down an X-rated avenue again. 'Okay, then … er, I don't even know your name.'

'Liam.' His voice was so deep, it gave an extra sexy sizzle to his name.

'Okay, then, Liam, you own a yacht here and you recognise the smell of a Sea Breeze cocktail. I guess you come here often?' Amusement glinted in the silver grey of his eyes and she realised what she'd said. 'Oh God, that's the cheesiest chat-up line in history.'

He gave her a long, searching look. 'Are you trying to flirt with me?'

Thump, thump went her heart, and she couldn't work out if it was nerves, or arousal. But nerves wouldn't create this squirmy feeling between her legs. 'I don't know.'

Silence fell between them, heavy with awareness. She was conscious that he was still standing, one hand in his pocket, the other holding a glass of whisky. Long, elegant fingers wrapped casually around it. *Stop imagining those hands on you.*

'To answer your earlier question, I'm a frequent visitor here, yes.'

He'd not taken the bait she'd unwittingly laid down. She pushed aside the disappointment. It was better this way. No flirting, just some company to help her feel less lonely on her first night. 'Maybe you could give me some tips for things to do while I'm here? I've read every guidebook I could get my hands on, but I could use some inside knowledge.'

'Sure.' He nodded towards the sofa. 'Mind if I join you?'

'As long as you don't mind the smell of fermented cranberry juice.'

A small smile tilted his lips as he slid effortlessly beside her, crossing one leg over the other in a move that seemed smooth and practiced. And yet … the edge she'd sensed in him earlier was still there. She smelt it in the unexpected kick of spice in his aftershave, saw it in the taut bulge of bicep beneath the sleeves of his T-shirt, the smattering of dark hair on his thighs. The callouses she'd felt on his palm as he'd handed her the drink. A sense of rough, of coarse, beneath the polish.

The rough didn't extend to his lips though, she thought with a jolt as her eyes settled involuntarily on his mouth. On closer inspection they looked soft, sensual. It was easy to imagine them sliding across her skin, over her nipples.

'You smell intoxicating.' Hooded grey eyes met and held hers. 'I imagine you taste even better.'

Holy moly. Her heart clattered against her rib cage. 'I … um, if that's you trying to beat my corny line, it's a terrible attempt.'

He shifted, the tanned forearm that had rested so close to hers, now stretched across the back of the sofa. 'Clearly, I'm out of practice.'

Oh, my God, *was* he interested? 'I don't think you need it. To be honest, you had me at the yacht.' He stilled, and belatedly she realised how that must have come across. 'Oh, God, that was meant to be a joke, you know, *Jerry Maguire*...' She hung her head, feeling the hot flush of embarrassment creep up her neck. 'I told you I was terrible at this. Way to seduce a hot guy, Jade. First barge onto his boat, then sit next to him smelling of rotting fruit juice and finally insult him by implying he's only attractive because he has a big boat. And no, that wasn't a euphemism. Not that I think you don't have a big... I mean I'm sure you do have... Oh fuckity fuck.' Beyond embarrassed now, she rose to her feet. 'Clearly, it's time I called it a night. Thanks for the drink and sorry about my word vomit. I wish I could blame the cocktail, but unless it's absorbed through the skin I think that was all me.'

'Wait.' His hand wrapped round her arm, giving it a gentle tug until she dropped back onto the sofa. '*Are* you trying to seduce me?'

Her tongue felt too big for her mouth, the words she wanted to say getting stuck as his inscrutable gaze raked hers. 'I think I was, or at least I was trying to flirt with you, which is probably a dumb idea but I'm the queen of dumb ideas.' His eyes narrowed, leaving her feeling unbalanced. She wished she was as good at hiding her thoughts as he was. 'It would help me hugely if you said something now because your face is kind of hard to read.'

His gaze went from cool grey to so inferno-hot, it scorched her insides. 'If you could read my thoughts, you'd be scared.'

Her heart thumped, but she ignored it and raised her chin. 'I don't scare easily. Try me.'

'Are you sure? Because for what I'm about to say to you, I need you to be really, really sure.'

Arousal burned through her. It didn't matter that getting tangled with a guy on her first night was the last she needed. She felt achy, giddy with lust. Just uncomfortable enough that it felt exciting. The thrill that came with being naughty. 'I'm sure.'

The air between them fizzed with an energy that was pure sexual tension. 'I'm wondering what it would be like to take you back to my boat and fuck you where I first laid eyes on you.'

Holy shit. Yet there was something very honest about the crude words. It left her in no doubt about what she would be letting herself in for if their flirtation was to go any further. Not a romantic encounter, or the start of a holiday fling. Just a raw, take-it-or-leave-it offer of sex.

And it was electrifying.

'Should I go on?'

She needed to say no. What had begun as a flirtation had gone wildly out of control. But when she opened her mouth to speak, no words came out. Instead, the images of them together shimmied through her mind, and as the heat of his gaze skated across her hypersensitised skin it felt like he was touching her, everywhere.

'I've also thought of ripping that damp dress off you,' he continued, clearly taking her silence for the encouragement it was. 'Running my hands over your slick, soapy curves as I help you clean off in my shower. Then, because I won't be able to stop myself, I'd carry you up to the top deck and fuck you again under the stars.'

Between her legs the ache he'd created was so intense she had to squeeze her thighs together. What on earth was she supposed to do? She'd come here on a three-month sabbatical to find her true self. Not be distracted by the first man she met. Especially as the impression he must have of her – the archetypal dumb blonde who found herself on the wrong boat, spilt her drink down herself – was exactly the stereotype she wanted to erase.

And yet…

What better way to help erase the memory of her last two shitty boyfriends than by having hot, island sex with an insanely attractive millionaire?

Chapter Four

He'd come on too strong. That's what several months of celibacy and a week of too much work and too little sleep did to him. Yet Liam had a feeling there was more to it than that. Something about *her* made him desperate to taste her, feel those soft, dynamite curves slot against all his hard edges. Hear the hitch of her breath again, see the bright flame of arousal in those huge blue eyes that had drawn him in right from that first meeting, despite how exhausted, how pissed off he'd been feeling. He went for classy over sexy, discreet over obvious, brunette over blonde, slim over curvy, but she'd smashed through all his usual preferences.

He hadn't made the same impression on her, though, as evidenced by the taut silence that followed his coarse declaration, broken only by laughter drifting over from the bar and the gentle sounds of the sea washing up the beach. He'd apologise, call it quits and wish her good night. She'd been unsure right from the start, and his crude talk had shifted her mood from unsure, to no fucking way.

She made a little coughing noise in her throat. 'That's a lot of … sex.'

Okay, so she hadn't jumped to her feet yet. 'Yes. But you asked what I was thinking. Not what I expect to happen.'

'True.' She glanced down at her drink.

'I'm happy just to sit here and have a drink with you.' She let out what could only be described as a dismissive snort and he felt a flare of annoyance. 'If you think I came out here searching for someone to have sex with, you're very much mistaken.'

Her eyes turned impossibly wider. 'That's not, oh God, I didn't think that at all. I just…' She glanced away, looking out to the now ink-black sea. 'Men look at me and see sex, not someone to chat to.'

'You're implying we're all the same.'

'You've just explained, in great detail, how you want to fuck me.'

'Can't I see both? A woman I want to engage with physically and verbally?'

A smile played around her mouth. 'I guess both works.' She took a long sip of her drink, her throat moving in a way that made him want to kiss the pulse there. 'So.'

Sex with this intriguing blonde might have slipped away, but he felt no great desire to shift from the sofa. What did he have waiting for him? Another night where he tried to sleep, but spent a good deal of time lying awake and staring at the ceiling? 'Top of your list, should be the whale museum.'

'Whale museum.' She looked at him blankly.

'You asked what you should do while you're here.'

'Ah, yes, before we got sidetracked by all that sex.' She sipped again at her drink, then eased back into the sofa in a way that made him think she was more relaxed now. 'I read about that. What about seeing actual whales. Do they do tours from here?'

'Whale watching is more popular from Cade Cod. But I could

take you out, if you like.' Where had that come from? He didn't have time to take tourists out on joy rides, no matter how attractive he might find them.

Laughter burst out of her. 'Last time I tried to cadge a lift with you, you weren't very happy.'

It was rare he was teased. 'I don't like people invading my space.' Her pretty eyes blinked and he realised he'd sounded too harsh. 'This time I would be inviting you.'

She seemed to study him, perhaps working out if she wanted to be taken out into the middle of the ocean by a stranger. 'Then sure, that sounds amazing. But will we really see whales?' Immediately she groaned and put her head in her hands. 'That sounds like I'm accusing you of luring me onto your boat to ravish me, but what I meant was what are the chances of actually seeing a whale? Because when I went to Spain we were talked into taking a boat trip to see dolphins but it was a real con because we didn't see any.'

'Either I'm conning you, or planning to have my wicked way with you? Are there any other options?'

She gave a shake of her head, blonde hair tumbling around her shoulders as she rolled her eyes. 'One day I'll think before I open my mouth.'

Automatically, his eyes were drawn to the mouth in question. As he imagined her lush pink lips parting for him, his groin tightened. 'I can't guarantee whales, but I'm pretty sure we could find some, yes.' His voice sounded rough, as raw as the sex he couldn't stop imagining. 'Humpbacks, finbacks, Minke, pilot whales,' he added, trying to focus back on the conversation. 'Probably some dolphins and seals, though the best place to see them is Muskeget Island. There are also three lighthouses to visit, plenty of opportunities to go fishing—'

She put up her hand. 'Whoa, hang on a second, let me make a note.' He waited as she picked up her phone from the coffee table, then promptly dropped it onto the sand. 'Oh, buggeration.' As she bent to pick it up, he cursed his bad luck that he wasn't sitting opposite, because if he had been, he'd have had a perfect view of the round swell of her breasts. 'Okey dokey.'

Christ, who said that these days? And why did he want to smile as he watched the diligent way she took notes, her tongue peeking out between her lips.

'Seals, lighthouses, fishing, whaling museum,' she repeated. 'I read that whales are a big thing on Nantucket.'

'I think you'll find whales are big wherever you are,' he responded dryly. 'But yes, for about a hundred years, Nantucket was the headquarters for the global whale-oil business. The whalers here were renowned as being the best in the world at hunting the sperm whale.'

She grinned. 'Maybe I don't need to go to the museum, I just need to listen to you.'

'The museum has visual aids to help the story.'

'I'm kind of a fan of the visual aid I've got now.' Her gaze slid over his face and he heard his heart thump against his ribs. 'In case you missed it, that was me flirting with you again.'

'I didn't miss it.' He did his own inventory, ending again on the mouth he was becoming obsessed with. It was no good reminding himself that he didn't need distractions right now, not with so much on his plate. Or that a few hours ago he'd been complaining he was beat. The tiredness had been drowned out by raw need, his body raging with arousal. In a bid to calm himself, he took a sip of his drink. 'Beaches.' He glanced towards her phone. 'That's another must.' She stared back at him and he gave her a wry smile. 'That was me trying to stick to my promise of talking.'

Soft laughter followed his admission. She was all big blue eyes and pretty dimples, approachable in a way that beautiful women weren't. Beauty drew the eye, but having been the recipient of the harsh side of it, he now found it easy to ignore. Sexy, though, with a side of funny and a slice of cute. Why was he finding it so hard to ignore that?

'Okay, hit me with the best places to sunbathe.'

Immediately he pictured her in a bikini. Something fun, like polka dots, but skimpy, those big breasts barely contained… Cursing inwardly, he gulped at his whisky. And rejoiced in the distraction of the burn as he rattled off a couple of his favourite beaches. 'How do you feel about sharks?'

'Er, like I only want to see them in 2D?'

'Then you should probably skip swimming off Great Point.'

Horror flitted across her face. 'Are there really sharks in the sea?'

'That is where they tend to spend most of their time.'

'Ha ha. I'd love to say something cool, like, I know how to handle a shark, or even better, it's the shark who needs to worry, but in reality, if I came across one, I'd totally shit myself.'

He lived in a world where people watched what they said around him – Jeremy and his grandma excluded. Jade was refreshingly unfiltered. 'Relax. If you keep to the main beaches the most frightening sea life you're likely to come across is the small human variety.'

Her face softened. 'Now that I can handle. Kids are so funny, they say the things we want to say but are too scared to.'

He thought back over their conversation. 'You don't strike me as someone who's scared to say what they think.'

'Maybe that's because I'm basically still a kid at heart.' Her eyes slid down to her phone and then back up to him. 'Thanks for the tips. I'll aim to give everything a go except the shark attack off Great Point.'

Silence descended between them. He'd finished his drink, she'd finished hers. Now was a good time to head back.

'Would you like another whisky?' She nodded down to his

empty glass. 'I know you own a fancy yacht and can afford to buy your own, but that doesn't mean you should have to. My way of thanking you for the tourist tips.' She gave him a hesitant smile. 'But no worries if you want to head off. You've probably got better plans for the evening.'

'Definitely not better.' He waited until she looked at him. 'Are you offering to buy the drink because you feel you should, or because you want to?'

She blinked, gaze slowing rising to meet his. 'Because I want to.'

There was only one way his thoughts were now travelling. 'And if I said why don't we have that drink on the boat, instead?'

Her breath caught, but the hand that carefully placed her glass back on the table was steady as a rock. 'I'd say I hope you can make a good cocktail.'

Sex. It hung, hot and heavy in the air between them. He was aware he was acting totally out of character. He didn't joke with strangers. Had never invited anyone back to his boat, let alone a woman. He also avoided hitting on guests in his own resort, too easy for things to become complicated. Yet for this guest, he was throwing away his rule book. Maybe because she was nothing like the women he usually came across who liked to play games, to be seduced, to pretend they weren't just out to do something as dirty, as basic, as hooking up for a night.

The less smooth he'd been with Jade, and fuck, he was seriously rusty, the more she'd seemed to relax.

Standing, he reached to take her hand and as her warm fingers clasped around his, he realised his heart was thumping loudly in his chest.

Chapter Five

She was about to do something stupid, yet whether it was the buzz of the alcohol, the punch drunkenness of jet lag, or the heady giddiness of arousal, right now, in this moment, she didn't give a rat's arse. She wanted to carry on the evening a little longer, to spend more time with this deeply attractive man with his brooding good looks and magnetic air of worldly confidence. A man so different to anyone she'd ever met.

She wasn't naïve, she knew he was hoping for sex, but maybe part of her was hoping for that, too. What she knew for certain was she'd enjoyed his company, felt flattered that he'd made the effort to engage with her. Most of the guys who tried to pick her up assumed all they had to do was give her a cocky smile.

Liam cleared his throat. 'If your sole purpose to come back with me is for a cocktail, you're in for a disappointment. The range of alcohol I keep on the boat is very limited.'

She glanced sideways at him as they walked back along the beach, her heart beating a crazy rhythm. 'I don't think I'll be disappointed.' Once again she was at the mercy of that piercing look, the one that made her skin prickle and her belly flip-flop.

'Not that I'm expecting you to make me a cocktail. I just said that to try and sound sophisticated, like I often get asked by hot guys to go back to their boat.' She started to laugh at the absurdity of it. 'Twickenham, that well-known magnet for luxury yachts.'

He quirked an eyebrow. 'That's where you live?'

'Yep, home of English rugby, but not home to many boats. Well not yet anyway. There are plans to develop part of it by the river…' Oh, my frigging God, what was she doing? 'But then I don't suppose you'll be heading to Twickenham any time soon so I won't bore you with the details.'

They reached the wharf. It stretched out into the sea, several large sailing boats and two more luxury yachts now moored against it. She recognised his at the end, looking resplendent in the flickering lights from the lamps along the waterfront. Wealth, class, sophistication. It was everywhere she looked … until her eyes dropped to her stained cotton dress. And her Primark flip-flops.

Suddenly she felt inadequate.

No, that's the old you.

She wasn't sure who the new one was, but tonight wasn't the time to find her. It was the time to shove all her insecurities in a box and be the heroine in her very own billionaire romance novel, only the rich guy wasn't an arsehole. And she wasn't going to fall for him. Instead she was going to flirt, to enjoy him. Maybe even use him for sex. Definitely use the experience of being chatted up by him to reconfirm she was worth more than the shitty guys she'd been dating. Then she was going to prove she was better than the shitty things they'd said about her. After that, she'd go home and find herself a man to fall in love with who valued who she was.

She felt Liam's hand rest low on her back. Not pushing her forward, just touching her. Reassuring her. 'We can go back to the bar.'

She glanced again at him, felt everything inside her tighten with longing. 'But then I'd never get to nosy inside this fancy boat you threw me off.'

He let out a bark of laughter and holy crap, if brooding Liam was irresistible, laughing Liam was *I need to jump his bones now*.

His hot gaze pinned hers, and his hand travelled up from her back and along her arm until it cupped her face. 'You are ... unexpected.'

Her heart bumped against her ribs. She was used to being told the opposite. That she was obvious. 'Unexpected, as in I've found a slug in my lettuce or as in that sprout flavoured ice cream didn't taste as bad as I thought?'

His mouth was tantalisingly close to hers, those impossibly soft-looking lips curved in a smile. 'Yet again, you provide only terrible options.'

No words were said as they walked the final few yards to the boat, yet it seemed as if their bodies were saying plenty. *Touch me*, her breasts demanded. His hand tightened on hers. *Soon*, it seemed to say.

She wasn't sure how far she wanted to go, but she needed something to take away the ache.

When they reached the yacht, he halted and turned to face her. 'The wobble you had a few minutes ago. It's over?'

Wow, he was perceptive. 'Seeing the boat again made me take a breath. I'm more used to getting in a guy's Ford Fiesta.' She cringed. 'Not to have sex, I mean there's not much room in the back of those things...' She let out a strangled laugh. 'I really need to stop talking so much.'

His eyes travelled to her mouth. 'I know a way to achieve that.' Then he grimaced and glanced back at her. 'Was that too corny?'

'Er, no.' She swallowed, heart fluttering. 'Actually, it sounded like something you should definitely follow up on.'

The word *please* almost left her mouth but she swallowed it as his lips finally, finally found hers.

And holy crap. It was like she'd been zapped with a live wire. Every nerve end tingled, her skin felt hot, her brain started to melt as his mouth teased hers, his tongue brushing her lips before slipping inside, his breath warm with a hint of whisky. Gentler than she'd thought he'd be, he seemed content to take his time, tasting her from every angle like he was *savouring* her. Just as her knees were about to buckle, he drew back, eyes a smoky grey as they stared into hers. 'I was right.'

'Sorry?' She could barely get the word out she felt so unsteady. Like he'd taken her world and, in one smooth, sensual glide, turned it upside down.

'You taste even better.'

With the fluid grace of a man at ease with himself, and with the boat, he climbed on board. She stumbled after him, only the hold he had on her hand preventing her from ending up flat on her arse. 'Think I need to find my sea legs.'

The look he gave her made her blood thicken. 'I know a way we can solve that.'

Her belly swooped. She knew what he was implying, and part of her was desperate to take him up on the promise in his eyes. The easy way he carried himself, the confidence he wore like an expensively tailored suit, the heat he elicited in her from just his gaze… Instinctively, she knew sex with him would be explosive.

'Relax.' He gave her a small smile, one that perfectly communicated he'd read her indecision, then held out his hand. 'Come, let me show you those stars I promised.'

I'll fuck you again under the stars.

His words from earlier flooded back to her, yet alongside the sharp tug of arousal, was the flutter of unwanted nerves. She was way out of her depth.

But then his warm hand enveloped hers and the nerves settled, leaving only the tug in her belly.

Liam handed Jade a glass of champagne and as he settled next to her on the sun pad, he felt the earlier tension start to leave her. People called him a cold bastard, and maybe at times he could be, but not where women were concerned. No, there he'd been too trusting. 'Nothing will happen tonight that you don't want to.'

She gave him a soft smile and his heart performed an odd skip. 'You clocked my hesitancy, huh?'

'I'm a stranger to you.' He shrugged. 'I'd be more surprised if you weren't wary.'

Her eyes searched his, and she smiled again. 'Yeah, I'm not wary of you. You don't look like an axe murderer.'

'How can you tell?'

She grinned. 'You're not carrying an axe?' Her eyes skimmed the deck. 'All I can see is an ice bucket and a bottle of champagne. I'm no detective but I figure that's more death by seduction, which is a far better way to go.'

'I'll bear that in mind next time I reach for my axe.'

She laughed, and it felt strangely satisfying to know he'd caused it.

'It's myself I'm wary of,' she added when her laughter died down. 'I've a tendency to rush into things without thinking first. It got me into trouble loads at school and if I'm honest it's still getting me into trouble now, especially where men are concerned.' He wanted to ask her what she meant, but she put her glass down on the deck, settled back on the sun pad and stared up at the sky. 'These stars I can see. Do you know any of their names?'

He shifted so he was lying down next to her. Not touching, but close enough he could feel the heat of her skin. His dick, which had been half hard most of the evening, stirred again. 'I know the Milky Way,' he offered, willing his body to catch up with what his mind had already worked out. Sex was not going to happen tonight.

'Yeah, I've heard of that.' Her head turned towards him. 'Just in case I'm not absolutely certain what it is, though, besides a yummy brand of chocolate bar, can you remind me?'

'It's the galaxy that includes our solar system.' He pointed at the sky to the left. 'You see the area that looks like a cloud?'

He watched as her eyes scanned the inky blackness, littered with thousands of twinkling stars. 'The one that looks a bit like an alien with a transparent head and a brain that is glowing in the dark?'

Amusement hummed inside him and he cleared his throat, not wanting to laugh in case she thought he was laughing at her. 'Astrologists say the Milky Way looks like spilt milk, but I guess an alien's brain works, too.'

'Split milk is kind of nondescript.' She sunk further into the sun pad. 'So, um, that's the Milky Way, then.'

'It is. About two-hundred billion stars. Plus a bit of dust and gas.'

'Holy crap, billions? Seriously?'

He hadn't realised those blue eyes could get any wider. 'There are too many to see individually, hence the glow. Nantucket is a great place to view it. There's hardly any light pollution here.'

'More than I can say for Twickenham.' She paused, seeming to take it all in. 'Makes you feel very small and insignificant, doesn't it, knowing all that is out there.'

'Yes.'

Again he felt her gaze on him. 'I bet it's the only time you feel insignificant.'

Christ, if only she knew how wrong she was. 'You think tall people can't feel small?' He could tell he'd surprised her, but because he didn't want her asking any more questions, he kept his eyes firmly up at the sky.

'When I was a kid I used to think I could wish on a star and it would all come true,' she said quietly after a while.

He turned to look at her, finding her expression unusually pensive. 'What did you wish for?'

'Oh, you know, the usual. Ten-year-old me wanted a pony, twelve-year-old me wanted to live in a castle made of books.'

'Ah.' Understanding dawned. 'It's a bookworm – that key ring you showed me – not a caterpillar.' When she didn't immediately reply, he glanced at her again and found her staring open-mouthed at him. 'What?'

'I'm surprised you made the connection, that's all. But Sparks thanks you for realising his worm credentials. My sister didn't get it. In fact, she laughed till her belly ached when I told her I bought it because I thought it was a worm.'

He couldn't miss the pain in her voice. 'Sounds like you don't get along.'

'Oh, we do, mostly.' She let out a deep exhale. 'But fourteen-year-old me wanted her to fail an exam, just one, so my parents could be disappointed in her for a change.' He was shocked, not by what she said, but the fact she'd openly admitted something so private. 'I don't know why I said that,' she added, face still turned up to the sky, like she was embarrassed to look at him. 'It's the first time I've admitted out loud how jealous I am of her.'

'We're strangers sharing a moment in the dark. It's not like I'm going to judge you.'

Finally, her eyes met his and she smiled. 'It's not even that my parents are horrible. I mean I know they love me, you know?' As he didn't, he kept his expression neutral. 'It's just Lauren has always been the shining star, the one who went to university, who became a doctor. I'm the one still trying to find my way.' She sighed. 'Have you got any siblings you're jealous of? Just to make me feel better.'

'No siblings.'

Silence descended, broken only by the occasional creak of the rope on the moorings and the gentle wash of water against the hull. He was usually happy with quiet, preferred it to conversation, yet after what she'd admitted, his cursory response felt churlish. 'But I was jealous of the boys in my class.'

'What were you jealous of?'

Fuck, what was he doing? His childhood wasn't something he talked about. In fact, screw that, he didn't talk about *himself*. Clearly he was too tired to put up his usual defence. 'Their swagger, their bond.' He kept his gaze up at the sky. 'They had money, and it made them important in the eyes of everyone around them.'

She scoffed. 'Being rich doesn't make a person important. It just makes them think they are.' As if she'd suddenly realised what she'd said, she added, 'Not that every rich person thinks like that. I'm sure there are some perfectly nice ones. Like, um, you.'

He wasn't sure if he'd just been insulted, or agreed with. He couldn't fault what she'd said, though. Only that she lacked a few vital insights. Money wasn't important unless it was what you were judged on. Judged, shunned, tormented, ridiculed. He felt the familiar knots tighten in his stomach and focused on the stars as he willed the memories to fade.

'So what did ten-year-old Liam wish for?'

He slammed his eyes shut and heaved out a breath. This evening wasn't going anywhere near how he'd imagined it when he'd invited her onto the boat. He'd thought they'd have a bit of a laugh, something he'd almost forgotten he was capable of. And yeah, okay, he'd hoped to make out with her, tempt her into sex.

Aware he'd not replied, he rolled over onto his side to face her. She looked fucking perfect, lying on his boat, beguiling blue eyes, blonde hair draped across the pad of his sundeck, her dress moulded against her curves.

Maybe he could put up with answering a few more questions if it meant he kept her here a little longer.

Chapter Six

Jade stared back at Liam, wondering what he was thinking. He'd hoped for sex, that much was obvious, yet here he was, talking about stars and now, clearly with great reluctance, his childhood. She'd withdraw her question, but he fascinated her. She wanted to peel back that defensive layer, get to know as much as she could about him. 'You don't have to tell me.'

'I'm aware.'

His guard was up, but she'd never been one to give up easily. 'I did admit that I'm jealous of my sister, though, which has to be way more embarrassing than anything you have to say, so you kind of owe me.'

He gave a shake of his head, but his mouth, the one it was impossible not to keep staring at, not to imagine pressing sensuous kisses down her body … twitched with amusement. 'Ten-year-old me wished he didn't have to go to boarding school.'

Warmth spread through her at his tacit agreement to continue a conversation he clearly would rather not be having. 'I hated school, too, but at least I could get away from it at the end of the day. What about twelve-year-old you?'

He hesitated, and she could imagine him carefully selecting his words to reveal as little of himself as possible. Unlike her explosion of the first words that came into her head. 'Twelve-year-old me wanted to fit in with his classmates. Be part of the gang.' He exhaled sharply. 'I don't know what I'm doing, telling you all this. I don't talk to people.'

'Well you seem to be managing just fine.' Finding his hand, she wrapped her fingers around it, feeling a zing down her spine at the contact. 'We're strangers, remember? No judgement, no repeating anything we say tonight to anyone else. Girl Guide honour.'

He eyed her sceptically. 'You don't look like you were in the Guides.'

She smirked. 'I was, for a few weeks. Until I was kicked out for spending too much time with the Scouts. And before you ask, it was because they did cooler stuff. So anyway, what did fourteen-year-old Liam wish for?'

He inhaled, letting the air out in a long, slow breath. 'To buy his grandma a house.'

And this was why she'd wanted to keep talking. To find these precious nuggets of information that set him apart from any other man she'd met. 'Are you sure you're not just saying that to get one over on me?'

'You want me to phone her and prove it?'

She sat up, swivelling to look at him, and felt something shift in her chest. Guarded, cool at times, but when he allowed her a peep beneath that aloof mask he wore? 'Did anyone ever tell you, you're dead sweet?' Laughter peeled out of her at his expression. 'I figured that wasn't what you were aiming for.'

His jaw tightened. 'Fourteen-year-old me also wished for power. And revenge. Neither of which are sweet.' He stared directly at her, eyes a flinty grey. 'I still do.'

And there was the hint of ruthlessness that made him so

compelling. 'Maybe sweet is the wrong word, but I think behind the brooding front you put up, there's a warm human trying to get out. And I'm not just saying that because you wanted to buy your grandma a house. I gave you plenty of chances to make me feel stupid tonight, but you didn't.'

'We all spill drinks from time to time.'

'What about mistaking a luxury yacht for a resort transfer?'

'Some might say that was cunning.'

She eyed him curiously. 'I bet you get women trying to pick you up all the time. Which I wasn't trying to do, by the way.'

'I know.'

She gave him a playful smile. 'At least not then.'

His long, powerful body stilled. 'And now?'

Her pulse jumped, a sharp thrill arrowing through her at the deep gravel to his voice. 'I'm crazy attracted to you, that much should be obvious, but I've only just got here and I don't want to make a mistake. Not when I'm jet-lagged and sloshing with cocktails.' She gave him a wry grin. 'Inside and out.'

He nodded, but his eyes didn't leave hers. 'What about if we kissed again? Would that be a mistake?'

A shiver skated down her spine. 'No. Definitely not.'

His hand reached to clasp her face and her belly did a long swoop as she stared into eyes that had darkened with desire. Then his mouth descended on hers and she couldn't hold in her moan of pleasure. This time he was less gentle, giving her a taste of his hunger, his need. On a groan his tongue pushed past her lips and plunged inside her, licking, tasting, firing heat through her blood. The weight of him pressed her onto the sunpad, his hands sliding from her face, down her arms, then across to her chest.

'Is this okay?' he whispered.

She couldn't speak, could only nod, her tongue stuck to the roof of her mouth as his fingers toyed with her breasts, kneading them, teasing the hard points of her nipples beneath her dress.

God, she was so turned on right now. And that was before she felt the rigid length of his erection against her thigh. She wanted it in her hands, to see the girth of it, feel the weight. Wanted him as excited, as hot, as he was making her with his mouth, his drugging, sensuous kisses, the glide of his hands.

Disappointment flooded her as he broke away, her skin instantly missing his heat, his touch. With a groan he slumped onto his back, his breath coming out in uneven pants, the muscles of his chest rippling beneath his T-shirt as she watched it rise and fall. Unable to help herself, her gaze travelled lower, to the huge tent in his shorts.

Between her legs she felt a delicious tug.

'Thank you,' she said. He raised a brow and she smiled. 'For stopping. I ... um ... I'm not sure I'd have been able to.'

'Another minute and I wouldn't have been able to, either.' She watched the sensuous glide of his Adam's apple as he swallowed. 'I know all about making mistakes. I don't want to be one for you.'

She'd had two serious boyfriends and a couple of other less serious ones, yet she'd never felt so *cared for* as she did in that moment. 'I don't think you'd be one.' When he stared back at her, she shrugged. 'My mistakes were believing I was in a relationship with guys who liked me, respected me, then finding out I was wrong.' It hurt to admit it, to hear the reminder of how foolish she'd been. 'If we were to have sex, I'd know it was a one-night stand.' She paused, watching him. 'I bet you have a lot of those.'

'Some.'

'I've never had one. In a way I wish I could, because I love sex, so how great to be able to live in the moment and just enjoy the act with an attractive stranger?' She sighed. 'But for me to really enjoy sex, I have to be relaxed, and I can't do that if I'm not with someone I have an emotional connection with. Someone I trust.'

His expression turned guarded again. 'I understand.'

'No, I don't think you do, not fully.' Her heart thumped as she sat up and looked down on him. 'I do trust you. Enough to know you won't take advantage of me if I ask you to kiss me again.' His eyes flared, sending goosebumps scattering over her skin. 'I'm not ready for sex, but I want to touch you. And feel you touch me.'

Liam saw Jade's cheeks flush and would have smiled, had he not been busy trying to control his breathing. Trying to control himself, because fuck, now his dick was raring to go again. 'I won't take this any further than you want to go.'

She nodded, and his pulse quickened as she got hold of the hem of her dress and pulled it over her head. Tits bouncing gloriously in front of his face.

The spike of lust was so savage it was painful. 'Gorgeous,' he murmured approvingly, gazing at the luscious globes, barely contained in the gossamer-thin bra. He slid his fingers up and down its straps, then around the edge of the lace before slowly pressing a kiss to her cleavage. Arousal hummed through him as he inhaled, savouring her smell, the softness of her skin. More. He shifted his attention to the swell of her breasts, kissing, licking though the wispy thin material.

She pushed herself further into his mouth. 'I can take it off.'

His gaze lifted to hers, finding her watching him. 'No.' He pushed himself up into a sitting position and smoothed his hands over her, cupping, feeling. 'I like to take my time.'

'I can see that.' Her breath hitched as his fingers toyed with her nipples. 'Most men just want to rip off the packaging.'

He ducked his head, tasting the skin of her cleavage again. 'Maybe they're more used to opening presents than I am.' Shit, why had he said that? To distract her from asking any questions, and to get his head back in the game, he deftly twisted the clasp of her bra, letting it fall to the deck. And now it was his turn to draw in a sharp breath. 'Fucking perfect.'

She laughed, which jiggled her tits and made him even harder. 'Not perfect, but they are all me.'

He could see that. Plump and round, they hung naturally, soft to touch, the skin around them paler – clearly she didn't sunbathe topless – the nipples a rose pink. 'I want to lick them, suck them, play with them for the rest of the evening.' He palmed them, burying his face in her cleavage, inhaling her; coconut, something citrusy and a hint of the sweet cocktail.

She moaned, shifting restlessly, fraying his control even further. 'That sounds way too tempting.'

Because he couldn't help himself, he sucked again at her nipples, tugging with his teeth until she cried out his name on a breathless whimper.

'Liam, please.'

'Please what?' He was hard to the point of pain. 'Tell me what you want from me.'

'I ... I don't know. Can I touch you?'

He groaned, afraid he was going to embarrass himself. 'You can do whatever you want with me.'

Shifting so his back rested against the edge of the sunken sunpad, he lifted her onto his lap, hissing out a breath as the globes of her ass settled against his groin.

Reaching for the hem of his T-shirt, she pulled it over his head, her eyes lighting up at the sight of his chest and giving his ego a powerful boost. His dick got a different boost as her fingers trailed across his pecs, rubbing at his nipples, all while her ass wriggled gloriously against his groin. 'Your chest is beautiful.'

'Yours is better.'

She smiled before sliding back a little onto his thighs. Just as he was about to complain, her hands dived into his shorts, finding him easily because he was that hard, that ready to burst out and take her. 'Holy crap, boats and cars, it's not the same.'

He grunted and pushed further into her grasp, his mind dizzy with lust. 'What?'

'You know, fast cars are driven by men with small dicks.' Her hand ran up and down his length, her soft touch a direct contrast to his raging hardness. 'But fast boats are clearly driven by men with frigging enormous ones.'

Christ, he was laughing, despite the fact his balls were ready to burst. 'Not drive,' he rasped. 'We established that.'

'Yes, sorry. It must be the fact I have this steel rod in my hands, it's making me forget.'

Control officially snapped, he gazed into her eyes. 'I want to make you come. Can I do that?'

She bit into her bottom lip. 'Please.' Her fingers grasped him tighter and he shuddered, full on shuddered like it was the first time a woman had held him.

Slipping his hands beneath her lacy underwear, he found her drenched core, igniting another bolt of lust. 'You are the sexiest fucking woman I've ever seen.'

Red stained her cheeks and she ground down on his hands. 'Thank you. But if that's true, you need to get out more.'

Sex could be moody, at times strained, intense. Two people trying desperately to get themselves and each other off. It wasn't fun. Wasn't something to be laughed at, yet here he was, sporting a smile *and* an aching erection.

He wanted to lift her up and onto him, to plunge into her soaked depths. No, wait, he'd taste her first and then plunge. While his fevered mind ran through all the things he wanted to do to her, her hand began to tug at him, her grip the perfect combination of soft and hard, soft skin, hard hold. Fuck, *this*, having her on his lap, staring at the most amazing tits he'd ever seen, his fingers sliding in and out of her heat. It was more than enough.

She gasped as he added another finger, his pace quickening… No wait, maybe the hoarse sounds were coming from him? Never had he felt so connected to another human, so immersed in them that he couldn't think straight. Restlessly he rubbed his other hand over the round curve of her gorgeous ass, squeezing, pulling her further onto him. He didn't know whether to put his mouth on her breasts, lick at her nipples, or kiss her again. Before he could make up his mind, she made the decision for him, drawing his head to her glorious cleavage. 'Please,' she murmured.

As if he needed asking. As if *he* was doing *her* a favour. 'Like this?' He tongued the delicate pink nipples and she gave a moan of pleasure, her hips shifting up and down, driving him crazy. The more he sucked, the more he nipped at them, the harder her hand tugged him. And the tauter the final thread of his control stretched.

'I'm going to come.' Her expression turned fevered, her eyes heavy with desire. 'Holy macaroni, I can't stop.'

With a final gasp she came, her walls clamping around his fingers, the breathy moans she unleashed triggering his own release.

Seconds passed, minutes, as he drew her against his chest, both of them breathing heavily. He just about had the presence of mind to reach for his T-shirt and wipe his release off her hands.

'You wrecked me.' Dazed, he stared at her, taking in the puffy lips, flushed skin. The huge eyes that blinked up at him, all sated and gently amused.

'Ditto.'

He ran a finger down the soft skin of her cheek. 'I've never been with a woman who says holy macaroni when she comes.'

She smirked. 'I bet the women you're used to wear perfume instead of "eau de stale cocktail" and know that boats are sailed not driven. Though why have a steering wheel if you're not going to drive?'

He let out a low laugh before sliding them both back down onto the sun pad. Of their own volition his arms locked around her, pulling her towards him, feeling her slot perfectly against his side.

'Just a few minutes.' She nuzzled his neck, her voice drowsy. 'Then I promise I'll go.'

He drew in a breath, felt his body give one long, satisfied exhale, all his muscles relaxed again, languid. His brain switching off as her curvy body nestled further into him. 'No rush.'

They were the last words he uttered.

By the time he woke, the sun was already up and he was alone on the deck, his body covered by a throw from his bed. It was the longest he'd slept since he could remember.

Chapter Seven

From the desk at the back of the bookstore, Jade watched the seagulls dive-bombing into the shimmering blue sea through the open doorway. Not a bad office backdrop. With a smile to herself, she glanced back at the computer and the document Daisy had put together, listing everything that needed to be done on a daily and weekly basis. She was slowly making her way through it, some of the items easy (make yourself a drink; big tick), some more difficult (check stock levels; she could count, but what was a *good* number?) and one or two of them made her stomach queasy (review budget, decide which new books to order for following month, devise and implement marketing plan to increase sales).

She got in a pickle working out if she could afford another pink top (yes, obviously), so being responsible for someone else's money didn't seem like the best idea. As for marketing plans ... she didn't even know where to start.

Her phone buzzed with an incoming message from her sister.

How's it going in Nantucket? Sold any
books yet?

Jade quickly typed out a reply.

Nope. It's not exactly busy.

Why? Too many holidaymakers with other things
on their mind besides reading…

What could be better than reading?!

If you have to ask, you've not had sex with the
right person yet.

A tingle hummed through Jade as she responded.

After last night, maybe I can think of one thing…

She laughed as her phone lit up with an incoming call.

'Oh my God,' said Lauren. 'You've only been out there one day and you've already found someone to shag?'

The smile slipped from Jade's face but she reminded herself Lauren didn't mean to make her sound cheap, easy. 'It's not like I went looking for a hook-up. It just happened.'

'Yeah, I know. It's just it *happens* to you far more than it does to the rest of us.'

Did it? Or was Lauren judging against her own, stricter values? 'We didn't actually have sex. Just … fooled around.'

It felt wrong, dismissing the evening like that, as if it had been trivial, inconsequential, when it had been frigging *magical*. Better than anything she'd ever experienced. So much so that she regretted not having sex, regretted giving in to her fear of feeling cheapened because now it felt like a missed opportunity. How many other chances would she get to have spectacular sex with an incredibly attractive man, on his yacht, under the stars? A man who'd actually shown her more respect, more care, than any of the guys she'd been out with.

'So, spill the beans, what was he like? Are you hooking up again?' Just as Jade was deciding how much to tell her, Lauren swore. 'Damn it, I'm being bleeped. Another life to save. Take care and I'll message you later to get all the dirty details.'

Life to save. Dirty details. After ending the call Jade swallowed, and swallowed again, but the bad taste was still in her mouth, the heaviness still in her stomach. Getting up from her chair she walked through the bookstore, taking in the shelves of bright book covers, and then to the outside where she took a deep breath. There was no room in her life for Lauren's ugly comparisons when she had books and the ocean.

Glancing at her watch, she realised it was one o'clock already. Time to close up shop for an hour and take a break, because she'd worked sooooo hard. And, okay, she wasn't saving lives, but this was a chance to *live* her life.

Switching the shop sign to *closed for lunch*, she locked up and glanced along the wharf. Which way to head? As it was her first full day, maybe she'd take Daisy's advice and grab her lunch from Provisions on Straight Wharf. Apparently their sandwiches were to die for.

She smiled as she strolled across the wooden boardwalk. It was a beautiful day, the sky a vivid shade of blue, the breeze off the sea keeping the temperature down to pleasantly warm.

Taking a left, she headed into town. As she neared the historic district, the tarmac roads changed to cobblestones, and with weathered old colonial buildings lining both sides, it felt like stepping back in time. Main Street was wide, yet the cobbles on the road, the redbrick of the pavements and the rows of trees providing dappled shade gave it an air of intimacy, of a past rich with history. Everywhere she turned, planters brimming with flowers were set outside boutiques with Georgian-style windows displaying artisan crafts or designer clothes. Bustling café's advertised homemade ice creams and fresh seafood. So many of the buildings were made from grey wood slats – she'd read that it was traditional for Nantucket, the wood being cedar shingles, which turned a soft grey as they weathered. Talk about New England charm – now she really understood what it meant. It was rustic and romantic, yet also rich and elegant. It was *captivating*.

Her pulse kicked up a gear as she spotted a familiar, tall figure walking away from Straight Wharf, a takeout coffee in his hand. Sporting a white linen shirt and chinos, his eyes covered by shades, Liam could have been a film star, or a model … and maybe he was.

Had she been rash, taking things so far with a guy she didn't know? *Day one and you've already found someone to shag.*

Sod it, no. Lauren could think what she liked. She'd known the previous two guys she'd dated a few weeks before she'd slept with them. *And look how well they turned out.*

Last night had been special. She and Liam had shared confidences, connected in a way she hadn't done with boyfriends she'd thought she knew inside out. When she'd left him in the early hours of this morning, she'd not felt cheap. She'd felt lucky to have spent a memorable night with a memorable man.

As if he sensed her staring, Liam looked up. He paused for a second before changing direction and walking towards her.

'Hi.' God, her mouth was dry, her heart pounding so hard he must be able to hear it. 'Used any bad chat-up lines today?'

She watched as he slotted his free hand into the pocket of his trousers. His face was hard to read anyway, but especially now with those expensive-looking shades covering his eyes. 'Is it hot out here? Or is it just you?'

It's a joke. 'Well, I did come outside for some fresh air, but you took my breath away.'

He smiled, wrenching the breath from her lungs and turning her joke into a reality.

'Thank you for last night.' She'd forgotten how deep his voice was, a low sexy rumble that sent a shiver of awareness down her spine. 'I enjoyed it.'

'Me, too.'

He pushed off his sunglasses and took a step towards her so he was just on the edge of her personal space, eyes raking her face before dipping down to her mouth. 'Are you free tonight?'

Her body responded to the smouldering grey gaze with a wave of heated arousal. 'Well, I don't charge, if that's what you mean.' He raised an eyebrow and she cringed, embarrassment flooding her. 'Crap, that was an awful joke. I was trying to play it cool, like pretend I'm not totally overwhelmed by bumping into the seriously hot guy I almost had sex with only a few hours after meeting him.'

His gaze was level, calm, but totally inscrutable. He could be thinking *steer clear of the crazy woman*, or *she's nuts but I still fancy shagging her* … no, fucking her. That's what he'd said he wanted. And oh God, why did her lower belly perform giddy somersaults at the thought?

'So, tonight?'

She swallowed to ease the dryness in her throat. 'Honestly, I'm not sure it's a good idea.'

'You're here with someone?'

'Oh, no, nothing like that. I'm single. Very, very single.'

He angled his head. 'Then can I ask what's stopping you?'

She wished they were back on the top deck of his boat where real life had seemed a million miles away. 'I have a habit of sleeping with men who are bad for me. Not that we'd be sleeping together, but … well, you know what I mean.'

He glanced away, as if trying to work something out. 'I used to have a similar habit, where women were concerned,' he said eventually, gaze returning to hers. 'It's why I don't date.'

You think tall people can't feel small? Despite his outward confidence, he understood about being hurt. He was also sending her a very clear message. 'So if tonight isn't a date, what are you suggesting?'

He raised his free hand to cup her face, his thumb rubbing gently across her bottom lip. 'A drink, Jade.' His voice was a low rumble, his breath warm against her skin. 'A drink and we'll take it from there.'

Her belly tumbled, his pull impossible to ignore. 'Okay, a drink. On your boat?'

He seemed to study her for a moment, eyes flicking across her face before he dropped his hand and slid it into his pocket. 'Are you staying at the resort?'

'Um, nearby, yes.'

'Okay, meet me at the wharf. We'll go from there.'

'Go where?'

His lips curved. 'The best place to have a cocktail in Nantucket.' His eyes focused once more on her mouth before he took a step back. 'See you later.'

As she watched his retreating broad back, the assured way he strolled down the cobbled street, she felt a hard flip in her belly. She would give herself tonight, and then she would focus on work, on the bookstore. On the reasons she came to Nantucket.

———

Liam gave himself a severe talking to as he strode back along the harbourfront to the resort. He didn't date, he'd just told Jade that, yet instead of agreeing to meet her on the boat, something she'd even suggested, he'd lost his fucking mind and offered to take her for a cocktail.

Not only that, he'd just turned a mutually agreed one-night stand, into a two-night stand.

Christ, though, the sight of her, all blonde and curvy in a sundress that skimmed her thighs, pink bikini straps peeking from the low-cut top, had been enough to stop him in his tracks. He'd literally been unable to nod in her direction and keep on walking. Not when he'd thought of how gorgeous she'd look, sitting on Galley beach with a cocktail in her hand, a delighted expression on her face, because he could tell how excited she was to be in Nantucket. Yeah, a drink on his boat had seemed too cheap, too easy when she'd deserved more.

Temporary insanity, that's what it was, brought on by intense sexual frustration after the best night of non-sex, ever. Sure, he'd come, and come hard, but not where he'd wanted to. Not between those sexy legs.

'A woman is waiting in your office.' May, who ran the front desk and also organised him with a ruthless efficiency he appreciated, interrupted his X-rated thoughts. 'She said you'd be happy to see her.'

His first thought was his grandma – she was the only woman, the only person, he was ever happy to see – but she currently lived on Martha's Vineyard and hadn't left it by herself in over a year. 'Thanks.'

Warily he walked towards the office, then let out a grim smile when he saw the woman sitting with her back to him. 'Brought me the signed contract?'

Flo turned and stood, holding out a large brown envelope. 'It's here, but before I hand it over I want your assurance you will do right by the girl who's just started her three-month stint in the bookstore.'

'She'll be compensated and given accommodation on the resort.'

Flo narrowed her eyes. 'And her work in the shop? Surely you can let her continue while you decide what to do with it.'

There was no deciding – not when the decision was obvious. 'You sell to me, and the shop and the wharf are mine to do what I want with.'

The older woman shook her head at him and he didn't like how that felt, like he was being chastised. 'I'm not talking about the legalities of the situation. I'm asking you to have a heart. To think about the wide-eyed, eager young lady who's travelled all the way out here to run a bookstore on Nantucket.'

And now he was getting pissed off. 'Maybe you should have thought about her before you agreed to let her come over.'

Flo nodded, her smile sad. 'I fully intended to sell after her three months were up, but my sons need the money now, so I don't have a choice.'

He'd like to bet her sons weren't destitute, queuing up at food banks for their next meal. They didn't need it, they wanted it. Jade was right, money didn't automatically make a person important, but by God, not having it, made you powerless. 'There's always a choice, Flo. I'm not forcing you to sell to me.'

'No, I know, but—'

'Are we doing this deal or not?' he interrupted.

With a deep sigh she handed over the envelope. 'Here. But try not to be a bastard about it. You could crush a young woman's dreams.'

'I'm not the one doing the crushing. You're the one breaking your contract with her.'

Flo's expression became pinched. 'I wanted it written into our agreement that the current contract for Little Bay Book Shack remained until her time was up. Your lawyers wouldn't do it.'

Because the wharf and the waterfront were all part of a carefully worked through plan that had already taken far longer than he'd wanted to come to fruition. 'Maybe you should have got yourself a better lawyer.' *Or told your sons to stand on their own two feet for three months.*

She looked daggers at him for a moment – again, water off a duck's back – before turning sharply and marching out.

Immediately, he tore open the envelope, allowing himself a satisfied smile when he saw it had been signed. Before he got down to business, though, he pressed call on the first saved number in his contacts, Grandma. When her voice echoed back to him after three rings, he eased onto the chair behind his desk, muscles he hadn't realised were tight, slowly beginning to loosen.

'I wondered where you'd got to.' Her tone was warm but gently reprimanding. 'Thought you might have called last night.'

He took a second to close his eyes, to recall the image of him lying with Jade on the foredeck. 'I got tied up in something.'

'Um, must have been a good something.'

He frowned. 'Why do you say that?'

'I can hear the smile in your voice. Not often I get that. You're usually in such a rush, dashing from one deal to the next.'

His smile – and fuck, he had been smiling – slipped. 'I'm never in too much of a rush to talk to you. I'm sorry if it's ever sounded like I am.'

'You don't need to apologise, you silly goose. I know you're busy. Now tell me how you are.'

'You realise nobody else on this planet would dare to call me a silly goose?'

'Which is a shame, because that's what you need more of, people standing up to you. Now answer the question.'

He had a sudden image of Jade, taking him to task over his poor chat-up line. 'I'm fine.'

'Really fine, or *I'm saying this to shut my old grandma up*, fine?'

A bark of laughter escaped him. 'I know better than to lie to you, but I am okay. Just tired. The deal I was trying to make in Cape Cod hasn't come off yet, but there are issues here I need to address so I couldn't stay.' He smiled, for the first time seeing the silver lining to his current problem. 'In fact you're going to be seeing a bit more of me over the next few weeks because I'm down a resort manager.'

'Oh, no. Ashley?'

'Yes.' Because he didn't want to get into a discussion about why she'd left, he moved the conversation on. 'How's Bardot? Keeping out of trouble I hope.' Aware his schedule was becoming more and more manic, he'd bought her the beautiful Persian feline several years ago. She had friends and a housekeeper who popped in most days but he'd wanted – no he'd needed – to make sure she always had company. In common with the fifties sex kitten, Bardot had long blonde hair, a slinky walk and oozed style.

Immediately, the image of another knock-out blonde sex bomb filled his head.

'Oh, she's good as gold.' His grandma gatecrashed his thoughts and with a flash of guilt, he forced his mind to focus on the woman he was talking to. 'She's curled up next to me right now. I swear she can hear your voice because her ears have perked up and she's listening in.'

Probably expected him to suddenly appear with a bowl of the ridiculously expensive cat food his grandma insisted on giving the pampered puss. He remembered a time she'd fed both of them for a week for the price of one of Bardot's damn sachets. 'Tell Bardot I'll see her tomorrow evening. And if you've nothing else better planned, I'll see you, too.'

Her laughter tinkled down the phone. 'As if anything would be better than seeing my darling grandson.'

Satisfied he'd made the one important person in his life happy, he ended the call. Switching back to business mode, he phoned his go-to architect.

'Flo has signed the contract so you can dig out those plans for the waterfront cottages again. I want work to begin as soon as the legal team give us the okay.'

Chapter Eight

Jade's stomach pitched as she stood on the wharf that evening. Day two and she'd agreed to have another drink with the man she'd nearly had sex with on day one.

God, she made bad decisions. No wonder Lauren had such a low opinion of her.

She was in half a mind to walk back to the bookstore when she spotted his tall figure striding towards her from the resort. He slowed when he neared her. Dressed in a sky-blue polo shirt, charcoal linen jacket and jeans that looked soft and expensive, he screamed rich and sophisticated. She looked down at her short denim skirt, her simple sleeveless top. She screamed clumsy and inelegant.

'Hi.'

Her heart let out a loud thud. 'Hi back.'

He tilted his head. 'Are you okay?'

'Er, I think I may have got cold feet.'

Liam frowned, moving forward a few steps. 'Why?'

Nerves jangled and she clenched her hands to stop them from shaking. 'What do you see when you look at me?'

He nodded, like it wasn't a really odd question. 'You mean besides a drop-dead gorgeous blonde with a body I thoroughly enjoyed exploring and want to see more of?'

The belly flutter returned, reminding her why she'd come here in the first place. 'I like that, but yes.'

His gaze scanned her face, and she wondered if he was searching for the right words to guarantee the sex he'd not been given yesterday. 'I see a woman who made me laugh, which is rare. Also a woman who surprised me, fascinated me. Enough that I was looking forward to seeing her again tonight.'

'For sex.'

He frowned. 'For a drink.'

'So you don't want sex?'

He let out a frustrated sounding exhale. 'I don't want anything you don't willingly want to do.'

'Good answer.' Oh God, why was she making such a big deal of this? This gorgeous man, who only had to look at her to make her knees weak, had invited her for a drink. So what if his motive wasn't pure, it's not like he was pretending it would be anything more than a hook-up. And if they did end up having sex, it would be her choice. Her choice to sleep with a guy who said she was *fascinating, surprising*. If she thought of her resolution about avoiding guys who underestimated her, he'd just seen more in her than anyone else ever had.

'So, where is the best place on Nantucket to have a drink?'

His eyes flared and he placed his free hand on her hip, turning her to face him. 'I'll show you. But first...'

His mouth inched closer and as his gaze pinned hers, her stomach felt like it did at the top of a rollercoaster, all squirmy, a little fear mixed with excitement, adrenaline pounding through her. She could feel the heat of his palm through her skirt, smell his expensive cologne on her every inhale. Feel the tickle of his breath across her lips as his mouth hovered over hers.

'Fuck, you're breathtaking.'

This was why she was here. He made her feel worthy of catching his attention. 'I managed to avoid the smell of stale cocktail this time.'

He let out a low laugh. A second later, his mouth descended and all the breath rushed from her lungs as he started to slowly devour her, his tongue driving between her parted lips, his hips pushing against hers, letting her feel how hard he was.

She whimpered – honest to God, frigging whimpered – when he drew away. 'Are you up for a walk? It's about three-quarters of a mile but we can take a car if you prefer.'

'A walk is good, providing my legs stop trembling.'

He smiled, taking her hand in his. 'Then let's go.'

He led her away from the wharf and onto a footpath. 'So where *are* we actually going?' she asked when she managed to catch her breath, though the way his fingers smoothed across her knuckles as they walked did not help to calm her racing pulse.

'Galley Beach.'

He glanced at her and she frowned. 'Is that supposed to mean something to me?'

'Just wondering if you've heard of it in any of those guidebooks you devoured.'

It gave her a burst of pleasure to know he'd been listening. 'I don't remember it, no.' She gave him a gentle dig in the ribs. 'That's why I wanted the inside knowledge. Why *do* you come to Nantucket so often?'

'I visit for business.'

'Um, business. Is that whale business?'

He shook his head, looking amused. 'Tourism. How about you? Holiday?'

'In a way. I'm going to be working in a shop for a few months, but because it's not my real job it doesn't feel like work. Just an amazing opportunity to do something different, to maybe, hopefully, make my mark on it.' She put a hand to her chest, feeling the increase in her heart rate. 'I'm so excited to be here, it's crazy. I want to make the most of it so while I'm not beavering away in the shop I want to explore everything Nantucket has to offer. The pictures in the guidebooks looked amazing, and what I've seen so far has been … I want to say, cute, but that's wrong because it's got this elegant air, but also old fashioned, like I'm in a different century. I mean, boardwalks, cobbles, buildings made of weathered wood, sand dunes and lighthouses. It's not like London, that's for sure.'

'You're a long way from home,' he murmured as they rounded a corner, giving her a peek of the vivid blue of the ocean between the perfectly maintained grey shingle properties.

'That's kind of the point. I've lived what you could call a sheltered life, but this is my chance to stretch my wings. See what I'm really capable of.'

Her head bopped from side to side as they walked past houses that seemed to get bigger and more impressive with every stride. The lawns were immaculate, the hedges precisely trimmed, white picket fences freshly painted. Some had tennis courts, many had a deck on the roof, presumably giving a fabulous view of the sea. There was even a ship's figurehead.

'It's from a merchant ship,' Liam remarked as he saw her starring. 'In the 1800s, it sailed six times to the Pacific.'

'Incredible.' She shook her head. 'Not just the figurehead, but —' she waved at the houses as they walked '—the whole street. There's no litter, no peeling paintwork, no overgrown gardens. It's all so perfect. So pretty…' She trailed off as she caught sight of the beach ahead. 'Oh, my God, that's beautiful.'

Between the grey shingle buildings was a magnificent stretch of sandy beach which seemed to glow gold, thanks to the glorious orange setting sun.

He paused, gave a little shake of his head.

'What?'

'I've seen it so often I've become blasé.' He turned to look at her. 'It's rare to see it through a fresh pair of eyes.'

'Well you should spend time in West London. Then you'd appreciate the hell out of this place.'

Her jaw continued to fall open as they walked through the entrance of the Galley Beach restaurant and out onto the beach, where groups of tables were clustered on the sand. Yep, actually on the sand. It was busy with people enjoying a drink in the evening glow of the sun, laughter drowning out the sound of the waves as they lapped up the shore. They were led to the only free table, the waitress not shy about ogling Liam.

Not that he seemed to notice. His gaze wasn't on the woman who pulled out his chair while giving him a flirty smile, nor was it on the setting sun, or even the drinks menu that was pushed into his hands. It was on *her*.

She had never felt so absolutely the centre of a guy's attention.

'I'm sorry about earlier.' He looked puzzled and she gave him a sheepish smile, looking around her, drinking it all in. 'The cold feet. I wouldn't have wanted to miss this for the world. Thank you for bringing me.'

She was like a kid in a candy store, Liam thought, as he watched the expressions of awe, of delight, flicker across her face as they drank their second cocktail and finished off the plate of butter-poached lobster he'd ordered so she could get the full Nantucket experience. All against the backdrop of a perfect sunset. It cast a shimmery light over her, making her skin look more tanned, her hair like fine-spun gold. The short capped sleeves of the silky top she wore fluttered in the breeze, drawing his gaze, which inevitably dipped down to her cleavage. No, not a kid. A fully developed, innately sexy woman who somehow also managed to look innocent, her enthusiasm a refreshing change from the jaded attitudes of the women he usually shared a drink with. She didn't try to act coy, or cool. She let him see everything she was thinking.

'What is it you do back home?' It wasn't polite conversation. He *wanted* to know. She intrigued him, this combination of klutzy, funny, vulnerable, brave, all rolled up in a blonde bombshell package.

'You want the fancy title or the real one?'

He mentally added down to earth and guileless to his list. 'Both.'

'I'm a publishing assistant, which basically means I'm an admin.' Her gaze fell to her drink for a moment before meeting his. 'I know I have to work my way up, but I've been there two years now and I'm still not doing what I want to do. They know I'm not happy, which is why they let me have three months off to come here.'

'And what *do* you want to do?'

She looked back at him. 'Do you really want to know this?'

'If I didn't, I wouldn't ask.'

She seemed to study him before nodding her head. 'Yeah, I can see that about you. You wouldn't bother to pretend to like something or enjoy it, so, well, thank you for being interested. Nobody has ever actually asked me what I want to do.'

'Not your parents?'

'They're the best, don't get me wrong, but they were more about what I was capable of doing.'

He thought back to his own childhood and realised in many ways he'd been lucky. His grandma had always shown an interest in him. 'You don't have to thank me for asking questions I want to know the answer to.'

'Okay. I hope you don't regret asking though because when I get onto this subject...' She grinned. 'I have this obsession with books, and when I say obsession I mean crazy, over-the-top passion for them. Obviously, I'm addicted to reading them, but I also love touching them, smelling them. God, there is nothing better than the smell of a new paperback. Well, maybe some things are as good. Like whatever aftershave you wear, that's a real belly flutterer.' He almost choked on his drink and she giggled. 'Nobody's ever told you how good you smell? Well, books also smell amazing but in a different way. Comforting, yet with a hint of promise because you know when you open it, you're going to be transported somewhere thrilling. And then there's the covers. There is nothing prettier than a stack of books.' She glanced around her and laughed. 'Okay, again you've got me there because this beach, in this peachy light, is probably the prettiest thing I've ever seen. In fact, it looks like it could be the backdrop to a raunchy romance novel. It just needs a tall, dark, handsome guy on the front wearing nothing but his shorts and a broody smile.' Her eyes caught his, mischief dancing in their blue depths.

His groin tightened. And yes, he wanted sex, but he also felt the impact of her grin under his ribs and all the way down to his toes. 'You want to work with books.' A thought niggled, but vanished at the sight of her uninhibited laughter.

'What gave it away? But yes, I do. And hopefully when I get home I'll be able to persuade my boss to give me more responsibilities in that direction. Maybe get the chance to proofread some books, start to learn how to edit. I don't know. I want to be more than a woman who juggles diaries, files documents and answers emails.' She stared back at him, face suddenly serious. 'And I want people to see more than a blonde, busty airhead when they look at me.'

He inclined his head, aware he'd judged her that way, too,

when he'd first seen her. 'I can't not see the blonde hair, or the sexy as fuck figure'—he gestured to the table they were sitting on —'but I don't do this. Or at least I haven't, not for a long time.'

'This?'

'I don't make drinks reservations. I don't ask questions of the woman I'm drinking with.' He made sure to catch her eye. 'I don't enjoy listening to her talk.'

'Oh.' A flush crept over her cheeks but then her mouth tilted in a playful smile. 'You want to hear more about books?'

'Not books, no.' They brought back bad memories. He glanced at her empty glass. 'Do you want another drink?'

She sunk her teeth into her plump bottom lip. 'What's the alternative?'

'I take you back to where you're staying.' He lifted his eyes to hers, let her see his desire. 'Or you come back to the boat.'

'Um, the cocktails weren't up to much, if I remember.'

Christ, she was teasing him. The sad part was he didn't even mind. Welcomed the flirting, even if it didn't end the way he wanted it to, because he was fucking enjoying himself. 'There's always champagne.'

'Oh, yes. I guess I could make do with that.'

She shot him another playful smile, this time added a wink, and he almost groaned out loud. Thank God he'd worn a jacket, so he could hide what he knew was an obvious bulge at his crotch.

When the bill arrived, he batted away the dollars she tried to push onto the table. 'I'm loaded, Jade.'

'So? When I sit down for a drink with my mates, we either share the bill or work it out on the basis of what we drank. Not how much we earn.'

He didn't have friends he went drinking with. 'I invited you, I pay.'

She thumped her small fist onto the table. 'Rock-paper-scissors.' When he just stared at her, she grinned. 'Come on, you must have played this game. Basically if you put your hand in a fist it's a rock, and if I put two fingers out like this—'

He placed a hand around hers. 'I'm aware of the game. Just not why we're playing it.'

'Duh, so I can have a chance at paying the bill, Mr Money Bags.'

Was he seriously about to play this dumb game while sitting in a sophisticated restaurant? She waggled her eyebrows, smiling playfully at him. 'Fine.'

He went with rock, figuring she'd go with scissors again. But a grin erupted across her face as she signalled paper. 'Yay, I win.' She grabbed at the bill, and her face fell. 'Holy shit, that's a lot of money. What was in the cocktails, gold leaf? Because I read about that, you can have a cocktail with gold leaf, which seems a real waste of gold. And money.'

Smiling, he took the bill from her and handed it, together with his card, to the passing waiter. 'Would have been easier to accept my offer in the first place.'

'Maybe. But then you'd have missed out on an important first.' He raised a brow and she grinned, blue eyes sparkling with humour. 'First time you've played rock-paper-scissors on Galley Beach.'

Laughter shot out of him. He could have told her laughing was also a first on Galley Beach but he'd already told her more than he was comfortable with. Instead, he took her hand and helped her to her feet. To his astonishment, she reached up on tiptoes and pressed a soft kiss to his cheek.

'Thank you.'

Her lips weren't even on his mouth. It shouldn't feel so good. Yet combined with the soft look in her eyes, the sweet smell of her, he felt an odd wave of dizziness.

Women didn't thank him for buying them a drink, like he'd done something special. They expected it.

Clearing his throat, he began to lead them back through the restaurant, his focus on putting one foot in front of the other. Not on the soft curl of her fingers around his hand, or the press of her body as it bumped against his. Definitely not on the weird sensation under his ribcage.

Or the throbbing heaviness in his groin.

Chapter Nine

Jade's heart began to gallop as they neared the yacht.

She'd made up her mind to go back with Liam the moment he'd asked her what she wanted to do with her life. When he'd admitted he had to make the reservation for their drink, it had sealed the deal. He could have made things easy for himself and accepted her suggestion they drink on his boat again. Instead, he'd taken her somewhere special. A place he clearly thought *she* would appreciate.

He didn't date, but he'd phoned ahead and booked a table.

He wanted to have sex, yet he'd listened to her rabbit on as if what she'd said was important to him.

The hottest man she'd ever met had treated her with respect. And enjoyed her company.

As he helped her onto his boat, the butterflies in her belly reacted like they were on speed, flapping their wings a million miles an hour.

And that was before he slid his hand against her lower back and drew her to him, close enough she felt the heat of his skin through her top. Far enough away she wanted to fling her arms around his neck and jump into his arms so she could feel that lean, hard body against hers.

'Kiss me.' Her voice sounded scratchy, rough to match the feel of her top against her aching nipples. 'Please.'

He groaned, dipping his head to do exactly that. Not a tentative first kiss now, but a full meeting of mouths, of tongues. She felt him everywhere, not just with the flicks of his tongue, the press of his lips, but his restless hands that smoothed up and down her back, then cupped her face. The press of his thighs, the hard length of him that pulsed against her belly.

'I've been thinking of undressing you all afternoon,' he rasped.

'I've been thinking of you undressing me for some of the afternoon,' she admitted, inhaling sharply as he slid off her top with a sure, deft touch before finding the zipper of her skirt and pushing it down.

'Only some?' As her clothes pooled at her feet, his fingers traced the edge of the lace of her bra before slipping under, his thumb rubbing her aching nipple.

'Um.' Her own hands dragged off his jacket before reaching into his jeans, their touch less practiced, less sure, but the need to feel him, to see him, driving her on. 'The rest of the time I imagined me undressing you.'

He gave a strangled half laugh, half growl as her fingers curled round his hard, pulsing length. 'What is it about you that I can laugh even when you're holding my dick?'

Class clown, needs to spend less time making people laugh and more of making something of herself.

'What do you usually do when someone holds it?' she asked. She squeezed, and his groan reverberated through her.

'I don't feel like I do now. Like I'm about to shoot my load after two good pulls.' He swore crudely. 'If you don't want this to end with you pressed into my mattress, you need to tell me now.'

Was she ready for this? Ready to have sex with a guy she'd be unlikely to meet again, yet would potentially ruin her for anyone else? 'I want to see your bed.'

'Thank fuck.' He lifted her into his arms, but then paused. 'Wait, is that *see* my bed or lie on my bed?'

Laughter bubbled out of her. 'I want to have a nosy inside your bedroom.' As his big body froze, she ran her nose up the side of his neck and inhaled. It was a close call, but he really did smell better than a paperback. 'And then I want to test out your mattress. With hot, sweaty sex,' she added, just in case it still wasn't one hundred per cent clear.

For a brief moment his body seemed to sag with relief and then suddenly she was being carried like a fairy princess through the cabin lined with cream-leather sofas and downstairs, to a bedroom with dark walnut panels and a huge bed with rumpled sheets.

'I wasn't expecting a visitor,' he huffed as he pushed the bedding aside.

'You weren't?' He seriously hadn't thought they'd end up here?

'Hoped, sure. Expected, no.'

He eased her carefully onto the bed like she was something fragile, then gazed down at her like she was something he wanted to devour.

'I want to taste you.'

Heat rushed between her legs and of their own volition her thighs separated. His eyes flared and he unfastened her bra before removing her underwear, sliding it over her hips and down her legs with a determination that caused her heart to thump against her ribs. She had a second to think it wasn't fair, he was still dressed, but then his head dipped and his tongue found exactly the spot she needed it to find.

Holy crap, he knew what he was doing down there. His lips knew where to press, his mouth where to suck, his tongue how to go from soft to hard, the rhythm he set slowly building until her hands grasped at the bed sheet, all sensation focused on one part of her body, pleasure building, building.

'Oh, my God. I'm going to come, like really detonate,' she panted, her hands flying to his head, tangling in his hair. 'Shit, that's it. Mother of everything holy…'

Pleasure ripped through her, dragging her into a vortex of colour, of stars. When she finally came down from it, she let out a long, satisfied breath. 'Whoa. What did you do to me? You are seriously good at that. Like one of those times I really want to give six stars but I know I'm only allowed five.' He stared back at her, eyes full of arousal, yet bemusement bumped around the edges. 'It's a book thing.'

He eased up, hot gaze raking her body. 'This needs to come off.' Nimble fingers undid the front clasp of her bra, and he groaned as her breasts spilled out, immediately burying his head in her cleavage, licking, sucking, his hips thrusting restlessly against her thigh, reminding her he hadn't come yet.

'Um, you're forgetting something.' She clasped his head, pulling it up. 'Much as I want your mouth to continue what it's doing, I want to see you without your clothes on, more.'

His eyes burned into hers as he undid the buttons of his shirt. 'You're sure?'

The saliva left her throat as she stared at the sculptured planes of his chest, muscles rippling beneath tanned skin, a smattering of dark chest hair adding to the very powerful male image. 'About you taking your clothes off?' She licked her lips, almost tasting the salt of his skin. 'Abso-flipping-lutely.' He huffed and she put her hand up. 'Yes, I'm sure I want sex with you.'

She barely had time to appreciate his wicked grin before he ducked to yank open a draw and pull out a square foil, which he ripped open with his teeth. A few moments later his jeans and boxers were shoved down, his eye-watering erection sheathed and he was levering himself over her.

Automatically her legs wrapped around his hips, pressing him against her core. She wriggled, trying to get more friction and he grunted. 'You feel me? How hard I am for you?'

One flex of his hips later and he slammed into her, stretching her, filling her, sucking the breath from her. 'Oh, my flaming God.'

Instantly he stilled. 'You okay?'

'I'm better than okay.' Her hands clutched at the tight globes of his arse. 'You feel so good. I mean big, really frigging *big*, like I can feel you everywhere, but so, so good.' Mindless, she pulled at him. 'More.'

He let out a deep, guttural groan and then his hips snapped, thrusting, thrusting, over and over, causing everything inside her to coil and tighten until she was a panting, needy mess. And then she broke, letting out a cry as pleasure spiralled through her again, flooding her senses, wave after wave until she dropped her head to the pillow, her body limp, her mind blank of anything except him, the feel of him still hard inside her.

A few thrusts later, he let out a quiet grunt of pleasure as he found his own release.

———————

Liam let out a satisfied sigh as he rolled onto his back, drawing Jade to his side. There had been a time he'd enjoyed cuddling after sex, before he'd learnt that letting people close allowed them to fuck you over. Still, there was no chance of that with a one … or two-night stand, and he liked the feel of Jade's skin against his.

'How many of your stars was that?'

He felt her smile against his skin. 'Definitely another six out of five.'

'I agree with the sentiment, but not the rating scale. You book people are strange.'

'I take it I won't see you in the shop then.'

The hand that had been stroking down the curve of her spine, stilled. 'Which shop is that?'

'I'm working in the bookstore on the wharf for three months. You know, the Little Bay Book Shack. Though it's hardly work, being surrounded by books in a cute shack overlooking the sea. More like the most exciting adventure of my life.'

His heart faltered, his mind began to race. It explained why she'd caught the resort transfer even though she'd admitted she wasn't staying at the resort. Ashley had told him of George and Flo's arrangement but she'd made him promise to let it continue, telling him it wasn't doing any harm. Technically, Jade wasn't an employee, though, at least not yet. Flo had signed, but until the money had been transferred, he didn't own the shop.

Still, it was … messy. And that was a fucking understatement. With mounting dread he recalled the conversation he'd had with Flo. *Think about the wide-eyed, eager young lady who's travelled all the way out here to run a bookstore on Nantucket.* He'd seen the dreamy look on Jade's face as she'd discussed her love of books, the excitement as she'd talked about working in the shop, making her mark. His stomach clenched. Fuck. How could he have not worked it out before?

Jade's hand wandered across his pecs, her fingers teasing his chest hair, and he sucked in a breath.

'Do you like reading?'

Christ, she was talking about books and he was torn between wanting to fuck her again, and jumping out of bed to put as much distance between them as possible so he could *think*. 'Not unless it's a contract.'

The warmth of her laughter caressed his skin, and he hardened further as her fingers circled his nipples. 'Oh, my God, that's so sad. Reading is the best. Why don't you let me find you a book? What are you into? Thrillers, action, autobiographies, travel…'

Dimly he was aware of her talking, but his mind was at war. Her breasts were cushioned against his side, her leg thrown over his, her fingers teasing the hairs on his abdomen, dipping lower…

I trust you. Enough to know you won't take advantage of me.

Fuck, this was wrong, wasn't it?

He groaned as her fingers curled around his girth, lust beginning to drown out all reason. The purchase hadn't legally been completed yet. It could still fall through. And besides, he'd be compensating her. She wouldn't lose out on her three months on the island. She could spend the time ticking off her tourist to-do list and reading all those damn books she loved so much. Hell, he'd let her raid the shop before he knocked it down. Take any of the books she wanted.

Automatically his hips shifted, pushing into her hand.

More laughter. 'Why do I get the feeling you're not listening to me?'

'If you want a conversation you need to take your hand off my dick.'

She smiled up at him, giving him a sultry look. 'Do you want me to?'

Mussed blonde hair, big blue eyes, large, naked breasts with rose-pink nipples puckered and begging for his tongue. She was the ultimate male fantasy.

You should use the balls she's stroking and tell her who you are, what you have planned. Give her the opportunity to decide if she still wants you.

But lust fired through his body, frying his brain. All he could think was how hard he was, how much he ached to bury himself inside her again. He was strong when it came to negotiating business deals, but pitifully weak when it came to resisting women he was fiercely attracted to. He'd paid the price for that weakness, had it shoved in his face, been ridiculed for it, yet Jade made him want to throw aside his common sense.

It's just sex, just a hook-up. They both knew that, so it didn't matter what happened tomorrow, did it?

'What I want,' he said gruffly. 'Is for you to sit on me and ride me until we both come.'

It was one in the morning and he was sitting on the aft deck, trawling through his emails. Sex had wiped him out for a good few hours but now his mind was alert, something he was well used to. The only time he'd slept through the night since boarding school was the night before, with Jade. He put it down to extreme exhaustion.

His eyes homed in on an email from his lawyer.

The funds had transferred. The wharf was now his.

He waited for the pulse of satisfaction, but all he felt was a wave of guilt. He should have told Jade who he was. Next time they met was going to be awkward as fuck. Casting an eye over another email, this one from Flo, he read that she was going to see the bookstore manager tomorrow morning to tell her in person and wanted him to come along to hand over.

What Flo didn't say, but heavily implied, was she was going to make it clear to Jade that he was expected to honour their contract.

The guilt settled like a lead weight in his stomach. *You're going to pay her. She'll be able to stay on the resort.* Yeah, he was worrying over nothing. Chances are she'd actually be pleased to hear she had three months to enjoy the island without the hassle of running a damn bookstore.

Ten-year-old me dreamt of living in a castle made of books.

Shit.

At the sound of footsteps, he jerked his head up. Jade walked towards him, her clothes back on, her blonde hair flowing wildly around her shoulders. 'I, um, thought I should head off.'

His body reacted to the sight of her, but now his mind was in control. *Too fucking late.* 'I'll walk you back.'

'Er, if you're worried I'll get lost, I can see the shop from here.'

'It's not a matter of getting lost.' He rose to his feet, closing the laptop, his grandma's voice echoing in his ear. *You treat women with respect, even if they sometimes haven't given you the same courtesy.* 'It's manners.'

The walk back along the wharf was quiet. He was all too aware of the unevenness of the current situation, yet now wasn't the time to confess who he was. Not in the moonlight, when his body still hummed from the sex they'd just enjoyed and their clothes were wrinkled from being discarded on the cabin floor.

Tomorrow, in the cold light of day, when they didn't both smell of sex.

She paused at the entrance to the shop. 'Well, thanks for the escort. Whoever taught you manners should be proud of you.'

'My grandma.' *But she wouldn't be proud of what he'd done tonight.* It was an uncomfortable thought.

'Well, thank you Liam's grandma.'

She smiled, and it was so guileless, so open, he felt a twist in his gut. Whether it was another dose of guilt or some other force taking over, he wasn't sure, but he touched his hand to her face, keen to make sure that at least for now, they would part as friends. 'Thank you for yesterday, and for tonight. I enjoyed spending time with you.' Dipping his head, he pressed a soft kiss to her lips. 'Goodnight, Jade.'

She nodded, her eyes darting over his face, making him wonder what she saw. 'No thanks needed. In case it wasn't totally obvious, I had a good time, too.' After giving him one final look, she pushed open the door to the bookstore.

Sliding his hands into his pockets, he set off back to the boat, not liking how he felt. Instead of relief at the amicable ending of a successful two-night stand, he felt unsettled, a sick feeling in his stomach that he knew would only get worse when she found out who he was. And what he had planned.

Chapter Ten

Jade hummed as she opened the box of books that had just been delivered. As per Daisy's instructions, she set about checking and logging the order. Flo was due any minute and she wondered what her boss would think to the display she'd spent the morning putting together, in between the customers she'd served. She'd gone rainbow crazy, and the colourful theme didn't just flow through the book stacks on the coffee table and display shelves, it extended to the balloons she'd bought and hung this morning (maybe that did look a bit like a kids party?) and the cushions on the sofa (some found, some borrowed from the resort).

If running a shop was all about making it look impactful, she had this nailed.

'Hello!'

Jade jumped to her feet, and smiled when she caught sight of the person stepping into the shop. 'Oh wow, I was just thinking about you, and here you are.'

Flo, looking funky and elegant in a flowing, brightly patterned jumpsuit, smiled back. 'Here I am.'

'It's so fab to finally see you in person after all those frigging Zoom calls.' Jade rushed up to her, then halted, letting out an embarrassed laugh. 'I was going to hug you, but then I realised that's probably not appropriate as you're my boss.'

Something flashed across the older lady's face, but before Jade could wonder what was wrong, Flo put her arms round her. 'We can hug.'

'I'm so grateful you gave me this opportunity,' Jade babbled, unable to stop the words flowing. 'It's totally awesome to be here. The shop is about the coolest thing I've ever seen, and I promise I'm going to do you proud and keep it looking amazing.' A deep sigh echoed from Flo and as she drew back from the hug, Jade felt a jolt of panic at the expression on her boss's face. 'Oh, God, have I mucked up already? I thought it would be okay to rearrange things a bit but—'

'Good Lord, you've done nothing wrong.' Flo clasped her hands, 'It's me who's mucked up.' With a tight nod, she indicated to the squishy sofa. 'Shall we take a seat?'

'Um, okay.' There was something about the pinched way Flo smiled, the stiff way she walked, that spread alarm through Jade as she followed her.

'There's no easy way for me to say this,' Flo began the moment she sat down. 'I've sold the wharf to the resort.'

'Oh.' Jade wasn't sure how to react.

'It means the bookstore belongs to the new owners, too.'

'So you're not going to be my boss anymore?'

'No.'

The door chime sounded, indicating another customer. They both turned to see who had walked in, and Jade sucked in a breath. She was dimly aware of Flo saying something but she was too distracted by the sight of the man striding in to hear what she said.

Liam, all business in chinos and an expensive-looking blue

linen jacket, slid off his shades and headed towards them with a purposeful air. *He knows you work here. This isn't a coincidence.* With her heart hammering, she took a moment to remind herself to breathe, another to smile in greeting.

'Hi. I wasn't expecting to see you here.' Had he come to ask her out again? She could barely speak past the wild fluttering in her chest. 'I didn't think you liked books.'

'I don't.'

His face was guarded, his eyes blank. As if they'd never met. 'Oh, you don't have to worry about talking to me in front of Flo. She's not a customer. Or even my boss, which she would have been if you'd come in five minutes earlier, but apparently she's sold the shop and now I've got a new boss.'

His expression tightened and she wanted to ask why he was acting so weird, but Flo was talking to her and demanding her attention instead. 'Sorry Flo, what did you say?'

Flo cleared her throat. 'I said Liam is your new boss.'

'He... What?'

'He's your new boss.'

Confused, she swivelled to face Liam again. 'You've taken over the bookstore?' This had to be a joke. 'But you don't even like books.'

A muscle flexed in his jaw and though his eyes met hers, they didn't linger, shifting instead to look at Flo. 'I'm the new owner of the wharf and this building, yes. It's going to be absorbed into the resort.'

'Oh.' She'd slept with her boss. Her stomach rolled. Yeah, that wasn't good, not good at all. She hadn't known he'd be her boss, though, so surely she could give herself a break. But ... the queasy feeling returned. 'Did you know? When we...' She trailed off as she realised Flo was watching them with obvious interest. 'Er, when we met, did you know you were going to be my boss?'

That muscle jumped again. 'When we first met, no.'

First? Did that mean he knew later? But she couldn't ask, not with Flo there. 'Okay, so this is a bit, er, unexpected. And awkward,' she tagged on, aware of a heavy tension in the air. Bad enough in a usual place of work, but in this place of calm, bibliophilic beauty, it felt blasphemous.

'I'm sure Flo will want to discuss this further with you. I just came to … introduce myself.'

A slight flush crept over his cheeks and if she'd hadn't felt so off-balanced, she might have found it interesting, even a little endearing, to see him so uncomfortable. 'Pretty sure we've already moved past the introduction phase, *boss*.'

The flush deepened and he looked as if he was about to say something but then gave a little shake of his head. 'Perhaps when you've finished talking to Flo you can come to my office in the resort.'

So business-like, impersonal. No trace of the man who'd walked her back last night. Who'd had his hands, and his mouth, on every part of her body. *Don't think about it.* She straightened her back, looked him in the eye. 'Is that an order?'

He let out a heavy exhale. 'It's a polite request.'

With an abrupt nod, he turned and strode out, leaving in his wake a lingering hint of very male cologne and a heavily charged atmosphere.

'I'm sorry to do this to you,' Flo broke the silence, her expression full of apology. 'When I hired you, I fully intended to let the contract run and then sell, but a few weeks ago my sons announced their business had taken another hit and they were going to become bankrupt if they didn't get a loan now. Of course, you'd already booked your flight and organised the time off work. Plus you were so excited about coming here.' She let out a deep sigh. 'Call me an old fool but I thought if I kept putting off the sale, things would work out and my sons would find the money another way.' She gave Jade a sad smile. 'I love my children, would do anything for them, but sometimes they drive me crazy.'

'It's okay. I understand. My parents would do the same for me and my sister.' Well, they definitely would for Lauren and they probably would for Jade, too, because they loved her – they'd just be less certain of ever getting the money back.

'He has promised you'll still be able to stay for the full three months, but I only have his word on that. His lawyers refused to put anything into the contract, and frankly they had me over a barrel because the wharf isn't worth the money he's paying to anyone else.' She smiled sadly, covering one of Jade's hands with her own. 'I want you to know I still have faith that you'll be a real asset to Little Bay Book Shack. I'm sure you'll be able to convince Liam Haven of that, too.'

Liam *Haven*. Holy shit, it was slowly sinking in. The yacht's name, *Ocean Haven*, which was the same name as that of the resort. She hadn't just slept with her new boss. She'd slept with a man who owned the whole frigging resort.

Flo coughed. 'It's none of my business, but I get the sense you two already know each other?'

'Sort of. At least, I thought I knew him a little bit. Now I'm not sure.'

Flo slowly climbed to her feet, bangles jangling. 'Well, I'm afraid this is goodbye, dear. Remember I'm always at the end of the phone if you want any advice.' She gave Jade a tight hug and started walking towards the door. When she opened it, she halted and glanced back at her. 'I know it's none of my business, but I'd be very wary of climbing into bed with Liam Haven. He has a reputation of being ruthless, both in business and his personal life.' She smiled, as if trying to soften her words. 'Good luck, dear.'

Ruthless. Yeah, she wasn't kidding. As Jade watched the woman she'd managed to convince to hire her disappear out of her life, anger mixed with a massive swell of self-disgust. Only a few days into her supposed life-altering three months, and already she'd fallen back into old habits, showing herself to be utterly stupid when it came to men.

———

At the tap on his door, Liam's pulse kicked up a gear, only to settle immediately when he saw his deputy's face.

'Jeremy.'

The man's ginger eyebrows flew up to his hairline. 'You don't sound happy. And there was me thinking that now you've secured the deal on the wharf, you'd be in a sunny mood this morning.' He waved a hand in Liam's direction. 'Let me rephrase that, because sunny is most certainly not a mood I could ever associate with you. How about instead I ask who pissed you off this morning?'

'Nobody.' It was himself Liam was annoyed at. He was accustomed to taking tough decisions, having difficult conversations, but the one he was about to have with Jade was causing his stomach to churn. 'What do you want?'

Ignoring his abruptness, Jeremy sauntered into the office and dropped elegantly into the chair opposite. 'I bring good news. The supply issue from yesterday is resolved, so we're running on full menus again and the shower in the presidential suite has been fixed. The couple moved back this morning and graciously accepted our offer of free food and drink for the rest of their stay.'

Liam baulked. 'Who agreed that?'

'I did. Better to be in the red with happy guests than in the black with angry ones. Happy guests will come back, spend lots of money on their return, and sing your praises to their rich friends who will then book their own holiday here and spend lots of money—'

'I get the picture,' Liam interrupted. He didn't like giving anything away free to people rich enough to squander ten-thousand dollars on a night in a hotel, but this was why he employed Jeremy. To be the light to his dark.

'Oh, I'm sorry.' They both turned to find Jade standing in the doorway, cheeks flushed. 'I knocked, and I thought I heard someone say come in, but obviously I just heard a voice, and assumed it said come in.' Her gaze jumped to Jeremy and back to Liam, before giving him a smile he knew to be forced because he'd seen her real one. 'I'll just turn right round and wait outside. Pretend I wasn't here.'

That, Liam thought with a flare of annoyance, was damn near impossible. As if he could read his mind, and Liam hoped to Christ he couldn't, Jeremy let out a low whistle the moment the door clicked shut. 'And who is that?'

If Jeremy wasn't a gay, engaged man, Liam had an unnerving feeling he'd have been annoyed at his interest. 'Jade. She arrived a couple of days ago to run the bookstore.'

'Ah, another of Flo's band of super-keen temps eager to leave their stamp on the Little Bay Book Shack.' Jeremy studied him a moment. 'Does she know you plan on bulldozing the place she's spent the last few months in a state of giddy excitement about running?'

Annoyance bubbled. 'Not yet, but it's hardly my issue. Flo employed her.'

'Yes, but now you're about to throw her dream onto a bonfire and light the match.'

'Was there anything else?' he snapped.

Jeremy rose to his feet. 'Nope, at least nothing more important than the conversation you're about to have.' He walked towards the door but instead of opening it, he turned back to Liam. 'Be kind.'

Jesus. Like he was some sort of big bad wolf? 'I'll be fair.'

'You always are.' Jeremy met his eyes. 'But that isn't the same thing.'

He ducked out of the room and Liam slumped back against his chair. Fuck. For the first time in years, he didn't feel ready for the conversation he was about to have. He'd asked Jade to come to the office in the hope the business environment would enable him to forget his attraction, forget all memories of the last two nights, and see her as another issue to be handled.

He looked up at the light tap on the door, and instantly knew it didn't matter where he met her. He wouldn't be able to look at her without thinking of sex. Heart thumping, sweaty, can't-get-enough-of-it sex. Mixed with bouts of laughter.

She wasn't laughing now. In fact, she looked as uncomfortable as he felt.

'So, apparently I slept with my boss,' she said.

'Apparently.'

She swallowed and glanced away from him. 'You said you didn't know the first time.'

'How could I? We didn't talk about anything personal.'

Bold blue eyes clashed with his. 'I told you something about me I'd never admitted to anyone.' She let out a pained laugh. 'To think I thought you were sweet.'

His skin felt it was too tight a fit for his body. 'I told you I wasn't.'

'And you were right. Because a sweet guy – heck, just a decent one – would have told me who he was after he knew I was working at the bookstore for three months.'

Guilt slithered into his gut. 'You had your hand on my dick. I couldn't fucking help myself.'

Her cheeks reddened. 'And I'm supposed to be flattered?'

Shit. He let out a rough exhale, pinching the bridge of his nose in frustration. 'Look, what is done, is done.' Except that it didn't feel done. She was technically now his employee, in his place of work, and wearing a simple short-sleeved blouse and Capri pants that should not scream sex. Yet he wanted to leap over his desk and crash his mouth down on hers. Then pin her against the wall, or to his desk and…

'Flo said you promised her I could stay the full three months.'

He dragged his mind out of the gutter. 'You can. I'll pay whatever Flo agreed with you, and you can stay in a room here at the resort.'

'Thanks but I don't need a room. I'm sleeping in a cute studio above the bookstore.'

He worked to make his tone flat, dispassionate. 'Little Bay Book Shack is being knocked down.'

Her mouth hung open, blonde brows coming together in a frown. 'You're getting rid of the bookstore?'

'Yes.'

'So I'll be selling books from a place in the main resort?'

Why did his stomach feel like it was weighed down with a week's worth of undigested, congealed take-out? 'There'll be no bookselling. You have three months on the resort with nothing to do but enjoy yourself.'

'*Enjoy* myself?' Her skin paled, her hands twisting as she stared back at him. 'Do you remember me telling you that running the bookstore for the next three months was the most exciting adventure of my life?'

That weight in his stomach doubled. 'Yes.'

Her face hardened, blue eyes spitting fire at him. 'So you didn't just have sex with me while being fully aware I had no clue you were my boss. You also had sex with me knowing you were going to stomp on my adventure before it had begun?'

Now it felt like acid was burning through the lining of his stomach. 'Yes.'

She let out a choked laugh. 'And I thought I'd reached rock

bottom with the last two guys I slept with.' Her eyes glistened. 'Way to go, Jade. You really know how to pick them.'

A band tightened round Liam's chest and he didn't know how to deal with the sensation. He knew all about being hurt, being betrayed, but somehow he'd managed to be the one doing the hurting. 'I'm paying you, you won't lose out.' He tried to smile. 'And you can have whatever books you want, for free,'

She snorted dismissively. 'It's not about money.'

'It's always about money.'

'Maybe in your world.'

He wasn't a stranger to being looked at with disdain, yet it had never felt this uncomfortable. 'What is it about, then?'

'For starters, it's about you treating me with the respect I deserve.'

It was his turn to be angry. 'I have. I *am*.'

'Are you?'

A tear began to creep down her cheek and that feeling that his skin was too tight? It was magnified, leaving him feeling itchy all over, unable to breathe properly.

'If you respected me,' she continued, her voice lacking the warmth, the vitality he was used to. 'You would have been upfront with me as soon as you knew I was working in the bookstore. You wouldn't have gone on to sleep with me again.' She laughed humourlessly. 'I think we can both agree you well and truly fucked me over in more ways than one.'

With a final, searing glance at him, she swivelled round and marched out of the room.

Rooted to the spot, Liam stared back at the open door. The scent of coconut lingered in the air, yet all he could taste was the acid that inched up his throat.

It felt like he'd ruined something special, trampled on something important.

Chapter Eleven

Tears blurred her vision as Jade dashed past the reception, avoiding the gaze of the receptionist. She'd come out here to prove she was better than everyone thought, yet she'd ended up sleeping with her boss, losing her job and shredding any lingering self-respect she may have arrived with.

Sod staying here for another three months, she wanted to go home *now*.

She swerved around a couple who were clearly so besotted they couldn't walk to the restaurant without stopping to kiss, and a pang of acute longing arrowed through her. What it must feel like to be that in love you couldn't go a minute without needing to touch, to kiss.

'Jade, wait.'

At the sound of Liam's voice, her heart lurched. No she couldn't face him again. Not until she'd calmed, found her balance.

Head down, she kept half walking, half running. He owned the resort, for God's sake. He wasn't going to be caught chasing some stupid blonde who'd been dumb enough to have sex with him.

'Please.'

That was harder to ignore. Her pace slowed and a few seconds later he appeared beside her.

'I'm sorry.'

He sounded genuine, but she was too hurt to accept it and too angry. And not just with him. She was livid with herself for being weak enough to sleep with him. 'Which part are you sorry for? Sleeping with me? Sleeping with me knowing you were my boss, or sleeping with me knowing the next day you were going to crush me?'

His tall frame stiffened, tension rippling through it. 'Not for sleeping with you.'

'Yeah, well I'm gutted about all of it.' Unwilling to look at him, she kept her gaze ahead, her chest pinching when she caught sight of the wooden pontoon, and the grey tiled roof of Little Bay Book Shack beyond it. 'Having sex with the first guy I met out here was unbelievably cheap, even by my standards.'

He reached for her arm, his touch burning her skin. 'Don't.'

She shook his hand off. 'Don't what?'

'Demean yourself, or what we did.' His gaze pinned hers. 'We had a rare chemistry, which lead to some phenomenal sex. I was wrong not to stop it as soon as I realised you were working in the bookstore, but I figured as I was going to pay you and let you stay, you wouldn't be too upset.'

She forced her gaze away from his, determined not to be swayed by those beautiful eyes. 'Of course you thought that. I was some blonde happy to go back to your boat and have sex with you even though we'd only just met. Why wouldn't I also be happy lazing about by the pool all day and taking your money?'

He let out a coarse oath, showing that rough edge again, at odds with his expensive good looks. 'Stop twisting what I say.'

'Am I twisting it? Or am I just saying what you really thought?' Once more, she felt the sting of tears. She needed to get away from him, to lick her wounds and regroup. 'Look, thanks for the offer to let me stay. It's decent of you. I mean, three months of paid holiday isn't something I should be grumbling about, right? So let me think about it, and meanwhile I presume there's stuff I need to do to close the shop, so I'll see if Flo can help me with that. Or Daisy.' Crap, she could feel the tears overflowing and made a desperate swipe with her hand. 'We spent the last few days pinging ideas back and forth for how to grow the business, but I guess learning how to wind it down is just as useful.' A sob squeezed past her throat, and she turned away, embarrassed. 'Anyway, I'll catch you later.'

Not giving him a chance to reply, she set off towards the wharf, praying he didn't follow her. The next time she talked to him, she needed to have her emotions under control.

The further she walked away from the resort, the quieter everything became. She knew he wasn't following her because she couldn't hear any footsteps. Couldn't hear anything at all but for the creak of the wharf as she walked across it.

Her heart melted at the sight of the grey-shingled building as it came fully into view. She'd arrived with such high hopes, a nervous bundle of anticipation and excitement, and now ... now she felt hollowed out. Sure, she could stay, but what was the point? Being paid to do nothing wouldn't help her confidence, it would make her feel like a scrounger.

With a sigh she unlocked the shop and stepped inside. As she walked across the wooden floor, her eyes drank in the driftwood shelves, the rainbow book displays she'd agonised over, and her heart twisted at the wasted opportunity, the utter disappointment of it all.

A buzz in her pocket alerted her to her phone ringing.

'Mum.' She swallowed down the boulder of emotion and

forced her voice to sound calm as she answered the call. 'Is everything okay?'

'Hello love, everything is just fine, but how are things with you? I can't stop thinking about you and wondering how you're getting on.'

Shame flooded her, followed by a pang of regret. She should have phoned home yesterday. That way she'd have given herself a few days before she had this awkward conversation. 'Sorry, I meant to phone, but there's so much going on.' *I've been shagging my boss and losing my job.* God, she felt sick. How could she explain this to her parents, to Lauren? To the team at work who'd been rooting for her?

It's not your fault Liam's closing the shop.

'Of course, you're busy,' her mum replied. 'Running a business, especially when you've not done it before, and it's in a foreign country, is not for the faint-hearted. We're so proud of you, Jade.'

Bollocks. Tears crept down Jade's cheeks and it was hard, so frigging hard, not to start blubbering. 'Thank you.'

'Well, I won't keep you. I just wanted to hear your voice and check everything was okay. I can't wait to hear more about the shop and how you're doing when you've got the time.'

Jade ended the call and slumped to the floor, hit by a wave of acute sadness. She wasn't the only one who was going to be disappointed when she went home without having achieved anything.

No. *Not happening.*

Reaching for the hem of her blouse, she wiped away the crappy tears. She was done disappointing her family. More than that, she was done being underestimated by everyone … *including* herself.

She was smart, capable. Maybe she didn't totally believe that yet, but the thing about faking it till you made it? She could fake the hell out of this.

Smart, capable women didn't take the money and go quietly.

They made things happen.

Settling onto the ocean-blue sofa, she scrolled through her contacts and found Flo's number.

Liam's gaze skimmed across the wharf, and the bay frontage beyond. Now it was all his, he could start to picture the cottages his architect had designed, in consultation with the HDC (Historic District Commission) who oversaw every build, preserving Nantucket's historic character. High-class buildings, each with a large upper balcony and lower terrace.

Luxury holiday accommodation for those prepared to pay top dollar for a little exclusivity, a lot of high-end furnishings and a private wharf to moor their yacht. Years in the making, it was a critical addition to his portfolio.

With an inward nod of satisfaction, he strode towards the bookstore. Tension, or was it anticipation, skated down his spine as he neared. He'd been surprised to get the message from Jade, via May, asking if he'd meet her in the shop after it closed. 'Wonder what that can be about,' the front-desk manager had mused, giving him a calculated look. 'When she left your office earlier, she didn't look like a woman who'd want to see you again for a long while.'

Liam had narrowed his eyes, waited until she looked away, then changed the subject. He actively discouraged talk about anything that wasn't work related. He wanted people to be a little afraid of him. That way they stayed away. It was why he couldn't understand how he'd blurted so much about his childhood to

Jade. He made a mental note to avoid picking up women when shattered, and under the influence of whisky.

His pace slowed as he pushed open the bookstore door.

Christ, he'd forgotten the place looked like a unicorn had vomited up rainbows.

'Hi.' Jade came into view at the back of the shop, giving him a guarded look. He immediately mourned her smile. 'Thanks for coming.'

'No problem.' His gaze drifted over the shop again, noticing things he hadn't before because he'd been too focused on Jade. 'Don't some of those cushions belong in the resort?'

'I borrowed them from the housekeeping lady.' Her left hand flew to cover her mouth. 'Crap, please don't be cross with her. I put her in an awkward position by asking for them. I promised I'd get them back by the end of today, which I totally will. I just wanted to create something different, you know, to try to impress Flo.' She gave him a stony look. 'Only it turns out she was too busy telling me she'd sold up, to notice.'

He'd let staff go without a ripple of unease. Why did this feel so difficult? 'The look is certainly … eye-catching.'

'It is, isn't it?' She seemed to have put her dislike of him aside for a moment as she stared back at the shelves. 'I see loads of rainbow stacks on Instagram and I love them, so I thought I'd try it out here. I got carried away though and ended up continuing it in everything I could.' Her gaze swung towards the white-washed walls. 'You're lucky I didn't have any paint or there would be rainbows all over the walls.'

He shrugged. 'It would make no difference to me. We'll be ripping it down as soon as we bring a construction company on board.'

Wrong thing to say.

'So you said.' She turned back to him, more than a hint of challenge in her eyes. 'I asked you to meet me here to remind you how special this place is. How many bookstores are there on Nantucket?'

'Not many, because they don't make money.'

She pulled a face. 'This place makes money. Otherwise Flo wouldn't have been able to run it for so long.'

'Luxury cottages will make a lot more money,' he countered flatly.

'And that's all you care about? I've been talking to Flo and she says the bookstore could be a real asset to the resort. She has loads of examples of how we've worked together to help give your guests a brilliant holiday experience.'

'If guests are that bothered about reading, they'll bring their own books.' He wasn't used to being questioned, and he let his frustration show. 'I'm running a business here, not an Instagram photo opportunity. A business that keeps hundreds of staff in employment. I need to maximise profitability.'

She looked less than impressed. 'Your boat, oh, sorry, your *luxury yacht*, tells me you're already making a heck of a lot of money out of the resort as it is. Do you really need to demolish a building with character, a place islanders *and* holidaymakers can enjoy, just to make even more?'

'Making money is what I do,' he answered baldly, angry that he sounded defensive. Fuck what people said, money was king. To anyone who didn't believe that, he'd say, try being poor. Better still, try being poor, surrounded by rich, spoilt brats who enjoyed reminding you how unimportant you were.

Disgust flashed across her face. 'Fine, if it's all about money, at least give me a chance to prove the bookstore could be an effective money-earning option. You've agreed to pay me for the next three months, anyway.'

'You think I haven't already done the math?' He knew, to the last decimal place, how much the resort would be worth with the addition of the harbourfront cottages. 'Keeping the bookstore is a non-starter.' She flinched, and the way she stared back at him, like he'd not just let her down, he'd totally wrecked her opinion of him, caused another wave of intense, skin-itchy discomfort. 'Look, nothing's going to happen in the next two weeks. Use the time to sort out the stock. Take what you want, sell off what you don't. You can keep anything you make.' She gave a little shake of her head, the gesture almost pitying. 'What?'

Her eyes blinked at his sharp tone. 'Nothing.'

He huffed out a breath. 'You didn't seem to have a problem telling me what you were thinking last night. Or the night before.'

'No, but then I thought I was having a hot fling with a rich guy. A *sweet*, rich guy. Turns out he was a ruthless resort owner.'

He recoiled, stung. Being called ruthless wasn't new, but coming from a woman he'd kissed every inch of, laid under the stars with, *enjoyed*, it hurt more than he expected.

'It's funny,' she added, though there was no humour in her voice. 'I joked to myself it was a bit like one of those romance novels, you know the ones featuring the sexy billionaires? Only I was happily using you for sex, too. But in the books, the heroine resists the billionaire hero because he's a bastard, then finds out he's a good guy. I slept with you thinking you were a good guy. It turns out you're a bastard.'

You don't know the half of it. Frustration fizzed through him, regret fast on its heels. 'I'm not a billionaire. Not yet.' He took a couple of steps towards her, his pulse scrambling as he looked into her eyes. Fuck, she was gorgeous. 'I messed up, and I'm sorry. I should have told you who I was the moment I realised you were involved in the bookstore.'

'You should.'

Unbelievably drawn to her, he trailed a finger down the soft curve of her cheek. 'It doesn't have to stop us enjoying each other while you're here.'

She gave a sharp inhale and he felt a stab of satisfaction. But then she swallowed and shifted away from him. 'Thanks for the offer, but no. I can have sex without love, but not without like.'

'You liked me well enough yesterday,' he pointed out gruffly, feeling as if someone was standing on his chest. 'Nothing's changed.'

Her mouth gaped open. 'Seriously? You think lying about who you were, having sex with me knowing you were going to shaft me, and destroying a place I clearly think is incredible, is *nothing*? Never mind that you've just had the gall to offer me sex as some sort of consolation prize.' She pulled up to her full five-foot-and-a-smidgen height and jutted out her chin. 'Thanks for the generous offer to keep the sales from the books, but I didn't come out here for the money.'

Pocket-size, yet she was the one making him feel small. 'What *did* you come here for?'

For a brief moment she looked crestfallen, but then she squared up to him. 'I told you when we were on Galley Beach, but probably all that interest you showed in me was just a way of making sure you got the sex you'd been deprived of the day before.' Her voice trembled a little, but her gaze was unflinching. 'Funny thing is, you didn't have to pretend to be interested. I'd have slept with you anyway.'

He felt like he'd been punched in the chest. 'I wasn't pretending.'

'Then you should remember what I said.' Her watery blue gaze pierced his. 'I came here to work with books.'

He gave her a curt nod. Message received. Then he turned away and marched back towards the resort – his resort, the place he'd created from nothing. A defiant statement to those who'd fucked him over. They'd not managed to cower him, to break him. The new waterfront would cement the statement, make it even more powerful. Not only had they failed to break him, it would say – *he had won.*

Yet even as he increased the distance between himself and the bookstore, the image of Jade wouldn't budge from his mind. Beneath the anger, she'd looked heartbroken, like he'd not just put an end to her little adventure. He'd ruined something vitally important to her.

It took a bag of mints and an evening with his grandma before the bad taste left his mouth.

Chapter Twelve

Jade read the name on the brass plaque in front of her: Jeremy Scott, Guest Services Manager. Then she sucked in a deep breath, checked she wasn't showing too much cleavage, and knocked on the door.

'Come on in.'

'Hi, I'm Jade Taylor.' She smiled at the guy behind the desk. Direct blue eyes, red hair, and a face that looked familiar. 'Oh, we've met before. You were talking to Liam … er, Mr Haven, yesterday when I kind of barged in on you.'

'I remember.'

His tone was dry, his expression warm, friendly, but also speculative. She tried not to think what conclusions he'd drawn about why she'd pushed her way into the resort owner's office. And called him by his first name. 'I run … er, I was employed by Flo to run the Little Bay Book Shack, you know, the place on the wharf. Or at least that's what I was supposed to come here to do, what I was really looking forward to doing, before she sold it to Liam … Mr Haven…' God, what was she doing? She'd rehearsed this on the way over and now she was making a total pig's ear of it. Ignoring Jeremy's amused look, she ploughed on. 'Anyway, I've been told the bookstore is going to be shut down, which is a totally misguided decision … in my opinion, obviously. I want to prove to Mr Haven—'

'My boss?'

Oh, shit, she'd kind of assumed from what Flo had told her, that Jeremy would be on her side. 'Um, yes. I want to show him that the bookstore could be a really valuable addition to the resort. I mean, surely I can't be the only one who thinks it's nuts to get rid of it and have a waterfront of boring new builds instead.'

Jeremy burst out laughing and continued to laugh, at one point wiping at his eyes, before slowly his guffaws turned to chuckles and finally to an amused shake of his head. 'I'm sorry, totally unprofessional of me. I just couldn't help wondering what the boss would think of you calling his exclusive luxury cottages *boring*.'

This was not going as planned. But she'd signed a contract to sell books for three months and she was not going give up without a fight. Drawing in a breath, she gave Jeremy her best flirty smile. 'You won't tell on me, will you?'

He looked amused. 'No. I value my job too much.' Jeremy stretched out his legs and regarded her. 'So what did you want from me?'

Giving him another smile, she nodded towards the chair. 'Do you mind if I sit?'

'Of course, my bad.'

She settled on the chair, crossing her legs in a way that showed them off to their best advantage. They weren't long or elegantly slender, but regular Pilates had given them definition. 'So, um, I wondered if there was any way we could work together to our mutual advantage.' Oh, crap, did that sound like a come-on? Gentle flirting was one thing, but she didn't want to come off as desperate. 'I mean, you're in charge of keeping guests happy, yes?

And books have to be one of the best ways of doing that, especially in a swanky place like this, where doing anything more than lifting a hand to turn over a page seems way too much effort.'

A smile hovered around his mouth. 'Keep going.'

Feeling more confident, she leant forward and was about to go into her sales pitch when there was a loud rap on the door.

She almost fell off the chair when Liam strode into the office, his tall imposing, annoyingly attractive frame making the place feel suddenly cramped. 'Why the fuck have we ordered fifty stuffed flamingos?' His gaze swept the room, and when it collided with hers, he visibly jolted. 'What are you doing here?'

She swallowed and glanced pleadingly at Jeremy, who looked like he was about to burst into another fit of laughter.

'Jade is here to discuss winding down the bookstore,' Jeremy replied smoothly. 'She thought I might be able to help.'

Liam raised a brow and studied his guest-services manager through narrowed eyes before turning his attention back to her. Her skin prickled as his eyes travelled down, skimming over her cleavage and making her very conscious of how it looked, her pushing out her breasts to the man opposite. Self-consciously she sat back.

Liam slid a hand into his pocket and regarded Jeremy. 'Has she met Leroy yet?'

Confused by his question, she turned to Jeremy, who seemed unsure whether to laugh or tell his boss to piss off. 'No, though I'm sure she will at some point.' With a casualness Jade could only admire, Jeremy leant back and threaded his hands behind his head. 'Do you want to discuss the flamingos now? And for the sake of accuracy, I should point out they're not stuffed, that would imply the birds were once alive. These are handmade resin sculptures. The type a bride might want as decorations for her island wedding.'

'Jesus.' Liam shook his head, like he couldn't contemplate the idea of anyone getting married, never mind in front of resin flamingos. Finally, his eyes found hers again, lingering a beat longer than was polite. 'I'll leave you both to it.'

Jade's skin heated under his perusal. She really had to give her body a strict talking to tonight. Remind it that Liam was the enemy.

Jeremy's sharp gaze swivelled between the pair of them, but thankfully he didn't comment on what she felt sure was the deafening crackle of charged molecules now bouncing through the air. 'So, where were we?' he asked as the door finally clicked shut behind Liam.

'I was trying to persuade you to help me prove the bookstore is an asset worth saving.'

'Ah yes.' He lifted his eyebrows. 'You were asking me to go behind my boss's back.'

Jade flushed. 'That's not, well not technically … bollocks, that's exactly what I was doing, wasn't it?' She let out a deep sigh 'Sorry, asking for your help was a stupid idea, of course you can't do anything to upset him.'

A slow smile crossed Jeremy's face. 'Lucky for you, upsetting the boss is something I do on a regular basis, providing the reason is justified.'

Shoots of hope began to take root. 'Obviously, I think it is, but as a fan of all things books, and someone who really wanted to manage this bookstore, I'm totally biased.'

'I'm also a fan of books, though not as much as my fiancé.' He gave her a look filled with humour. 'Leroy.'

Holy cow, she'd been flirting with an engaged man. Who was gay. Heat scalded her cheeks and Jade groaned. 'You must think I'm the most ridiculous person you've ever met.' No wonder Liam had asked if she'd met Leroy.

'On the contrary.' Jeremy's voice interrupted her spiralling thoughts. 'Anyone prepared to go up against the undeniably sexy but also distinctly surly Mr Liam Haven has my full admiration.'

Ignoring the 'sexy' remark – she could spot a fishing expedition when she saw it – Jade gave Jeremy a hopeful smile. 'Does that mean you'll help me? Obviously, I'll do all the work, but just to have another brain on the job would be amazing.' Especially as she wasn't totally confident how useful her own would prove.

'Oh, you won't just get my brain, you'll get Leroy's, too.' Jeremy picked up his phone and tapped on it for a few seconds before grinning back at her. 'Come to the beach bar tonight and we'll pool some ideas.'

'Oh, my God, that's awesome, thank you so much.' She was gushing, but it was hard not to when, for the first time since Liam had crushed her dream and then insulted her with an offer of consolation sex, she saw a sliver of hope.

Jeremy laughed. 'It's me who should be doing the thanking. I think I'm going to enjoy watching you and Liam lock horns.' He angled his head. 'What do *you* think of flamingos?'

Jade winked. 'I have flamingo wallpaper on my bedroom wall at home. Only a person with no soul wouldn't like flamingos.'

It had been another brutal day. The sooner he found a new resort manager to replace Ashley, the sooner he could get back to the job he loved. The one that didn't involve conducting staff meetings, or pacifying entitled guests. Liam relished hard work – aside from his grandma, work was his life – but the stuff he loved to do, negotiating terms, agreeing contracts, sourcing new land to purchase, he did alone, away from people. People were a fucking headache. Employees who needed handholding, customers who wanted special treatment. Guest-services managers who took delight in winding him up, he added sourly.

Bookstore temps who flashed their cleavage at said manager but wanted nothing more to do with him.

Scowling, Liam ignored the path to the wharf and headed towards the beach. He'd work off some of his angst by taking the long way back to the yacht. No, he hadn't decided to stay on the boat instead of reclaiming his suite at the resort because the sheets still smelt of Jade. And he definitely wasn't now on the lookout for a woman with long blonde hair and curves he'd spent far too much of last night thinking about.

He came to an abrupt halt as his gaze cut to three figures sitting at one of the beach-bar tables. It was as if she was deliberately haunting him.

Without thinking, he marched up to the table. 'Jeremy. Leroy.' He nodded in their direction before his gaze found hers. 'Jade.'

She looked defiantly back at him, but the way those big blue eyes then skirted away from his? Yeah, she was up to something. And the silence that followed his greeting added to the whole they-were-talking-about-him vibe.

'Well, if it isn't the big boss.' Jeremy saluted him with his beer bottle. 'What's gone wrong now? Or, wait, maybe you've actually come to be sociable and join us for a drink?'

The man not only knew which buttons to press, he took delight in pressing them with great regularity. Now he was left awkwardly making something up and walking away, or awkwardly accepting the offer. Why the fuck hadn't he ignored them?

Because you can't ignore her.

Resigned to an uncomfortable half hour, he caught the eye of Carlos at the bar and nodded to indicate his usual, before pulling up a spare stool and easing onto it. 'I didn't mean to interrupt.' He gave them all a pointed look. 'Please carry on with whatever you were discussing.'

They all looked at each other. Jade appeared embarrassed, Leroy gave an indifferent shrug, and Jeremy's face held the expression of a man holding back a tidal wave of laughter.

Carlos slipped a glass of Macallan onto the table in front of him and Liam slowly raised it to his lips and took a sip. 'To save you making up an elaborate lie, I'm well aware I was the subject.'

Jade covered her face with her hands and let out a low moan, which had the unfortunate effect of reminding him of the way he'd made her moan the other night.

'Technically, the subject wasn't you, but the bookstore,' Jeremy answered. 'Don't want you thinking we spend all our evenings gossiping about you.'

'No?' He arched a brow. 'What's the latest theory on why Ashley left?'

Leroy gave him a half smile. 'She's pregnant with your baby.'

He grimaced, feeling a flare of anger on Ashley's behalf.

'And being the son of a bitch everyone knows you to be, you sacked her and sent her packing,' Jeremy added cheerfully. 'I should add the more discerning staff don't buy into this rumour because they know Ashley was too smart to have sex with you.'

And that was when he found out that Jade was a terrible actor. Neither Jeremy or Leroy could have missed the way she stiffened and sucked in a breath. Ignoring the very speculative glances his employees were now giving him, Liam took another measured sip of whisky. 'What about the bookstore, then?'

Finally Jade turned to look at him, and prickles darted across his skin as her gaze met his head on. 'You said nothing was going to happen with it for two weeks, so instead of using the time to wind it down, I'm going to use it to show you what an asset it is to *your* resort.'

'I thought we'd already had this conversation.'

'We have.' She tilted her chin in his direction. 'But you gave me two weeks and I'm going to use them how I see fit.'

Irritation vied with a grudging respect. He wasn't used to people ignoring his orders, yet technically he had given her two weeks. 'Fine, but it's a waste of time. The bookstore will never be able to give me what the cottages can.'

'Money.' She gave him a look that he'd not seen since the nurse at boarding school had patched him up after yet another one-sided fight. Pity.

'How else do you think I bought my grandma that house?' Her eyes widened and he felt a jolt of surprise. Why had he reminded them both of the night he'd opened up to her?

'Well, it's my time I'm wasting,' she said finally. 'So I don't believe you have a say.'

A humming silence followed their exchange and he knew, without looking at them, that Jeremy and Leroy were bursting with questions he had no intention of ever answering.

Jeremy cleared his throat. 'Jade has been going through some of the ideas she's had to increase business. They're good. You should hear them.'

Liam glared back at Jeremy but the man shrugged, like he hadn't just turned traitor and firmly planted his flag on the side of Jade and the damned bookstore.

To Liam's horror, Jeremy then climbed to his feet and smiled over at Jade. 'Excuse us sweetheart, but I'm going to drag my fiancé off for an evening dip. Let's chat again tomorrow about how we can help you put some of those ideas into action.'

He slid Liam a final glance, mouth twitching in a smirk he made no attempt to hide. Leroy let out a resigned sigh, swallowed down the rest of his drink and rose to his feet. 'Guess I'm about to get wet.' He inclined his head in Liam's direction before shooting Jade a wink. A fucking wink, like he was Mr Playful when Liam had only ever seen the man in serious mode. 'See you around, Jade.'

Jade gave him a little wave and the pair of turncoats proceeded to walk off hand in hand across the sand, which looked golden in the glow of the setting sun, and towards the sea.

'Isn't that romantic.'

He turned to her, expecting to see a wistful expression, but instead she simply looked happy for Jeremy and Leroy. As he had no wish to talk about the men who'd so easily chosen Jade's side, he picked the slightly less irritating conversation. 'So, these ideas you've had.'

She huffed, the softness disappearing from her face. 'You don't have to listen to them.'

He glanced down at his glass before locking eyes with her. 'I still have to finish my drink.'

She let out a snort of laughter. 'I could swig that down in one gulp.'

'You don't swig Macallan.' Her cheeks flushed and too late he realised he'd sounded condescending, when he'd been trying for dryly amused.

'Fine, I'll rattle through what I'm going to be wasting my time doing over the next two weeks while you,' she waved down at this drink, 'take your teeny tiny sips.'

He forced a tight smile. And cursed himself for not taking the direct route back to the yacht.

Chapter Thirteen

Jade glanced around the small group gathered in the bookstore. It was Saturday afternoon and day one of Operation SOB (Save Our Bookstore – she had to think of a better name for it). As they'd promised the other night, Jeremy and Leroy had invited a few locals to help.

'We're fed up with property developers swooping in like vultures and turning large parts of our charming town, rich with historic heritage, into a sprawling resort full of vulgar modern buildings.' Henry, who Jade guessed was in his early thirties, steepled his hands, the gold signet ring on his left pinkie catching the light. With his elegant, sharp cheekbones, carefully styled hair and faded red chinos, which according to Jeremy were a Nantucket status symbol, the guy oozed wealth and privilege. He'd also taken over the meeting, droning on for the last fifteen minutes about everything that was wrong with the Haven Resort. 'We already have sufficient accommodation on this island for every type of holiday maker,' Henry continued. 'The Chase Resort has been serving wealthy tourists for over a hundred years.' He glanced at Jeremy. 'Why you turned down the chance to work there, I don't know.'

Jeremy shrugged. 'I'm happy where I am.'

'Happy working for a soulless, modern resort that wants to rip the guts out of our shoreline?' He snorted and turned back to Jade. 'Whatever you can do to stop that son of a bitch getting his way, has the full support of me and my family.'

'Um, that's great, thanks.' Nerves fluttered in her belly. Enlisting some people with clout had seemed like a great idea the other night, after a few drinks, but today, facing this group of angry residents out for blood, her little stand against closing the bookstore felt like it had morphed into something bigger. Nastier.

'Here, here.' This was from Adam, who'd once owned a business on the waterfront near the bookstore, before, in his words, being forced to sell up. 'I realise Haven has already bought the wharf, and the whole bloody frontage either side of it now, but in highlighting the plight of the bookstore we can rally the rest of the town – hell, the island – into realising it's time to take a stand against these developers and stop any further desecration of our precious shoreline.'

'Absolutely.' Mary, who Jade guessed was in her early fifties, was one of the town librarians, and judging by the way she'd kept looking crossly at Henry as he'd droned on, also had an awful lot to say. 'We don't want the likes of Haven taking over any more of our island. I know my Sarah is employed by him, but after all that business with Ashley, my opinion of him has gone even further downhill. Sarah says rumour at the resort is that Haven made Ashley pregnant then pushed her out. Poor girl didn't even feel she could stay on the island. She's in Australia now.'

'I'm not sure we know all the details,' Emma murmured. On the board of the Heritage Society, she was quieter than the others and, Jade had found to her delight, was the wife of George, the water taxi man. 'But it was a shame to lose Ashley. She was always ready to help the community.'

'Unlike her boss,' Philip chimed in. In his sixties, according to Jeremy, Philip was one of those people who like to get involved in anything and everything. 'I remember Liam Haven's grandma, Pat. She was a hard worker, kept herself to herself. Difficult to believe they share the same DNA.'

As she listened to the collective murmur of agreement, Jade looked pleadingly over at Jeremy. She was on a mission to keep her job for three months and hopefully stop the bookstore from being knocked down. Not declare a public war on Liam Haven.

Jeremy caught her eye and nodded. 'I know emotions are running high regarding the amount of real estate being bought up by developers, but can we park any personal vendettas for a moment.' He turned to Jade and smiled. 'We're here to help our new Little Bay Book Shack manager promote the store, not carry out a character assassination of the man both she and I happen to work for.'

All eyes turned to Jade and her heart began to thump. 'If I'm honest, I've never managed a shop before, never mind tried to save one, so I kind of need as much advice as I can get.'

Adam gave her a slow smile and leant back against his chair. 'No worries. Use us however you see fit.'

He winked, and Jade felt a flush of embarrassment. She didn't want to be flirted with – she'd already made one colossal mistake with the opposite sex in the *not even a week* since she'd arrived.

Then again, if she wanted to be taken seriously, she had to earn that right. Pushing down the jittery feeling in her stomach, she started talking. 'So, as I was telling Jeremy and Leroy.' Her gaze drifted over to Jeremy and she took some comfort from the reassuring smile he gave her. 'To generate interest in the shop I thought we could have a themed book week where we focus on a different genre each day.' Did it sound trite, coming after Henry and Adam's big speeches? Liam hadn't laughed when she'd gone through the details the other night, though that was likely because he wasn't listening. He'd sipped at his whisky, said a quiet *thank you* when she'd finished. And left.

Pushing the man out of her mind, she squared her shoulders. 'Monday could be mystery day and involve a murder trail around this part of the town. Tuesday would be for travel and I could set up stalls in the resort and the town containing books and maps for different destinations. Wednesday could be women's fiction; Thursday, thrillers; Friday, fantasy; Saturday, um, maybe science fiction…' She could feel the energy drain from her the further she went through the week. What on earth had she been thinking? She couldn't pull this off. From the nonplussed look on the faces in front of her, she couldn't even convince them to help her, either. 'I've not got it all planned out yet,' she ended lamely.

'It sounds excellent,' Mary said finally into the silence. 'Ambitious, perhaps, but there's nothing wrong with aiming high.'

Unless you're biting off way more than you can chew. Jade's hands began to sweat and she had a strong urge to rush to the loo and puke her guts up.

'Let us know how we can help,' Emma added. 'And if you think of a way to include historical fiction, we could advertise it at the Heritage Society.'

Frigging hell, she'd missed off a major genre. That desire to puke intensified.

'Well, keep us informed.' Henry rose to his feet, eyes fixed to his phone. 'Sorry, got to take this, important call. Catch you later.'

He walked out without even making eye contact, and Jade felt dismissed. Like she wasn't worth his while. The others drifted out after him, though at least they had the decency to smile at her, and promise to help.

'I look forward to seeing more of you,' Adam murmured as he shook her hand.

Yeah, she wasn't sure about that, either. Had he meant the innuendo?

When only Jeremy remained, Jade slumped onto one of the chairs she'd dragged down from the studio flat upstairs. She felt as if she'd been chewed up and spat out.

'Sorry, that didn't go quite as I'd anticipated.' Jeremy sighed and sat down opposite her. 'I invited Adam when I met him downtown, but Henry was with him and expressed an interest. I didn't think it would harm having someone with his wealth and connections on board – his father owns the other big resort on the island – but I didn't reckon on him being such a gargantuan asshole.'

Relieved, Jade laughed. 'I'm glad it wasn't just me thinking that.'

'Nope. The man clearly wants to get one over on Liam in whatever way he can. Of course, the boss can also be a gargantuan asshole, but…' He shrugged, as if he knew there was a difference but couldn't explain it.

'Liam … Mr Haven, never made me feel small. Angry, yes.' And cheap, she reminded herself, though he'd been cross when she'd said that. 'He never made me feel like I was less important than he was.'

Jeremy slid her a speculative glance. 'You can tell me to mind my own business, but did something happen between the pair of you?'

Heat scorched her skin and she cursed her fair skin. 'Um, why do you say that?'

His eyes skimmed her face and he gave her a kind smile. 'Well, if I hadn't already guessed from the undercurrent between the pair of you that night at the beach bar, those red cheeks have just given it away.'

Crap. She could lie, tell him he had a vivid imagination, but he wouldn't believe her and besides, there was something about Jeremy that made her want to be honest with him. If she was going to stick out these three months, she badly needed a friend on the island. 'We hooked up the first night I was here. Before I knew who he was,' she added hastily.

Jeremy stilled for a moment, then he started to laugh. Real, bend at the waist, belly laughter. 'Sorry, this probably isn't the right response to that piece of information,' he wheezed, clearly trying to rein in his amusement. 'But holy shit, that's, er, interesting. And no doubt highly embarrassing, for both of you.' His expression sobered. 'Did he know who *you* were?'

'Not the first time.'

Jeremy made a choked sound. 'There was more than one occasion?'

'Twice.' More if she counted the orgasms, she added silently. Not that she'd kept a tally. Or was going to think about it ever again. 'Um, two nights. But that was before I realised he wasn't nearly as nice as he came across.'

'Nice isn't a description I'd ever associate with him.' He gave her a wry smile. 'He's also not as bad as he's painted, though he makes it hard to see that because he's not one for joking around. He keeps us all at a distance.'

He let you in. On the boat, staring at the stars, again on the beach, in the glow of the sunset; both times he'd allowed her to see another, more vulnerable side. But then he'd gone on to sleep with her knowing he was about to crush her. Maybe it had all been an act. 'Now I just want to focus on the reason I came, which is to manage this shop. I know he's going to stop me at some point, but I'm not going to roll over for him.'

Jeremy cleared his throat. 'No.'

She saw the twitch of his lips and let out a huff of laughter. 'Bad choice of words.' Bending her head, she thumped it onto the table. 'Bollocks, bollocks, bollocks. Why did I succumb to those ridiculous good looks. I feel so stupid.'

She felt Jeremy's hand slide across her shoulders and squeeze. 'Don't. The boss can be an asshole, as we've already concluded, but he's also an undeniably sexy asshole. Now, let's have one of those cups of tea you Brits are so certain solves everything, and work out a plan of action.'

Liam frowned at the poster on the wall behind the activities desk. It had only been a few days since he'd sat and listened to Jade's earnest plan for how she was going to turn the book shack into a million-dollar empire in a week. From the description on the poster, the transformation would start on Monday.

Why couldn't she see reason and enjoy a paid three-month vacation on Nantucket like any normal person who found themselves in her situation? He wasn't so much of a bastard that he wanted to see her fail, yet that was the only possible outcome. No matter how much effort she put in, keeping the bookstore would never be a viable option for him.

He looked up at the sound of whistling and saw Jeremy ambling towards him. 'Is this your doing?'

'I agreed she could promote the book week within the resort, yes.' Jeremy ignored the dark look Liam gave him and smiled at the poster. 'Looks good, doesn't it? The guy who runs the art society designed it.'

'Adam.'

'That's the one. Jade managed to persuade him to do it for free.'

He didn't like the tight feeling in his chest. 'I'm sure she can be very persuasive.'

'Oh, I have no doubt you know exactly how persuasive she can be.' Clearly immune to the death glare Liam gave him, Jeremy carried on talking. 'You're aware the sexual chemistry between the pair of you is so hot Leroy and I nearly got burned the other night?'

'She's an employee,' he gritted out.

'Barely. And according to rumour, that hasn't stopped you before.'

Anger coiled, like a rattlesnake waiting for a reason to pounce. '*You* think I was fucking Ashley?'

Jeremy met his stare face on, then let out a slow breath. 'Actually, no. But I think you have been fucking Jade. And if you hurt her I'm going to be seriously pissed with you because she's a lovely woman who doesn't deserve to have her dream crushed by this crazy obsession of yours.'

The anger began to uncoil, humming through his blood. 'You mean my obsession with making money, which keeps you and your fiancé employed?'

'It's more than the money,' Jeremy countered.

'Oh?' Jeremy didn't know. He *couldn't* know. Liam kept his expression impassive and tried to ignore the knots forming in his gut.

'Fine, I'm guessing it's more than money. No sane person checks out the competition as often as you do.' Liam opened his mouth to argue but Jeremy rolled on. 'I'm not talking about looking at the Chase Resort restaurants, their rooms, their on-site activities, which is what you pay me to do, by the way. I've seen your computer screen, boss. You're checking their financials, their net worth.'

'What I do is my business,' he gritted out. 'I suggest you butt out and stick to yours.'

Most people would take offence, at the very least take the hint, but Jeremy just smiled. 'Sure, but while you're going about your *business*, spare a thought for the woman who's about to bust a gut working at that shop because she thinks she has a chance of convincing you to keep it.'

He had to work hard not to flinch. 'It's her choice to work there. I told her I was happy to pay her to do nothing at all.'

'Maybe instead of convincing yourself you've done the right thing by her, you should find out why it's so important for her to keep working there.'

With a sharp nod in his direction, Jeremy calmly strolled past him, as if he hadn't just dropped a stink bomb and then dodged the foul-smelling fallout.

Because he'd planned on doing it, anyway – fuck you, Jeremy – Liam set off towards the bookstore.

The bell jangled as he pushed open the door, and his heart lurched as he saw two blonde heads look up. One gorgeous and distinctly female. The other … his hand clenched and he shoved it into his pocket.

'Adam.' He nodded coolly towards the guy whose art shop he'd bought six months ago. The pair of them went way back, and Liam fucking hated the reminder.

Adam looked annoyed, like he'd been interrupted mid chat-up. It made Liam want to take out his clenched fist and shove it in Adam's smug face. He shouldn't be jealous. Jade had been a hook-up, nothing more.

'Hi *boss*.'

She didn't look pleased to see him, either. He gave her an ironic smile. 'I'd like a word, when you've finished with this *customer*.' Two could play at the emphasis game.

'Actually, I've already got what I came for.' Adam gave a laconic shrug before turning back to Jade. 'See you tonight, sweetheart.'

Liam watched the bastard walk out, his insides feeling like he'd swallowed a bag of jumping beans. 'Tonight?'

Jade's blonde brows flew up at his barked question. 'How can I help you?'

'You can start by telling me what Adam is doing in this shop.'

She rolled her eyes. 'Technically, I don't think I have to.'

'It's my shop, I have a right to know what goes on inside it.' He was being a prick but he couldn't seem to stop. He told himself it wasn't because she'd been flirting, but because she'd been flirting with *Adam*.

'Oh, my God, you really are an arse, or should I say *asshole*.'

'Your American accent needs more work.' He exhaled, pinching the bridge of his nose. 'Look, I came here to see how you were getting on. Not to pick a fight.'

He watched her shoulders drop. 'Well, as long as we're not fighting, I can tell you Adam was here because he's helping me promote the book week. He and a few others. He designed the poster for me.' Her eyes found his. 'A lot of people want the bookstore to stay. Apparently you're not liked very much.'

'I don't care what they think of me.' His gaze rested on hers and that pull he'd felt from their first meeting? It was still there. An unwanted guest he couldn't ignore. 'I find I do care what you think.'

She looked momentarily surprised. 'I liked the man who talked to me about the Milky Way on his boat. Who took me to Galley Beach and made love to me as if I was special. But the man who slept with me, and apparently other employees, without giving a fig how much he was about to upset me? Yeah, him, I wished I hadn't met.'

'I've never slept with an employee.'

'You slept with me.' She looked away, and instantly he missed her eyes on him. 'And anyway, that's not what I've heard.'

'I didn't sleep with Ashley. I can't say what happened, it's her business, but we had a working relationship, nothing more.' Those blue eyes found his again, and he experienced a sudden and acute desire to regain her trust. 'I don't know what other rumours are going around but I did once, in a moment of weakness brought on by tiredness and alcohol, have a one-night stand with a fitness instructor temporarily employed at the resort.'

'That sounds familiar.'

He met her accusatory stare head-on. 'It wasn't. I bitterly regretted it the next day. I don't regret you.'

She blinked slowly. 'Why did you regret her?'

'She found out who I was and came looking for me, suddenly deciding she wanted more.' He gave her a level look. 'You found out who I was and don't want anything to do with me.'

The door chime sounded and a group of tourists wandered in. It was hard to rein in his disappointment, but became easier when he saw how relieved Jade was. She didn't want to discuss what had happened between them. She wanted him gone.

He nodded towards her. 'I'll see you around.'

She gave him a stony look in return. 'Not if I see you first.'

He walked out before she could see how much her dislike bothered him.

Chapter Fourteen

M urder Mystery Monday. Last night, and the night before, when Jade had been working to prepare a trail of mystery and intrigue around the wharf and along the waterfront, helped by Jeremy, Mary and a flirtatious Adam, she'd been convinced it was a great idea.

So far today, she'd had two more sales than the same time yesterday. Not exactly what she'd had in mind when she'd bragged she was going to use the next two weeks to show Liam what an asset the store was to his resort. He'd probably made as much money in the last second as she had all afternoon.

'Hey, don't look so glum, these things take time to gain momentum.' Adam, who'd breezed into the shop a few minutes ago to "check on progress", patted her hand. And took the opportunity to look down her top. Or had that been accidental?

Pulling her hand away, Jade took a step back. 'Thanks, and on one level I know it was never going to have immediate results, but on another level, I really wanted to be unable to move in here for the mass of people.'

The door opened and two customers strolled in. Relieved to

have something to do besides worrying if Adam was going to ask her out, Jade breezed past him and gave the elderly couple a bright smile. 'Have you come to take part in the murder mystery?'

'Oh, no, who can be bothered with that?' The woman glanced around her. 'I'm looking for Richard Osman's latest. Do you stock it?'

Well, that told her. Keeping the smile on her face, Jade found her the book and consoled herself with the fact that at least it was another sale.

The couple made a swift exit, ignoring the displays she'd agonised over. Her heart fell when a tall, dark-haired figure strode in after them. Hard enough to deal with Liam when she was feeling her best. Right now, her confidence was so squished she wasn't sure it could ever unsquish.

It really wasn't fair that he looked so bloody yummy. Or that her stomach started performing happy somersaults the moment her eyes registered his presence. Or that she spent way too much time remembering how earnest he'd looked when he'd told her he cared what she thought.

Like she could trust any words that came out of the mouth of a guy who'd had sex with her knowing he was about to screw her over.

His gaze swept the shop, expression tightening when he saw Adam, before he carefully rearranged it into a neutral mask.

'Have you come to gloat?'

He halted, dark brows coming together. 'Sorry?'

Crap, why had she said that. 'Nothing.'

'I suspect he's here to check *Ocean Haven* is the only boat moored to the wharf.' Adam turned, slotting his pockets into his chino shorts. 'We didn't have time to talk about this when we last met,' he continued, glancing in her direction before staring back at Liam, 'but not content with getting rid of Little Bay Book Shack, the new owner of the wharf has declared the moorings private property, stopping the rest of us from using it.'

'Oh.' She wasn't sure she could get worked up over something that sounded like a rich guy problem.

Liam's mouth twisted as he stared back at Adam. 'How does it feel to have something you thought was your right to use, taken away from you?'

Adam's expression lost some of its cockiness. 'For Christ's sake, Haven, that was nearly twenty years ago.'

'Seventeen, to be exact.' Liam turned to her and indicated towards the blue sofa. 'I'll wait here while you finish your meeting with Adam.'

'Oh, we're not having a meeting,' Adam countered, regaining some of his swagger. 'We were planning tomorrow.' He gave Jade a flirty smile. 'I'll see you later.'

The door closed behind Adam, and Liam slowly rose to his feet again, a muscle flexing in his jaw.

'I know what you're thinking.'

He raised a brow. 'Try me.'

'You're thinking I'm a flirt. Probably on account of my blonde hair and the way I dress.'

His mouth formed a tight-lipped smile. 'Wrong.'

'Then you're thinking that because I slept with you without knowing you, I must be continually jumping into bed with guys.'

'Whom you sleep with is none of my business.'

'Good, I'm glad we cleared that up.' It was hard to fight when the person you were fighting refused to hit back. 'Look, I don't know the history between you and Adam, but obviously there is one. He's using me to try and wind you up.'

'It's working.' Liam let out a deep sigh. 'I don't like the idea of him using you.'

'That's rich, coming from you.'

He let out a humourless laugh. 'Okay, I deserved that.'

Swallowing, he shifted on his feet. 'I also don't like the idea of him flirting with you.'

Okay, she was going to ignore that little bubble of pleasure. 'Why? We hooked up, that's all. No biggie. Well, aside from the small matter of what you didn't tell me in the second hook-up, but that's all water under the bridge. Or I guess I should say under the wharf.'

His gaze locked with hers. 'It doesn't feel like it's over.'

'What, the hook-up? Or me being mad with you?'

'Both.'

She let out a squeal of frustration. 'Stop trying to confuse me, okay? We had sex, you were a git, you apologised. Let's move on.'

'Move on to what?'

'A polite, professional relationship.'

'Fine.'

A few beats of tense silence followed.

'Was Adam one of those people fourteen-year-old you wanted revenge against?' Liam rocked back on his heels at her question and she rolled her eyes. 'I'm crap at maths but even I can do fourteen plus seventeen equals about the right age for you now.'

'I'd … forgotten I shared that with you. I don't make a habit of sharing my private thoughts. Especially not with people I only have a polite, professional relationship with,' he added, mocking her words.

He might have hurt her, yet it was clear he'd also connected with her in a way he didn't with others. 'We both shared things that we've never shared before.'

He nodded and glanced away. 'To answer your question, yes.'

'So you bought the wharf to get back at him?'

'Them.'

'The classmates?' she hazarded. 'The gang twelve-year-old you wanted to be part of?'

A shadow crossed his face. 'It was *a* reason, and yes.' He

exhaled heavily. 'It sounds petty, I know. Poor kid vows to take revenge on group of entitled rich pricks.'

It wasn't what he'd said, but what he hadn't said. This imposing, impressive man had once been bullied. 'What was the "something" they took away from you?'

'Somethings.' He emphasised the plural.

'Give me an example.'

'Why?'

'Because I want to understand why this wharf is so important to you.'

His mouth flattened in a thin smile. 'There was a small private cove we used to go to every summer. Nobody else used it, just me and my grandma. One day, we turned up to find the path fenced off.' She watched his Adam's apple work up and down in his throat as he swallowed. 'They knew it was our place, and they decided we'd enjoyed it for long enough.'

He only ever mentioned his grandma, she realised. Not his parents. 'So now they can't moor their boats to the wharf. How does it feel to get your own back?'

'On this occasion?' He exhaled heavily. 'Not as good as I'd hoped.'

'Well they say revenge is a dish best served cold, but seventeen years … that's like being in a deep freeze.'

'That isn't the reason…' He started to pace around the store, as if he couldn't keep still. 'I didn't come here to discuss the past. I came to warn you that the construction team will be here tomorrow to survey the waterfront. They may need access to the shop.'

'Of course. I wouldn't want to get in the way of the eagerly anticipated luxury holiday cottages that Nantucket is absolutely crying out for.'

He gave her a level look as he passed a book display.

'Come on,' she said. 'You know I'm going to give you a hard

time about this. Just like I know the reason you're really here is to remind me I'm wasting my time trying to promote the store. Why else would you, Mr Haven Resort himself, come here in person to tell me something you could have emailed or sent a minion to inform me?'

———

Yeah, Haven, what other reason could you possibly have for coming to the book shack twice in three days?

'I might have come *in person* because I'm aware I wasn't upfront with you before, and I want to make amends.' It was partly the truth, and saved him having to admit he'd spent the morning fighting a compulsion to see her. And finally given up.

Silence followed his words and he turned to find her staring at him. 'Okay, maybe I can believe that. But as I need to hate you for a bit longer, I'll reserve judgment for now.'

He halted in his pacing – something he'd had to do to keep his mind occupied and prevent himself from blurting out that his revenge hadn't felt as good because she'd been hurt in the crossfire. 'Why do you need to hate me?'

'You might be my boss, but I don't have to answer every question you ask me, do I? Don't you Americans have something about pleading the Fifth?'

A slow smile spread across his face as he watched her try to squirm from his question. 'You need to hate me so you won't be tempted to sleep with me again.'

She rolled her eyes, but her cheeks reddened. 'Even if I did get past hating you, and past the bit that you're my boss—'

'Temporarily,' he qualified. 'It's an important distinction.'

'Whatever, I'll still not get past being disappointed in myself for succumbing.'

'*Succumbing*?' Like he'd set out deliberately to lure her into his evil web. 'This from the woman who said she was trying to seduce me?'

'God, okay, I didn't mean it like that. I meant I succumbed to your stupid looks and limited charm.'

'After that description, I can see why you did.'

She waved a frustrated hand at him. 'Just … shut up, okay? I am officially immune to you.' Her gaze swivelled towards the coffee table. 'What do you think of my latest display?'

He trampled on the desire to grin and walked over to the … what the fuck?

She burst into laughter. 'You should see the look on your face. It's Murder Mystery Monday, remember?'

'It looks more like *Bloody* Monday,' he countered, his terrible British accent pulling a reluctant smile from her.

'I imagined what I wanted to do to you when I was putting it together.'

'I see.' He stared down at the grizzly assortment of items. 'The rope is to…?'

'Tie your hands behind your back.'

'That's a relief. I thought you were going to hang me.'

'I figured that was too easy.'

He ignored the sting and picked up the black balaclava and leather gloves. 'And these?'

'The gloves are so I don't get blood on my hands, obviously. The balaclava is for you, so I don't have to look at you while I'm doing the deed.'

Curious, he picked up the plastic knife covered with red splashes of paint. 'This is to cut off my head I presume?'

'No, your balls.'

The parts in question shrivelled inside his boxers. 'When I think of you holding my balls, it's with something entirely different in mind.'

She let out a spluttering sound. 'Oh no, we're not going there.'

'Going where?' Discreetly – it might only be plastic but a guy couldn't be too careful – he slipped the knife into his trouser pocket.

'We're not going to the place where I ask if you often think about me holding your balls—'

'The answer is yes.'

She muttered a few swear words under her breath, followed by something that sounded like *where are the bloody customers when you need them* before letting out an audible sigh. 'This conversation is closed.' Her eyes strayed to his pocket. 'I would ask if that's my knife in your pocket or if you're just pleased to see me, but I'll spare us both another cheesy line and wait while you put it back.' Feeling like he was about five years old, he pulled the toy knife out and grumpily shoved it onto the table. 'Did you really think I could cut off anything with that?'

'I didn't want to risk it.'

A smile almost broke free across her face. 'For a not-quite billionaire, you can be kind of a muppet.'

'I can be a green, hand puppet that looks like a frog?'

'You can be a right plonker.'

'Just so I have the translation correct, that means?'

'A dumbass.'

'Got it.' He could point out he'd built a whole company from nothing, but he didn't think she'd be impressed and besides, not telling her who he was that second time? It was one of the dumbest things he'd ever done.

What he'd never know, was what would have happened if he had been up front. Would she have continued to like him? To sleep with him?

Would he, a man who'd sworn never to let anyone get close to him again, have wanted that?

'You need to go.' Jade's voice cut through his inner ramblings. 'Any minute now I'm going to be inundated with customers who've read the flyers and want to do the murder-mystery trail. I'd hate for you to be trampled in the crush.'

Behind the bravado of her words there was an unexpected vulnerability. 'You never told me why managing this shop is so important to you.'

'Actually, I did.'

He frowned, his mind churning through their conversations, feeling a hint of alarm at how easy it was to recall everything she'd told him. *I'm the one still trying to find her way* sprang into his head first. 'You told me you love books, that you're currently frustrated you're not involved with them more, but that's why you're here. Not why this job is so important to you. Is it about proving something to yourself? Your family?'

'Maybe you were listening to some of the things I said.' Her lids lowered over her eyes for a moment before she looked back at him. 'I wanted to see if I could do it. Not just manage a bookshop, but do it while living away from home, standing on my own two feet.' Her chin jutted. 'Lauren aced all her exams and went on to become a doctor, but she's never worked abroad, never moved that far from home.'

He'd spent most of his life working to prove that he was better than the people who'd dismissed him, shut him out, treated him like shit. Now, here he was, denying Jade the same chance. The realisation settled heavily over him, yet what could he do? He owed it to his fourteen-year-old self to finish what he'd started.

'You're, what, twenty-eight?'

'Twenty-five.'

No wonder she was so wide-eyed and eager. 'You'll have other opportunities.'

'Oh, sure.'

The weight of her disappointment hung between them. She was all woman, yet it was easy to see the girl who'd wanted to live in a castle made of books.

But that was *her* dream. And being suckered into it, into her, was dangerous. He'd not spent ten years working his ass off, only to have his own goal derailed by a woman who was only here for three months, as gorgeous as she was. He was too fucking close to achieving it.

'Good luck with the stampede.' He gave her a careful smile and exited sharply before he let those big blue eyes suck him in any further.

Chapter Fifteen

T ravel Tuesday had been a flop, the rest of the week not much better, though Mary and Emma were doing their best to help.

'Don't you worry about tonight. There are flyers in the library, posters everywhere I was allowed to stick them, and some in places I wasn't,' Mary added on a hearty chuckle as they set out chairs in the bookstore ready for the presentation from the local romance author. 'I also told the book-club president who messaged all the members. Steamy Saturday will be a triumph. We'll be beating the crowds off with a stick.'

Jade caught Emma's eye and the woman gave her a sympathetic smile. 'Claire is bound to attract a lot of interest.'

'Of course she is,' Mary bristled. 'The entire female population of Nantucket have read at least one of her books, and most of the men, too, though some of them just for the naughty bits.'

'They weren't naughty,' Jade protested. 'They were hot. Beautifully, orgasmically, hot,' she added, eyeing up the bottles of wine she'd stashed by the till while trying not to think how much those descriptions also matched the real-life sex she'd had recently. Did posh Nantucket readers frown on alcohol while listening to a book talk, or did they enjoy glugging it down and discussing raucous sex scenes?

'That, too.' Mary sighed and patted at her short, greying hair. 'I used to tell my Doug to read her latest, thought he'd get some ideas, but he's such a slow reader he never reached the parts about tying me up and spanking me. Maybe if he had, we wouldn't have divorced.'

Jade spluttered with laughter. She hadn't expected that from the buttoned-up looking librarian. But she should have, she realised, because she'd been guilty of exactly what she hated others doing, making a judgement based on how someone looked.

'Did you know Claire was friends with Ashley?' Mary continued, unaware Jade was looking at her in a totally different light. 'I'm sure that's partly why she agreed to come and do a talk. She'll want to help kick Liam Haven where it hurts.'

Jade had an unwanted vision of Liam holding the plastic knife she'd splattered in red paint and telling her he often thought of her holding his balls.

'Hiya!'

She shook the image away and turned to greet the tall, dark-haired lady who'd just swanned into the shop looking, frankly, exactly how Jade wanted to look. Cool, sophisticated, elegant.

'I'm Claire—'

'Our marvellously talented local author.' Mary immediately set on her. 'Are you a wine drinker? We have red and white. Oh and I brought two bottles of a really nice rosé. Jade will fetch you a glass. Maybe you'd like to try one of each?' she added with another of her rumbling laughs.

Jade cleared her throat. 'Um, thanks, Mary. I've got it from here.' Ignoring Mary's huff, she smiled brightly at Claire. 'Let me take your jacket.'

'Don't worry about Mary,' Claire whispered once Jade had

dragged her out of the older woman's clutches. 'She just likes to be involved in everything.' She smiled. 'It was great to get your invite, thank you. It's been a while since I did a talk. I used to do them at the resort, but since Ashley left I've not been asked.'

'Ashley was the manager of the Haven Resort, right?'

'Yes.' Claire's gaze swept across Jade's face and she laughed. 'Oh dear, I can see from your expression you've heard all the gossip. The Liam Haven haters believe he's a cross between Satan, Casanova and Gordon Gekko. Now then, where can I freshen up?'

Jade showed her upstairs to the bathroom, wishing she'd had more chance to quiz her further. Deciding she needed a tiny break from Mary, she perched on the bed and took a moment to scroll through the messages on her phone before heading back down.

There was another one from Lauren on the family chat group.

> You need to phone home soon, Sis. We want an update on the shop and everything else you've been up to. And I mean EVERYTHING xx

Guilt washed over her. She'd deliberately not phoned her mum back since their quick chat the other day, because what could she say? She didn't want to worry her, and she couldn't bear the thought of disappointing her yet again. She'd hoped if she waited, she'd be able to turn the bad news story into a good news one. *Guess what, Mum, the shop was bought out and the new owner (who I absolutely didn't sleep with) was going to get rid of it but by running a massively successful marketing campaign I managed to persuade him to change his mind.*

She stared back at her phone and typed:

> I'll phone soon – just been sooooo busy xx

Just as she was about to put it away, her phone pinged with an email notification from LHaven@Havenresorts.com. Frowning, she clicked on it.

> *Jade*
>
> *I hear you're hosting a 'meet the author' event in the shop this evening. Hope you've removed all sharp, and not so sharp, implements.*
>
> *Yours sincerely*
> *The Boss*

Damn the man. She didn't want to smile, but she couldn't help it.

She clicked on reply.

> *Dear Boss*
>
> *All knives removed. Replaced with handcuffs and whips.*
>
> *Yours sincerely*
> *Temp manager of shop you want to knock down*

The bathroom door opened and Claire slipped out on a cloud of sophisticated scent. 'Okay, I think I'm ready.'

'Great.' Jade pushed her phone into her pocket and eyed her curiously. 'Are you one of those Liam Haven haters you mentioned?'

'I've only met him a couple of times, so I don't know him well enough to like or dislike him.' Claire winked. 'Though I will say he is one seriously hot guy and, I don't mind admitting, the inspiration behind a few of my heroes.'

Just as she was about to follow Claire back downstairs, Jade's phone beeped with another email notification.

Jade

Was that an invitation to attend?

Yours sincerely
The Boss

PS: I'm much happier with you using the whip and handcuffs on me than the knife.

Liam tapped his fingers restlessly on the desk, his attention wandering, yet again, to his inbox. Why had he emailed her?

And why was he waiting for a reply like some hormone-driven teenager?

Sex, that was all it was. He wanted to have sex with her again. And maybe some fun because God knows, she was definitely that. She was also an *employee* who knew more about him than he should have allowed, and who was actively working against him, trying to fuck up his carefully laid-out plans.

So the wise course of action was to close his email and ignore the voice telling him he could walk back to his boat via the bookstore; he could check in on the presentation that he knew, thanks to Jeremy, was taking place right now with Nantucket's illustrious romance author, Claire Kennedy. Just to see how many people had turned up.

Damn it. He shut his laptop with a snap and jumped to his feet. Minutes later, he found himself pushing open the door to Little Bay Book Shack.

The door chime sounded – shit that was loud – and everyone turned to stare at him. A sea of mainly female faces, expressions ranging from annoyance to surprise, horror to amusement. He scanned the space, desperately seeking out bright blonde hair.

'Liam.' Hearing his name, he turned to see a face he recognised, Ashley's friend, the author. 'Good to see you, do come and join us.' Her mouth twitched in a way that made his stomach sink. 'We were just discussing sex.'

Jesus Christ. His face must have spoken volumes because, from the back of the store, he heard a soft explosion of giggles. *There* was his blonde. The sole reason he'd apparently lost his mind and stepped into a presentation given by an author of romantic fiction when he didn't even like books, never mind romance books.

Jade stood up and pointed to her chair, clearly indicating for him to sit on it. Taking a breath, he ignored the very interested stares of those already seated and weaved his way towards her.

Thankfully, Claire started talking again, diverting the attention back to where it should be. Even if that did involve asking the audience what they thought made a good sex scene.

'I'm only taking your seat if you sit on my lap,' he murmured.

She gave him a pointed look. 'I don't think that's appropriate. Boss.'

He sighed, cursing his slip. It was hard to take the wise, stay away, course of action when she looked so cute, so perky, so *tempting*.

He watched as she eyed up the counter behind them and, in one nimble motion, levered herself onto it. 'Ouch!'

A few of the women sitting within hearing distance turned in her direction and she gave them an apologetic smile. 'I sat on the stapler.'

Deciding he preferred to stand, he moved behind her and bent to whisper in her ear. 'You've sat on larger recently and not complained.'

She twisted to stare back at him, eyes a cool blue. 'I got hurt then, too, the pain was just more delayed.'

He hissed in a breath. Why the hell had he come? Jade didn't want him here. The readers who'd turned up to have an open discussion with their favourite romance author didn't want him here, either.

'Perhaps we should have a male point of view.' Dread settled in his stomach as Claire's eyes found his, humour dancing across her face. 'Have you read much erotica, Liam?'

Erotica?

Jade let out a noise that sounded like someone strangling a cat.

'I don't read books.'

Claire continued to look highly amused. 'Interesting. I suppose I assumed, as you've come to the Steamy Saturday book presentation, that you had an interest in the subject.'

Now Jade's email about whips and handcuffs made sense. 'My interest was in a presentation from one of Nantucket's highly acclaimed authors.'

Claire laughed. 'Smooth catch. We were just discussing the importance of an emotional connection between our characters during sex scenes as well as a physical one. Do you have a view on that?'

Three rows from the front, a woman he recognised as Mary from the library, gave a dismissive grunt. 'I doubt Mr Haven understands the term.'

'Which term?' Claire asked, though he could have saved her the bother. He knew exactly where this was going.

'Oh, I'm sure he knows all about sex. But he didn't show much emotion when he forced Ashley back to Australia with his unborn child,' Mary added.

Yep, right on queue.

'With respect Mary, that's a load of bollocks.' Jade's bold statement was met with a few gasps, and just as many sniggers. 'Um, what I meant was, you're repeating gossip as fact, and that's not cool.'

'Careful,' he murmured. 'You're in danger of ruining my hard-earned reputation.'

'You deserve it for what you're doing to the bookstore,' she hissed back. 'But not for stuff that's just rumour.'

'Nobody forced Ashley home.' Claire's quiet voice cut through the murmurings. 'And Liam is most definitely not the father of her unborn child. She would be appalled to hear the rumours circulating.'

Mary sniffed. 'Well, you can't blame us for believing the gossip. What has Haven ever done for this island? It doesn't need more of his flashy accommodation for rich tourists. It needs houses for people who live and work here.'

The animosity was nothing he hadn't come across before, yet as a ripple of *hear, hear* ran through the group, his insides scrunched inwards, as if absorbing the blow. Had it hurt more tonight because his guard had come down, thanks to Jade and Claire's surprise defence of him?

Exactly why he needed to keep his fucking distance.

Yet when Jade's eyes met his, sympathy swirling in their depths, he couldn't resist tilting his head so his mouth brushed her ear. 'Thank you.'

A shiver ran through her, enough to cause an answering tingle down his spine. He wanted to haul her back against him, to settle his mouth on the soft skin of her neck. To lift her into his arms and carry her up the narrow staircase behind them to the bed he knew was up there. But she was no longer the sexy stranger he'd found himself unbelievably drawn to.

She was a woman actively stirring up antagonism against him and his plans for expansion. A woman who'd defended him because she was fair, not because she liked him.

Ignoring the mutinous/curious glances of those sitting, he walked towards the door, pausing when he got there to catch

Claire's eye. 'I apologise for interrupting your talk.' With a curt nod at the rest of the room, he made a swift exit.

Flashy accommodation. The words jarred, rubbing against wounds that should have healed yet still felt raw. He had money now, but he still wasn't accepted because it was nasty new money, not sophisticated old money. It shouldn't bother him. He didn't want it to bother him.

With a frustrated sigh he wrenched his phone out of his pocket and stabbed out a message to Jeremy.

> Erotica? You didn't think to tell me??

Within seconds a message pinged back.

> Thought it would be a nice surprise.

With a grunt of annoyance, he messaged back.

> Next time you think of surprising me, think again.

Chapter Sixteen

Jade could feel her face start to ache as she continued to smile into the camera on her laptop. Her mum was chatting away still, her dad rolling his eyes. Lauren had also joined the Zoom call, from the breakout room at the hospital. No doubt she'd have to leave soon to deal with another lifesaving emergency.

'Heavens, what am I doing, rabbiting on when really we want to hear about you, Jade.' Her mother's expression turned soft, her smile kind. 'How is the shop? And Nantucket? Is it everything you'd hoped it would be?'

A lump rose in her throat. 'The island is beautiful. Well, what I've seen of it so far. I've been working a lot since I came out here but I'm free this afternoon so I'm thinking of doing something touristy, maybe checking out the whaling museum. Apparently, whales are big round here.'

'They're rather large wherever you are,' her dad interrupted drolly, unhelpfully reminding her of the night Liam had made the same comment.

A different Liam to the one she knew now.

'You need to get yourself on one of those tourist tours where they take you to see them,' Lauren said.

I could take you out, if you like. Gah, why couldn't she stop thinking about him?

'Yes, I will,' Jade said.

'Never mind the aquatic mammals, what about the human talent?' Lauren waggled her eyebrows. 'Any further developments after that first night?'

Jade gave her sister a hard glare through the screen. Surely she realised she didn't want to discuss her rash hook-up with her parents listening in?

'Developments, what developments?' Her mum's eyes widened. 'Is there something you've not been telling us, Jade?'

'Nothing important.' She tried to swallow her frustration, and failed. 'Why is it that when we discuss Lauren it's all about her job, but when it's my turn, it's about men?'

Her mum's face fell and Jade felt a dart of guilt, which sharpened when her dad replied quietly. 'Your mum did ask about the shop.'

Crap, she had. And Jade had deliberately not answered. 'Yes, I know, sorry.'

'Hey, I didn't realise the subject of men was off the agenda,' Lauren protested. 'You were the one who brought it up last time we messaged. I was only showing an interest.'

Double crap. Everything she was feeling, every fear, every insecurity, had all come to a head. And instead of dealing with them, she was taking her issues out on her family. 'You're right, you're all right. I'm the one who's a frigging disaster. I fooled around with a guy on my first night, and he turned out to be my new boss, because my old boss sold the shop to him. Now this new boss is getting rid of it and I told him I was going to prove he was better off keeping it.' The words tumbled out messily, all control gone. 'He said I was wasting my time and I know he's right because as well as the shop, he owns a flipping hotel chain so he's hardly going to listen to me, but I'll not be able to know one way or another anyway, because I've been trying for the last hour and I can't work out how to use the flaming spreadsheets so I don't know what profit the shop made last week compared to before I started.' She wiped her eyes. 'And if all that wasn't enough, even though he slept with me knowing he was about to shaft me over the shop, I'm starting to not hate him.'

Her mum looked confused. 'Isn't that a good thing?'

'No, it's a frigging disaster, because what if I start to like him? Then I'll want to sleep with him again and I haven't come all this way to get my heart broken. I managed that pretty well at home.'

Her dad cleared his throat. 'Maybe we should go back to discussing the shop.'

'We'll discuss that in a minute,' her mum cut in. 'First I want to know why my gorgeous daughter believes she'll get her heart broken.'

Jade groaned. 'Come on, Mum. I've had ordinary guys think I'm not good enough for them. You really think I could sleep with a not-quite billionaire and not get trampled on?'

'Technically,' Lauren piped up. 'You've already slept with him.'

'Yep, and I got trampled on, so I rest my case.' Jade let out a long breath. 'Can we change the subject? I don't want to talk about men, and actually, I don't want to talk about the shop either. Tell me what's going on in Twickenham. Did you manage to sell all those raffle tickets, Lauren?'

Her sister picked up the baton and ran with it, because her saintly sister wasn't just a doctor who saved lives, she was also a volunteer for the local homeless charity. A charity Jade had also helped with, but Lauren was the one with the ideas for fundraising. Jade was the one who got drenched waiting in the rain to work on the stall, only to find the venue had been switched to the hall and nobody had bothered to tell her.

Still, when the time came to say goodbye, she didn't want to end the call. Her family wasn't perfect, but she missed them fiercely. Missed talking without thinking, missed being with people who knew her, even if that included knowing her failings. Who understood her. Who loved her no matter how much she cocked up.

'Jade.' Her dad's voice cut through her misery. 'Those spreadsheets you talked about. You can't be expected to understand them if you've never used one. Ask the people who worked there before. Or ask the new owner. Part of the role of a boss is to help his employees.' He smiled. 'If he doesn't, it will be a reason to keep hating him.'

'Thanks, Dad.'

'Oh, and we never want to hear you're not good enough ever again,' he said quietly. 'This guy, *any* guy, would be bloody lucky to have you.'

Emotion gripped her throat and she could barely scratch out her goodbye.

When she'd closed the call, she pulled up the Reasons to Hate Liam Haven list she'd compiled a few days ago. After yesterday, *bastard who disowns his unborn child* had been removed. Thankfully she still had *lied to me*, and *arrogant rich guy only interested in money*. Revenge and money, she corrected with a flourish. Neither were attractive.

Feeling better, she opened up the spreadsheet again. Her dad was right, she needed to get help, though she wasn't going to go with his crazy idea of asking Liam. She had Daisy and Flo, but she wasn't sure how easy it would be to go through it virtually. There was Adam, who seemed super helpful at the moment, but she was worried he'd see it as encouragement. Mary, Emma and Philip were also options but there was one other member of their group who she felt far more comfortable approaching.

Picking up her phone, she messaged.

> Am in a pickle. Are you any good with spreadsheets?

A messaged bounced back five minutes later.

> Can't abide them. But I know a man who is a whizz at them. He's on his way X

> Bless, thank you, Jeremy ... and thank Leroy!

> It isn't Leroy...

Jade reread the message. Weird. Who else could Jeremy have persuaded to drop everything and come to help her at a moment's notice? On a Sunday.

Liam knew if he stopped to wonder why he'd just abruptly curtailed his meeting with the journalist, he'd turn right round and head back to his office. But from the moment Jeremy had called to tell him Jade needed help with the bookstore spreadsheets, he seemed to have lost his mind. Again. It was becoming a dangerous habit where the cute blonde book lover was concerned. His reply to Jeremy should have been *tell her to forget it, the shop is closing in a few days*. Instead he'd told Jeremy he'd handle it.

Jeremy had chuckled, like he knew something Liam didn't, which hadn't helped the queasy feeling that he was losing his grip. Nor did the fact he felt no hum of satisfaction as he registered that *Ocean Haven* was the only boat moored at the wharf.

How does it feel to finally get your own back?

Damn it. Maybe seventeen years *was* too fucking long to harbour a grudge.

With a grunt he pushed at the shop door before realising it was locked. Of course, it closed on a Sunday. So why was Jade working?

Suddenly the door opened and his mind stuttered of all thought, leaving him staring at her. Dressed for a day off, her blonde hair was swept into a messy ponytail secured with a pink ribbon, and her face was free of make-up. She looked fresh, yet intoxicatingly sexy, the sight of her tits straining against the material of her vest top making him lose the use of his tongue.

'If you've come to stock up on your erotica, I'm afraid the shop's closed.'

He unglued his tongue from the roof of his mouth. 'Sorry?'

She slid her hand onto her hip, drawing attention to a bottom half which, with shapely legs, toes painted in neon pink and a pair of denim shorts that must barely cover the plump globes of her gorgeous ass, was no less mind blowing. 'I assume you're here for a book after your interest in Claire's talk yesterday.'

'I … no.' He scrambled to clear his brain. 'Didn't Jeremy tell you I was on my way?'

Her eyes popped. *'You're* the one he sent?'

'Sent?' Like he worked for the guy? Yet, did it sound any better to admit he'd volunteered to help? 'I was headed to the yacht,' he lied. 'He asked if I'd mind calling in on you. Something about spreadsheets.'

She sighed as she stood aside to let him in. 'Jeremy sure knows how to embarrass a girl.'

'Embarrass?' His arm accidentally grazed her as he walked past, the fleeting feeling of cushioned warmth sending a bolt of arousal through him.

'Would you want your boss to know you can't do something?'

'I don't believe the occasion has ever arisen,' he murmured, taking care to keep more distance between them. His very visceral attraction towards her was fucking awkward. 'Do you want some help, or not?'

Her gaze drifted over his shoulder while she seemed to wage some sort of internal war with herself. 'Do I want it? No. Do I need it?' She sighed again. 'I suppose beggars can't be choosers.'

'I'm flattered.'

Finally she looked at him. 'I guess you'll want a drink.' With that she let out another deep exhale and headed towards the back stairs.

He made a determined effort not to watch her ass as she climbed the staircase ahead of him. 'Is this your usual warm welcome for visitors, or am I a special case?'

'Oh, you're special, all right.' When he reached the top, he found her looking at him warily. 'Actually, maybe we should do this downstairs.' He glanced around the small studio, taking in the kitchenette, the two-seater sofa. The... 'No, don't look at it.'

Amused, he stared back at her. And that, he realised belatedly, was a mistake. It was easier to handle the sight of the bed than those huge blue eyes. 'Don't look at what?' He asked dryly.

'Exactly.' She grabbed the laptop from the worktop and shoved it into his hands. 'You sit on the sofa and study the spreadsheet thingies while I make a drink. Good old Tetley tea from home, or some dubious coffee that was already here and even if it is in date I will probably ruin because I don't drink the stuff?'

'Water.'

'Are you sure? Can't beat a good mug of tea. Helps everything from hangovers to heartbreak.' He stared back at her and she gave him a wry smile. 'Yeah, the heartbreak part is a lie. At least it didn't help me.'

'The men who were bad for you.' He didn't like thinking of her with other men. *And I thought I'd reached rock bottom with the last two guys I slept with.* Liked it less when he remembered he'd treated her worse than they had.

'Yep. So anyway.' She waved a box of teabags. 'Is that still a hard no for the tea?'

'I prefer my drink not to resemble a dirty puddle.'

She shrugged her shoulders. 'Your loss.'

He watched as she reached up into the cupboard for a glass, the stretch revealing a sliver of the soft curve of her belly. The one he'd traced with his tongue.

Dragging his gaze away, he turned his focus to the spreadsheets Flo had put together, recognising them from the ones she'd sent him when he was buying the bookstore.

Jade set a glass of water on the small coffee table in front of him. 'Bet you're not used to numbers that small.'

He glanced up at her. 'I wasn't always rich.'

Her cheeks went pink. 'Sorry, yes, I got that from when you were talking about wanting to buy your grandma a house. I meant when you look at the finances for your fancy resort.'

She came to sit next to him and it was like a million neurons fired off in his brain. He was kidding himself if he thought this was just a casual attraction, one that would conveniently disappear the more he saw her. It felt like he was hooked, and his choices were to fight the inevitable, or save himself the angst and admit to it.

'My fancy resort has bigger numbers, but the principle is the same. This column is where you put the sales recorded from the till.' He pointed to the screen, but when she leant in to follow the direction of his finger, her breasts came into contact with his arm and he groaned. 'You realise not looking at the bed isn't going to stop me from wanting to fuck you in it.'

She inhaled sharply, scooting away from him as if he'd suddenly announced he had rampant herpes. 'I don't want to know that.'

'Trust me, I'm aware. And I'm not exactly happy about the situation, either,' he added grimly. 'But the genie is out of the bottle, and we can't just shove it back in, no matter how much we might want to try.'

'Genie, what genie?'

She looked panicked and he let out a frustrated breath. 'You know what I'm saying. I don't have to sit here and imagine what it would be like to roll around with you on a bed. I *know* what it's like. And it's really fucking hard to ignore that.' He stared back at her. 'Really hard to tell myself I don't want to experience it again.'

She shot up from the sofa and started to pace up and down the small loft space. 'Well you need to, because you and me are not happening again. No, no, no. Definitely not happening.'

'You're sure about that?'

'Absolutely.' He took satisfaction from the fact her gaze didn't meet his. 'I'm working on being a different version of me than the one who walked onto your boat wondering if she was good enough. Wondering if the guy she was about to sleep with just saw her as an easy lay.'

He winced. 'I told you, that's not what I thought.'

'It's what part of you thought. You asked to fuck me, Liam. Not to take me out to dinner.'

'Yet I took you out for cocktails.'

'You did. Even though you don't date.' She frowned, bright blue eyes searching his. And seeing too much. 'You've been hurt, too. So maybe we should both get better at picking the people we do decide to let close.' She paused, looking down at the floor for a moment before meeting his eyes again. 'Do you know what I overheard my last boyfriend saying to his mum when she asked him what he saw in me? "*Every guy goes through a dumb-blonde phase. Jade is mine.*"'

'What an asshole.'

'And an arsehole.' She raised her chin. 'I'm tired of being

KATHRYN FREEMAN

underestimated. Especially by people who should know me better.'

'That's why these three months working at the shop are so important to you.'

'Yes. And I need you to give me longer than two weeks. I deserve longer.'

Easy to make decisions based on numbers on a spreadsheet, but when the consequence of one of those decisions was looking at him as if he held the power to her happiness in his hand? Yet if he gave in to her, he'd be putting a halt on his own goal, his own ambition. And the likes of Adam would believe they'd been successful in stopping him.

Exhaling sharply, he nodded down to the computer. 'You're not going to be able to see the screen from over there.'

Chapter Seventeen

He hadn't said yes. But he hadn't said no. Jade gave Liam another furtive glance as he continued to talk in his deep, low drawl, explaining how the spreadsheet he'd taken the last hour going through, was supposed to be kept updated on a daily basis.

Oops.

The fact she'd taken anything in at all was a miracle considering her mind kept jumping back to what he'd said about how not looking at the bed wasn't *going to stop me from wanting to fuck you in it.*

She snuck another peek at him and felt a hard flip in her lower belly. She'd dated some good-looking guys – Rob, before he'd called her his dumb-blonde phase, had all her girlfriends swooning over him – so she knew looks were overrated. Still, it was hard not to be sucked into Liam's powerful aura. It wasn't just his almost brutally handsome face, or the mesmerising eyes, the assured *I don't care what you think of me* swagger. It was the rough, unvarnished edge beneath the smooth surface that tugged at her.

A pair of light grey eyes locked onto hers. 'I seem to have lost your interest.'

She shook herself. 'Nope, definitely not. Expenses are … fascinating. They should make a film about them. Maybe put Ryan Gosling in the lead role, though.'

'You'd pay more attention to him?'

He looked insulted, which made her want to laugh. 'Probably, but it wouldn't change the outcome. I'm hopeless when it comes to numbers.'

He shrugged. 'You're people, not numbers.' He said it so easily, like it was obvious. As she tried to work out how to reply without flinging her arms around him and sobbing out her thanks, he peered at her curiously. 'You're looking at me like I just said something right.'

'I liked the way you put it, that's all.' Damn, her voice was scratchy. 'You know, that being crap at maths is okay, because I'm good at other things.'

He leant back, eyes still on her, and still curious. 'Does this come back to what you were saying, about being underestimated?'

It was both unnerving and flattering to be the focus of his intense gaze. 'I told you about my sister being a doctor. My parents used to joke she was the brainy one and I was the pretty one.' She dragged her eyes away from his, unable to hold his stare. 'When I was a kid, I didn't mind it. In fact, I was happy to be the one the boys were after. Go me, I was in demand, the girl the others envied. But then I grew up, and I realised being popular just because I looked good actually sucked. My sister, my friends, they were liked because they had something interesting to say. Me? I was dated because I had blonde hair and big tits.'

'Sorry?' His voice sounded strangled, like he was trying not to laugh.

'It's not funny,' she said crossly. 'How would you like to be arm candy?'

'You're saying I'm not?' he murmured before crossing one leg over the other and giving her a long, measured look. 'Do you think I have these conversations with everyone?'

She blinked. 'What do you mean?'

'Jade.' He ran a hand through his hair, a hint of exasperation in his voice. 'The only person I talk to, outside business talk, is my grandma.' He let out a low laugh. 'And now you, apparently.' A dozen questions tripped onto her tongue but he held up a hand. 'I'm only telling you this because you thinking you have nothing interesting to say is frankly ridiculous.'

She searched his handsome face. 'Aw, Liam Haven. Are you saying you *like* me?'

He shut his eyes briefly before staring straight back at her. 'Yes, Jade. I like you.'

It was impossible not to smile. Not to feel the warmth that seeped through her chest, or the excited flutter of her heart.

Not to be aware of the sparks that fizzed in the ensuing silence.

He gave a small shake of his head. 'I refuse to ask the question.'

She had to fight not to smile. 'What question?'

He huffed. 'I feel like a fucking teenager.'

'I can't believe teenage you ever asked anyone their opinion of you.'

A shadow passed over his face. 'I didn't need to.'

She wanted to stay angry at him, stay hating him because then she didn't have to worry where this humming attraction might lead. But he kept giving her glimpses of the man she'd first been attracted to. 'Well, I'll answer the question anyway. Despite the fact you're planning to put an end to my adventure and knock down this shop, I'm beginning to not hate you.'

The corner of his mouth tilted upwards. 'Good enough.'

Sparks she'd been at pains to dampen fired dangerously into life. Suddenly all she could see was the shimmering silver of his eyes, the small scar that bisected his eyebrow. The curve of his sensuous lips. 'Just because I don't hate you doesn't mean we're heading for the bed,' she qualified hastily. 'I'm on a mission to feel better about myself, and being the boss's fuck buddy won't help me with that.'

He visibly winced. 'That's not how I see it.'

'But it is how it will look and how I will feel.' She swallowed, her nipples hardening as his gaze continued to press hers. 'You need to stop staring at me like that.'

'Like what?'

'You know what. Like you want to devour me in one easy bite.'

His hand touched her cheek, thumb rubbing gently over her skin. 'I want to devour you, but not in one bite. In lots of small, carefully placed, slowly savoured, bites.'

Her breath caught in her throat and despite what her head was telling her, she leant into his touch. Just one more time. She could kid herself it was possible. One more night and then she'd focus back on the shop, on saving it from being knocked down.

The doorbell chimed.

'Oh God.' She leapt back, pulse hammering. A quick glance at her watch and she swore.

'Expecting a visitor?'

'Well, not a visitor, as such. It's a SOB meeting. And I can't believe I've not thought of a better name for that yet.'

'SOB?'

'Save Our Bookstore. It's the group who helped me promote the book week. There's Adam who you know, Emma from the heritage society. Mary and Philip…'

'Nantucket's own grapevine and busybody.'

'Well, yes, but they're also sweet when you get to know them. Oh, and there's also a guy called Henry. We don't see him very much but Jeremy tells me he's useful to include as he has wealth and connections.'

'Henry *Chase*?'

Gone was the sexy, smouldering man she'd been seconds from caving in to. Liam was sitting rigidly, his expression stony.

'That's the one. Why? Do you know him?'

Did he know Henry Chase? 'These are the people you're colluding with?' he asked tightly, ignoring her question.

'No, these are the people who are *helping* me prove to you the bookstore is worth saving,' she countered.

'The same people who, in your words, don't like me very much?' She could dress it up however she wanted. She was working with his enemies, against him.

She went to open the window and waved to whoever was down there, telling them she'd be down in a sec, before turning back to him. 'They don't know you like I do.'

'They don't want to know me.'

'Maybe you haven't given them the chance.'

He let out a snort of disbelief. Adam, Henry, others whose names and faces still remained fresh in his mind ... they were the ones who'd never given him a chance. 'You're taking their side?'

'There are no sides.' She went to dig a jacket out of the wardrobe and shrugged it on before turning to face him. 'Look, I know you have history with Adam, but did you ever stop to wonder if you're turning into the very people who tormented you as a child?'

Anger flooded him and he surged to his feet. 'You're saying I'm a bully?'

She flinched at his tone. 'No, of course not.' Her expression softened. 'Bullies are mean and nasty, and you're neither of those things. But can't you see the similarity? By preventing Adam and others from using the wharf, and by turning the shops on the waterfront into cottages for your resort, you're stopping the people who live here from enjoying places they used to think were theirs.'

'You think I'm an arrogant rich prick?'

'I think you're rich. And may have tunnel vision.'

The parallels between what she was saying, and what he'd said about "his" beach were too close to be comfortable. But it wasn't the only part that stung. Jade had been on the island for less than two weeks, yet she'd been taken into these people's confidence. *Accepted*. Something he'd never achieved.

But at least he could make them take notice.

'You say there are no sides, yet you've clearly picked yours.' He stalked past her to the stairs, almost falling down them in his desire to get away from those baby blue eyes, the soft lips that could deliver such a cutting appraisal.

This was why he didn't let people get close. Because it fucking hurt when they rejected him.

'Liam, wait.' He heard her footsteps chasing down the stairs after him. 'What about the shop?'

'I want it closed by this time next week.'

She blinked, looking first confused, then shaken. Finally, she nodded and went to unlock the door. 'Whatever you say. Boss.'

Avoiding Mary and Emma who were waiting outside, he marched off towards the resort. It was Sunday, but the only way he knew to quieten his mind was with work.

He'd built his business from nothing, but all that everyone around here saw was a man who'd wrecked their island. Didn't matter that his wasn't the only resort on Nantucket, or that many of the locals relied on the income from the very tourists who stayed in his resort. He didn't have the right name, the right connections. The right sort of money.

By the time he yanked open the door to his office, he'd worked up a full head of steam. The last person he wanted to see was the man who waltzed in behind him wearing a disgustingly cheerful sunshine-yellow shirt. 'I'm busy,' Liam barked.

'Oh dear.' Jeremy floated to a stop. 'Did the spreadsheet lesson not go well?'

'What part of I'm busy did you not hear?'

Ignoring him, Jeremy slid breezily onto the chair. 'You are aware that a problem shared is a problem halved.'

'I don't have any problems.'

Jade was no longer an issue. He would avoid her for the next week, after which the shop would be closed down and she'd no doubt scurry off home, leaving him to get back to being himself again. Not a guy who looked up at fucking stars with a woman he barely knew and talked about things he'd spent a lifetime locking up tight.

'I get it,' Jeremy replied, interrupting his sulk. 'Life is all hunky dory in your world. Except if it was, you wouldn't be sitting there with a face like thunder. Of course your usual expression is hardly sweetness and light, but this one.' He flapped a hand towards Liam. 'This would frighten small children.'

'It's intended to,' Liam muttered, irritated. 'Also to frighten employees into leaving me alone. Why isn't it possible to upset you?'

Jeremy smiled. 'When you grow up hearing every insult under the sun being directed at you, it soon just becomes noise that no longer holds any power.'

Liam paused, taking a moment to study the man opposite him. 'Maybe we do have something in common.'

'You mean aside from our fabulous good looks?'

He huffed out a laugh, surprising himself. 'Aside from that, yes.'

'Well, you're dark, not ginger, and much to the disappointment of a couple of staff who will remain nameless, you're not gay, so what insults were you forced to endure?'

Was he really going to do this? 'It doesn't matter.'

'Clearly it does, or you wouldn't be sitting there like a grouchy bear.'

Jesus. 'I was poor in a school of rich kids.'

'So they weren't won over by your sunny personality alone? I am surprised. Which school of monstrous children did you go to?'

'Phillips Academy. It's a—'

'Boarding school.' Jeremy whistled. 'A very prestigious boarding school attended by most of the Massachusetts elite.' He eyed Liam. 'If you were poor, how did you get there?'

Why the hell had he started this conversation? Spending time with Jade had made him soft in the head. 'I doubt my life story is relevant to this meeting. What did you want?' he asked brusquely, putting a line under his temporary lapse in judgement.

'Oh, I just wanted to find out how you'd got on with Jade.'

'Is this the same Jade who, thanks to you, has joined forces with the likes of Adam and Henry to campaign against me? Against the expansion of the resort that employs both you and your fiancé?'

'Ah.' For once, Jeremy looked uncomfortable. 'To be fair, she set up the group to persuade you to give her a chance to manage the bookstore. That's all she's interested in, not island politics. Which is why I agreed to help.'

Despite the fact you're planning to put an end to my adventure and knock down this shop, I'm beginning to not hate you. Liam pressed a hand against his shirt, surprised to find it wasn't the thing constraining him, making his chest feel tight and achy. She was standing *up* to him, not standing *against* him. And he'd just told her he was going to close her down in a week.

She was right. He was turning into the very people he despised. They'd used their money to make him feel small, to bully and intimidate him. And now he was doing the same to a woman who'd only ever been sweet and funny and sexy and good to him.

'I'm going out this afternoon.' He shot Jeremy a look. 'Try not to do too much damage until I get back.'

'I think I can manage without your superior wisdom for a few hours. Can I ask where you're going?'

'No.'

'Fair enough.' He eased up from the chair. 'Jade said she was off to see Sankaty Head Lighthouse after the meeting.' He winked at Liam. 'You know, just in case you were interested.'

As he watched the man saunter out of his office, Liam wondered how he'd gone from the boss who nobody dared talk to, to one Jeremy felt comfortable enough to wink at.

And why he was trying to fight a fucking *smile*.

Chapter Eighteen

Meetings were infinitely better without Henry. It was the third time the SOB group had met, and without his dominating presence it had been much more productive. Of course it could have been down to the fact they were in one of the local cafés, gorging on lattes and pastries. Or to the fact Claire had joined the group, too, and brought with her a much more positive energy – someone else who wanted to make saving the bookstore the focus of the meeting instead of hating Liam Haven. Although when Jade thought of the version who'd trounced out of the shop an hour ago, she was tempted to jump into the other camp.

'I totally agree with Emma,' Mary stated. 'What better way to spend an evening than knocking back wine, munching nibbles and talking about books? I'm sure the library would be on board with supporting that. In fact we should hold it at the library because there's more room there.'

'We could promote it as a social event,' Claire added. 'A great way for islanders and tourists to mingle over a common interest.'

Jade nodded, excitement building. 'We could run it like one of those speed-dating sessions.'

'Pardon?' Philip looked at her aghast.

'I just meant it can be a way of mixing people up, but instead of looking for a date, you're asking about books,' she explained, curbing the desire to shake him out of his judgemental box. 'We can pair up people who love crime, romance, literary fiction and so on. Give them a set time to ask quickfire questions.'

'I like that.' Emma again, who seemed to have found her voice now that Henry wasn't there to talk over her.

'It sounds tacky. I can't see many people buying into it,' Philip argued.

As Jade felt her face heat, Mary elbowed him in the ribs. 'Don't be such a snob. You won't be forced to date anyone, heaven forbid you'd want to do that. It will be fun, and goodness knows we could do with a bit of fun around here.'

There was a bite to Mary's words that made Jade wonder if the older woman had an ulterior motive in trying to shove Philip out of his comfort zone.

'I thought this was meant to be about selling books,' he grumbled.

'Actually, about that.' Jade cleared her throat. 'I don't think increasing book sales should be our focus anymore. Liam's made it quite plain the bookstore will never be able to compete financially with his other plan.'

'You mean the one that will rip the heart out of this part of the waterfront?' Adam interjected sourly.

'That's one viewpoint.' Was she really going to defend the man who, less than an hour ago, had coldly given her a week to leave the shop? But she couldn't stop seeing his face just before he'd left, the hurt in his eyes when he'd concluded she'd taken sides against him. He was stubborn and hard-headed, yet if a barb snuck through his armour, he hurt like anyone else. 'Another view would be he's doing what he wants with his property.' She looked pointedly at Adam. 'Something I know you can understand.'

Adam flushed. 'I was a kid when we did that.'

'Did what?' Mary interrupted, clearly sensing gossip. 'Oh, are you talking about the infamous boat incident? I never did understand what really happened.'

'That boat would never have sailed anywhere,' Adam fired back, body language defensive.

'Boat? What boat?' Jade frowned. 'I thought you stopped him from going to a cove?'

Adam shifted awkwardly on his chair. 'It was a private beach that my family owned. He had no right to be using it in the first place.'

'And now he owns the waterfront, so really we have no right to tell him what to do with it,' Jade countered, earning a smile from Claire. 'What happened with the boat?'

All eyes were on Adam now and a red stain crept up his neck. 'Haven was trying to repair some heap of crap that was never going to be seaworthy. Another way to look at *that*, is to say by torching it, we probably saved his life.'

'Oh, my God, you burned his boat? Why on earth?' Jade demanded, horrified.

Adam's eyes shifted away from hers. 'Look, the guy was annoying, even then, always putting himself where he wasn't wanted. Bad enough on land, but we didn't want him following us out to sea.'

The twelve-year-old boy who'd wanted to fit in. Be part of the gang. Her heart lurched and as she scanned the room she could see the others were as shocked as she was, the view of the world they'd happily lived with, suddenly tilted. Adam of the warm hazel eyes and flirty smile had been a bully. Liam, of the wintry eyes and cool, *do not get close to me* expression, had been the one bullied.

'I remember Liam as a quiet kid,' Philip said into the stunned silence, his brow wrinkling as if he was trying to picture him. 'Mother was highly strung. Used to be a housekeeper at the Chase

Resort, like her mom. But then she just upped and left, leaving Pat to bring Liam up.'

'A tough woman, Pat.' Mary interjected. 'Too proud to accept any help. I always wondered how she managed, suddenly faced with having to take care of a young kid at her age, and on a housekeeper's salary.'

'Well he went to the same boarding school as me so he wasn't that poor,' Adam muttered. 'And he's hardly short of cash now. Not content with buying up this part of the island, he's bought a plot in Siasconset and is building a huge fuck-off mansion.'

'Which he's entitled to do, surely?' Jade sighed. 'Look, I'm only a visitor but I can see there's a lot of tension around what's happening to the island. I'm not sure being antagonistic is going to help though, because he's not doing anything wrong. It's up to us to show him what he could do with the waterfront and the bookstore that would still benefit his resort but also the island. Appeal to his heart, rather than his finances.'

'Assuming he has a heart,' Mary added dourly, but then she batted her hand in the air. 'I'm not sure I feel right saying that after what I've just heard. But he is still hellbent on expanding his resort at the expense of parts of the island that many of us born and bred here hold very dear.'

'So let's continue with the plan to hold a book evening at the library, but let's promote it as being a collaboration between the library and Haven Resorts, because technically the bookstore is part of that now, whether we like it or not.' Jade couldn't tell whether the group were with her, only that it felt right. That somehow her dream to prove she could manage the bookstore had morphed into a desire to get Liam and the island community working together to help them both. 'It might begin to shift people's opinions of him and he in turn could then see the value in getting the island on side, rather than always against him.'

'It's a nice sentiment.' Adam shrugged. 'It won't work but

you're not going to take my word for it, so hell, why not. Nothing to lose at this point.'

'Doubt you'll get his agreement,' Philip added.

'Leave that to me.' She was an expert at doing first, asking permission later. If she got found out.

The meeting wrapped up, and as the others left, Adam strode up to her. 'How come you're taking Haven's side now?'

What was it with these men? 'I'm not taking sides. I'm also not an eight-year-old. Maybe it's time you guys tried to act your ages, too.'

He reared back. 'Wow, for a cute blonde with a sunny smile, you sure pack a nasty punch.'

Gah. 'Well, for a passably handsome fair-haired bloke, you say some pretty juvenile, sexist twaddle.'

She left him standing, jaw open. Feeling mighty proud of herself, she headed down the wide cobbled main street towards the bike rental shop. This afternoon, she was finally going to do some sightseeing.

Was he really driving across the island to look at a lighthouse he'd seen a million times before, on the off chance he might also see a short blonde figure? He should be going through the applications he'd had for the manager post. A post that once filled, meant he was no longer tied to spending every day on this goddamn island.

Yet here he was, chasing after a woman, when he knew damn well the only way he'd remain unscathed was to keep well away from her.

He was only here to apologise, he reminded himself. And felt marginally better.

Driving past the golf course, he turned into a residential lane and parked the car at the top. The red and white cylindrical lighthouse stood tall and proud on the cliff, the sweeping greens of the golf course to the left of it, and the vivid blue ocean to the right. But there was no sign of Jade. Had he missed her... His heart gave a little kick as he spotted a female figure on a bicycle cycling up the lane towards the lighthouse, blonde ponytail flying out of the back of a pink baseball cap, shapely legs peddling away beneath a pair of denim shorts.

Unable to help himself, he smiled and honked the horn.

She turned to look at him and, to his horror, began to wobble.

Then promptly fell off the damn thing.

Heart in his mouth, he lunged at the door handle and threw himself out of the car.

'Shit, Jade, are you okay?'

Relief washed through him when she began to sit up. 'I'd be better if you hadn't scared the crap out of me.'

'It was a hello honk, not a scary one,' he protested, squatting on his haunches.

'And I'm supposed to tell the difference how?'

She shifted, and guilt wriggled through him as he saw the long graze from her elbow to her wrist. Gently he lifted her arm to examine it, wincing at the combination of blood and dirt. 'We need to get that cleaned up.'

'Yeah, *I* need to do that.' She jerked her arm away from him. '*You* need to go back to whatever it was you were doing before you decided to scare people off their bikes with your nasty horn-blowing.'

He sighed and pulled the bike to one side so he could help her to her feet. 'I came here to apologise.'

'Oh.' She stumbled a little, holding on to him as she balanced her weight away from what was clearly a tender ankle. 'Well, I'm kind of busy right now, so maybe you can save it for another day.'

'Jade.' He exhaled, trying to keep a lid on his frustration. 'You need to come back with me.'

'Um, actually I don't. It's my day off today so you're not the boss. I can do what I want.' She shuffled away from him and bent to pick up the bike.

As he watched her struggle to lift it while balancing on one foot, blood dripping onto the ground from her scratch, the frustration bubbled over. 'For fuck's sake, Jade. Leave the bike, I'll pick it up later. Get in the car and we'll get you cleaned up and that ankle looked at.'

'Actually, no.' She brushed a few stray hairs that had whipped across her face in the breeze. 'I came here to see the lighthouse.'

She began to limp off towards the damn thing, wheeling her bike.

Frustration bumped up against amusement, and both gave way to admiration as he watched her slowly make her way along the path. 'Fine, if you insist on being stubborn, let's do this in a way that will at least make me feel slightly less terrible.' Carefully he prised the bike out of her hands, settled it against the fence, and lifted her into his arms.

She squealed, wriggling. 'Oh, my God, you can't just kidnap me. Let me down.'

'You wanted to see the lighthouse, I'm taking you there.'

He started to walk, annoyance quickly giving way to a simmering arousal as his hands curled around the soft skin of her thighs. When she threw her arms around his neck to steady herself, he was done for, his erection jamming against the zip of his chinos.

'This is ridiculous,' she muttered.

'The ridiculous part is you refusing to let me take care of you.'

Her shoulders rose and fell. 'Fine. I'll come back another day.'

'Good decision.'

He swivelled and began to march back to his car.

'It's not like you could have carried me all that way, anyway.'

He halted. 'Want to bet?'

She rolled her eyes. 'Just get me into your car without dropping me.'

He eased her carefully into the passenger seat, trying not to touch or look at her any more than was necessary. He didn't want to be this attracted, this aroused by her. This *unbalanced* by her.

'Did you really come out here to apologise to me?' she asked as he pulled back onto the road.

He glanced sideways at her. 'What do you think?' He let out a long breath. 'I shouldn't have given you an ultimatum like that. I … lost my temper.'

Her gaze skimmed over his face and she seemed satisfied with what she saw because she gave a little, pleased smile. 'How did you know where I was?'

'Jeremy told me.' He cleared his throat. 'We … talked. He seemed to think I might be interested.'

He caught the curve of her mouth. 'Careful. If you keep that up, you and he might become friends.'

'I don't do friends.'

Again he felt those eyes on him. 'Why not?'

He briefly considered veering off the road and pretending he had a flat tyre. 'It wasn't a conscious choice. More the way things worked out.' Memories from his childhood swarmed through his mind like wasps, stinging as they went; shunned by classmates, ridiculed for his cheap clothes, laughed at when asked about his family, where he lived.

'But that was at school,' she said softly, guessing correctly. 'What about after that?'

He shrugged. 'I stopped trying. It was easier that way.'

'What do you mean, easier?'

Easier than being rejected. He let her question hang in the air.

A beat later her hand covered his on the steering wheel. 'Well, you have a friend in me.'

Emotion burned a trail through his chest and lodged like a

rock in his throat. He couldn't even speak past it. All he could do was wrap his fingers around hers and squeeze.

He'd come to apologise, yet here she was, in pain from injuries he'd caused, comforting him.

With a flash of terror, he realised his attempt to keep his distance had totally failed with Jade. His heart was letting her in, whether he liked it or not.

Chapter Nineteen

Gingerly, Jade climbed the steps up to the studio flat, very aware of Liam's presence behind her. He'd given her a week's ultimatum, then caused her to fall off her bike. It was enough to stay angry with him, wasn't it?

Okay, she'd not ridden a bike for over ten years. And he'd only been at the lighthouse because he'd wanted to apologise for the ultimatum.

Yep, she was basically screwed. If she couldn't hold on to the anger, she had no defence against the new parts of him she was slowly unravelling. The soft underbellies to his hard shell. He had no friends because he'd stopped trying... Her heart had frigging melted at that, leaving a gooey mess of emotions in its place. She'd not needed his answer as to why, it was obvious. Everyone carried a threshold for pain, beyond which they couldn't tolerate it.

It didn't help *her*, though, because she'd suffered her own pain, let men into her heart only to find Prince Charming was actually King Prick.

In the few weeks she'd known him, Liam had already swung from one to the other. It was impossible to know where he would finally land. There was also the small matter of him being her boss, of them being at loggerheads over the bookstore. And of her home and her life, her real life, being over three-thousand miles away.

So staying angry was really her best bet of surviving her time out here without having to go through another epic heartbreak.

'I told you, I can manage,' she protested as he clasped her elbow and led her towards the sink like she was a frail eighty-year-old.

'And I told you, I'm not leaving until I'm satisfied you're okay.'

She gingerly put some weight on her left ankle and grimaced. A beat later he was typing into his phone.

'Who are you messaging?'

'May.' He glanced up at her. 'I want you to be checked by a medic.'

Oh, my God. She snatched the phone from his hands. 'Are you totally insane? I've slightly twisted it, that's all. If you want to make yourself useful, you can get me some peas.'

'Let's clean your elbow before we start making dinner,' he muttered, turning her so she faced the sink. His chest a warm, hard wall of delicious muscle behind her.

'The peas are for my ankle,' she retorted, giving him a glare over her shoulder, only to find his smoky grey eyes smiling straight at her. 'Okay, you knew that. You were making a poor joke.'

'A reasonably amusing joke,' he corrected, turning on the tap.

'By your standards, maybe, but they must be pretty low because I have it on good authority that Liam Haven doesn't joke.'

'Let me guess: Jeremy.'

'Maybe.' With a gentle touch she hadn't thought him capable of, he brought her elbow towards the warm flowing water. 'I can wash my own flipping arm,' she grouched, trying to pull away. 'Amazingly, I've been doing it since I was three.'

Ignoring her, he kept her arm in his gentle grip and began to carefully wipe at the crusted blood with some kitchen roll.

His body seemed to surround her, caging her in, so all she could think, smell and feel, was him. His coiled strength, the expensive sandalwood cologne he wore, his—

'Oh my God, are you really hard right now?'

'I'm touching you.' The rough timbre of his voice resonated through her. 'Of course I'm hard.' She tried to squirm away from him but his hips pressed against her, his body remaining locked around her. 'Ignore it. I'm here to take care of you, not fuck you.'

The gravelly words, the insistent, pulsing heat of him, all caused arousal to pool between her thighs. 'You're kind of hard to ignore,' she grumbled.

'Now you know how I feel.' Surprised, she turned and caught his eye again. This time there was no amusement. If anything, he looked annoyed. 'Don't look at me like this is news to you.'

She was saved having to reply when he turned off the tap and scooped her into his arms, placing her on the sofa like she was something delicate, breakable. To her astonishment, he knelt on the floor and began untying her trainers.

'Jeepers creepers, stop.' She jerked her foot away. 'I can do that.'

He sighed. 'Why are you turning this into a battle?'

'Because I'm still cross with you. Because you're my boss and this isn't appropriate. Because I'm not comfortable with guys handling my smelly feet.'

Because I'm going to fall for you if you keep showing me these sensitive, caring sides to you.

His hands settled on her foot, clasping it gently. 'It's your day off, I'm not your boss today. And I remember you having no qualms about me handling your feet when we were on the boat. In fact, you were happy to put them on my shoulders, to dig them into my ass—'

'Stop it.'

He must have read the mess of emotions on her face because he closed his eyes and drew in a deep breath. When he opened them again, his expression was full of apology. 'Sorry.' He swallowed, staring down at where his fingers wrapped tenderly around her ankle. 'I just want to make things right between us. I didn't like what you said, about me turning into a rich arrogant prick. And I didn't like the fact you were siding with people who don't like me.' He lifted his gaze to hers. 'But by reacting like I did, I proved you were right with both.'

The anger she wanted to feel, she *needed* to feel, fizzled out. 'You're not arrogant. But I do think you're so focused on money, on seeing some people here as your enemy, that you don't see the bigger picture.' She bit her lip. 'Philip said your mum left when you were small.'

'Had a good time gossiping about me, did you?'

'We *talked* about you.' Annoyed, she tried to pull her foot away again but he held firm.

With tension cracking through the air, he began to slowly undo her trainer. Realising he needed to do this to make up for what he saw as him knocking her off the bike, she gave in and let him. His fingers were gentle as they twisted the ankle, checking how far she could move it before she winced. Clearly satisfied it was as she'd described, a slight twist, he pulled the coffee table closer, placed a cushion on it and then shifted her ankle onto it.

Still, without speaking, he walked over to the fridge and dug into the small freezer compartment to find the peas. Once he'd wrapped them in a tea towel, he pressed them onto her ankle.

And finally he began to talk.

'I was an unplanned pregnancy for my twenty-two-year-old mom. The guy she had an affair with paid her off. She took half the money and fled, leaving her mom, my grandma, to bring me up.' His eyes met hers, searching, as if trying to judge her reaction. 'Don't you dare feel sorry for me, because she's the best person I know. She was a cleaner; my pop, a fisherman who died far too early. Instead of using the other half of the money to have a comfortable life, she used it to send me to a prestigious boarding school near Boston, thinking she was doing the best for me.'

It was the shadows in his eyes, the edge to his voice. 'But?'

'But she hadn't factored in how cruel some rich kids could be. Especially when they came across a poor kid with zero connections.' He gave a shrug of his powerful shoulders. 'In the end I gave up trying to make friends. It was easier to keep myself to myself.'

Her heart tumbled in her chest. 'That's awful.' Unconsciously, her gaze shot to his eyebrow, the one with the scar.

He gave her a wry smile. 'One of many skirmishes. I won some, this one I lost. Again, don't waste your time pitying me. If anything, they did me a favour. I learnt to rely on myself and only myself. Thanks to them, I put all my energy and focus into my studies, determined to make something of myself.' He looked down at her ankle, at where his fingers gently smoothed across her skin. 'Adam, and others like him who went to the same school, are part of the old wealth on the island. I'm the worst combination – new wealth. They hate that I made it by purchasing part of the harbourfront instead of inheriting a ready-made business. They hate that I flash my wealth around by buying land to build my own house in the same area they're living in their big inherited houses.' His jaw hardened. 'They consider me vulgar, and they pollute the minds of others to their way of thinking.'

When he raised his eyes to hers, she felt another hard tug on her heart. 'I don't listen to other people's opinions. I make up my own mind.'

He nodded, and rose to his feet. 'I haven't told anyone what

I've just told you. Not even my grandma. How could I tell the woman who thought she was giving me the best start in life, that I was miserable?'

'Why did you tell me?'

He paused a moment, eyes holding hers captive. 'When it comes to you, a lifelong habit of keeping my distance seems to fly out of the window.'

The air between them crackled and she held her breath, a sudden sense that they were at the edge of a precipice. Ahead was a potentially life-altering thrill, but it came with a great degree of danger. Did she take a huge, terrifying move towards it? Or retreat, as fast as she possibly could, to safety?

Liam broke the heavily charged silence. 'You know, this'—he pointed back and forth between them—'it doesn't work for me either. I have plans, carefully constructed plans I've spent years putting in place, that you're trying your hardest to derail. I don't want to spend my days thinking about you. Nor do I want to keep spilling my guts to you. I especially don't want to like you, because I know I'll get shafted further down the line. But it's happening, and I can't stop it.'

With a final incline of his head, he turned and headed down the stairs.

She was left wondering if the decision whether or not to move towards the danger was even in her hands.

———

The iconic clay cliffs of Martha's Vineyard came slowly into view and Liam felt some of his tension start to recede. Light from the setting sun danced across the water, casting shimmering reflections as he powered towards the shore. Minutes later he secured the yacht on its mooring and walked up the private wooden jetty towards his grandma's house.

He always looked forward to seeing her, but after the day he'd just had, more than ever he felt the need to be close to the woman who was his anchor, his family.

The one person in his life who'd ever given a damn about him.

A flash of white fur darted towards him and he bent to stroke the sleek cat who purred like an expensive car as she rubbed against his legs. 'At least someone's pleased to see me.'

'Stop fussing over her and give your grandma a hug.'

He felt a rush of warmth, of deep affection, as he marched over to the figure standing in the open French doors. With her short white hair, which she dyed blue, pink or purple depending on her mood, but was today a bright silver, his grandma was still a knockout at seventy-five. He bent to hug her, lifting her feet off the ground and twirling them both around. And earning him a delighted chuckle. 'It's been too long since a man swept me off my feet.'

Carefully he settled her back on the ground. 'And why's that? You know Pop would never have wanted you to live alone.'

'I'm not alone. I have Bardot. And I have you.'

'What about John?' In his early seventies, the man lived around the corner and had been attempting to persuade his grandma into a relationship for two years. 'Is he still breaking his back, and his bank balance, trying to convince you to give him a chance?'

She chuckled and threaded her arm through his as they walked inside. 'He's bored and I'm his entertainment. Now tell me your news. What are your plans for the waterfront, now that your purchases are complete? And for that lovely old store on the wharf?'

He peered down at her curiously. 'Why do I get the feeling you already know?'

'I still have my spies on the island, you know. And they tell me the new bookstore manager has started a campaign to get you to keep the shop.' She smiled. 'I always liked that place.'

'You liked browsing the books there,' he corrected. 'And then you'd borrow the one you wanted from the library and if they didn't have it in, you'd ask them to order it.'

'Only because I couldn't afford books back then. It was always my dream to be able to go in and just buy whatever I fancied. It's such a delightful shop, all that driftwood, the position of it.' She let out a long, dreamy sigh. 'A real paradise for book lovers.'

He knew she was coming from a place of sentimentality, but he couldn't ignore the feeling of hurt. 'Not you, too.'

She squeezed his hand, her expression full of love. 'If by that you mean I'd like it if the bookstore remained, then, yes, but I'm sure you have very good reasons for knocking it down.'

'I do.' He could hardly build a row of exclusive luxury cottages, each complete with its own private mooring, and leave a damn bookstore in the middle of it all.

She walked to the kitchen and reached into the cupboard, bringing down two wine glasses. 'Well, then, you just have to explain your reasons to this new manager.'

'She's not as reasonable as you.' His conscience niggled. Jade only knew it was about money. If he told her everything, would she understand? He recalled the sympathy in her eyes as he'd opened up to her this afternoon. Maybe she would, but was it really in his best interests? He'd be laying himself bare. Leaving himself defenceless.

A shudder ran through him.

'I hear she's very pretty.'

Sliding his hands into his pockets, he set his expression to neutral. 'You could describe her that way.' Luscious, devastatingly sexy, utterly unique were other descriptions. 'Do you want me to open a bottle?' he asked, hoping to change the subject.

'Of course. I bought a lovely Merlot for you.'

He went to grab the bottle sitting on the worktop, and frowned down at the label. 'It's a Pinot Noir.'

'Oh, is it? Silly me, I must have misread it.'

Worry shifted through him. If it had been the first time she'd made a mistake misreading something, he'd brush it off, but this was getting too regular. 'Merlot and Pinot Noir aren't exactly similar.'

'They are when you're old and in a hurry.'

She busied herself getting cheese out of the fridge and the worry deepened as he recognised her behaviour. She was avoiding looking at him. Walking up behind her, he took the cheese from her hands, set it on the island and closed the fridge door. 'Talk to me.'

'I know you prefer the Merlot, but I'm sure the Pinot Noir will be fine. I remember a time when having a glass of wine at all was a luxury we could only afford on special occasions—'

'Stop.' He clasped her face, more wrinkles now than when they'd shared the occasional bottle on his breaks from university, yet still so very dear to him it made his heart hurt just looking at her. 'Is it your eyesight? Is that why you're misreading labels and have stopped driving?' He thought back to his visits over the last three months. 'Is that why you haven't asked me to bring you a new book?'

Blue eyes, dimmed with age, darted away from his. 'You always did know when I was struggling.'

'It's my job to know.' He bent to kiss her furrowed forehead. 'My job to take care of you.'

She humphed. 'I don't want you wasting your time on me. I want you living your life.'

Christ. When he'd told Jade his grandma was the best person he knew, he'd only scratched the surface of how lucky he'd been to have her. 'How can I live my life if I'm worried about you? Now tell me what's happening so I can fix it.'

She patted his cheek. 'My dear boy, this is something you can't fix.'

She took his hand and led him to the sofa, sitting down first before patting the space next to her. He dropped into it, wrapping his arms around her, his mind immediately making similarities between her frail, bony body and the youthful curves of the last woman he'd held. 'The doctor says I have age related macular degeneration, the common one, and there's no treatment. I just have to find ways to adapt to it.'

Fuck. His mind buzzed. 'How long has this been going on?' Why hadn't he noticed? He'd just said it was his job to take care of her, yet he'd done a piss-poor job of it.

'For a while I've noticed my eyesight has become blurred. It's just the bit in the middle, but it makes it harder to read.' She smiled sadly. 'I think that's the worst part. You know how I love to read my books, but it's proving a bit of a struggle now.'

'Have you seen a specialist? Of course you haven't,' he muttered, answering his own question. 'First thing tomorrow morning, I'll make you an appointment with the top guy. From now on, no more handling this on your own. Together we'll find a way through it.'

She patted his hand. 'I don't want you worrying about me. I'm taking all these fancy vitamins the doctor suggested and I bought myself a magnifying glass and brighter light bulbs.'

Brighter bulbs? She couldn't see to read and she thought brighter bulbs was the answer? 'From now on we're in this together,' he repeated. Because he could see she was about to argue, he shot her his best smile. 'Batman and Robin.'

'You silly goose.' She shook her head, but he could see amusement chase away some of the shadows. 'Bonnie and Clyde.'

'Woody and Buzz Lightyear.'

That got a chuckle out of her. 'Abbot and Costello.'

It was a game they'd played when he'd been down, usually the day before he had to go back to school. It was only later he'd realised it had been her way of reminding him she was always there for him. 'Scooby-Doo and Shaggy.'

She sighed, her body relaxing against his. 'Fine. You win. Make me an appointment.'

He poked her gently in the ribs. 'Snoopy and Woodstock. And I'm doing more than making you the appointment. I'm taking you to wherever we need to go, and throwing vast amounts of money in whatever direction will get you the best possible care.'

Her eyes glistened and she squeezed his arm. 'You're a good grandson.'

He hadn't been, not over the last few years, he realised with a rush of shame. Oh he'd seen her regularly, and phoned when he couldn't, but he hadn't paid attention, his mind too focused on business.

It made him think of Jade, and her earnest expression as she'd told him he was too preoccupied with money to see what was important.

She'd been right, but it wasn't the community he needed to become his priority. It was his grandma.

Chapter Twenty

F riday evening, and Jade was in the library with Claire, making sure everything was ready for *Bookish Speed Dating – find your book match*.

No, not the library. That was far too dry a word for such a glorious building. She was in the Nantucket Atheneum. Even its correct name, written in regal gold lettering on the front of the building, was majestic. Nestled in the heart of downtown Nantucket, the neoclassical building resembled an historic mansion with its tall, imposing white columns framing an entrance reached by a series of regal steps, flanked either side by shrubs in giant pots. It was elegant, it was *magnificent*. Absolutely the perfect homage to books and reading.

'Are we expecting Liam?' Claire asked as they surveyed the Great Hall.

Yep, her little meeting was being held on the second floor in a room known as the frigging *Great Hall*. And with its high ceiling, ornate cornices and the grand gold-framed oil paintings lining the walls, she could not argue with the *great*.

Her gaze rested on the lines of tables, each set with two chairs, and nerves buzzed in Jade's belly. *It sounds tacky.* Her stomach rolled. Please God it wouldn't be a flop. 'Um, I don't think Liam will come.' She glanced guiltily at the poster advertising the event. 'At least I hope not.'

Claire eyed her curiously. 'I thought the pair of you got on? It certainly looked that way at the talk I did.'

Do not blush, do not blush. 'I don't dislike him, if that's what you mean. Not like some of the others.'

'Good, because he really doesn't deserve the bad press. Ashley sent me a letter to give to him so I was hoping to see him here. She was worried if she sent it to the resort his admin would open it, and it's very personal.'

'Oh?' Had she hit the casual interest tone she'd been aiming for?

Claire gave her a knowing look. 'I told Ashley about all the rumours circulating and she was horrified. Hence the letter to Liam, thanking him for not saying anything. She also gave him and me permission to tell people the truth, so I'll save you having to ask the question you're clearly dying to ask,' she added dryly. 'Ashley had a fling with one of the regular guests. He told her he was single but when she accidentally got pregnant he admitted he'd been lying and actually had a wife and family he had no intention of leaving. Gutted, she decided to go home to Australia. Liam was a rock throughout and let her go with a glowing reference and without having to complete her notice. He even gave her a very generous lump sum that he insisted was the bonus she'd accrued, even though he'd already paid her a bonus the previous month.' Claire met her eyes. 'He told Ashley he knew what it was like to be toyed with.'

'Oh.' She had to do better than one-syllable answers. Claire was a frigging genius with words. 'That's awful, poor Ashley.' And *yay, go Liam*, she added silently.

'It was a tough time for her but she's doing okay now she's home. Getting excited about being a mom.' Claire's phone buzzed and she gave Jade an apologetic look. 'Sorry, I should take this, it's my agent.'

Jade smiled and watched her go, her eyes connecting once again with the poster. Crap, she should have asked permission.

'Having second thoughts?'

She startled. 'God, you scared me.'

Jeremy laughed. 'Feeling a bit jumpy are we? Wouldn't have anything to do with that, by any chance?' He gestured at the poster she'd been staring at. The one declaring *proudly sponsored by Haven Resorts* in big, bold letters across the bottom. 'The *proudly* was an interesting touch.'

'I figured go big or go home.' She let out a strangled laugh. 'And if he sees that, I probably will be going home.'

'Um.'

She narrowed her eyes at him. 'What's that supposed to mean?'

'I was just wondering if we were talking about the same *he*. I was talking about the man who, the moment I sent him a message about you needing advice on spreadsheets, cancelled a meeting and dashed over to you.'

'Bollocks.' She sucked in a breath, feeling a flutter in her chest. 'He really cancelled a meeting?'

'He did. A meeting with a journalist looking to give the resort some free publicity.' He gave her an assessing glance. 'You know I have hundreds of questions, don't you?'

'Maybe.' She bent to straighten the already perfectly straight table in front of her. 'But I wouldn't have the answer to them.'

'You might have an answer to why you chose to put his name to a meeting he doesn't know about, designed to raise the profile of a bookstore he's planning to shut down?'

'Crapity crap, when you put it like that...' The nerves in her belly stopped buzzing and began to scream.

'Of course, it could be looked at another way,' Jeremy continued. 'You're helping improve his image because he's too bull-headed or proud or blinded by whatever feud he's got going on with the Chases, to do it himself.'

She pressed a hand against her stomach, felt it quieten. 'Let's go with the second one. It also happens to be the truth, although I didn't realise he had an ongoing feud with all the Chases. I thought it was just Henry.'

'Maybe feud is the wrong word, but it seems more personal than the healthy dislike of a competitor.'

She recalled their discussion about her dating the wrong men. *I had a similar bad habit, where women were concerned.* 'Maybe they clashed over a woman?' At this, Jeremy let out a bark of laughter, causing Mary to look over at them curiously. 'Shhh,' Jade hissed. 'Mary's going to want to know what we're talking about.'

'And you don't want her to know you've still got the hots for the man you hooked up with, before you realised he was the big bad wolf and you were supposed to hate him?'

'I never said I had the hots for him,' she spluttered, aware she was probably the colour of a tomato by now.

Jeremy gave her a smug smile. 'Why else have you expertly weaved a question about his past relationships into the conversation?'

'God, you've got a devious mind. I should just walk away.'

'But you're too keen to find out the answer to your question.'

'You probably don't even know,' she grumped. 'It's not like you and he are besties. He doesn't even have a bestie.'

'And you'd know this, how?'

'Oh no, you're not getting anything out of me. I am a vault.' She mimed zipping her mouth shut.

'Yet you expect *me* to dish the gossip on our boss?'

Our boss. It was a timely reminder that the thoughts she'd been having about him, the unprofessional, at times downright carnal thoughts, were not appropriate. Even if he wasn't also ridiculously out of her league and a moody, complicated man fixated on business who didn't let anyone close. 'Yes.'

Jeremy chuckled. 'I like you, Jade Taylor. You're a breath of fresh Atlantic air wafting across this sometimes-stale island.'

'Yeah, I definitely don't waft, I'm more a charge full speed ahead and fall arse over tit sort of girl.' She turned to face him. 'And you still haven't answered the question.'

He pursed his lips. 'You're right, I've tried, but so far the man has stubbornly refused my overtures of friendship so I don't have any information on his personal life that can be considered as being direct from the horse's mouth.' He bent closer to whisper in her ear. 'However, the hotel grapevine is buoyant with rumours that he once dated Sabrina Ellis, heir to the international Ellis Hotels and Resorts chain for which, interestingly, our boss used to work.'

She felt her eyes grow wide. 'He slept with the big boss's daughter?'

'Apparently.' Jeremy smirked. 'So he's hardly going to be fazed by, let's phrase it more delicately than I did earlier, how about "interwork non-curricular relations"?'

Even as she tried to get her head around Jeremy's convoluted phrasing, she knew it didn't matter. Being her boss's booty call was not going to do her self-respect any favours.

'Have you two come to help, or to gossip?' Mary bustled over, giving them both a very school-teacherish look. 'And if it's the second, why am I not included?'

Jade laughed. Mary was one of those women who took a while to warm to you. Once she'd decided you were okay, though, a twinkle was never very far from her eye. 'No gossip,' she lied. 'Just wondering if Liam Haven is going to turn up.'

'Well you should be more worried about the line Claire tells me is building at the front door.'

'There's a *queue*?' Jade felt a bubble of unrestrained joy.

'No, I'm just making it up to get you back for not including me in your little tittle-tattle.' Mary must have seen her bubble burst, because she patted her arm. 'Actually, the queue isn't just outside the entrance, it's winding round the side of the building.'

'Oh, my God.' Jade squeezed her hands together, feeling a kick of adrenalin. This was happening. 'We have real people wanting to come and talk books.'

'Better hope one of those real people *isn't* you-know-who,' Jeremy whispered. 'Or you'll have some explaining to do.'

She watched as he made his way elegantly across the room, bestowing smiles to everyone who looked in his direction. A good friend to have, she mused. How sad that his boss didn't have the sense, or was too burned by past experience, to see it.

Would Liam turn up? She shook off the worry. He'd only be annoyed if the evening was a failure, and how could it possibly fail when an army of book lovers were chomping at the bit to talk to each other about their specialist chosen subject?

———

Liam had a business to run and three resorts to oversee; Nantucket, Martha's Vineyard, and the newest in Provincetown. He was also managing the Nantucket resort until he chose a replacement from the so far very unappealing list of candidates the agency had supplied. Despite that full-on workload, he knew exactly which meetings his company had agreed to sponsor.

Bookish Speed Dating was not, and would never be, on the list.

So why was he currently staring at a poster for the event, with 'Haven Resorts' splashed across it in awful purple font?

He yanked out his phone and called Jeremy. 'Why the fuck am I sponsoring a fucking speed-dating event at the fucking library?'

There was a pause on the other end, followed by the sound of footsteps. 'Can you repeat that please? I couldn't quite hear what you were asking between the f-bombs.'

He pinched the bridge of his nose. 'Why is "Haven Resorts" plastered all over a poster advertising an event I have no knowledge of?'

'Maybe the email asking your permission slipped into your junk mail?'

'I check my junk mail twice a day.'

'Ah.' He couldn't be sure, but he thought he heard Jeremy mutter, *'Should have guessed'*. 'Maybe you should go to the library and see what the meeting is all about before you jump to inappropriate conclusions. You might find it was something you would have agreed to put your name to had you not missed the request which I'm almost certain would have been sent to you.'

'I'm *almost certain* you have direct knowledge of what's happening here,' he retorted. Just like he was almost certain Jade and her merry band of Haven haters were behind the poster and the meeting.

Damn it, he had enough on his plate with his grandma right now. He did not need a public confrontation.

But you'll get to see Jade. He hated that he felt a bump of pleasure. Hated too that his legs began to propel him towards the library before he'd started to consider the pros and cons of turning up.

The sun was low in the sky as he wound his way through the cobbled streets of the historic district towards the Nantucket Atheneum. As he always did, he took a moment to admire the building, and another to wonder why it wasn't used for a higher purpose than housing books.

Thankfully, once inside, he didn't have to ask the way to the event – it was painful to say the words *bookish speed dating* in his head, never mind out loud. The sound of lively chatter guided him straight up the stairs towards it.

Lined up on the highly polished wooden floor of the Great Hall were small tables – he hazarded about fifteen of them. At each table pairs sat opposite each other, having animated conversations.

He'd barely had time to take it all in before a buzzer sounded.

'Time to swap!' Jade, cheeks flushed, blonde hair tied back in a ponytail, creeping loose at the sides, waved her right arm in a circular motion. 'Clockwise to the next table please.'

His pulse rocked up a few beats as he stared at her. Was it okay to be angry and yet mesmerised at the same time? Because he couldn't take his damned eyes off her. Nor could he fail to spot how easily she talked to people, a smile here, a press of an arm there. Exaggerated horror, followed by laughter, the other person – a guy, he noticed with a flare of jealousy – joining in on the joke.

He was torn between stalking over to her and dragging her away, or retreating to his yacht to have the argument another day. One when he didn't feel exhausted, drained from all the research he'd been doing on AMD. A day when he didn't desperately feel the need to talk to someone about it all.

And when he didn't feel so raw from seeing the woman he couldn't get out of his head, using his name to further her own ambition.

He was about to take the *retreat* option when a pair of big blue eyes clashed with his across the room. He watched as she blinked, even saw her draw in a breath. Then she smiled apologetically at the young guy she'd been talking to and walked purposefully towards Liam, drawing the eye of every male, and some females, in the room.

Even those supposed to be fascinated by the books, he thought waspishly.

'Hi.' She bit down on her bottom lip, and his blood temperature rose a few degrees. 'Good to see you here.'

'Is it?' He nodded towards the poster. 'Or were you hoping I wouldn't attend the meeting I'm apparently proudly sponsoring?'

'Ah. You noticed.' She gave him a cute little smile. 'I may have forgotten to ask your permission.'

Mary shoved a tray of food for tiny people – he freaking hated canapés – under his nose. He waved her away, annoyance humming through him. 'I presume I'm paying for those?'

'Well, the bookstore is, so technically, I suppose yes, but according to your precious *spreadsheets*,' the way she emphasised the word told him he wasn't the only one now irritated, 'there is money for promotion.'

'You used my name and money to promote an event designed to save a bookstore I own and want to close down?' She couldn't have made him look more stupid if she'd tried.

Her cheeks reddened. 'I realise it sounds a bit off when you say it like that, but if you'd just let me explain. It's true the goal of the event is to persuade you to keep the bookstore, but—'

'There you are.' Liam's hairs stood up on the back of his neck as Adam slid up to Jade and kissed her on both cheeks. 'I see we've got a great turnout.'

We? Liam's annoyance turned to anger, reinforced as Adam smirked.

The screech of the buzzer sounded again and Jade gave him one last, worried glance before ducking off to announce another rotation.

'She's quite a woman.'

Liam snapped his gaze away from Jade's ravishing figure and back to Adam, who was giving him a calculating look. 'She's an employee.'

'Hasn't stopped you in the past, by all accounts.' He gave him a sly smile. 'It must hurt to know the woman you're clearly obsessed by, is doing her best to rally the island against you.'

The barb pierced but Liam kept his body relaxed, his voice steady. This was familiar territory. 'Do I look like I'm hurting? Because it feels like I'm running a highly successful multi-million-dollar business.' He gave him a sardonic smile. 'How are you doing?'

Adam's face flushed a fiery red. 'How do you think? You stole my business from under me.'

'I bought your business for a fair price,' Liam corrected.

He turned to walk away, but was stopped in his progress towards the exit by two women who gave him a tentative smile. 'Mr Haven?'

He eyed them warily. Usually when he was accosted, his accuser wore a scowl, but these two seemed more curious than angry. 'Yes?'

'I thought so. We just wanted to thank you.' The older one with curly hair looked at her companion, but when she didn't say anything, just kept staring at him like she was trying to work out what species he was, she spoke again. 'We had a fabulous time tonight. Met so many like-minded people and we've come away with a long list of book recommendations.'

'Which we'll buy from Little Bay Book Shack, obviously,' her companion piped up. Apparently now finding her voice.

'I hope you can put on another evening like this. Maybe make it a regular feature.' The curly-haired woman smiled. 'It's such a great way to meet new friends. Plus, of course, it brings the locals and tourists together, which is lovely.' She glanced at her friend, who nodded vigorously.

'What Anne said.'

They both laughed, and the older of the two patted his arm –

yep, actually touched him. 'We won't keep you, but thank you again. It's been wonderful.'

They drifted off, leaving Liam staring after them, an emotion he couldn't identify settling in his chest. As several more people stopped to thank him for helping put on an evening he'd done nothing towards, it was quickly superseded by an emotion he did recognise. Guilt.

Jade hadn't made him look stupid. She'd made him look generous, *benevolent*.

Chapter Twenty-One

Following the speed-dating evening, Saturday in the shop had been the busiest Jade had known it, full of people wanting to buy the books they'd been recommended.

She'd felt chuffed. Pleased enough with herself to instigate a family chat on the Sunday, *and* remain calm when Lauren kept trying to turn the talk towards her love life. 'There is no love life. I'm here to focus on the shop,' Jade told her. 'And I think I've made some real progress in that direction.'

It had felt good talking about a success for a change. Her little team – she was running a *team* – had been buzzing after the library event. When the last person had drifted out, Mary had attacked the leftover bottles of fizz. Then she'd found some awful music on her phone and badgered them all to dance. Philip, included. The man had actually shown some decent moves once he'd downed a few glasses.

The only low point was Liam and his determination to twist everything. Of course Adam hadn't helped, but then he hadn't helped with the whole event, either. Just swanned around telling people they should support the store because otherwise Haven was going to close it down, like he had other thriving businesses on the waterfront.

If only Liam had bothered to hang around long enough to listen to *her* explanation, she thought for the umpteenth time, rather than slink off to stick pins in her voodoo-doll replica.

That's if she was even important enough for him to have a voodoo doll of her. Or to have remained in his mind after he'd walked out of the frigging door.

I don't want to spend my days thinking about you.

Okay, maybe he did think of her. But he didn't want to.

Just like she did not want to keep thinking of him. Especially not on her day off.

Exasperated with herself, she stood up from her prone position on the beach and shook the sand off her legs. The book she'd been reading fell onto the sand. Great. She'd be picking the stuff out of it for days.

She quickly gathered her things and shoved them into her rucksack, taking a moment to take a final look at the stunning stretch of soft, golden sand that was Madaket Beach. It was so peaceful here, clear blue sea ahead of her, large sand dunes behind her. No rows of loungers, no tacky beachfront cafes. Just beautiful sand as far as the eye could see, a few couples strolling along the beach, a handful of swimmers … and a seal. Yes, a seal had bobbed its head out of the water straight in front of her. God, she loved this island. Forget the issues with the bookstore, with Liam. She would make the most of being here while she could.

Tugging the rental bike off its stand, she began to peddle back past Millie's restaurant towards the bike path. And no, she was not going to remember this time a week ago, when Liam had shocked her into falling off. Then carried her in his arms and proceeded to care for her.

Nope, definitely not remembering that.

Instead she focused on her surroundings, the smell of pine trees and the glisten of small freshwater lakes, known as the Great Ponds, that nestled between the swathes of lush green countryside. She stopped at one small lake and squealed when she saw what was swimming in it. Turtles. Snapping turtles according to the sign. About a foot long, they were so ugly, they were beautiful.

As she neared the town she climbed off her bike and walked it along the cobbled main street – no way could her bum stand cycling over the smooth stones which, together with the grand old tree-shaded mansions lining either side, gave a real sense of times gone by.

When she reached the wharf she tried not to look at the gleaming white yacht moored at the end.

Her eyes had other ideas though, and her heart lurched as she spotted a male figure hunched over, head in his hands. Without thinking, she clattered the bike to the floor and ran across the rickety wooden slats. 'Liam?'

His head snapped up, and she heard him mutter a curse before dragging a hand down his face. 'Go away.'

'You look awful.'

He let out a humourless laugh. 'And you look fucking gorgeous. But you need to go.' He bent and picked up a glass from the floor. That's when she saw the bottle of whisky.

'Drinking already?' It was only just gone five o'clock.

He smirked, his next words slurring. 'Who are you? My mother?' As soon as he'd said the last word, his expression turned haggard. 'Like she'd ever cared. She fucked off and left her mother to pick up the pieces. And she did. Christ, she was awesome at it, being my mom, my dad, my grandma, my whole fucking family. But now she … she…' He shook his head and took a huge gulp of the amber liquid.

Jade climbed onto the boat and went to sit next to him, her hand curling around his. 'She what?' she asked quietly.

He hung his head lower, his long, lean body shuddering as he dragged in a few breaths. 'Fuck off.' But it was said without heat.

'Why?'

Slowly he raised his head, eyes meeting hers for the first time. And that's when she saw the red rims, the telltale glisten in their stormy grey depths. 'I don't want you seeing me like this.'

'You mean like a human being for once?'

He grunted, taking another swig of his whisky. Silence descended and she wondered how long he'd been sitting here, how much he'd drunk. Whether he would open up to her or tell her to fuck off again, only with more heat.

'I took her to the specialist today, my grandma.' His voice cracked through the quiet. 'Fucking AMD.'

Advanced Macular Degeneration. Jade may not be Lauren, but she'd heard of that. 'She's having problems with her eyesight?'

He kept his gaze firmly ahead. 'Problems.' His shoulders heaved up and down as he let out a sound of disgust. 'That would suggest there was a solution, but according to the supposed top guy in his field, there is no solution for the type she has. If she's lucky, she'll keep her peripheral vision and learn to adapt to using it. If she's unlucky, she'll lose it altogether.'

Jade's heart faltered. She didn't need to know his backstory to understand how important his grandma was to him. She only needed to look at his distraught face. 'I'm so sorry.'

'Yeah, me too.'

Of their own volition, her arms reached up to wrap around him. Let him push her away. She couldn't sit here and not offer comfort. Not let him know she ached for him.

To her surprise, he leant into her.

'She loves reading.' His voice cracked again. 'Loved, past tense.

God, I hated those books of hers, it was always a sore point between us. She used to say they offered her an escape but I'd see her in tears reading them.' Briefly his eyes lifted to meet hers. 'How was that helping? Sure, they were a temporary respite from her own crappy life, but then the book ended and bang she was back to reality working all hours at a shitty job just to keep our heads above water.'

Through the strained words, Jade heard his guilt, the tortured knowledge that he was the extra burden his grandma had not accounted for. 'Just because she cried didn't mean she was sad. Books, good books, draw emotion from us.'

'Yeah, well, now she can't read them. Can't do a lot of stuff, like driving, being independent. But she just sat there, smiling at me and patting my hand, telling me not to worry. She'd be fine.'

'Of course she will.' Jade nudged his side. 'She's got you taking care of her.'

The compassion in Jade's eyes, the certainty in her voice ... it nearly broke him. He'd never been this close to bawling his eyes out. Not since that night at boarding school in the middle of the first term, when he'd known he was never going to fit in, never be anything other than the butt of jokes. The victim of pranks – like the hilarious bucket of cold water falling on him when he opened the door to the dorm.

Now, though, with Jade's arms wrapped tightly around him, like she was trying to shield him from pain, his emotions were dangerously close to the surface. 'The specialist mentioned some new treatment that might slow the progression.' He wanted to talk, he realised, wanted to tell her. 'She's down to have it next week.' He huffed out a breath. 'I know there are worse things, but Christ, she does not deserve this, not after the life she's had. She should be living it up now, not reduced to staying in her own home because she can't see enough to leave it.'

'But she has you to help her. And if I know you at all, you'll move heaven and earth to make sure this diagnosis doesn't cramp her style.'

'Too damn right.' He drained the rest of his glass and said a silent prayer of thanks that the build for the Sconset house was already underway. She'd wanted, in her words, to die on the island where she was born. Well she wasn't doing that alone. She'd do it living with him, in a house fit for a queen. He'd agonised over the design with his architect, making sure everything she loved had been incorporated; big windows with views of the sea, rambling roses around a sheltered porch, a grand fireplace. If he'd had time to build it with his own hands, he would have. Instead he'd done the next best thing and overseen every aspect of its build, much to the annoyance of his vastly overpaid project manager.

Jade's hand curled around his, her other hand removing the glass from his grip. 'Come on, let's walk some of that alcohol off.'

It was probably a good idea, but… 'Wait.' He lurched to his feet, feeling the effect of the whisky as he staggered inside to grab a baseball cap, which he secured firmly on his head. He did not want anybody else to see him like this.

Apparently he'd drunk enough to make him compliant because she threaded her arm through his and led him off the boat like a mother taking care of a difficult child. 'I thought you were mad at me, anyway,' he said grouchily as they turned away from the resort and towards Brant point.

'I usually am,' she agreed with a smile bright enough to burn his poor, raw retinas.

'You didn't splash "Sponsored by Haven Resorts" across the poster to make me look stupid.' Saying it like a statement felt easier. He fucking hated apologising.

He caught the curve of her lips out of the corner of his eye. 'Finally twigged, did you?'

'After the tenth person thanked me for putting on an event I had no clue about, and would have vetoed if you had asked me. Yeah.' She didn't say anything, just kept that small smile on her face. 'Why?' he asked eventually when it was clear she wasn't going to volunteer the information herself.

'Why hold the event? I wanted you to see how valuable the bookstore could be—'

'Why say Haven Resorts sponsored it?' he interrupted.

She gave him a side glance. 'To show you that you don't have to remain on the outside. You can become part of the community.'

'By *buying* their affections?'

She let out a sound of exasperation. 'By funding projects that can help both Haven Resorts and people who live on the island. Forget the past and those who did you wrong. There are so many good people living here, if you'd just give them a chance to get to know you. And you all have one thing in common, you love the island. If you didn't, you wouldn't have built a business here.'

'Did you forget about the boy who wanted revenge?'

Another noise of suppressed frustration. 'Fine, you stayed here to stick two fingers up at certain individuals. But the fact remains, Haven Resorts needs Nantucket as much as Nantucket needs you. Why not work together to make it a better place for locals and tourists?'

He tried to focus on her words, and not on how gorgeous she looked, all fired up. 'And I suppose one of the projects I should be funding is the bookstore?'

'That would be for you to decide, obviously.'

'But you're determined to make it difficult for me to close it.'

'If by difficult you mean getting you to realise that you're wrong to get rid of it then, yes, that's my aim.'

How was he supposed to keep a level head when all this

whisky was sloshing around in his bloodstream and she was staring at him with a smile full of mischief, and eyes that sparkled with defiance. 'Didn't I give you one more week? By my reckoning, that ends today.'

Her smile dimmed and she looked away from him. 'That's one interpretation.'

'Give me another.' Fuck, how much whisky had he drunk? And for how long was he going to convince himself it was the alcohol influencing him, and not *her*. Her determination not to give in. Her diabolically sneaky methods of getting him to change his mind.

She halted and turned to face him. The breeze ruffled her blonde hair and a stray strand whipped across her face. Before he had a chance to stop himself, he'd taken hold of it, letting the silky lock slip across his fingers before he tucked it behind her ear. His heart pounded, his blood heated and his eyes wouldn't shift from her mouth.

He wanted to kiss her more than he wanted to take his next breath.

She swallowed as his thumb came in to contact with the soft skin of her jaw. 'Let me manage the shop until the end of my contract and then, if you're still not convinced it's an asset to Haven Resorts, you can close it down.' She gave him a dry smile. 'But wait till I'm on the plane, or you might find me chained to the door.'

A wave of acute sadness rolled through him at the thought of her leaving. There were good reasons why he kept people at a distance. Reasons he needed to remind himself of before he started making a big fucking mistake with Jade. 'I'll think about it.'

'Good. But think about it fast because I have lots of other ideas for things I want to do. If you'll give me the chance.'

He studied her, his chest shifting in a way he hadn't felt in a long time and didn't want to feel now. 'You know you've already done what you set out to do.' She wrinkled her brow and he had to clench his fists to stop his hands from reaching up to smooth the lines. 'You're living away from home, standing on your own two feet.'

'True, but the success of the book evening—'

'The one I sponsored?'

'Yes.' She gave him a shy smile. 'It's made me greedy. I want more of that. I want to go home knowing I've achieved something.'

He had something to prove, too, and his own demons to bury. Yet deferring the work for the next few months seemed a small sacrifice for a woman he'd wronged but was still talking to him, trying to help him. 'Fine. I won't close the bookstore until the end of your contract.'

A smile split her face and she bounced on her toes. 'Oh God, I'm so excited right now, I could kiss you.'

'You won't find me stopping you.'

'Oh no.' She wagged her finger at him, and all he could think was how right she was to keep away but how disappointed, too. 'Kissing you is dangerous.'

'It doesn't have to be.'

'You seriously think we could get that close and not, you know, want more?'

'No.' His groin tightened as he stared into her beautiful eyes. Before there had been want, pure and simple. Now there was also like and respect. If he wasn't careful, that would morph into feelings that would leave him exposed again, vulnerable. 'Doesn't stop me remembering. Or wishing for a repeat.'

Her breath hitched. And when her teeth sunk into her lower lip, he went from half hard to painfully pressing against his zipper. 'I wish you were uglier.'

He let out a bark of laughter. 'Back at you.' Could he trust himself to sleep with her again and *not* fall for her? His walls were higher now. And their end date was a certainty he could guard against. 'Come back to the boat with me,' he whispered, self-preservation flying out of the window.

He had an ache that needed to be soothed, a want that needed satisfying. A lust that could only be sated by her sweet, hot body.

Chapter Twenty-Two

Jade knew going back with him was a mistake. A great, big, hairy one with knobs and bells on the end of those knobs, plus a few whistles.

So why had she turned away from the Brant Point Lighthouse, which had looked so cute on the beach guarding the entrance of the harbour, and instead found herself walking hurriedly towards Liam's frigging boat, her belly doing somersaults, her lady parts fired up and ready to go?

'This is a mistake.' She muttered the words out loud to make them real, yet still kept putting one foot in front of the other, her hand clasped tightly to his, as if she was afraid of letting go. Afraid of being sensible.

'Probably,' he agreed in that husky drawl that did not help her decision making. 'A hot, sweaty, mind blowing one we'll both feel better for making.'

Oh God. 'I need that to be true.'

'With the things I've been lying awake at night thinking of doing to you?' He gave her a look weighted with heat, his jaw set with determination. 'It's a certainty.'

Was lust fog a thing? Because her brain was struggling to work. 'I don't mean the sex part, I know I'll enjoy that.'

'Enjoy?' He halted, eyes pinning hers, smoky swirls of grey and flashes of white-hot flames. 'If you only *enjoy* it, I've not done my job.'

Her knees started to buckle. 'I mean the after-sex part.' She gulped. 'The part when you're sober and my brain isn't addled with Haven-induced lust. *Will* we feel better? Or will we wish we'd stuck to ignoring our *I want sex* hormones?'

His lids closed briefly before he lifted them again and touched her face, tracing the curve of her cheek with a gentleness at odds with the fire in his eyes. 'I don't want you to regret this.'

'Me, neither.'

Her words hung like a heavy shadow over the idyllic setting; a rustic wooden wharf, his yacht bobbing gently at the end of it. Sun slowly setting in the sky, casting a beautiful romantic pink light over them. It was too easy to fall under its spell, and under the magnetic pull of the man in front of her.

'What would make you regret it?'

She worried at her lower lip, brain cogs trying to engage. 'If I feel cheap afterwards, like you push me out of bed, ignore me, or people find out and think I only slept with you to persuade you to keep the bookstore.' She swallowed. 'Or if I lose all sense of self-preservation and want to do it again. Maybe even start to fall for you.'

He nodded, eyes scanning the horizon behind her before settling back on hers. 'I didn't push you out of bed before. You left.' He counted the points down on his fingers. 'I can and have happily ignored everyone on this planet except my grandma, yet for some reason I can't ignore you. Believe me, I've tried.'

Her heart flipped over. She liked that admission.

'You shouldn't waste your time caring what others think,' he continued, another tap of his fingers. 'Especially those prepared to think the worst of you. As for falling for me, you won't.'

'How can you be so sure? I mean, I know you can be a grouch but beneath that is a good guy trying to come out.'

He gave a little shake of his head, lips twitching. Then he sighed, jaw muscles snapping together. 'Look, trust me, it won't happen.'

It was a reminder there was a reason he kept himself aloof. He'd been hurt, by women, by his mother, by his classmates. 'So what would make you regret this?'

'Nothing.'

The certainty in his voice made her core tighten. She glanced over his shoulder to the yacht, listening for the voice to tell her not to go. Maybe it was drowned out by the endorphins screaming through her blood, because she couldn't hear it. 'Last one to the boat is a hairy nincompoop.'

She let out a bark of laughter at his confusion, but didn't have time to enjoy it because suddenly she was racing across the rickety wooden planks of the wharf as fast as her legs could carry her.

Something about this felt better than the last time. Like they were more evenly matched. No longer the rich, almost too perfect guy and the clumsy blonde goof. Instead a man and a woman who had both been underestimated and were out to prove a point to the world.

The closer she got to the boat, the giddier she felt. And when she heard a growl behind her, a delicious shiver ran down her spine. 'I'm not a nincompoop,' he rasped, his heavy footsteps sounding closer and closer. 'Whatever the fuck that is.'

Laughing, she made the mistake of turning to look at him. What happened next was a blur, but as she lost her balance she watched with a kind of suspended dread as her fate was spelt out in the changing expressions flashing across his face. Worry, confusion, horror, panic.

She had a split second to scream. Then she was plunging into the cold water of Nantucket harbour.

Smack! The water hit her stomach, the most undignified belly flop ever imagined. As she spluttered to the surface, she groaned. 'Shit, this is cold.'

She looked up to the wharf, only to find Liam pulling his shirt off over his head, then yanking off his shoes. As she gaped in shock, he executed a neat shallow dive into the sea, coming up to the surface just next to her. His hands slid firmly around her waist.

'What are you doing?'

'What do you think?' Treading water, hands still on her hips, wet hair plastered across his forehead, his eyes flashed with irritation. 'I'm saving you from drowning.'

She started to giggle. 'Er, I can swim.'

'How was I supposed to know that?' he asked indignantly, hands still on her hips, though the death hold had loosened.

'Maybe ask before flinging yourself in to save me?'

'You didn't like the idea of swimming with sharks,' he countered, looking like a drowned, very pissed-off male.

'Er, duh, that was the shark part.' Unable to resist, she pressed a kiss to his face. 'Thank you.'

He didn't look mollified. 'You screamed. Was I supposed to wait and see if you sunk?'

He'd not hesitated, she realised, just gone with his instinct, and that had been to save her. 'Again, thank you.' She kissed him again, this time a fleeting glance on lips that were warm despite the cold sea. 'Cool dive, by the way.'

'Better than your belly flop,' he muttered. Letting go of her, he swam the few yards towards the yacht and hauled himself athletically up onto it. She took a moment to admire the ripple of his back muscles before letting out a sigh and swimming after him.

Looked like the evening had come to a soggy, anti-climactic

end. And maybe it was for the best. Maybe she'd just had a lucky escape from what would have been a colossal error in judgement.

Yet as he held out his hand to haul her on board, and as she watched the drips of water slide across his perfect pecs, it didn't feel like a lucky escape. It felt like a wasted opportunity.

Good God. She looked like a freaking mermaid, Liam thought as he reached to clasp her hand. Wet blonde hair dragged back from her face, bold blue eyes appraising him, clothes plastered against a body that would tempt any man with blood still flowing through his veins.

The lust that had receded during his unexpected evening swim smacked into him again with full force as her wet, slippery body collided against his.

A towel, that's what she needed he reminded himself as he dragged his gaze away from her chest. Not him gawking at the hard nipples he could see poking against her soaked top.

'Come with me.' He took her hand, insides doing an unexpected jig as her fingers wrapped around his.

'No, wait.' She halted at the door to the cabin and he swore he could hear his hormones deflate in disappointment.

'I was going to get you a towel.'

'Oh.'

Did she sound disappointed? He peered at her more closely. 'Or you can have a hot shower?'

'Sounds good.' She stared down at the highly polished teak. 'But I don't want to drip all over your snazzy floor.'

'It's a boat. It's designed to be dripped all over.'

'Ah, obviously. Silly me. Not as silly as tripping over my feet and bellyflopping into the sea, but—'

Okay, he was done. 'Do you want to shower and call it a

night?' She blinked, and he instantly regretted his tone. Too harsh, too full of the sexual frustration he should not be showing a woman who'd just had a nasty shock. 'Sorry, it's just I'm shit at reading female signals. Tell me what you want to do.'

She dipped her head, eyes widening when she saw the obvious erection outlined by his wet linen trousers. 'Is there another option? After the shower I mean, because that water was frigging freezing.'

His libido started to dance again. 'We go back to plan A.'

Her eyes glinted. 'Remind me what that involved again? I mean after the race to the yacht, which went spectacularly well, I think.'

Laughter rumbled through him. 'If I'd known it involved an evening swim, I'd have settled for being a … whatever a nincompoop is.'

He followed her inside, gaze glued to her spectacular ass as it swayed ahead of him. 'A ninny, a fool.' She glanced over her shoulder at him. 'Kind of like a guy who jumps into the sea after a woman without checking first if she can swim.'

With a grunt he lunged for her, hauling her up and over his shoulder. 'I was heroic.'

'You were,' she laughed, wriggling in his hold.

'You should thank me for rescuing you,' he added as he marched down the stairs to the master bedroom.

'Oh, yes? And how should I do that?'

'Taking your clothes off would be a good start.'

He pushed open the door to the master cabin and slid her carefully back onto the floor, taking a moment to drink in her appearance. Dishevelled blonde hair, sparkling blue eyes, a grin that could light up a room from a hundred yards. Carefully he smoothed the wet strands behind her ears. 'I never know what's going to happen next when I'm with you.'

'Is that a bad thing?'

He shook his head. 'It's just not something I'm used to. I'm usually in control, but with you it's like I'm on a rollercoaster ride and I'm not sure what's going to happen around the next corner.'

'Life should hold some surprises. It's what makes it interesting.'

He went to turn on the shower before slipping the soaked top over her head. 'You're definitely that.' As his eyes caught sight of the red sting on her stomach, he winced. Instinctively he knelt in front of her and began dropping feather-light kisses across the soft skin of her belly. First it was to soothe, but when she let out a moan of pleasure, his body woke up again and the kisses turned sensual. With fast movements he dragged off her shorts and underwear, his breath catching at the sight of her fully naked. 'Fuck. It's no wonder I can't keep away. Not when I know what you're hiding beneath your clothes.' His tongue began to trace lazy circles around her belly button and then lower, revelling in her sharp inhale, in her low moan of pleasure as he reached his target.

'I thought we were showering...' Another moan. 'Forget it, doesn't matter, keep doing that.'

Smiling to himself he continued to feast, getting harder and harder the wetter she became. When she unleashed a series of fast, hot pants before letting out a cry of pleasure, he was moments away from embarrassing himself.

'Oh, my God, you are a bloody master with your tongue ... no, a virtuoso. Is that more skilful than a master? Whatever is most skilful, that's what you are.'

At the end of his arousal tether, he lurched to his feet and kissed her, diving straight in, hands sliding over her damp body as he pulled her more firmly against him. 'What I am,' he said roughly when he broke for breath. 'Is horny, hard and desperate to be inside you.'

'Then take your frigging trousers off and get in the shower with me.'

With a sultry wink over her right shoulder, she sashayed into the bathroom.

He almost fell over in his haste to rid himself of his wet pants, ending up hopping in a very undignified manner. Something the giggles from the shower told him she'd witnessed. 'If your staff could see you now, they'd not be so terrified of you.'

Finally, he dragged the damn things off. 'You're technically staff and you don't seem that scared.'

'That's because I know your *don't mess with me* scowl is all for show.'

He whipped his boxers off and flung them on the floor on top of the soggy clothing pile. 'It's not.'

'So how do you explain letting Ashley go without completing her notice? Sounds like something a caring, considerate, *softie* of a boss might do.'

'There's nothing soft about me,' he protested, the part of him that was painfully hard bobbing in agreement as he marched towards to the bathroom. 'And where did you hear about that, anyway?' He could guess, having read the hand-delivered letter Ashley had sent him via Claire. His eyes caught sight of the water cascading over those glorious curves. 'Forget it, doesn't matter.'

She squealed as he ducked into the shower, her legs automatically wrapping round his hips as he lifted her. 'Need to be inside you,' he muttered, dipping his mouth to hers, nibbling on her plump lips before delving into the sweet depths of her mouth with his tongue.

Her hips shifted and he slotted himself home.

Then froze. No.

'Hey.' Her eyes searched his. 'Everything okay?'

'Condom.' And damn, he'd forgotten that, too. Just like he

seemed to have forgotten he was not supposed to be thinking of any part of this woman as *home*.

'It's okay. I'm on the pill.'

'Thank fuck.' Worries that his walls weren't high enough to protect himself from her were shoved aside as he let his body do what it wanted. Push into the heat of her. She gasped when he was fully seated. 'You good?'

'Yes.' Her eyes glittered down on him. 'But I want to spend the rest of the night being very, very bad.'

He didn't think it was possible for him to get any harder. 'That control I said I had, but I always lose around you?' He thrust into her again, and again, pushing her back against the wall with the force of his hip movements. 'It's just snapped.'

He turned into an animal, mindless with the need to bury himself inside her, to spill his seed. To claim her in the most primitive way.

'Yes, yes.' Her voice egged him on. 'I'm close, so frigging close. Don't stop.' A few seconds later. 'Holy moly.'

Feeling her release clamp around him, he let out a howl of pleasure, legs buckling under the force of his orgasm. *Mine*, his body seemed to say. *Mine*.

Please, God, let him be strong enough to stop his heart from thinking the same.

Chapter Twenty-Three

As Jade watched the customers leave the shop, each clutching a book they'd been recommended at the library event the other evening, it was hard to keep the smile of satisfaction off her face. Not only had her idea been a success on the night, it had led to a definite increase in sales.

It wasn't the only thing she had to smile about.

Her heart fluttered as she recalled Liam's face as she'd left him early this morning. He'd been fast asleep, the harsh lines of his face relaxed, hair askew thanks to her restless fingers running through it, tugging on it when his tongue had reached exactly the right spot...

She gave a guilty start as the door to the shop opened.

'Well, someone looks like they were having a raunchy daydream.' Mary grinned. 'I might be old but I still recognise that look. Anyone I know?'

Christ on a cracker. Her cheeks were so hot she was scared she might melt. 'I wasn't ... um...' Her eyes landed on the book next to the till. 'I was thinking of the book I'm reading,' she improvised, picking up Claire's book.

Mary nodded approvingly. 'I've read that one. Got me all hot and bothered, too.'

Desperate to change the subject, she pointed to the bag the older woman was carrying. 'Is that what I think it is?'

Triumphantly, Mary pulled out a series of audio books and some large print books. 'I tried to get a selection, like you said. What age did you say this woman was again?'

'I don't know, but you might. It's Liam Haven's grandma.'

Mary's eyebrows bobbed upwards. 'Pat Haven?'

'I presume so. Liam only refers to her as "Grandma".'

'Well, well. It's been a long time since I saw Pat. She moved to Martha's Vineyard years ago. Can't say I blame her. Must have been tough, bringing up her daughter's child. There was a lot of sympathy for her, back in the day. But then her son decided to buy up the waterfront.'

'I guess you could say that's the price of progress,' Jade argued. 'Nantucket is a popular place for visitors, and they need somewhere to stay. If it hadn't been Liam buying it, someone else would have done it. At least he was connected to the island.'

Mary eyed her quizzically. 'The man's got to you, hasn't he? First you're helping his grandma, next you'll be rolling over and letting him take away this store.'

Jade could see both sides, and knew there had to be a middle ground that both she and Liam could be happy with. 'I won't be rolling over for anyone.' To take the sting out of her words, she smiled and reached to take the books. 'All I'm doing is helping a lady who's losing her sight, continue to do what she loves, which is read.'

Mary pursed her lips together, then sighed. 'Sorry, you're right. Every time I saw Pat she'd have a book in her hand. Must be awful to have something as important and special as your eyesight, snatched away from you.'

Behind Mary, the door opened, and Jade's heart jumped into her throat at the familiar large frame now blocking the doorway.

Liam nodded, his mouth curving in a slight smile which, together with the warmth in those silver eyes, unleashed a swarm of butterflies in her belly.

Presumably interested to see who'd caused Jade to lose the power of speech, Mary looked over her shoulder. 'Ah, Haven. Sorry to hear Pat's eyesight isn't so good. Send her my love, won't you? Hope she enjoys the book package this one here,' she nodded at Jade, 'is getting together.'

A guard immediately dropped over his eyes and his expression turned blank. 'Thank you.'

'Well, then.' Mary's head swivelled between the pair of them. 'I'll leave you to it.' Under her breath she muttered, 'Claire's book, my ass.'

Liam held the door open as Mary marched out of the shop. It closed behind her with a loud clunk, the sound echoing off the whitewashed walls.

Jade's head buzzed with things she wanted to say. *Last night was incredible. I want to do it again but I'm scared I might be falling for you. I think Mary knows about us.*

'You *told* her?'

Her head jerked back at his frosty tone. 'About your grandma? I didn't think it was a secret.'

He stepped further into the shop, tension radiating off him. 'It's a private health matter. Now the whole island is going to know her eyesight is fading.'

'Does that matter? People will want to help, like Mary did.' She held up some of the books Mary had left. 'She brought over some audio books and large print books from the library. I thought I'd add them to those we have in the shop and maybe I could take them over to her, see if it helps. If they work for her, we can order in whatever she's into.'

227

A jaw muscle jumped. 'You were planning on visiting her?'

'Well, not if you don't want me to, obviously. I mean, you can take them if you prefer.' She stilled, embarrassment stinging her cheeks as she finally twigged what was going on. 'You think this is all part of some clever plan of mine to infiltrate your life, don't you? Like I'm somehow going to use your grandma to put in a good word for me with you. Gah.' Feeling stupid and unbelievably hurt, she stomped towards the back of the shop, dragged out a cardboard box and began dumping the books Mary had given her, plus ones she'd found in the shop, into it.

'What are you doing?'

'I'm getting a collection of things for you to take to your grandma that might help her read. The easiest thing would be to listen to audio books on her phone or computer, but I don't know if she's tech savvy so I've included a few CDs, plus some large print books.' She threw her spare Kindle in there, too. 'And this is my Kindle, which she can borrow. You can change the font size so that might help, too.' Feeling tears burn her retina, she thrust the box at him, and when those stupidly long fingered hands grasped it she definitely didn't think of the way they'd played with her body last night. 'Here. I hope some of it helps.'

He'd fucked up. Liam didn't know how he'd gone from anticipating giving Jade one hell of a good morning kiss to make up for the one he'd missed when he'd found himself waking up alone, to this. Her staring at him with scorn in her expression and fire in her eyes.

He needed to apologise. She didn't think she'd done anything wrong, he could see that. Could even understand she was trying to help, but right now it felt like a betrayal. He was only just getting used to the idea of letting Jade see parts of him others didn't. He certainly didn't want her giving that information to others.

'We're private people,' he said quietly, taking the box from her. 'We don't need or want help from anyone. Especially not people here.'

She nodded stiffly. 'Sure, my bad. I'll make sure to keep well away in future.'

'That's not what I meant.'

'Oh, sure, you still want to sleep with me, but outside that I should forget everything you tell me and pretend like we don't know each other.'

This was spiralling out of control and he didn't know how to stop it without sending the wrong message. And it would be very wrong to march over and kiss her now. To tell her he missed her in his bed this morning. Part of him was so incredibly touched she was doing something to help his grandma, yet a bigger part was terrified by the squeeze on his heart he'd felt when she'd talked about going to see her. Jade wasn't supposed to be kind as well as funny, smart and sexy as fuck. She was supposed to be a woman he could enjoy and forget. Not one he could feel wrapping her silky blonde tendrils around his heart.

Panic surged through him like a bolt of high-voltage electricity and he set his shoulders, taking an invisible step back from the emotional black hole threatening to suck him in – and inevitably suck him dry. 'Look, I came to thank you for last night. It was just what I needed.' Bile rose to the back of his throat as he watched the hurt slide across her face and his hands gripped tighter to the box. 'And thanks for this. It was very … thoughtful. I'll be sure to give them to her.'

'You do that. And while you're there, tell her I'm happy to help in any way I can, but to come to me directly. I don't want to have to deal with her jerk of a grandson.'

Okay. He deserved that, revelled in it, in fact; because her hating him meant there wouldn't be a repeat of last night. He wouldn't get sucked any further into that place he swore never to visit again, where he gave someone the power to hurt him, reject him.

Yet when he turned to walk back out, clutching the box in his hands, everything felt wrong. Like he'd taken a bad turn into a dark, lonely alley. The sense of wrong intensified when he knocked into the stand near the entrance and felt a burn of hot liquid on his thigh.

'Fuck.' He hissed, shaking his leg.

'What is it?'

He ignored her. He just needed to get out.

'Wait, I'll open the door for you.'

He did not want to smell the coconut shampoo she used. Or feel the brush of her breasts as she reached for the door handle.

'There's something wet...' Her voice trailed off and mortification shot through him.

Did she think he'd pissed himself? 'There's a drink in my jacket pocket,' he told her through gritted teeth.

'Oh.'

He inhaled sharply, gripping tightly to the box as she rummaged in his pocket. Finding the take-out cup, she peeled off the lid and sniffed.

'Tea?'

'Must have got it by mistake.' Christ, he was usually a better liar than this. 'You keep it.'

Her expression softened. 'Thank you.'

With a sharp incline of his head, he marched out as fast as his pounding heart and rubbery legs would allow him.

———————

By the time he reached the safety of his office, he was a hot, wet mess. Literally. And finding Jeremy loitering outside did not help the maelstrom of emotions burning in his gut one little bit. 'Is there a fire?' he snapped. 'A flood?'

Jeremy smiled in his unique, laconic fashion. It made Liam's temper flare that little bit more. 'I don't believe so. Nor do we appear to be plagued by swarming locusts today.'

'Then what are you doing here?'

'Would you believe I've come to update my boss on the week's activities, like I do every Tuesday at this time?' His gaze fell to the box Liam was clutching as if his life depended on it. 'Have you brought me cake?'

'What?'

'I thought you might be carrying a treat for your favourite employee.'

'I don't have a favourite,' he muttered as he settled the box on his desk. 'You're all as bad as each other.'

'Oh dear.' Jeremy paused, a glint entering his eyes. 'Surely there's *one* employee you like?'

Liam was not in the mood to be teased about a woman he was terrified he'd already let get too close. 'Tell me what you came here to say.'

Jeremy ambled up to the desk and took a look inside the box. Then smirked as he carefully sat down, crossing one neatly pressed cotton chino leg over the other.

'What's the smirk for?'

'Just wondering what our Jade has done to put you in such a spin.'

Our Jade? Like Jeremy and the little band of Haven haters owned her. 'What has she got to do with anything?'

'Well, I added *Liam* plus *box of books* and got *been to see Jade*. Of course there's also the fact that you appear to be, how shall I put this politely, not quite your usual self, which does seem to have become rather a habit since she started here.'

Liam glowered. 'We are not discussing this. Or anything beyond your work here. Ever,' he added, determined to push the point home because Jeremy had a habit of ignoring what he wanted to. 'Understood?'

'Absolutely. You've put your point across eloquently, as usual.' Jeremy cleared his throat. 'There is just one small thing I'd like to ask, before we definitely don't discuss anything of a personal nature ever again.' His gaze slid to Liam's and there was enough of a twinkle in it to make the hairs on the back of Liam's neck twitch. 'Would you be my best man?'

Chapter Twenty-Four

Jade flipped the signed to *closed for lunch* and set off towards the resort, praying she wouldn't run into Liam. It had been four days since their encounter in the shop and so far she'd managed to avoid him. Jeremy had assured her Liam wasn't around today – Saturday – but it wasn't until she saw his yacht not in its usual mooring place that she breathed a huge sigh of relief.

To think she'd defended him, thought there was more to him than that cold, aloof façade. Turns out once again she'd shown appalling judgement when it came to men.

Frustratingly none of that stopped her mind from flashing up images of the mortification on his handsome face when he'd seen the takeout cup of tea in her hands. The one they both knew he'd come into the shop to give her. If Mary had come in five minutes later... *No!* She was not going to think about him anymore. She was done with the guy.

Spotting Jeremy's red hair from across the courtyard she marched towards the resort café, smiling for the first time in four days when she saw the people sitting, waiting for her.

Friends, she thought, a warmth invading her chest, pushing away the hurt over Liam. Mary, Emma, Claire, Jeremy and Philip all greeting her with cheery smiles. Thankfully, the two men who made her uncomfortable, Adam and Henry, couldn't make it. Good. She didn't need their negativity.

'We got you a drink.' Jeremy waved at the empty seat and it was only then she saw a teapot in front of it, together with a cup and saucer.

'Where on earth?'

He laughed gleefully. 'They don't call me the best guest-services manager on the planet for nothing. Anything a guest wants, I can provide.'

Touched, she sunk into the chair. 'That's the second cup of tea I've been bought this week, though definitely the best presented.' Too late, she realised her error.

'Who bought the first?' Emma asked, but it was Mary that Jade made the mistake of looking at. And Mary who chuckled.

'I've a feeling it was the enemy. At least I assume that was a takeout cup bulging out of Haven's pocket when I bumped into him in the shop, and he wasn't just pleased to see you.'

The table erupted at Mary's awful joke and Jade groaned, putting her hands over her face to hide her blush. 'Cancel what I was thinking. You guys aren't friends. You're wicked.'

Mary reached to pat her arm. 'We are totally your friends. That's why I knew I could make that joke. I wouldn't dare have made it with someone I didn't feel comfortable with.' Her face creased in concern. 'But I didn't mean to upset you.'

Jade shook herself. 'Sorry, I just...' *Think I'm halfway in love with the man you just called the enemy.* 'I'm feeling a bit homesick today.' She pasted on a bright smile and picked up the teapot. 'But nothing a cup of tea won't fix.'

Her gaze slid to Jeremy, who gave her such a sweet, understanding smile she felt tears prick her eyelids.

She took a moment to pour the tea, to take a sip and push all thoughts of Liam Haven out of her head. 'So, after first congratulating you all on an awesome event in the library last week, which I hope we can repeat, I'm going to drink lots of tea, while you guys throw some ideas at me for our next campaign.'

Jeremy narrowed his eyes. 'Let's have your ideas first, because I know you've got some.'

'I may have.' And why was she being so coy about this? The bookstore was her responsibility, the team her idea. She was the leader, so it was about time she stopped cowering in the second row and pushed herself to the front. 'I was thinking we could do like a pop-up book clinic where we give book recommendations for people in a reading slump.' She gazed around the table. 'We're all here because we have an interest in books, and I reckon we also know people who read, so we should have all the genres covered. I'll man the clinic, but if it comes to questions on genres I don't think I've got enough knowledge on, I could have a list of people to contact.'

Emma smiled. 'Phone a friend.'

'Exactly.'

Jeremy nodded. 'Sounds good. Why don't you try it out at the resort? We've got hundreds of tourists who spend their days with a nose in a book.'

She flashed him a warning look. 'I'm not sure Liam would go for that.' In fact she knew he wouldn't. Tough enough to sell when they were talking to each other – *by the way, can I use your resort to try out my next idea to boost interest in the shop you want to get rid of.* After the way they'd parted … any day now she was waiting for the letter to terminate her contract.

Following a bit more discussion it was agreed Jeremy would sound out Liam – yeah, good luck there – and Emma would ask her mum, who happened to be the town manager, about gaining agreement for a pop-up clinic in the town centre.

As everyone said their goodbyes, Jeremy caught her eye. 'Don't rush off.'

She grimaced. 'Don't take this the wrong way, but I'm not sure I'm up to your form of gentle, torture with kindness, interrogation.'

'How about if I use the Liam Haven version and just ask what the fuck happened between you two on Tuesday?'

She waited a beat, felt annoyance rather than upset, and smiled. 'That worked. He came into the shop, saw me talking to Mary about trying to get some books together for his grandma, and flipped.'

Jeremy frowned. 'Had he asked you to help his grandma?'

'God, no, as if the great Liam Haven would stoop so low.' It earned her a smile from Jeremy. 'But he had told me she was finding reading more difficult, so I thought large print books or audiobooks might be worth a shot. I knew the library had a better collection than the shop, so I asked Mary to help. Which was apparently the wrong thing to do because they're private people and do not want others to talk about them, or, God forbid, receive help from anyone.'

'The man is more prickly than a cactus cross-bred with a holy bush.' He sighed. 'And I asked him to be my best man. I must be a few fries short of a happy meal.'

She gaped at him. 'I thought you couldn't stand each other?'

Jeremy chuckled. 'Maybe you're right, at least on his side, but from my side.' He shrugged. 'Can't help but see a man wearing an aloof suit that's not an easy fit. I think he wants to shrug it off, make attachments, but habit and history keep him from doing it.'

'And pig-headedness,' Jade added sourly.

'A good dollop of that, too.' He smiled. 'But I've got used to his grumpy ways over the last five years and hey, no man who loves his grandma as much as Liam does, can be all bad.'

'True.' She let out a frustrated sigh. 'I've seen him without that suit, and he's kind of adorable. But then he acts like a total arsehole and I wonder which is the real Liam Haven.'

'Define asshole … arsehole in this context.'

'Aside from telling me off for trying to help his grandma? He thanked me for sleeping with him, told me it was just what he needed and walked out.'

Jeremy shuddered. 'That comes under the definition of asshole, all right. Maybe it's a good job he didn't accept.'

'He was rude enough to turn you down?'

'He totally ignored my question and asked me about the budget, which I'm taking as the same thing.'

Beneath the careless shrug she saw his hurt and squeezed his arm. 'He might come to his senses yet. And failing that, sod him. You can find a better best man.'

He looked at her quizzically. 'The wedding is at the end of next month, when you'll still be here.'

'Second best am I now?' She laughed and kissed his cheek. 'I'd be honoured to be your substitute, but give Liam time. You probably surprised the hell out of him.' She thought back over what he'd told her about his childhood, about what she knew of the man. 'I don't think he's ever had a close friend before.'

Maybe it was why he'd pushed her away, too. But it didn't excuse his rudeness.

Liam's first thought, when he saw his grandma waving at him as he secured the yacht to its mooring was that she looked happier.

At least one of them was having a good week.

Of course his had been all right until he'd sabotaged his friendship with Jade. And then ignored Jeremy's shocking request. As if he knew anything about being a fucking best man.

But for Jeremy to ask it of his boss, it must have taken balls as well as a lot of thought.

'What's wrong?' Damn, he'd forgotten his grandma was watching. He'd barely opened his mouth to reply when she interrupted. 'And don't you tell me nothing. I know when you're upset. I knew it when you were a boy, pretending you were quite happy to go back to boarding school when I'd already heard you sobbing your heart out, and I can tell it now.'

He double-checked the boat was secure, mainly to give him something to focus on besides the swell of emotion that had found its way into this throat. When he thought he had himself in check, he marched up to her and gave her a big hug. 'Hello, you.'

She shook her head at him, chuckling. 'Hello back. But don't think you're going to avoid my question.'

'I wouldn't for one minute.' He threaded an arm around her waist. 'But first answer me this. If you knew I hated boarding school so much, why did you keep sending me there?'

Sadness crept across her face. 'I kept thinking you'd settle and make friends. I called the head once and he assured me you were fine and doing well academically. And you were so good at putting on a brave face I guess in the end it was easy for me to pretend you were fine.'

'I was fine,' he asserted.

'Academically, yes, but we both know it left scars.' She bustled him inside. 'Now tell me what's wrong because I'm older and wiser now and I won't stop until I hear the truth.'

He decided to go with the easiest of his issues. 'I was asked to be a best man the other day.'

Joy lit up her face and she clasped her hands together. 'That's marvellous. By who?'

'Jeremy.'

'The delightful guest-services manager?'

'Your words.' He let go of her and walked into the kitchen, busying himself with getting a glass of water so he didn't have to look at her. 'I didn't accept.' He waved a hand in her direction. 'Before you get all up in my face, I didn't turn it down either. I...' Guilt, hot on the heels of shame, cannoned through him and he had to take a breath before he felt steady enough to face her. 'I ignored the question.'

'Liam Haven.' He didn't know which was worse, his own feelings of guilt, or seeing the disappointment on her face. 'I didn't bring you up to be graceless or rude. Being asked to be a best man is an honour and you should have treated it as such. Especially as it must have been hard for him to ask his boss such a thing.'

'I know. It just took me by surprise.' Understatement of the century. He'd have been less shocked if Jeremy had asked him to strip off and do a naked tour of the resort with him. How the hell had he allowed both Jeremy and Jade close enough to upset his equilibrium this week?

Had to be something mystical about the letter J.

'Well, now the surprise is over, I hope you'll apologise. If he's got any sense he'll have asked someone who appreciates the honour,' she grumbled, rubbing salt into the wound.

'Okay, message received.' He took the glass of water he didn't need and set it on the island. 'Let's talk about you.' His eyes skimmed over her face, the pink dye in her hair, the shine in her eyes. 'You look happier than last time I visited.'

'Do I?' She frowned. 'Well I'm not sure why that is... Oh—' She clasped her hands together. 'It must be the books you brought over. I didn't realise how much I'd missed reading until I got stuck into some of them. I'm not sure how to set that electronic thingy up, I'll leave that for you to show me, but the big print really helped. And at night, when my eyes are tired, I listen to one of the audiobooks. Did you say you can get more titles?'

'Yes.' But only if he pulled his head out of his ass and apologised to the woman he'd wronged. His heart did a familiar, painful flip. He'd tried ignoring it but it didn't make the ache in his chest any duller. He missed her. Missed seeing her smile, listening to her, and yes, even fucking *talking* to her.

Bardot appeared, weaving around his legs. Grateful for the distraction, he bent to lift her into his arms. 'That's what you wanted, huh?'

Bardot purred, squeezing her eyes shut as he stroked her ears.

'You can give that cat all the attention you want, but it won't let you off the hook.' His grandma walked over, gave Bardot a smile and then lifted her gaze to him. 'Something else is going on with you and the way you've suddenly gone quiet tells me it has to do with this new shop manager. Jade, I believe her name is.' To drive the point home that she still had plenty of contact with the island, she added, 'A gorgeous blonde with a sunny attitude who, I assume, was sweet enough to get these books together for me.'

He sighed, wondering how he'd got this transparent recently. For years he'd been able to hide everything, now he had his grandma, Jeremy and Jade all thinking they could read him. 'You need to feed a man first before you expect him to spill his guts.'

'Fine. I made you a fish pie. It's in the fridge all ready, just needs warming up. You sort it out and pour us both a glass of wine. Then we'll talk.'

A steel edge ran though her voice and he knew she wasn't going to be happy with anything less than the truth. With the sluggish movements of a man on his way to the gallows, he slipped the pie into the oven, sliced some bread to go with it, then poured out two glasses of sauvignon.

Bardot gazed up at him with her big copper-coloured eyes and he took pity on her, feeding her a few of the treats his grandma wasted her money on. 'Only fair, considering we're about to eat fish pie in front of you.'

Fish pie had been his favourite as a kid and it touched him that she'd made it again for him tonight, even though the last time she'd cooked it she'd put a tin of the cat's salmon into it because she'd forgotten to get some. God knows what she'd substituted tonight.

'So, this Jade who has you all in a bother,' his grandma announced the moment he handed her a glass. 'Are you dating her?' *Nope, we're just fucking.* Christ. He couldn't have this conversation with anyone, let alone her. 'Oh, I see, it's like that, is it?' Eyes fading in terms of their sight, still saw too much. 'You're having sex with her but haven't bothered to ask her on a date?' Disappointment threaded through her voice. 'I'm sure I brought you up to respect women more than that.'

Should he try to explain that was how Jade wanted it too, even though he wasn't convinced it was true anymore, for either of them. Something had changed between them that last time. She'd seen him distressed and come to help. He'd been rude, tried to push her away, but she'd refused to budge. More, she'd listened, consoled him … gone out of her way the next morning to gather large print books to try to help. And in return, what had he done for her?

His stomach rolled over, acid inching up his throat.

He'd asked what would make her regret sleeping with him again, and then done exactly what she'd asked him not to. Made her feel cheap.

Agitated, he rubbed at his face, feeling like the shit he was. 'I've treated her badly and she doesn't deserve it,' he admitted.

His grandma gave him a sober look. 'Are you going to apologise and make amends?'

'Yes.' He didn't have a clue how, but he did know this raw ache inside him wouldn't let up until he did.

'Good. Then I hope she's as warm-hearted as everyone says.' She took a sip of her wine and settled back against the sofa. 'By my reckoning the fish pie will take forty minutes to warm up. Plenty of time for you to tell me the whole story, from the start.'

Bardot jumped up onto the sofa and curled into his lap, looking up at him as if to say *yep, I want to hear this, too.*

Damn, the women were ganging up on him.

He sighed, took a big gulp from his glass, and started to talk.

Chapter Twenty-Five

Buzzing. That's all she could hear, a buzzing in her ear. Barely conscious, she reached her hand out towards where the noise was coming from… Her phone? Bleary eyed, she tried to sit up. Was it her alarm?

No, it was Sunday … lie-in day, except, damn that buzzing.

She picked the phone up, and realised it was an incoming call from her sister.

'Hey?' She glanced at the time and felt a ripple of alarm. Lauren wouldn't call her at seven in the morning unless it was an emergency.

'Jade, thank God you're there. I need help.'

Her sister needed *her* help? 'What is it? Are Mum and Dad okay?'

'Of course they are.'

'Then what's wrong? Are *you* in trouble?'

'Sort of.' Lauren's voice was a whisper, like she was trying not to be overheard. 'I need some advice, sis. I did something really stupid last night and I'm freaking out right now. I don't know how to handle it.'

Jade shook herself awake. Lauren had come to her for advice. This was not the time for her brain to still be in sleep mode. 'Whatever you did, we can work it through together.'

'I slept with one of the guys I work with.'

Her heart, in overdrive since the start of the call, began to slow. 'You woke me at seven in the morning to tell me you had a one-night stand?'

'I forgot what time it was for you, okay? It's my lunch hour and it's the first chance I've had to phone you. One-night stands might not be a big deal to you, but they are to me. I don't do them.' She groaned. 'At least I didn't, and I don't know why I suddenly decided to so something so frigging stupid.'

It was hard to stay annoyed when Lauren sounded so distressed. She might wish she'd called for her help with something else, something less *frigging stupid*, but the fact was, her sister hadn't phoned her mum, or her friends. She'd phoned her. 'Sorry, that was me in *I've just woken* Godzilla mode. I'm wide awake now. So, give me some details.' An awful thought occurred to her. 'Is this something you wanted to happen? I mean he didn't force you?'

'Quite the opposite,' Lauren muttered. 'We were at a party, I'd had maybe two glasses of wine, tops.' She sighed. 'He's one of the nurses in A&E. I've seen him around, hard to miss him really because he's tall and well built and, um…'

'Handsome? Cute? Sexy?'

She let out a deep sigh. 'All of those.'

'Aw, Doctor Lauren Taylor, you *like* this guy?'

There was a long pause on the other end. 'I don't know,' her sister said finally. 'I mean I don't know him well enough to know, do I? I spent a few hours talking to him at a party and then lost my mind and went back with him to his room. And yes, the party was in his house, which he's still sharing with friends, because that's how young Ned is.' She groaned. 'God, even his name sounds young. He's nearer your age than mine.'

Jade smiled. 'You mean he's a whole three years younger than you?'

'Fine, I know that sounds dumb, but I don't do this. I'm … sensible. I date mature men, and I only sleep with them after I've got to know them, which takes at least five dates.'

Aware her sister was genuinely struggling, Jade reined in her annoyance at the implication that anyone who didn't follow Lauren's methodical dating process was, by her definition, *not* sensible. 'We all act stupid when we meet someone we feel an overwhelming attraction towards. Even the intelligent among us,' she added dryly, easing out of the bed and padding towards the kitchen.

'I don't,' her sister protested.

'You haven't done in the past,' Jade corrected, filling the kettle and popping it on the hob. 'But only because you've never met a guy you feel such a connection with that he robs you of all your senses.'

Silence echoed on the other end, and for a moment Jade thought they might have lost the connection. 'Is that what happened for you on that first night, with that man who turned out to be your boss?'

'Yes,' Jade admitted quietly.

'What did you do when you saw him again?'

She laughed sadly. 'I repeated the mistake. And then only a few days ago I repeated it again. But you're a lot smarter than me, so I'm sure you'll be fine.'

'I'm not. I worked harder, but I'm not smarter. And when it comes to emotional intuition, I'm light years behind you.' As Jade reeled from the shock of those words, Lauren continued to talk. 'I judged you when it came to men, and when I heard you'd slept with someone on your first night out there, I was bitch enough to think you were cheapening yourself. But at least you slept with a rich resort owner, not a guy younger than you, who is supposed to look up to you. I mean, who is the cheap one now—'

'Stop it,' Jade interrupted. 'Is there a rule at work that you can't fraternise with other staff?'

Lauren laughed hysterically. 'Are you mad? The hours we work, the only people we ever meet are other staff.'

'Then stop beating yourself up over this.' She thought of Liam, of her own mistake and all the things she'd called herself afterwards when actually passion, love, attraction … sometimes the force was just too strong for rational thought. 'Sleeping with a guy we fancy doesn't make us cheap. It makes us human. Have you bumped into him since?'

'No. I saw him briefly, from across the canteen. I didn't know what to do, so I ran out.'

Her confident, strong sister reduced to a cowardly mess of emotions. Because of a man. 'Were you repulsed when you saw him? Did you wonder what on earth you'd seen in him?'

'I wish. My heart did some gymnastics that I know are anatomically impossible.'

Jade put a hand over her own heart and sighed. 'Then welcome to Team Inconvenient Crush.' TIC? Gah, she was terrible at this. 'I can't offer you advice, just warn you you're in for a bumpy ride because this is not something you can brush under the carpet. You can try, but it's not going to let you, because every time you see him, you'll go giddy and lose your mind.'

'So what, I can't fight it? I have to give in to it?'

'You could try enjoying it.'

'Is that what you're doing with this resort owner. Enjoying it?'

Jade smiled sadly. 'No. But hopefully Ned is less … complicated than Liam. You never know, if you keep an open mind, and an open heart, this could be the start of something wonderful.'

'It doesn't feel wonderful right now. It feels scary and out of my control.'

'Yep, those are the symptoms,' Jade assured her. Thousands of miles separated them but, in that moment, she'd never felt closer to her sister.

'So basically you're saying I'm fucked, but not to worry because it happens to all of us at some point.'

'That's about the long and short of it.'

Lauren let out a long breath. 'Well, thanks for picking up the phone. I'd say I'm sorry I woke you, but I'm not because I couldn't have had this conversation with anyone else.'

Emotion clogged her throat. 'No problem, I'm always here for you. Good luck and keep me updated.'

'I will. And good luck to you, too.'

It wasn't luck she needed, Jade thought miserably as she ended the call. It was a vault to put her heart in so Liam Haven wouldn't be able to get anywhere near it.

———

Liam paced restlessly up and down the sidewalk. He'd checked the address he'd noted down from Jeremy's file, five times. This was definitely where he lived.

Once again, he looked at his watch. Ten o'clock. Was that a reasonable time to visit someone on a Sunday morning? Or … maybe it was never reasonable for a boss to knock on his employee's door on his day off.

He turned and began to walk away. He'd talk to the man tomorrow, when he came in to work.

It's been five days since he asked you to be his best man, his inner voice had the temerity to remind him. *Five days you've spent avoiding your fucking deputy.*

Exhaling sharply, he straightened his shoulders and turned

back, marching up to the door he'd spent the last five minutes staring at, and punched the bell.

Silence.

He jammed on it again, for longer this time.

The sound of muffled voices filtered through the door, followed a few seconds later by the heavy clunk of feet on stairs.

A beat later, he was staring at Leroy's bemused face. 'Oh, it's you.'

The man was wearing a pair of loose sweats that looked like they'd been tossed on in a hurry and … nothing else. 'Yes.' Shit, awkward did not cover this. Even painful did not cover this.

Leroy opened the door a bit wider. 'Guess you'd better come in.'

'Only if this is a … good time.'

Leroy chuckled and indicated for him to head up the stairs. 'The boss is here,' he shouted up. 'Wants to know if this is a good time.'

'I hope you told him we were trying to have a good time until he interrupted us— Oh.' Jeremy's head appeared at the top of the stairs, similarly clad in sweats, only at least he'd put a T-shirt on. 'Good morning, boss.'

Liam sighed heavily. 'It's a Sunday, I'm standing in your home. Call me Liam.'

'Well that depends. Are you here as my boss or—'

'I'm not here as your boss.' Warily he climbed the stairs, taking a cursory look at his surroundings. 'You *both* live here?'

As usual, Jeremy didn't take offence. 'Of course. And before you say anything rude—'

'You mean ruder than implying the place is small?' Leroy interrupted with a smirk.

While Liam cringed, Jeremy laughed. 'Good point. Before you make any further rude remarks about our humble home, we like it.'

'We like that it takes us two minutes to walk to work,' Leroy added dryly. 'Want a drink?'

'Coffee, thanks.' Liam edged onto the sofa, Jeremy sitting opposite him on the only other chair. 'I pay you both decent wages. Don't you want somewhere with more space?' The place was smaller than his freaking boat.

'Boss, have you seen the price of houses on this island? Only multi-millionaires can afford them. Sure, we could get somewhere slightly bigger further out, but we want to be in town.' Jeremy shook his head. 'And you've not come here to discuss the Nantucket housing situation.'

'No.' Liam parked the tumbling thoughts, though they provided a neat diversion to what he needed to say, but didn't know how to start. Thankfully he was given a reprieve when Leroy, bare chest now covered by a faded T-shirt, shoved a mug in his hand.

'Black, no sugar.'

'Thanks.' He eyed the man curiously. 'How'd you know?'

Leroy shrugged his wide shoulders. 'You pay me to pay attention.' His gaze fell on Jeremy and some silent communication ensued because Leroy nodded. 'I'll catch you later.'

A few seconds later, the door banged closed.

'That's Leroy's subtle way of giving you privacy to say ... whatever it is you came to talk about.'

Liam half smiled. 'You know why I'm here.'

Jeremy leant back on the chair. 'Wondered how many days you could avoid me.'

'Turns out five is my max.' He took a sip of the coffee, set it down on the small glass table in front of him, and looked the man straight in the eye. 'Yes. If you still need me, I'd be honoured to.'

Jeremy's eyes widened comically. 'Are you saying what I think you are? You really want to be my best man?'

He had a sudden flashback to his second term at boarding

school. The day he thought he'd turned the corner because he'd been asked to join some new society. He'd walked proudly into the venue only to find he was the only one still there, half an hour later. He hadn't freaked out, just thought he'd got the wrong room, wrong time. It was only when he was greeted with laughter as he stepped back in the dorm room that he finally realised. *You really thought we'd want you in our group, Haven?*

You really thought I wanted you to be my best man?

Bile rose up his throat and he lurched to his feet.

'Whoa, are you okay?' Jeremy looked utterly confused.

'Why did you ask me to be your best man?' he gritted out, heart pounding.

'What do you mean?'

He knew from the concern on Jeremy's face that he was making a fool of himself but he had to be sure. 'You must have friends? People you're closer to than you are me.'

Jeremy nodded. 'Sure, I have friends. Those from before I came out, who navigate carefully around my sexuality for fear of offending me. Those from after, who look at me and wonder how I managed to snag the hottest gay guy on the island. Then there are those who see me as a part of a mis-matched couple, the weird white, ginger guy and the sexy Black guy.' He shrugged. 'You've only ever treated me as me.'

Christ. He dropped back to the sofa, so many emotions flooding him he couldn't think straight. 'You deserve more out of a friend than someone who spends most of his day barking at you.'

'Maybe.' Jeremy gave him one of his wide, guileless smiles. 'And maybe I think one day you'll forget to push me away and just accept our relationship for what it is.'

'And what's that?'

'Work colleagues, sure. Boss and employee, sometimes.' He paused. 'But beneath all that, I trust you to have my back. Many times you could have fired me, you haven't. I'd like to think it was because you didn't want to be without my winning personality, though I suspect it's more that you can't be bothered to find a replacement. One day, though, I hope you'll realise I have your back, too. And in my book, that makes us friends.'

Was it really that easy? He'd tried to make friends, and been shunned. Now he was supposed to accept this man's offer? Yet in the five years since he'd first recruited him, Jeremy had never let him down. They'd worked together directly for the first few, until Liam had gone on to open two more hotels in Martha's Vineyard and Cape Cod, recruiting Ashley to do the day-to-day management of the Nantucket resort. 'Friends.' He swallowed. 'And do friends talk about … issues?'

Jeremy's mouth curved upwards. 'You want to talk through a problem, I'm your man. Especially if it's to do with Jade Taylor. I kind of have a brotherly soft spot for her.' He leant forward and clasped his hands on his knees. 'If I had to guess, I'd say you pissed her off on Tuesday. Seems it was quite the day for you pissing people off,' he added with a snigger. 'Anyway, now you realise what you've thrown away and you want to know how to win her back.' His brow scrunched, eyebrows coming together like a fury ginger caterpillar. 'As her self-appointed brother, I need to know how honourable your attentions are towards her.'

'Dishonourable. Very.' When Jeremy kept looking at him, Liam waved his hands in defeat. 'Fine. I like her. I want to … date her.'

A wide grin stretched Jeremy's face. 'Then I know just the way to get you back into her good books.' He chuckled. 'Books being the key word, eh?'

What the hell was he doing in this cramped flat, talking not just about a woman, but one he wanted to *date*? Yet as scared as he was about the thought of his life changing course, and of the dangers he could see all too vividly ahead, Liam wasn't prepared to turn back.

Chapter Twenty-Six

Jade could taste the salt in the breeze as she wandered through the resort towards the garden where she'd been told her pop-up book clinic had been set up. The fresh smell of the ocean still gave her a kick of pleasure every time she stepped outside, even though she'd been on Nantucket for a month now. Time was flying by so fast.

What a month it had been, though. That first week had been tough, the themed book week that had turned out to be a lot of hard work for little reward. Not to mention the whole finding out she'd slept with her boss fiasco.

Since then she'd started to get to grip with the shop, even knew how to fill in spreadsheets, thanks to *the man she wasn't going to think about*. She'd also made some good friends, used her creative writing skills for the first time since school and penned a couple of blogs, plus had the idea for and overseen a very successful book evening at the library. Mary had already pencilled it in the diary to repeat in the second half of the year. Of course, she'd be back in Twickenham then. Back to her old job, her old stomping ground. Her old life.

'Hey, where's that sunny smile we're used to?'

She shook off the sad thoughts and turned to give Leroy a wide grin. 'Better?'

'A bit scary, if I'm honest, but beats the scowl.' His dark brown eyes slid over her face. 'You okay?'

This time her smile was more genuine. 'I'm good. Ready to rock this pop-up book surgery Jeremy somehow persuaded Liam to agree to. Oh, shit.' A thought occurred. 'He definitely did get his agreement this time, yes? Because I know we skated over it at the library but that was before…'

'Before you two had a fight,' Leroy supplied, giving her a gruff chuckle. 'Boss man definitely gave the all clear. Heard it with my own ears. Seems the Ginger Wonder has managed to tamé the Big Bad Wolf. At the least he's some sort of wolf whisperer.'

'Um, I heard he asked Liam to be his best man.'

'Did you also hear the boss accepted?'

She blinked. 'Oh, wow. No.' It felt like a seismic shift in attitude. 'I'm glad, for Jeremy's sake. I hope Liam proves up to the task.'

'Looks like the substitute isn't needed.' He winked. 'How about being my best man?'

'God, what is it with you two? You must have friends you've known longer than me and besides, much as I'd be honoured, it would probably mean me having to do some dance or something with the other best man and that is definitely not happening.'

Leroy smirked. 'I'll leave it as a maybe for now.' Before she could say anything, he took her by the shoulders and pointed her towards the garden courtyard where a white gazebo decorated with multi-coloured balloons stood in the centre. Outside it were rattan sofas, grouped around low coffee tables furnished with stacks of hardback books. Inside, more chic seating was surrounded by colourful pots of flowers and display shelves that overflowed with paperbacks. There was even a flamingo with a book between its beak.

Hung across the gazebo was a big silver sign proclaiming *Welcome to the Book Surgery*.

'Wow, that's fabulous.' She had to blink to stop the tears escaping. 'I don't care what you say about your fiancé, in my eyes he's an absolute superstar.'

Leroy let out a huff of laughter. 'Wasn't all his doing.' Then he gave her a gentle push. 'Go get 'em.'

She almost skipped to the gazebo, but then came to an abrupt halt, her heart faltering when she saw not one, not two, but it must have been a dozen green furry caterpillars, haphazardly shoved onto the shelves and tables, each with its head angled so it was looking at a book.

There was only one person on this island who knew about Sparks.

Behind her, someone cleared their throat. Immediately her pulse began to race, and butterflies burst into her belly... Yep, her body recognised the deep, rumbly noise before her head turned to confirm. 'Turns out caterpillars are easier to find than bookworms.'

Her eyes gobbled him up even as her mind tried to draw a big steel cage around her heart. White open-collared shirt, shades that hid his eyes and gave him an air of film star mystery. Suddenly the gazebo felt cramped, like Liam was crowding her, even though he stood a respectful distance away.

Why did he have to be so tall? And so frigging drop-dead handsome?

As she struggled to find her words, silence stretched between them.

He slipped the shades off, revealing a pair of turbulent grey eyes. 'Say something. Please.'

Breaking away from the magnetic pull of his gaze she glanced around her. 'Did you organise this or Jeremy?'

'That depends. Do you like it?'

Do not get dragged back into his orbit. 'Yes.'

'Then I'll claim partial responsibility.'

'Why?' She forced herself to look at him again. 'A week ago, my only purpose was a cheer-you-up fuck.'

He flinched, jaw muscle bunching. 'You were getting under my skin, creeping under my guard. I … panicked.' His shoulders rose and fell as he inhaled a deep, shaky breath. 'I had to push you away.'

'So why are you here now?'

'To apologise.' He cursed and rubbed at his face. 'What I said was shitty, inexcusable, I know that. I don't deserve another chance.' His eyes lifted to hers. 'But I want one.'

The tug on her heart, the one she didn't want to feel? In that moment she'd have been grateful for it, because what she got instead was a full-blown yank. It terrified her how easily her heart forgave him. Like he'd just had to turn up and smile in her direction and it was ready to lie at his feet. Thank God, her head was smarter. 'We don't always get what we want. It wasn't that long ago I asked if I could stay on at the bookstore for the whole of my contract and you said no, I could have two weeks.'

'I told you, it's yours until you go home.'

'Yes, I remember you saying that. I also remember the next day you made me feel cheaper than anyone else has ever managed, and believe me, that's one hell of an achievement.' Anger burned inside her again, and she welcomed it, *channelled* it. 'Did I tell you that my ex, Paul, thought it was okay not to let me know he was actually dating someone else while sleeping with me because *I looked the type who wouldn't mind?*' Liam's face blanched and she let out a strangled laugh. 'Yeah, such a charmer, but apparently, arseholes are my go-to type because he didn't hurt me nearly as much as you did. I was trying to help,' she hissed, on a roll now, a week's worth of pent-up emotion bubbling over. 'Not infiltrate your precious privacy, not try and wheedle my way into your life through your grandma.' He looked like he might be sick, but she reminded herself she didn't care. 'God, the fact you thought I was the sort of person who would even do that.' That had hurt most of all. Despite all the sweet things he'd said to her, he still actually thought she was some sort of scheming cow out to snare him through sex and his grandma.

He was losing her. Liam hadn't realised how important it was that Jade gave him another chance, until he saw that chance slip through his fingers.

'I didn't think you were like that.' He dragged a hand through his hair, feeling totally unbalanced, like he was swaying against the ropes after a few heavy punches. 'Of course I didn't think that.' Taking a big risk she'd actually punch him, he stepped towards her, eyes pleading with her. 'I told you, I panicked. You were doing this amazing, touching thing for the most important person in my life, and it suddenly felt too much, like I was in real danger of falling for you. Then there was Mary knowing something acutely personal about me, a woman who's been part of the Haven-hating gossip machine that drove me and my grandma off this island... Fuck, Jade. For a few minutes I lost all sense of proportion.'

Her blue gaze raked his, like she was trying to get inside his head. Then she huffed out a breath and turned away from him, walking to pick up one of the caterpillars he'd insisted on, much to Jeremy's amusement. 'What do you want from me?'

Okay, this was the billion-dollar question. This was where he cut and ran, or stared fear in the face and decided she was worth making himself vulnerable for. Worth putting himself out there to be rejected again. 'I want to date you.'

She gaped at him. 'You don't date.'

'I used to. Then, like you, I was hurt, so I stopped.' His heart was racing, his stomach felt like it was filled with grit. 'But you're special, Jade. I become a different person when I'm with you, a man who laughs, who talks about himself. Who's starting to realise the impact of his actions and wants to change.' Her eyes held his and she nodded, as if to say *you have my attention, now convince me it's something I want, too*. 'You only have two more months out here. I want to be selfish and spend them getting to know you more and maybe in doing that, I'll also get to know myself more. The real me, not the bitter, closed off me I've become.' His heart sank as he played back his words. 'And that's all about what I'll get out of it, and not about how you can benefit.'

'Don't I get sex?'

He couldn't read that look in her eye. 'I don't know if you're teasing me, or throwing my words back at me.' Frustrated, he jammed a hand into his pocket. 'I get it, I'm a complicated mess. Why would you want to spend more time with me? Plus, with the way I've acted, you have no reason to trust me. But I'm trying to open up to you. Trying to offer you a version of me I thought I'd buried.' Emotion balled in his throat and he struggled to keep his voice steady. 'I won't blame you if you think he's not worth your while. Others have thought the same.' Fuck, now he sounded pathetic. Angry with himself he inclined his head. 'You're here to work and I've taken up too much of your time. Good luck today. I hope it goes well.'

He turned and began to walk away, legs feeling stiff, like they'd forgotten how to move.

'Wait.'

Heart thumping, he turned to face her. Blonde hair curling

around her face, hands clutching a toy caterpillar wearing an inane grin, she looked stunning and sexy and … unsure. 'I'll be in the shop tomorrow. You know … if you want to find out how this event went?'

It was an olive branch, and he grasped it as if it was the last life raft. 'Thank you, I will.'

He weaved his way back through the resort to his office, his legs unsteady. She hadn't agreed to date him, but she *hadn't said no*. Considering at one point he thought it was game over, he'd take that.

He pushed open the door to his office and slumped onto the chair, taking a moment to let the tiny victory settle over him. Yet as he went to turn his computer back on, his mind wouldn't focus, his tangled emotions distracting him. He needed to unpick them, separate them into a different compartment in his brain, before he could carry on.

And there was only one person he knew who could help.

Climbing back to his feet, he marched towards Jeremy's office, but the bastard wasn't there. Unreasonably annoyed, he set off towards the beach bar, figuring he might find the man… Yep, there he was. Sitting as cool as you like at a table, glass of something tall and fruity in front of him.

'Do I pay you to sit here?'

Jeremy glanced up at him. 'You pay me to keep the guests happy, and as I've just waved goodbye to a couple of guests who were unhappy with their room as it was only a pool view and not a sea view as advertised, but are now deliriously happy, courtesy of a chat with yours truly, a couple of free rum punches and a promise of an upgrade to a suite, then yes. You pay me to sit here.'

'Fine.' He threw himself down on the chair opposite. 'Ask me how it went with Jade.'

'Ah.' A slow smile crossed Jeremy's face. 'I like this new arrangement where you come to me for relationship advice.'

'I'm not. I don't.' Aware they both knew he was lying, Liam slumped against the back of the chair. How had he gone from keeping his distance, to wanting to share every minute of the conversation he'd just had with Jade, in the hope Jeremy would see the same thread of encouragement he had? 'I apologised, she listened, took apart my behaviour with a cool precision that made me feel two-foot tall. She didn't say no, but she didn't yes, either.'

'Of course she didn't. She's got far too much self-respect to allow the man who insulted her to just pick up where he left off without an element of crawling.'

'That's what it's going to take? She wants me on my knees, begging?' He'd only come close to doing that once, at the end of that first term when he'd been woken in the middle of the night by a bucket of cold water for the fifth night in a row. Instead, he'd guzzled caffeine drinks and forced himself to stay awake. Gradually his body had got used to having less sleep.

'Well, probably not literally, though you on your knees does make rather an intriguing picture—'

'What, then?' Liam interrupted before he did something humiliating, like blush.

Jeremy laughed, eyes glittering with humour. 'I never thought I'd see the day that Liam Haven was all twisted up over a woman.'

'I should have learnt my damn lesson,' he muttered, then made the mistake of looking up at Jeremy.

'Sabrina Ellis?'

'Gossip machine still going strong as I see.' Even the name had Liam's stomach rolling. 'Bad enough I'm talking to you about Jade. I'm not, under any circumstances, discussing past relationships with you.'

'Message received. Too soon.' Jeremy smirked. 'I'll make a note to ask you again in a few months, when the benefits of having me as a friend, confident and wise counsel will be more obvious.' He waved away Liam's attempt to interrupt his ridiculous monologue. 'With regard to Jade, she's been treated appallingly by men, and that now includes you, so if you still want to date her, you need to give her time. Show her you're serious, and treat her like the amazing woman she is. Not the one she sometimes thinks she is.'

Liam pieced the words together with what he knew about Jade. 'You're good at this.'

'You sound surprised. I'm a gay ginger man. I've been ridiculed, ignored, called every name under the sun. Instead of cowering away, I chose to talk to my detractors to try and understand how they thought. Engage with them.' He smirked. 'That's why I'm the confident, together, beautifully presented man you see before you now. So, when do we begin Operation Double BJ?'

Liam groaned. 'I don't want to know.'

'Oh, but you do.' Jeremy grinned. 'Bring Back Jade.'

'Christ.' Abruptly, Liam rose to his feet. 'I've got it from here. And if you ever use that acronym again, I *will* fire you.'

Chapter Twenty-Seven

J ade was surprised to find Henry sauntering into the shop on Thursday lunchtime. She'd not actually seen him since that first SOB meeting. She'd included him on the group chats and occasionally he'd added a thumbs up to whatever had been suggested, but he'd always excused himself from the subsequent meetings. She'd kind of hoped he'd fade away.

'Hi. Looking for some reading inspiration?'

'Oh, no, I've not come for a book.'

He scanned the shop, and Jade didn't know what it was about the man that instantly put her on edge. Like he was carefully making a note of what he saw and putting it into some sort of algorithm, *judging* her. Books not straight, empty mug ... his gaze settled on her ... hair too blonde, top too tight.

She shook the thought away. It hardly mattered what he thought of her. 'Then how else can I help you?'

'Thought I'd pop by and find out how the campaign against Haven is going.'

'You mean the campaign to save the bookstore.'

Henry smiled, showing a row of perfect white teeth to match

the perfectly styled fair hair. 'Come on, we both know it's more than that, at least for the rest of us.' He chuckled. 'You'll be heading home in a couple of months, but we've got to live here. If we don't stop the man, pretty soon we won't have an island to live on. He'll have bought it all up.'

'Sorry, Henry, but I'm only interested in keeping the bookstore open.' Liam might have agreed he would keep it open for the rest of her contract, but she couldn't bear the thought of it being demolished. It was too quaint, too important to book lovers living on the island and visiting. Plus, if he'd stop being so damn stubborn, she could see it helping to mend relationships between the resort and the island community.

'Looks like I'll need to set up another group then.'

She blinked. 'Another group?'

'A group to prevent Haven from desecrating any more of Nantucket with his awful resort.'

'Doesn't your dad own a resort on the island, too?'

Henry gave her the sort of look she'd had before from people who believed she was too blonde, too pretty to grasp what they were saying. 'I hope you're not comparing the timeless elegance of the historic Chase Hotel and Resort Group, with Haven's soulless, modern imitation?'

'I guess it depends what you're looking for. One person's *elegant historic* is someone else's dated. One person's *soulless modern*, someone else's perfect luxury holiday.' Thankfully the door opened and another customer walked in. 'Excuse me.' She turned to smile at the new customer, uncaring that she'd left Henry with a scowl on his face. She no longer needed his help, in fact she'd never needed it. All Henry Chase wanted to do was take down his dad's main rival.

Customers continued to keep her busy for the rest of the afternoon, but the pang of disappointment she felt when they turned out not to be tall, dark and grumpy-looking with mesmerising silver-specked grey eyes, became more and more acute.

I'm trying to offer you a version of me I thought I'd buried. I won't blame you if you think he's not worth your while. Others have thought the same.

His words had played round in her head all night. Maybe it was for the best that he wasn't going to show because she didn't have any defence against the man when he opened up to her like that.

The door swung open and her heart ricocheted off her ribs when she saw who it was. She had to press a hand to her chest to stop the damn thing flying across the room towards him.

He gave her a cautious smile. 'Is now a good time?'

'For what?' Oh God, it sounded like she was contemplating dragging him upstairs for a quickie.

He gave her a quizzical look. 'Is there more than one option on the table?'

'I … er, just meant I assume you're here to ask how yesterday went?'

He nodded, those beautiful eyes never leaving her face. 'Jeremy informs me you were a hit with the guests.'

'Wow, that's good to know. The team will be delighted.'

'The team.' His shoulders twitched. '*You* were the hit, Jade.'

'Oh.' He was hard to resist even when he was being an arse, impossible to resist when he decided to seduce her. This serious, intense yet secretly very kind man? He was one she could easily fall in love with.

'It can't come as a surprise.' He took a few steps towards her, his thumb caressing her cheek in a light touch that turned her insides to mush. 'The guests loved you. Everyone loves you.' His hand shifted to tuck a curl of hair behind her ear. 'You have a natural way with people, a wit, a charisma, a smile we try to encourage, hoping it will be pointed in our direction.'

Butterflies flapped crazily in her belly as the liquid silver-grey eyes pulled her dangerously under their influence. 'Thank you.'

He nodded and took a step back. 'Would you recommend a book for me?'

It took her a moment to gather herself. 'I thought you only read contracts.'

His eyes darkened. 'If I recall, you once promised to find me a book, but then we got … distracted.'

Unhelpful images of how she'd distracted him flew through her mind. He'd been naked, hugely aroused and throbbing in her hand…

She didn't know whether to scream with disappointment or cheer with relief when the door opened. And Adam walked in.

'Am I interrupting anything?' Adam's gaze bounced between the pair of them, a slow smirk crossing his face. 'Looks like I am.' He turned to Liam. 'I thought you said she was *just an employee*?'

Ouch.

Liam exhaled sharply, and a flash of frustration crossed his face. Clearly whatever he'd said to Adam wasn't necessarily the truth, but she'd had so many mixed messages already from him, it was impossible to know where she stood. Really, the only healthy way forward was to spend the next two months untangling herself from him. Not getting herself in deeper.

But then she looked at him again, at the fresh lines of tension on his handsome face, and her heart didn't see the man. It saw the lost, shunned young boy.

Liam shoved his hands into his pockets before he did something he'd regret, like grab Adam's shirt and shove him against the wall. Not that he'd regret the action, but he would regret embarrassing Jade. 'What do you want?'

Adam chuckled. 'Not content with continuing to meddle in the tourist industry, you're now working in book sales?'

Liam's hands twitched, forming into fists.

Jade turned and gave Adam a polite smile. 'How can I help, Adam?'

'I came to apologise for not being at the meeting the other day. I hear you're doing book surgeries now.' A broad smile crossed his face. Cocky and smug were the adjectives Liam would have used to describe it. Someone who liked the son of a bitch might say 'charming'. 'What do I have to do to make an appointment?'

'No appointment needed.' At Jade's reply, Adam's smile grew, and Liam's fists clenched tighter. This was excruciating. 'You just need to stand in line at the next pop-up clinic.'

Adam's smile froze. 'I see. When is that?'

'I'll be outside the visitor centre in the historic district on Saturday from one p.m.'

He nodded curtly. A man who'd momentarily stood eight-foot tall before being expertly cut down to size. 'I might see you there, then.'

The door banged shut behind him.

A charged silence settled between them. Liam knew he needed to get out and regroup. Let his emotions settle. He was prepared to beg for another chance, but to put himself through that when she had no intention of granting him one? Humiliation wasn't new to him, but could he knowingly put himself through it again? 'I'll see you on Saturday.'

'Sorry?'

'For the book recommendation,' he clarified. 'Outside the visitor centre, one o'clock.'

'Oh.' She bit into her lip, a faint red to her cheeks. 'You don't need to come to the clinic for that. I only said it to Adam because he was being a twat.'

A low laugh escaped him, but jealousy still twisted inside him. 'He likes you.'

'I think he likes winding you up, more.'

Their eyes met and the weight of the moment felt heavy on his shoulders. Somehow, without his knowing it, he'd handed her the power to hurt him. He could, and had, also hurt her.

Neither was remotely acceptable.

He should forget her, forget this humming attraction for a woman working against him, causing him to delay his dream so she could fulfil hers.

'You told Adam I was just an employee to you.' Jade's voice cut through his swirling thoughts. 'I'm not saying that's wrong, but my head is spinning with all this *I like you Jade, the sex was just what I needed. I want another chance with you. You're just an employee.* She slid her hands onto her hips. 'Be straight with me. Which should I believe?'

Why did she have to look so magnificent, boldly staring him down? 'Come out with me on the boat on Sunday. Let me show you.' Humiliation and pain be damned, he'd never backed down, only ever stepped forward. 'You show me books. I'll show you whales.'

Her quiet blue gaze held his. 'Is this just a ruse to push me overboard so you can get on with knocking down the bookstore?'

'I can bulldoze it any time I want.' He exhaled, matched her calm stare with one of his own. 'It's a ruse to spend time with you. To show you that the first and third statements are what you should believe. The second I apologised for, the last I said to Adam because I didn't want him knowing how infatuated I am.'

She sucked in a breath and automatically his eyes were drawn to her luscious breasts. Fuck, he wanted to bury himself in them again so much, he ached.

'What about sex?'

Guiltily he looked back up at her face. 'You are the sexiest woman I've ever seen, and my body remembers every second of how much it enjoyed being tangled with yours. Of course I want to sleep with you again. But if we spend the next two months only as friends, I can handle that. What I can't handle is knowing you're around the corner and not being able to talk to you.'

Her expression softened, the blue of her eyes deepening. 'That's because I'm such awesome company.'

This was why he'd allowed her to distract him. She made him smile, made the self-imposed burden he carried around with him – the need to prove he was successful in the most visible way by making Haven Resort the biggest and best on the island – feel less heavy. 'Sunday morning. I'll knock on your door at ten a.m.?'

'Pretty sure I can make it down to the yacht with no mishaps.' He stared back at her. 'Oh, crap, you're remembering my unplanned swim.'

'I'll knock on your door,' he repeated. 'Bring a sweater, it can get chilly out on the ocean.'

'Aye, aye captain.' She gave him a wonky salute, which made him want to bundle her into his arms and spend the next hour kissing her.

Just as he was debating whether kissing was allowed in the new friendship he was trying to navigate, another customer walked in.

The lady looked him up and down. 'You're Liam Haven.'

His heart sunk. That question was rarely the start to anything good. 'I am.'

'We used to moor our boat on this wharf and enjoy shopping along the waterfront. Now we can't moor it here and even if we could, this is the only shop left to enjoy.' Her gaze darted to Jade. 'Is it right that he's going to knock it down, too?'

Jade slid him a glance. 'Unless we can persuade him otherwise.'

The woman sniffed. 'Well, I hope he'll listen to reason. All this focus on tourists. Why doesn't anyone want to build places for those of us who live and work here?' She sighed. 'Sorry, I didn't come in to rant. I actually came to see if you have a copy of a book I was recommended by a friend who'd been to your book clinic...'

Jade gave him an apologetic glance before focusing back on the customer and Liam slunk out of the door.

Haven Resort needs Nantucket as much as Nantucket needs you.

Was Jade right? Was his crazy obsession – yeah, now he was quoting Jeremy – to get the island to respect him, actually doing the opposite? By expanding the resort, making it more and more an exclusive enclave for the rich, was he turning into someone no better than the assholes he'd spent half a lifetime hating?

Chapter Twenty-Eight

Jade's body went still as she watched the whale surface in front of them, then glide back down into the indigo blue of the Atlantic Ocean.

It was so beautiful, tears burned her eyes.

Liam stood behind her, the warmth of his chest against her back adding to the moment. His hands rested loosely on her waist, holding her in a way that was both respectful, yet possessive. He'd been like that all day, keeping a distance too far away to be lovers yet too close for mere friends.

'Tell me again which whales we've seen today.'

'The smaller ones with a white band on each flipper were the Minke whales.'

The whisper of his breath against her neck caused a swoop in her belly. 'White tummy,' she murmured.

'That's right. The much larger, long, slender one was the Finback or Fin whale.'

'The males have a one metre-plus penis.'

She felt the vibration of his laughter as it rumbled through his chest. 'That's what your book claimed. Way to give a guy a complex.'

'But they're over ten times longer than you, so actually…' *Holy crap Jade, where are you going with this?*

'Actually?' he prompted, mouth closer to her ear now, his voice an octave lower.

'I was going to say speaking proportionally, you could hold your head up high in a whale pod.'

And now his lips brushed her ear as he spoke. 'Thank you.'

Oh God, she wasn't going to survive much more of this. Her nipples were like bullets and there was so much heat between her legs she was worried he'd see steam. 'Maybe we should stop talking about penises.'

She almost groaned with disappointment when she felt his wall of heat leave her back. 'The chunky whale with the really long pectoral fins and tubercles on its head, is the humpback.' He was stood beside her now, eyes searching hers. 'He's the one who just made you cry.'

She hadn't realised he'd noticed. 'Yeah, well that's your fault for bringing me here, showing me these guys who look so majestic when they erupt out of the water. I mean, they're the kings of the belly flop, but somehow they make it look regal. And I bet their stomach doesn't go red.'

'Only because they have tough skin. Yours is soft, delicate. Smooth to touch.' He cleared his throat. 'It's probably time we headed back.'

'Yes.' Beyond time. Her body had spent all day being primed for sex, and was ready to fire the moment he touched her. *Really* touched her, rather than the glancing caress of a hand against her back, fingertips down her arm. A flutter of hot breath against her neck.

He was driving her insane, yet it was hard to tell whether he was as turned on as she was. At times she caught him looking at her with hooded eyes, yet then he'd glance away and she wasn't sure if she'd imagined it.

Of course I want to sleep with you again.

He'd said that, hadn't he? It was entirely possible he was trying to show her he wanted her for more than sex.

They walked back to the bridge and she tried not to be impressed by the confident way he handled the array of buttons and switches, hands sure on the wheel as he turned the boat around and headed back towards Nantucket.

They made easy talk on the way back, Liam proving to be an excellent tour guide. She'd expected the businessman in him to know about the area, she hadn't expected him to be so knowledgeable about the wildlife that inhabited it. Yet another sign he wasn't as cold-hearted and uncaring as he'd been depicted.

Her pulse kicked up a gear when Nantucket came into view. As the boat powered closer, she saw the now familiar white tower and black roof of Brant Point Lighthouse at the entrance to Nantucket Harbour, dozens of boats of various descriptions bustling in and out; yachts, ferries, fishing vessels. Along from the harbour were stretches of golden beach, interspersed with lush green vegetation. It wasn't just pretty, there was a serenity to it that, like the whales earlier, caught at her throat. She would miss all this.

But you're here now.

'How's your grandma?' she asked as they drew closer to the wharf.

He slid her a glance. 'Enjoying the books you collected for her. I set up the Kindle, which she says is the best invention in the history of inventions because it's a modern gadget she can actually use. It was thoughtful of you to get her CDs, but I'm working on setting her up with the audiobooks, even though she curses a lot when I try and show her how to find and play them on her smartphone.' His face softened, his voice warmed with such affection her heart gave a hard flip. 'What?'

Belatedly she realised she must have been staring. 'I was wondering about the woman who inspires such devotion in Liam Haven that he turns into a ball of goo when he talks about her.'

He grunted. 'She's my family. My world.'

'I can see that.' She paused, wondered whether to ask, then decided if he clammed up on her it would be a good thing. Stop her from making a rash decision to fall back into bed with him. 'How many other women have turned you into a ball of goo, even if only temporarily?'

His eyes narrowed. 'Is that your way of asking me about my exes?'

'You saw through my subtle line of questioning, huh?'

His mouth twitched. 'You have many attributes. Subtlety isn't one of them.'

'Noted, but I've told you about my exes, and you haven't said anything about yours, other than the fact you've been hurt in the past.'

'That's all there is to say. Two serious relationships, one with a childhood sweetheart who turned out to have no heart. One further and final mistake which ended six years ago.'

'Which one was Sabrina Ellis?'

He stilled, hands gripping tighter to the wheel. 'Jeremy told you.'

'To be fair, he only mentioned it because I asked him.'

'You asked Jeremy about my past relationships?'

Jade slunk into the plush leather of the seat. 'Yes, okay, I was interested to know who you'd dated.'

A small smile played around his mouth. 'How long ago was this?'

'At the library event,' she muttered.

'Um … and what juicy information did Jeremy manage to impart about Sabrina?'

'He was pretty useless, actually. Said she was the daughter of the owner of the Ellis Hotel empire so go you, and that was it. He only brought her up so he could reassure me that you wouldn't be fazed by … how did he put it … "interwork, non-curricular relations"? Something like that. I was too busy memorising her name so I could Google it later to really listen.'

He nodded, eyes now watching her curiously. 'And were you reassured?'

'By knowing the fact I worked for you wouldn't bother you? Sure. But that diving into a hot affair with you was a good idea? No way, José.'

———

Liam slowed the boat and turned to face the woman next to him. The one he'd driven himself half mad trying to keep his hands off all day.

'April was my first mistake, but I was young and inexperienced. Sabrina was the second. I was older and should have known better. She was the hardest to recover from.' He paused, staring out at the harbour as he tried to gather his thoughts. 'We've both been hurt in relationships, so we both have our reasons for being wary about what's happening here. But the difference is, we'd go into this knowing it will end when your three months is over.' It was the first time he'd thought of her going, and it caused a disconcerting tightening in his chest. 'We talked before about what would make us regret it. What we didn't ask ourselves was whether we'd regret *not* taking this further. Not spending the next two months enjoying each other.' He put his hand on her cheek, taking satisfaction from the hitch of her breath, the widening of her pupils. She wasn't immune to him. 'I know I would, but maybe I have more to gain.'

'What do you mean?'

'I told you, I feel like I'm a better version of myself when I'm with you. I want to see more of that guy.' *See if he can be brave enough to lower some walls, risk letting someone close again. Not someone. Her. He was prepared to risk it for her.* Gently he ran his thumb down her cheek. 'You told me you came out here to find yourself, prove you were every bit as smart and capable as your sister. Is there any way I can help with that, other than letting you work out your contract?'

She laughed. 'Well, you could give me some of your "I don't give a shit what you think of me" attitude. And a dollop of your "I'm so frigging successful nothing can touch me" confidence.'

She was joking, but he wondered if there was some way he could make her see what he did, what others did. 'That attitude, the so-called confidence, I didn't have as a kid. It came from building the business. Once you have belief in yourself, it matters less what others think.'

'I can see that.' Her eyes darted away. 'And I'm starting to think maybe I'm not the worst manager the bookstore has seen.'

'You're a fucking great manager,' he asserted, then laughed as he met a pair of blue eyes shining with mischief. 'You deliberately put yourself down so I'd say something nice.'

'Maybe.' She smirked. 'Worked, too.'

'Newsflash, I'd have said it anyway.' He studied her. 'Do you enjoy managing the shop?'

'Yes. Well, I enjoy interacting with the customers, talking about books, trying new stuff. The spreadsheets are a form of torture that should be outlawed.'

'What if we spent some time together going through the business model? I could help you plan the next two months so you get the most out of it. If you want,' he added, acutely aware she'd not actually said she even wanted to see him again after today, never mind continue to build a relationship, even if it was only as friends.

'Would you really?'

She didn't get it, he realised. 'Of course. Christ, Jade, have I not made it clear enough that I want to spend as much time as I can with you? That I'm borderline obsessed with you?'

A smile spread across her face. 'Well, if you put it like that, I'd love to take some business lessons from you.'

'I have a feeling we'll be learning from each other.'

'Good. One-sided relationships never work.' For a few beats there was silence, just the gentle hum of the engine and the slap of the waves against the hull. 'You didn't tell me what happened with Sabrina,' she said eventually. 'How did it end?'

He preferred the silence. 'I wasn't rich enough.'

'Seriously? She had some figure you didn't match up to? Like she'd carry on dating you if you were worth ten million but not one million?'

'Her dad told her she needed to ditch me and date someone *appropriate*.' The word still stung, as did the memory of how naïve he'd been to think it would ever have ended any differently. Especially after what had happened with April. Only his grandma had ever really wanted him. 'Stupidly, I thought she might fight for me. Turns out she loved the sex, the illicitness of fucking one of the staff. But not me.'

Her hand settled over his arm and she squeezed. 'Lucky escape. She sounds like a right cow.'

Laughter huffed out of him, and he realised it was the first time he'd been able to laugh about that time in his life. 'Now you have some gossip for Jeremy.'

'Oh, no, you should tell him. I hear you're besties now.'

'God, no.' Yet even as he denied it, he had to concede that as his only friend, it was likely Jeremy counted as a best friend.

'Aw, come on, you're going to be his best man. Can't get more bestie than that.'

'You heard, huh.'

'I was down as substitute if you turned him down.'

'That makes much more sense.' Was he seriously jealous that his gay guest-services manager was close to the woman he was infatuated with?

'Why would it make more sense?' Jade demanded. 'The man has a secret, totally platonic, crush on you. Why else would he put up with you for all these years? And don't tell me it's because you pay him. I happen to know he was offered a job at Chase and turned it down.'

'He was?'

'Yes, so stop fighting with Jeremy and start to realise you're both on the same side.' She grinned. 'And beneath all the sniping, you really like and respect each other.'

He made the mistake of looking at her again. The amused smile, the dazzling blue eyes… His heart tripped.

Fuck.

He knew the signs. He was falling for her, and this felt even more frightening than before because he was actively trying *not* to. It was like he was driving a truck downhill, trying desperately to slam on the brakes but the pedal didn't work and the damn thing kept hurtling forward, gaining momentum.

All he could see ahead was a mangled mess.

'Liam? You look like someone's walked over your grave.'

Just glimpsing into my future.

'Sorry. All this talk about Jeremy being my bestie. It's disconcerting.'

'The Jeremy part?' Her expression softened. 'Or the fact you now have friends?'

'A friend,' he corrected.

Her fingers interlaced with his. 'You have more than one, remember.'

His heart squeezed, emotion ploughing into him. Was there a way he could do this and avoid the mangled mess? If they stuck at platonic friends, would it take the momentum out of their relationship and steer it towards somewhere safer? 'Thanks.'

She rested her head against his shoulder and for a moment he felt a pulse of contentment. But then he accidentally looked down, caught sight of the valley of her breasts and that pulse turned hotter, needier. It was not going to be enough to spend time with her, talk to her. Not if he couldn't wrap his arms around her, smooth his hands over her skin. Slide into her heat.

The crash was inevitable. The only question was whether he would make it out of the twisted mess alive.

Chapter Twenty-Nine

Jade rechecked her appearance in the mirror. Was the outfit she'd chosen too much? Not enough? Was it too clingy, too low cut? She sucked in a breath and smoothed her hands down the bright yellow sundress. Why was she doubting herself? Looking attractive was something she was good at. The one thing she'd always had.

She stared back at her reflection. Not the one thing. She had a list of things she was good at now; networking, building relationships, growing a book business ... she was a *fucking great manager*.

Her reflection smiled back at her.

Had there ever been a longer, sweeter kiss than the one Liam had given her after he'd walked her back to the bookstore from their day on the water? Instinctively, her fingers brushed across her lips, still feeling the imprint of his. The gentle press of his sensual mouth, the tease of his tongue. Drugging kisses that had gone on for so long her lips had become swollen. Yet his hands had stayed on her hips, keeping them a tantalising distance from each other. Oh, she'd known he was hard, could see the magnificent outline of his erection, but that was all she'd been able to do, look.

If this was his way of torturing her until she gave in, then mission frigging accomplished. She was ready to wave the white flag, would even wear a T-shirt saying *I want sex tonight*, if it pushed him over the edge. The fear of falling for him, getting hurt … it was a worry for another day. She was only interested in now.

The rap on the door made her jump.

She grabbed her handbag and a lightweight shawl before racing down the stairs to open it.

'Hi.'

His gaze skimmed over her face, eyes darkening as they focused on her lips, then turning even stormier as they travelled down her body. 'Fuck.'

'You don't like it? I can change—'

'No chance.' He heaved out a sigh. 'The dress shows off the dynamite curve of your ass, the swell of your spectacular tits. It's perfect. You're perfect.'

'Oh.' Confidence fully back in place, she eyed him curiously. 'Then what's the problem?'

'The problem is I'm going to spend all night with a hard-on.' He dragged a hand through his hair. 'Bad enough, but where we're going…'

He trailed off, muttering something under his breath as he took her hand and began to march them back down the wooden pontoon towards his boat.

'So where *are* we going?' He'd not said yesterday, just asked her out to dinner.

'Martha's Vineyard.'

'Oh, wow, okay.' She pushed down the niggle that he didn't want to be seen with her in Nantucket. 'I've not managed to visit there yet. This will be fun.'

'Fun?' He exhaled a long breath. 'It's going to be torture.'

'Um, is that torture because of your, er … predicament?'

He snorted, jumping onto the boat before helping her. 'My permanent state of arousal when I'm around you?' His eyes flicked to her dress. 'Especially when you wear something like that. Christ.' He drew a hand down his face. 'Maybe I should wrap you in a blanket or something.'

'Well I have my shawl. The restaurant might not like it if I sit there surrounded by bedding—'

'We're not going to a restaurant.'

'You're taking me all the way to Martha's Vineyard to eat, but not at a restaurant? Oh, is that why I need the blanket? Is it a picnic on the beach? Because that's great. I love a picnic, though I should warn you, me and sand don't always get on. It gets everywhere, and I mean *everywhere*. Not just in my food, but, you know…'

'We're having dinner at my grandma's.'

Oh, my God. Her heart thumped against her ribs and she stared back at him. 'You're taking me to meet her?'

His jaw clenched and he looked away from her. 'This was a stupid idea.'

'Well, it was only stupid if you don't want me to meet her.'

Slowly his silver-grey eyes found hers. 'Of course I want you to. That's why I set this up.' His Adam's apple slid down his throat as he swallowed. 'The question is, do you mind spending the evening eating questionable fish pie with a seventy-five-year-old or would you rather go to dinner at a restaurant and dine on something infinitely more edible?'

She was aware of the giant step he was taking. Just as she was aware of the vulnerability behind his throwaway words. He wanted her to meet the most important person in his life. The person a few weeks ago she'd thought he was actively avoiding her meeting. 'What's questionable about the fish pie?'

'Likely to have one or two main ingredients missing. Or replaced with cat food.'

'It sounds delicious.' She reached up to put a hand on either side of his guarded, ridiculously handsome face. 'I'd be honoured to meet your grandma.'

His gaze jumped to hers, eyes narrowed. Whatever he saw must have reassured him because his expression lost some of its tension. 'Yeah?'

'Absolutely.' She grinned. 'Does this mean I also get to hear lots of tales of Liam Haven as a boy because I seriously can't wait for that. I might need to take notes, so I can tell Jeremy, so he can tell Leroy, so he can spread it to the rest of the staff.'

His eyelids fluttered closed as he heaved in a breath. Mumbling something about bad ideas, he went to untie the ropes from their moorings. She watched on, appreciating the perfection of his bum, outlined by the smart dark jeans and the play of muscles on his forearms, revealed by the rolled back sleeves of his white linen shirt.

The hard pull on her heart could not be ignored, yet neither could the fear that, unlike Rob, unlike Paul, this complicated, brooding man, whose own damaged heart held a fierce love for his grandma, had the power not just to break hers, but leave it shattered and unable to be repaired.

His grandma loved Jade. Of course she did. It had never been in doubt, because everyone loved her, yet seeing the pair of them laughing together as they discussed their favourite books had a profound effect on Liam. She'd put on an act with April, and with Sabrina, the only other women he'd brought home. It had been subtle, but he'd seen it in the polite smile, the way she'd put on her best dress.

Put fresh flowers in the vase.

She was herself with Jade. The flowers were there, the best dress was on, but the smile wasn't polite. It had been wide, warm and welcoming from the start. And now there was added laughter. He could put it down to their shared love of books, but somehow he knew Jade would have found a way to connect with his grandma whatever her interest.

He cleared his throat, and they both looked over at him. 'Just checking you both know I'm here.'

His grandma smiled. 'Of course we do. Have you checked on the fish pie? And we could both use a top off.'

'Isn't the whole point of going to someone's for dinner, that they serve you?' he grumbled, rising out of his chair.

'You're not here for the food. You're here so I can get to know this charming young lady you keep talking about.' She pinned him with a glare. 'And how can I do that, if I'm fussing about in the kitchen?'

Suitably chastised – how had he suddenly turned ten again? – he slunk into the kitchen. It didn't help that Jade looked like she was trying not to erupt into laughter. As he rummaged in the fridge for the open bottle of wine, he felt an arm slide around his waist. 'She thinks I'm charming.'

He gave Jade a sidelong glance and scowled. 'Doesn't mean she's right.'

'Aw, come on grumpy pants.' She plucked the bottle out of his hands. 'I'm a natural with people, you said so yourself. But don't worry, you're going to teach me business, and I'm going to teach you how to be more human.'

With a wink, she turned and walked back out, hips swaying mesmerisingly. Groaning, he adjusted his hard-on. He should have taken Jade out for a quick bite to eat at the resort, then invited her back to the yacht for dessert. Then spent the rest of the evening fucking her senseless.

Except she wasn't sure about him, so sex was off the table. And he'd already hurt her by making her think sex was all he was interested in, so he had to suck this up. If all he got out of the next two months was her friendship, and the knowledge he'd helped her see herself for the amazing woman she was, then he would have achieved something remarkable.

And if the way she'd just teased him was anything to go by, she was getting there.

'So how come you live in Martha's Vineyard?' he heard Jade ask as he slipped back into the room having ascertained the fish pie was coming to no harm. At least no more than it had probably come to already in the preparation. 'Didn't you both used to live in Nantucket?'

'We did,' his grandma confirmed. 'But Liam decided it was time for a change of scenery.'

'Oh?'

'It's a different vibe here. Nantucket can be … snobby, stuffy. It's more laid back on Martha's Vineyard.' His grandma looked at him, as if for agreement. He gave her a small nod of his head. 'When Liam bought up the land to build his first resort on Nantucket, some were against him. They didn't like so-called "new money" demolishing their history and replacing it with modern monstrosities. Of course, one person's monstrosity is another person's chic, modern resort that employs plenty of locals and encourages tourism to help many other businesses on the island. But some are too shortsighted to see that. And some couldn't handle the fact that the boy they'd shunned, was actually doing well for himself.' She smiled proudly. 'I was happy to stay, give them a piece of my mind, but Liam didn't want me upset by the nasty talk, or ostracised, so he bought me this lovely place.' Her expression softened as she caught his eye. 'But lovely as it's been, it's time to go back to my roots. To go home.'

'So you're moving back to Nantucket?' Jade's gaze swivelled between the pair of them.

'Liam's finding me a house in Siasconset.'

'I'm building *us* a house,' he corrected. 'We've been through this.'

'And I told you, no.' She batted a hand in his direction. 'You're a single guy in his prime. You don't want to be living with a silly old woman.'

'True. But I do want to live with you, so deal with it.'

Jade cleared her throat. 'This is exactly what I talked about in the kitchen.' She patted his grandma's hand. 'Excuse me while I give him his first lesson in how to be more human.'

His grandma sat up, all perky now. 'This, I want to hear. You go ahead, sweetheart. It's about time somebody dared to stand up to him.'

Stand up to him? Between Jade, Jeremy and his grandma, he'd never been put in his place so frequently. Or so effectively.

Jade grinned before turning to him. 'Why do you want your grandma to live with you?'

'So I can take care of her.'

'And?'

Christ, it felt like he was in the dock. 'Keep her out of trouble.'

Jade raised her eyes to the ceiling. 'And?'

What was he, five now? 'And because I fucking love her and I want to keep her close to me.'

'Bingo.' Satisfaction lit up Jade's face. 'Now I could be wrong, but I believe that's what she wanted to hear.'

'Oh no, you're not wrong dear. In fact you're very, very right.' There was a glisten to her eyes when she looked at him, and a tremor to her voice. 'Do you really want me with you? I won't be a burden?'

For the love of God. 'Of course I do. I told you I did.' He saw Jade's smirk and sighed. 'Fine. If I didn't make myself clear before.

We're a team. Always have been, always will be. Where you live, I live. End of story.' Because he felt his own voice begin to crack, he jumped to his feet. 'Now let's go and eat this damn fish pie.'

He set off to the kitchen, but not before he heard his grandma thanking Jade. 'I really thought he was just doing it to make me happy.' She sniffed. 'Didn't realise it would make him happy, too.'

He glanced back over his shoulder, expecting to find Jade giving him a triumphant smile, but instead she looked troubled. 'I can't imagine your grandson does anything he doesn't want to.'

A few months ago, he'd have agreed with Jade's statement, but now he was starting to wonder. He'd wanted to knock down the bookstore. Instead he was contemplating not just keeping it, but changing all his plans for the waterfront.

He'd also wanted to keep everyone at arm's length, protect himself. Now he was going to be a best man for Jeremy, and had let a blonde dynamo get so close he was worried he'd not be able to let her go when the time came.

Chapter Thirty

The boat ride back to Nantucket was mainly silent, and Jade knew that was down to her. She was the chatty one, but her mind was such a whirlwind of emotion, she was afraid if she opened her mouth, she'd say something stupid. *I think I'm falling for you.* Yep, something like that.

And it was all his fault for taking her to see his grandma. The sight of this hard, uncompromising man getting choked up when he'd told her they were a team... God, even now she felt her eyes blur with tears.

He held her hand to help her off the boat, expression full of concern. 'You're quiet.'

'Thought you might appreciate some silence, after enduring me and your grandma chattering all evening.'

'I enjoyed watching you together. She loved you,' he added. 'But then I knew she would.'

'The feeling was mutual. She's one amazing woman.'

'She is.' He peered down at her. 'So you're not annoyed I didn't take you to a restaurant?'

'Annoyed? Of course not.' Scared shitless more like.

He halted, turning to face her. 'Then what's the matter?'

'Nothing.' She swallowed. 'Well, except for the fact that taking me to see her wasn't fair.'

His browns scrunched together. 'What do you mean?'

'It was like you brought out the big guns.'

'You're calling my grandma a big gun?'

'I don't think you could get any bigger.' She worried at her bottom lip. 'Flipping heck, Liam, it was like watching Simba and Mufusa, Nemo and Marlin … damn, I can't think of any grandson/grandmother comparisons but you get my drift.'

'Honestly?' The tension that had crept into his expression eased away, replaced with bemusement. 'I have no idea what you're talking about.'

She let out a huff of frustration. 'I loved watching you with her, all right? It made me see a whole other side of you that I actually wish I hadn't because I don't know how I'm supposed to stop falling for you now, which is going to make things incredibly awkward for the next seven weeks.'

His throat moved as he swallowed. 'Seven weeks?'

'Yes. I counted it the other day.'

He inhaled a deep breath, letting it out slowly as his eyes locked with hers. 'It doesn't feel nearly long enough.' As her heart thumped wildly in her chest, his hand slid slowly up her neck to cup her cheek. 'You think I'm *not* freaking out about this? You aren't the only one in danger of losing themselves.'

She didn't know which was going to explode first, her brain or her heart. Both were racing like the clappers, pumping endorphins and adrenalin into her overheated blood. 'Honestly, I don't know whether to jump you, or run inside and lock the door.'

He let out a harsh exhale. 'Ditto.' His thumb smoothed across her cheek, eyes darkening to charcoal. 'But I've never run from anything.'

Her heart thumped louder. 'So we're doing the jumping thing?'

He groaned. 'If you want to jump me, you'll get no complaints.' He brushed his mouth against hers, sending a zing of awareness through her. 'But you could also invite me in for a drink and we'll see where this goes.'

'We've been here before, so we both know exactly where it's going if you come inside with me.' But she took his hand and they walked together to the bookstore, her fingers trembling as she unlocked the door and waved him inside. Resisting Liam Haven was impossible. God knows she'd tried, A-plus for effort, but it seemed so pointless when she only had seven weeks left here. Sod sensible. She'd come here for an adventure, to find herself, and he was part of that. It was time to stop being scared and take the leap, because even though the landing would hurt, the journey would be extraordinary.

Her legs felt like jelly as his long fingers curled around hers and he led her towards the stairs. 'This is crazy,' she mumbled as she climbed ahead of him.

'What is?'

'My heart's racing.'

When he reached the top of the stairs, he drew her jacket off her shoulders and laid it carefully over the back of her chair. 'Are you nervous about having a drink with me?'

'Yeah, you're not here for a drink. At least I hope not.' She rested a hand on her belly, trying to quiet the butterflies. Not nerves, she realised. Excitement. 'This reminds me of that first time, when you invited me back to the yacht for a cocktail, and then you said if I really wanted one, I'd be disappointed.'

He smiled, hands sliding up her arms until they reached her shoulders where he slid them under the straps of her dress. 'I remember.' She gasped as he bent to kiss her neck. 'Were you disappointed?'

'You know I wasn't.'

'We were strangers that night.' He dropped another soft kiss on her neck, only this time he didn't stop, instead continuing across her collarbone, moving the material aside. 'Now I'm kissing a woman I care about. A woman who knows me more than anyone else ever has.'

It was a reminder that he didn't allow people close, and for a good reason. As his grandma had confirmed tonight, he'd spent most of his life being shunned, both the boy and the man. He too had fears to push aside, pain that was hard to forget.

'I know you, but you also know me.' Needing a distraction from the emotions he pulled from her, she smiled and reached for the buttons of his shirt. 'So you should know you need to get naked because I'm a big admirer of the body you keep hidden under your clothes.'

His breathing quickened as his smouldering gaze met hers. 'It's yours to do what you want with.'

———

At his words, a gleam entered Jade's beautiful blue eyes. But then she ducked her head and focused on undoing his shirt, mumbling a curse as her fingers snagged on the buttons. It made him smile, which quickly turned into a hiss as her knuckles brushed against the sensitive hairs of his happy trail.

'Maybe I should take over,' he muttered, erection hard and pulsing against his zip, begging to be released.

'Nope, I've always wanted a sex toy.' Her tongue came out to wet her lips as she undid the button of his trousers and pushed them down over his hips, struggling to work them over his swollen dick.

'Is that all I am?' He wanted to be offended, but the thought of her playing with him, only made him harder.

Her tongue peeked out, wetting her bottom lip. 'You don't like the idea of being used for sex?'

'I like the idea of *you* using me for sex.' It was a reminder that, though it had always felt more than sex for him, he'd not always let her know that. And neither had her past boyfriends. Her hand curled around him, giving him a squeeze, rocking him right back to the here and now. 'I want you naked, too.' He grabbed at her dress and lifted it over her head before deftly undoing her bra, inhaling sharply as her breasts spilt into his hands. 'Fuck, I can't get enough of touching these.' He bent to kiss them, sucking at the nipples, adding a little nip that caused her to cry out his name.

But then she pushed him away. 'On the bed.'

He wasn't used to being ordered about, but one look at her flushed, beautifully animated face, and he was helpless to do anything but lay down on the mattress, hands behind his head.

Waiting.

And sweet mother of God, he was not disappointed. She followed him onto it, crawling towards him like a goddess, blonde hair sliding over her shoulders and down across her breasts which hung like beautiful ripe globes, begging for his touch. But when he reached for them, she batted his hand away.

'You're the toy, remember. I'm the one playing.' She gazed down at him, a teasing smile on her face. 'And from where I'm sitting, you've got an awful lot I want to play with.'

He was suddenly terrified he wouldn't be able to last through this. 'You're killing me, here. I need to touch you, feel you pulse around my fingers.'

'Later.' Her hands slid up his chest, resting on his pecs. 'I want to make you feel good.'

Christ. 'Trust me, having you near me and naked makes me feel fucking incredible.'

She smiled, gave his nipples a little rub, which sent a zap of arousal through him. 'I want to do more. I want to make you feel cared for, appreciated.'

Emotion jumped into his throat and he almost couldn't breathe for the pressure on his chest. 'You don't need to do that.'

'I *want* to do it. Far too many people have been mean to you. It's time to redress the balance.' She slid down and squeezed her breasts around him, sending his hips punching off the bed, as if an electric bolt had gone through him. 'Oh, wow, you like that huh?'

'If it involves your naked tits anywhere near my body,' he replied roughly, 'you can be certain I'll like it.'

'Good to know.' She licked her lips, squeezed again. 'Now let's find out what else you like.'

She did exactly that, stroking him, fondling him, worshipping him until he finally grasped her hips and seated her over him. Seven weeks, he thought as he rocked into her. It wasn't nearly long enough. As the pleasure coiled inside him, tightening his balls, squeezing his chest, he wondered what time would be long enough. Six months, a year?

She threw back her head, her core convulsing around him, and moments before she drew his own orgasm out of him, he tried to imagine a time when he would ever have enough of her.

And couldn't.

He woke to an annoying, jangling sound, followed by a groan from the warm, curvy woman he'd wrapped himself around like a blanket.

'Frigging heck Lauren, it's only seven.'

'Oops. I keep forgetting the time difference.'

Bleary eyed, he lifted himself up on his elbows, only to see Jade staring into her mobile phone. And a very shocked, less vibrant version of Jade, staring back at him.

'Oh, my God, is that a man in your bed, Jade Taylor? Who is it?'

Jade glanced at him over her shoulder, her hair a riot of blonde waves, lips swollen from having spent the best part of the night locked with his. 'Liam, meet my sister, Lauren.'

He gave a self-conscious nod before flopping back down on the bed, figuring there were worse places to hide than behind Jade's naked body.

'You didn't tell me he was so hot,' Lauren whispered, either unaware or uncaring that he was still in earshot. 'Now I can understand why you shagged him on day one.'

He didn't like the tone. He considered moving so they could have some privacy, and so he didn't say something Jade might not be happy with, but he didn't want to give Lauren an eyeful of his junk.

'How are things with Ned?' Jade asked, clearly used to Lauren's eloquent descriptions.

Liam heard Lauren sigh. 'We've seen each other a few times but it's difficult. You'll understand when you get yourself a career. There's a certain professional responsibility.'

He sat bolt upright and glared at Lauren through the screen. 'You don't count managing a bookstore a career?'

There was a beat of silence. Long enough for him to realise he'd just done what he'd told himself he wouldn't and interfered in Jade's business.

'Well three months of a job is hardly a career,' Lauren retorted finally. 'And aren't you the guy who tried to stop her doing even that?'

Point to Lauren. 'It is a career if she wants to continue managing it.'

Instantly, the atmosphere in the room changed from easy Sunday morning to ... *what the hell had he just said*? Slowly Jade turned to look at him. 'What do you mean?'

He was winging this, and he *never* winged. He thought long and hard before making decisions. 'You've shown me how the bookstore can benefit the resort. It can stay, and you can run it. If you want.'

'You're keeping it on?'

If it keeps you here. He couldn't say it. What if he showed his hand, only to be crushed, to have her reject him? Could he really risk going down that path again? And what about his dream, the one he'd been working towards his whole life? If he didn't knock the shop down, didn't build the cottages he'd planned, who the fuck was he turning into? The man who'd built Haven resorts was driven, determined. He didn't let anything get in his way. He'd created that man, knew him inside out.

The man Jade wanted him to be? The one who forgot about revenge, who worked with the community who hated him … he didn't know who that man was. And though he hadn't lied to her about wanting to find a different version of himself, he wasn't sure he could be *him*. 'It's something to think about.' Desperate to get away, he nodded towards the screen. 'Lauren, nice to meet you. I'll leave you guys to your chat.' He kissed Jade on the shoulder. 'See you later. And if you don't want your sister to get an eyeful of what you were playing with last night, I suggest you angle the phone.'

Chapter Thirty-One

Jeremy reached for Jade's empty glass and made a great show of turning it upside down before shaking his head and tutting.

The man was at his most mischievous this evening, no doubt aided by the three cocktails he'd already downed.

'What sort of guy are you, Boss Man, if you allow your date's cocktail to dry up?'

Liam, looking especially gorgeous tonight in a black open-collared shirt and charcoal grey jacket which made his eyes pop, sighed. 'I'm working.'

It was Saturday night and Jeremy had asked her and Liam to join him and Leroy in a wedding-planning session. Liam had immediately pulled the *I'm on duty* excuse, which Jeremy had just as immediately dismissed. *You're the boss man. You can work from the bar.*

'In which case, be a good best man and order another round of cocktails for us. And a water for yourself,' Jeremy added generously, causing another heavy sigh from Liam.

The man she'd spent every night with this last week, ever since the trip to see his grandma, slowly rose to his feet. 'Fine. But only if it gets me out of picking menus. And flowers. And cake. And fucking seating plans,' he added over his shoulder. Hands shoved into his trouser pockets, he ambled towards the bar.

'We won't be seeing him again for a while,' Leroy noted dryly.

Jeremy nodded and turned to her with a sly grin. 'Hopefully just enough time for us to interrogate our bookstore manager, starting with the most burning question. What did Operation Double BJ entail?'

She gawked at him. 'Sorry?'

'Ah, I'm not supposed to use that name. Such a shame, but he wasn't as impressed with it as I was.'

Leroy let out a low chuckle. 'I'm not sure which I find hardest to believe, that you asked him to be your best man, or that he accepted.'

Jeremy shrugged. 'He doesn't see it yet, but we're peas in a pod.' It was easy to laugh at the comparison yet Jade knew that beneath the light words was a serious acknowledgement that they'd both, in their different ways, been treated as outcasts. 'Speaking of vegetables, come on, spill the beans. How did he win you back?'

God, it was good to have friends. She'd only known these two for six weeks, yet Jeremy with his warmth and humour, and Leroy with his quiet interest, his steadiness, had rapidly become important to her. People she could talk to about anything, without judgement. 'He took me to meet his grandma.'

'Ah, the famous Pat Haven. Got to admire a woman who single-handedly brings up her grandson.' Jeremy studied her. 'So you're together now? Officially dating or just hooking up?'

Leroy groaned. 'Damn, my fiancé is a nosey son of a bitch. You don't have to answer, Jade.'

She laughed. 'I'm used to him by now. And yes, you could say we're officially dating, but...'

'You're only out here for three months.'

'Yep, and six weeks have gone already.' Her heart lurched. How was time racing away so quickly?

'Ever thought of staying longer?' Jeremy's question earned another groan from Leroy but Jeremy just grinned. 'Hey, you don't ask, you don't get to find out. And Jade's perfectly capable of telling me to mind my own business.'

'I am, but you've got the kind of adorable puppy expression that it's impossible to say no to, so to answer the question, yes, I have. Liam told me I could stay on and run the bookstore after the contract finishes, if I want.'

'He did?' Jeremy's face lit up. 'Well I'll be damned, sounds like the man is finally softening up a bit. So does that mean he's decided to keep the bookstore on?' He gave her a sly smile. 'Or does it mean he wants to keep *you* on?'

The squirmy feeling she'd had in her stomach ever since Liam had mentioned it, returned with a vengeance. 'I don't know.' She'd tried to talk to him again about what he meant, but he'd just repeated what he'd said that morning to Lauren, that if she wanted to stay and run the place, she could.

A warm hand settled on her shoulder. 'What don't you know?'

A few beats of silence met his question, and Jade's stomach fell. She didn't want to lie, but she did not want to discuss this now.

'She was telling me you said she could stay on at the bookstore after the contract is up,' Jeremy answered for her, correctly interpreting her bunny-in-the-headlights expression. 'I asked her if she wanted to.'

A muscle jumped in Liam's jaw. 'I thought we were here to discuss your wedding.'

'We are, but you disappeared and we knew you'd be upset if we made any plans without you.' Jeremy smiled sweetly and Jade smothered a laugh. But just when she thought they'd successfully navigated the subject that had never been far from her mind, Jeremy spoke again. 'Out of interest, have you made a decision to keep the bookstore, then?' Liam stared back at him, face impassive, and Jeremy winced. 'Ah, I can see it's not a subject up for discussion. It's just, as a founding member of the SOB group and also your deputy, I have a vested interest.'

'No decision has been made.' Liam exhaled heavily. 'I never thought I'd say this, but can we please now discuss your goddamn wedding?'

'No more talk about the bookstore, got it.' Jeremy reached into the bag by his feet and plonked a folder onto the table. 'Now, what do we think about a flamingo theme?'

Jade stifled her laughter.

'You've got to be kidding me.' Liam stared across at Leroy. 'Tell me you're more sensible.'

Leroy smiled and looked adoringly at his fiancé. 'Whatever Jeremy wants is fine by me.'

Jade felt a squeeze on her heart as Jeremy reached across the table and planted a smacker of a kiss on his husband-to-be's mouth. 'And that's one of the reasons why I love you. I'd go into all of the other reasons, but Liam might get even tetchier than he is now, so let's save it for later.' He glanced across at Jade. 'So, flamingo?'

'Of course. A perfect theme for a beach wedding.'

'Whales.' Liam levelled them both a look. 'Nantucket is all about whales.'

'But flamingos are pink.' She grinned back at Jeremy. 'Three votes for flamingos, motion carried. What's next?'

Beside her, Liam sighed. 'Fuck, this is going to be a long evening.'

'But you're here with your besties, and your…' She faltered, regretting opening her big mouth. They'd not given each other labels. 'With me.'

'My girlfriend.' His expression softened and he reached for her hand, raising it to his lips. The gentle kiss on her knuckles sent all the butterflies in her stomach into a spin.

Sex was easy between them – incredible, without doubt the best she'd ever had, but it didn't require anything more than acting on a primal, basic attraction. Affection, though, that was earned and very new. A simple look, a brush of fingers across her skin, the press of his palm on her back, holding her hand … the public gestures were every bit as heady as the passion that took place behind closed doors.

'Notice he didn't deny we're his besties.'

Jeremy's delighted voice cut through the moment, yet as Liam turned to reply, his hand curled around hers, resting them both on his thigh.

She tried not to read too much into his gestures, to live in the moment and not think into the future. As the days ticked down, though, as the time she had left on the island became less than the time she'd already spent, it became harder and harder not to panic.

Harder and harder not to think about postponing her flight home. Or even cancelling it altogether.

———

Liam sipped at his beer – he'd handed over to the night manager an hour ago – and gazed around the crowded bar as Jade continued to argue with Jeremy and Leroy about the way to make a cup of tea.

As if when the milk was added made the insipid drink any more appealing.

KATHRYN FREEMAN

It was the first time in years he'd been to a bar in Nantucket outside the resort and he couldn't shake the feeling that he was being watched. Scrutinised. Maybe it was paranoia.

Nope. The guy strolling up to their table was definitely staring him down.

'Liam Haven.' Grey hair, clothes that spoke of inconspicuous wealth, which was the Nantucket way. Anywhere else, people were impressed by labels, visible signs of wealth. On Nantucket, it was considered flashy. Gauche.

Liam nodded in greeting. 'Stuart Johnson.' He recognised Adam's father because he'd made it his mission to put a name and face to everyone on the island who'd deemed the Haven brand one they could dismiss, or ridicule.

If Stuart was surprised Liam recognised him, he gave no outward indication. 'What gives you the right to stop people using the wharf to dock their boats?' He looked towards Jade. 'And putting this young woman out of a job by knocking down the Little Bay Book Shack? Never mind whatever hideous plans you've got for the waterfront.'

He felt Jade stiffen and slid a hand onto her thigh, squeezing gently. *I've got this*. 'You own the Westside Club, yes?'

Stuart frowned. 'So?'

'How would you react if I told you what to do with it?'

'It's my damn club, I can do what I want with it.'

Liam inclined his head. 'And I own the wharf.'

Stuart grunted. 'You might have conned Flo into selling the bookstore to you, but it's been used by locals for years, and it's one of only two on the island. When are you going to stop destroying things we islanders hold dear?'

'With respect,' Jeremy interrupted. 'One of the things we islanders hold dear is our privacy and right now you're intruding on ours. You're also disrespecting a man in front of his friends, which doesn't seem like a sensible idea.'

Friends. Liam felt a burn at the back of his eyelids. It was like Jeremy had just thrown a protective wall around him.

Stuart looked incredulous. 'You're on his side now?' He nodded towards Jade. 'Aren't you two part of a group that campaigned to keep the bookstore?'

'Hi, Stuart. I'm Jade, good to meet you.' She gave him a sweet smile. 'You're right, I did set up a group to save the Little Bay Book Shack.'

'So what are you doing drinking with Haven?'

'Do you always see eye to eye with all of your friends?' She waved down at Stuart's wedding ring. 'Your wife?'

His expression faltered. 'Not always, no.'

'Then you'll understand that people can be friends, lovers, husband and wife, and still disagree on some things.'

'Yeah, but not when one of them is a jackass,' Stuart asserted.

Liam felt the anger vibrate through Jade's body. Anger on *his* behalf. 'Liam is quietly enjoying a night out with his friends. And his girlfriend,' she added loudly – and damn if his heart didn't cartwheel. 'You're the one who's stomped over here and thrown insults at him. Who's the jackarse?'

Liam found his lips twitching. 'Jackass,' he whispered under his breath.

She shrugged. 'He sounds like an arse to me.'

Stuart gave a disparaging shake of his head and sloped off. Liam could almost see a tail between his legs.

'Well.' Jeremy spoke into the silence. 'Never a dull moment when you're around, Boss Man.'

'Liam.' He felt some of the tension begin to leave his body. 'For God's sake, call me Liam.'

'Will do, Boss Liam. No, Liam Boss, that's better. Way more dignified.' Jeremy sprang to his feet. 'Right, more alcohol is called for.' He slid Liam a look. 'And as I know you generously put your card behind the bar, I'll get you one of those overpriced Macallans you're so fond of.'

Leroy slowly rose from the table. 'I'll come with you. Make sure you get it right.'

The moment they were out of earshot, Jade groaned. 'I'm so sorry.'

He was shocked to see tears brimming in her eyes. 'Why?'

'When I started that campaign, I didn't realise what a hornet's nest I was stirring up. Oh, sure, I knew at the first meeting that the group were there for more than the bookstore, but it was only later that some of them made it clear they didn't just want to stop you closing it, they wanted to stop you.'

'Shhh, it's okay.' He drew a hand down her cheek, feeling his body settle as she leaned into his touch. 'I deserve some of the hatred. Stopping people using the wharf to moor their boats was petty. You were right. I've been so focused on making Haven Resort the biggest and best resort on the island, I've been blind to who or what I'm trampling on in the process.'

'Are you saying you're going to keep Little Bay Book Shack?'

He gazed at her gorgeous face and felt his heart swell. Blonde and impossibly cute, but able to cut a rich bully down to size with an ease that left him humbled. 'I don't know what's going to happen between us, but I do know you fit here. If you choose to stay, the island would be lucky to have you. And if you can do for others what you did for Grandma, then the bookstore should stay.'

'And if I choose to go home, what happens to it then?'

It felt like a vice was crushing his chest. 'I don't know. I can't imagine anyone else running it.'

But he didn't want her to stay for the shop, he wanted her to stay for him.

'It would be good to keep it on, if you can,' she told him quietly. 'For the island, for the resort but also for you. Might make people like Stuart stay in their corner and not come out swinging.'

'I don't give a fuck about people like Stuart.' He swallowed. 'But I give a whole lot of fucks about you.' More than he'd planned, far more than was healthy for him. 'If you want the bookstore to stay, it stays, whatever you decide to do.'

Her smile melted his already embarrassingly mushed-up heart. 'Thank you.'

'Well, look who we found at the bar,' Jeremy interrupted, giving him a considering look before settling the drinks on the table – one beer, two pink coloured cocktails, one whisky.

He stepped aside to reveal Mary and Philip … and behind them, Adam. *This* was why he didn't go out in Nantucket. Too many reminders of his past. Too many people he didn't want to talk to.

'I've invited them to our wedding,' Jeremy continued, either oblivious to the tension currently zipping through the air, or uncaring. 'I told them to tell Emma and Claire to come, too. Thought we could have a little unofficial SOB gathering.'

Liam didn't need Jade's whispered, *can I?* She was almost bouncing with the need to announce it. He nodded and was rewarded with a radiant smile.

'Maybe we could turn the gathering into a celebration. Not to take away from your wedding, obviously,' she added, glancing at Jeremy and Leroy.

'Are you're going to say what I think you're going to say?' Jeremy cut in.

'You won't know if you keep interrupting her,' Leroy said dryly.

'Little Bay Book Shack is going to stay.' She squealed then, leaping to her feet and doing a silly dance, delight written across her face.

Jeremy let out a whoop and threw his arms around her. Mary,

who Liam would never have had down as a hugger, followed suit. Philip gave Jade a handshake, though even his smile was warm.

Adam bent to kiss Jade's cheek, and Liam felt the tension roll through him, every muscle tight and poised to fight. For her.

He expected them to ignore him but Mary caught his eye and inclined her head, raising her glass in salute.

Shocked, he acknowledged her gesture with a nod of his own.

'Jade got you to change your mind, did she?' Adam smirked over at him.

'Yes,' he retorted bluntly, earning him a rueful smile.

'Can't say I blame you for wanting to keep her sweet.' Adam took a sip of his wine and then, like Mary, raised his glass. 'Credit where credit's due. You made the right decision in the end.' He shrugged. 'Dad's still got beef with you, but from my side, we're quits. I was a shit to you when we were kids, you were a shit to me when you stopped me mooring my boat.' He glanced down at the glass of whisky. 'Why don't I buy you a drink and we'll bury the hatchet?'

'Fine. And you should know I'm shifting the private mooring sign on the wharf to the first two moorings on the left. Rest of it can be used by anyone. Johnsons included.'

Adam laughed and saluted him, too.

As the man walked to the bar to buy him a drink, Liam's gaze fell on Jade. She'd stuck up for him even when she'd not liked him, even when he'd been a prick to her. She'd also stood up to him, made him see the man he was turning into. 'Thank you,' he whispered.

The smile she shot him slipped right under his defences and wrapped tightly round his heart.

Fuck, he was sunk. How had he let her in so readily, in such a short space of time? He was either in massive denial, or the dumbest guy on the planet if he thought things would end any differently than they had with the other women he'd let into his heart.

His mom, April, Sabrina … they'd all left in the end. Hell, Jade even had one foot already on the plane.

And if I choose to go home. She'd not exactly leapt up and down with joy when he'd asked her to stay on and run the bookstore. Not like she had when he'd agreed to keep it on, regardless of what she did.

She loved the shop. Her feelings for him were much less clear.

Chapter Thirty-Two

J ade flipped the sign on the bookstore to *closed for an hour* and jogged along the waterfront towards the resort. The colours were so vibrant, the blue of the water in the harbour, the white of the boats, red of the walkway, green and pinks of the plants that burst out of the planters. Seagulls squawked overhead, the sun beamed down from a cloudless blue sky and the air was crisp with the smell of the ocean.

What a frigging awesome day.

She'd spent the morning replying to emails asking her to give a talk to various groups; the school, who'd just received an anonymous donation to build a new library, the new mother's group who were looking for book recommendations on the early years, and The Heritage Society, via Emma, who wanted to expand their reading into historical fiction. It was amazing how the bookstore had integrated into the community.

And she, Jade Taylor, still blonde, still inclined to clumsiness and dizzy moments, had led that change.

She wasn't just managing a business, she was expanding it. Thanks to the evenings Liam had spent taking her through

309

business planning and strategy, she even felt confident that she could replicate the success elsewhere. Okay, those fiddly spreadsheets weren't totally locked down, but Liam had agreed she'd tripled the sales compared to the same time last year.

Her phone buzzed with a message. From Liam.

> You have been spotted running away from your post. I hope you have a good reason. I hear the boss is an asshole.

Smiling to herself, she quickly typed back.

> He used to be an arsehole. Now he's very forgiving of his staff taking a quick break to calm the nerves of a groom-to-be 😬

Liam sent a face-palm emoji, then:

> Why does he get a visit and not the best man?

Her smile turned into a grin. The last few weeks Liam had definitely relaxed, let her see some of the man behind the very significant walls he'd built. There had been no declarations, not since he'd announced she could stay and manage the shop, if *she* wanted. Yet in little ways, she felt cared for. Appreciated. Like wanting to see her in the middle of the day even though they'd woken up together and would see each other tonight. Taking her to Smith's Point to watch the sunset. Hiring two bikes to cycle back to Sankaty Head Lighthouse because she'd not seen it properly the last time. Including her when he went to see his grandma. Patiently helping her put together the Little Bay Book Shop business plan even though she wasn't sure she would still be here to implement it.

Pushing the miserable thought to the back of her mind, she typed back a reply to Liam.

> Do you need help deciding where to put a dozen fibreglass flamingos?

Liam sent another face-palm then a message.

> If that's what it takes to get a visit from you, I'll buy a damn flamingo.

Oh yes, she felt wanted. It's just … he hadn't said he loved her. And time was marching on. Only two weeks before she was due back home and she really needed to make a decision. Could she leave her job, her family, on the whim of a *you can stay if you want?*

She'd achieved what she'd come to Nantucket to do. Could she risk her newfound confidence by hanging on here, when the reason she'd be staying was wrapped up in her feelings for him? What happened when he decided to get rid of the shop, get rid of her?

Her phone buzzed again. Liam.

> Am I buying a flamingo?

Laughter bubbled and she pushed the worries aside. They had no place interfering with such a glorious day.

> No need. YOU are enough. See you in a bit.

She hurried the rest of the way to the resort beach, the sight that greeted her enough to send the bubble of laughter whooshing straight out of her.

Waves lapped up the pale gold sand where Jeremy stood. Surrounded by a pile of pink flamingos.

'Don't say a word,' he cautioned as he spotted her. 'And nope, I don't want to see that big sunny smile, either. Or the twinkle in your baby blues. This is a legitimate emergency.'

She tried to school her features into that of concerned friend. 'Where's your fiancé? Shouldn't he be here to help?'

Jeremy pouted. 'He told me the flamingos were my idea so I had to sort them.'

'Ah, okay. And what, exactly, is the problem?'

'The problem is the stupid things keep falling over on the sand.'

'Right. And you need them to be on the sand rather than the grass because…'

'Because we're getting married on the beach.' He looked at her like *she* was the crazy one. 'That's the whole point of a beach wedding. Otherwise, it would be called a garden wedding, or a wedding near the beach.'

At the scrunch of footsteps on the sand they both twisted their heads around to find Liam strolling up to them, shaking his head. 'How many Haven Resort staff does it take to sort out a few pink birds?'

Her belly tumbled as his hot gaze fixed on her, the message clear. *Sort Jeremy out fast or I'll carry you out of here.* 'Three…' She cleared her throat, liquid warmth pooling between her thighs as his gaze darkened. 'Three staff,' she repeated. 'That's if you're joining us.'

'Oh, no.' Jeremy looked horrified. 'I don't want him hanging around, smouldering at you like some sex-starved adolescent. I saw the pair of you rocking that yacht this morning.'

Liam pinched the bridge of his nose. 'For the love of God, tell me the problem so we can fix it and I can get my girlfriend to myself.'

Jeremy frowned. 'You do know I'm gay and about to be married? No need for the possessive he-man act.'

Liam let out an exasperated breath and Jade giggled. 'You two should be on stage. You're the best comedy act out there.'

Jeremy took a bow. 'Thank you, but this situation is far from comedic. How am I going to make my flamingos stand on the sand?'

'Move them to the grass?'

Jade burst out laughing and Jeremy glared at Liam. 'We've been through this. It's a *beach* wedding, not a garden wedding.'

'Fine.' Liam waved at the area they were standing in. 'This is where you want to get married?'

'Yes.'

He tapped into his phone and held it to his ear. 'Mike, Liam here. Can you come and build me a deck on the beach this afternoon? Yes. Thanks.' He slipped the phone back into his pocket. 'Any more issues?'

Jeremy swallowed. 'Nope, that's it. I guess I'll just wait for Mike.'

'Right, good.' Liam marched up to her and clasped her hand. Smiling deeply into her eyes, he whispered, 'Grab your coat. You've pulled.'

The reminder of their early meetings, when they'd traded corny chat-up lines, elicited another bark of laughter from her. Immediately followed by a deep flip in her belly. 'Oh, goody.'

She held tight to his hand, leaning into him as they began to walk away. Why did it always feel like this? Thrilling, butterflies flapping, all combined with a giddiness usually only achieved with several cocktails on an empty stomach.

Suddenly, Liam halted and looked over his shoulder at Jeremy. 'By the way, you're in charge.'

'Yes, sir, Boss Man. Least I can do.'

Liam turned around. 'No, I mean you're in charge from now on. You're the new Resort Manager.'

Jeremy's jaw gaped open. 'You can't promote me just because you want to sneak off to do some horizontal tango-ing in the middle of the afternoon.'

'I can do what I like. I'm the boss.' Liam shrugged. 'To be clear,

I'm promoting you because you'll make a damn good resort manager. I'm doing it now so I can fuck my girlfriend in the middle of the afternoon.'

Jade did not want to think of the state of her underwear after hearing *that* statement.

'Well, that was super clear. Crystal.' Jeremy still looked stunned. 'Oh, and I forgot to thank you for the decking,' he shouted as Liam started marching in the direction of the hotel again. 'Enjoy your … 'lone time.'

Laughter vibrated through her. 'Where are you taking me?'

'Somewhere I can lock the door.'

Oh God. Her stomach swooped. Sex. It wasn't important enough to factor into her decision about whether to stay, of course it wasn't. She could live without, but living *with* it, when the man providing it had such an insatiable appetite for it, for her … it was terrifyingly addictive.

He slipped a key card out of his pocket and her heart picked up a pace. 'Here? In one of the hotel rooms?' Where any of the staff could spot them going in together. Coming out, all sex dishevelled. 'We can't do that.'

'Are you forgetting I own the place?'

Power, she thought dizzily as he opened one of the rooms with a quick, efficient movement. Why only now was she realising what a turn on it was?

He'd have to tell housekeeping to come back and change the sheets, yet as Liam threw his shirt back on, he didn't care how much the staff might gossip about his mid-afternoon activity. He'd needed to see Jade, and when he'd seen her, sexy as sin in her pink capris, he'd needed to have her.

Had some of his primal need to own her been down to

knowing Jeremy had been the recipient of her attention and not him? Yes.

And had some of it been down to the ticking clock that was sounding louder and louder in his head?

Without a doubt.

It was like he needed to pack a lifetime of being with her, into the next two weeks.

Unless she decided to stay.

Dragging on his pants, he zipped up before turning to help her fasten her bra. 'For future reference, I prefer taking it off.'

'I noticed.' She glanced down, pushed her fantastic tits further into the lace, and honest to God, he felt his dick twitch. It was like he was sixteen again, but with a major difference.

He was *happy*.

Tilting her head up to his, he stared into her pretty blue eyes. 'Have you made a decision yet?'

Her lids lowered. 'No.' She shifted away and bent to pick up her top from where he'd thrown it onto the floor. 'But it makes sense for me to use my ticket and go home, anyway, at least for a while.' Seemingly oblivious to the devastating hammer blow she'd just inflicted, she slipped the top over her head and stepped into her capris, her blonde tresses obscuring her face. 'I haven't seen my family in ages, and I need to catch up with work. Find out if it's even possible to extend my stay here.'

Extend her stay. 'So that's it, then?'

'Sorry?'

He forced his tone to stay measured, even. 'You won't even consider staying on permanently?'

'Of course I'm considering it.' Finally she met his eyes. 'But are you asking as my boss, or my boyfriend?'

His stomach lurched. He was being unfair, he knew he was. How could he expect her to make a life-changing decision based on knowing him a few weeks? 'Forget it. Of course you need to go back. Your life is there.'

'Is it?'

She held his gaze and his heart gave a violent twist. What was she asking him? And why was he so fucking terrified of finding out? In business he was blunt, got to the heart of the matter, yet standing here he felt naked, vulnerable. He wanted to ask her to stay, to make a life here with him, but the walls he'd spent a lifetime building and living behind couldn't be easily dismantled. It was one thing him knowing she'd snuck under them, another letting her know. He had to keep part of himself back. Otherwise, he wouldn't survive her leaving.

'Only you can answer that,' he answered quietly. 'If you want to stay, there's a job for you and a place to live.'

'And what about you? Will you be here for me?'

'Do you want me to be?'

She looked him square in the face. 'Yes.'

His heart tumbled in his chest. 'Then I will be.'

'For how long?'

For as long as you want me.

His walls were too strong to admit it, past experience shoring them up, pushing back against his desire to go down on his knees and beg her to stay. For him. For ever.

He could give her something to think about, though, and maybe it would be enough. 'That's an impossible question to answer,' he told her roughly, cupping her face. 'But you need to know that I care deeply for you. That I want you to stay. I want us to have more time together.'

Tears filled her eyes. 'I want more time with you, too.'

Hope danced around the edges of his consciousness, but he pushed it away because hope had got him into trouble before. 'You can't stay for me, Jade, or for what I can promise you, because I can't make those promises.' He heaved in a breath, touching his forehead to hers. 'I've never felt so unbalanced, like I'm spinning out of control, unravelling. In business I know exactly where I'm going, what I'm doing. Here, now, with you, I have no fucking clue about any of it. I'm terrified if you go home, you won't come back. But I'm also terrified if you come back, you won't stay. I don't know if I can open myself up to that rejection.'

She let out a shaky breath. 'I'm terrified that if I stay you'll become bored of me, or realise it was only about sex.' Her voice began to crack. 'Or you'll realise others were right after all and I'm just blonde and pretty with no substance. Then everything I've achieved here, the confidence I've gained, the belief in myself, will vanish and I'll be left broken-hearted and just plain broken.'

Christ. He'd spent so much time thinking of it from his side, he hadn't factored in her insecurities, her doubts. 'Don't we make a great couple.'

She let out a strangled laugh. 'I know.' Her lips brushed his. 'But at least we're talking to each other. If we keep doing that, and explaining how we feel, then we can get through this without hurting each other because I think we've both endured enough of that.'

He bundled her into his arms, squeezing tight, emotions spiralling. 'It won't be easy. I've spent my life hiding my feelings so I'm bound to fuck up.' He leaned back a little so he could look at her. 'If I do, you need to remember I would never intentionally hurt you. These last few months have been the happiest of my life, and that's the honest-to-God truth.'

'For me, too.' Suddenly, she stepped back. 'Crap, I've got to get back to the shop.' She gave him a tremulous smile. 'The boss doesn't like us skiving off in the middle of the day.'

'Really?' He drew in a breath, tried to steady himself. 'I thought he positively encouraged it. As long as the sneaking off is done with him.'

She smoothed a hand through her hair. 'How do I look?'

'Like a dream.'

Reaching onto her tiptoes, she pressed a kiss on his lips. 'Flattery will get you everywhere you want to go. See you later.' As she reached the door, she glanced over her shoulder. 'And don't forget, it's Jeremy and Leroy's stag do tonight.'

'Bachelor party,' he corrected. 'Do we have to go?'

'As best man, attending is the least you can do. You should have organised it.' Her eyes softened. 'But you did sort out his flamingos, so I think he'll forgive you.'

He snorted. 'Jeremy is far too much of a control freak to let someone else organise his night out.'

She winked. 'Is he? Or is he just careful about who he asks?'

'*You've* organised it?'

'Yep, and you can redeem yourself by swinging by the bookstore as soon as you're done for the day. We've got about a hundred flamingo-pink balloons to blow up, a few jugs of pink-flamingo cocktail to prepare, and a gazillion flamingo decorations to put up.'

With that she blew him a kiss and sashayed out. He watched her with a bemused smile and, despite the flamingo-fest ahead of him, a sense of cautious optimism.

It was possible that the end of her three months wouldn't mark the end of their time together, but instead be the start of a new, deeper relationship with no expiration date.

Chapter Thirty-Three

J ade breathed in a lungful of fresh sea air and relaxed against the cream leather seat at the back of the yacht … nope, aft. When she failed to get the lingo right, Liam would simply stare at her, eyes gently amused, until she corrected herself. Turns out it was quite an effective teaching method. If only her own teachers had employed it. Then again, it was likely only effective when the person doing the staring was a broodingly sexy guy she spent a disproportionate amount of time picturing naked.

Handsome man, blue sky; anticipation hummed through her. What a perfect start to her Sunday.

'Where are we going?' She glanced over at Liam, who was busy doing something with ropes. He'd tried to teach her, but as she'd pointed out, quite reasonably, why would she want to learn when it was such a treat to watch him work, forearms rippling with muscle, biceps bunching and relaxing?

He said something, but her brain was too focused on the sexy rope show. 'Sorry, what did you say?'

He gave her a knowing smile. 'We're going to the other side of the island. 'Sconset.'

'The most picturesque place on Nantucket. So I read.'

'I would agree.'

'Is that why you're building a house there?'

'It is. Plus, it's also the most exclusive place on the island.'

She rolled her eyes. 'Okay, Mr Money Bags.' She followed him through the salon to the bridge, noticing a couple of large cool bags. 'Are we having a picnic?'

'Do you want a picnic?'

'Definitely. I love eating sandwiches on the beach. I'm sure that's where they get their name from. I bet they started off as wiches, but were renamed after they were eaten on the beach and everyone realised it was impossible not to get sand in amongst the cheese and pickle.'

'They're named after the Earl of Sandwich.'

'Ha, I knew that.' She winked at him. 'Just checking you did.' He laughed, and it was hard not to swoon. He made her heart flutter when he was serious, but when he relaxed, when that laugh came out to play, he was devastating. 'What if I'd said I didn't want a picnic?'

He pushed a lever and the boat eased away with a smooth surge of power. 'Then I'd have asked what you did want.'

'And we'd have done that?'

'Yes.'

How on earth was she supposed to keep from falling in love with a man so hellbent on pleasing her? 'Lucky for you, I'm a cheap date.'

His intense grey eyes rested on hers. 'There is nothing cheap about you.'

Holy mackerel. 'You're good at this.'

'What?'

'Making me feel good, yet really, really turned on at the same time.'

'I'll keep the turned-on bit in mind.'

Her belly did another low flip. 'So...' She cleared her throat and tried again. 'So we're having a picnic on the beach. Any other plans? I'm wearing my bikini, in case swimming is involved, and in my beach bag I've got a towel and my book in case sunbathing is part of the deal.'

'Wearing the bikini is a given. Anything else we do is up to you.'

'But I have to be in the bikini.'

'For at least some of the day, yes.'

'Sounds reasonable, as long as you're in trunks. No T-shirt.'

He flicked her a look. 'That can be arranged.'

'Good. Equality at last.'

He gave a little shake of his head, but she noticed his mouth curve upwards.

A little while later the beach came into view, flanked by rugged cliffs and rolling dunes. He drew the boat to a stop and dropped the anchor.

She gazed across at the beautiful stretch of deserted sand opposite, waves lapping gently up to it. 'Is this the part where we swim to shore?'

'If you like, but I'm taking the dinghy.'

She felt like she was in one of Enid Blyton's adventures as he stowed the cool bags into the small dinghy and then helped her on board. 'Oh, no oars.' She mock pouted as he started the small motor. 'I was looking forward to seeing your rowing prowess. Plus watching your muscles ripple.'

'I thought you'd done that earlier, with the ropes.'

She sighed dreamily. 'You noticed, huh? But surely my viewing isn't rationed.'

He looked bemused for a moment, and then let out a low laugh. 'Fuck, you're good for my ego.'

She was about to argue that his ego didn't need any help, but then remembered the difficult childhood he'd had, the way he'd been cruelly ditched because he hadn't been rich enough, and decided she was glad she'd massaged it.

He cut the engine and leapt into the knee-high sea, pulling the dinghy out of the water and onto the sand before helping her out. 'Wow, this beach is beautiful. And there's no one on it.' Her gaze drifted ahead, to a huge grey house surrounded by a white picket fence, with steps down to the sand. When she turned back to Liam, she saw he was watching her. 'Oh, my God, that's it, isn't it? Your new house?'

He nodded. 'It was finished two days ago.' He lifted a set of keys out of his pocket. 'Want a tour?'

And that's when she realised why he'd been so cagey about today. He'd wanted to show her his house. Unbelievably touched, she smiled and reached to kiss him. 'Do the Brits love tea?'

They strolled up the steps, Liam carrying the cool bags while she took it all in. It wasn't the only house along the beach, but there was enough space between them that it felt like it was. He'd kept to the Nantucket tradition of grey shingles with white trim, the steps leading up to a wide porch, rose bushes planted along the right side.

'Grandma's got her own entrance.' He pointed to an attached wing. 'I would have built her more, but she was happy with a kitchen, bedroom, living room and bathroom.' He smiled. 'And a door that gives her access into the main house.'

'Adam called it your fuck-off mansion,' she murmured as he pushed open the front door to let her in.

'I'm not interested in what he thinks.' Liam dropped the cool bags on the floor and turned to her. 'I want to know what you think.'

'Bloody hell, Liam.' She walked around the ground floor in a daze, peeking into the rooms one by one. White walls, dark wood floors, feature grey-stone fireplace. Giant windows that overlooked the sea. 'It's incredible. Tasteful. Homely, but with a giant dollop of blow your socks off.'

She wandered into the huge kitchen, all white wooden units, chrome range cooker and luxury white-marble worktop streaked with grey.

When she turned, she found him staring at her, an expression on his face that was hard to read. But then his eyes fell to her mouth, and when they met her eyes again, what he was thinking was obvious.

Obvious enough to make her breath catch.

'Would you like to see upstairs? To be clear, I mean the master bedroom.'

She swallowed. 'Yes please.'

She gasped as he swept her into his arms, heart pounding as he carried her easily up the stairs. Burying her face in his neck, she wondered how on earth she was going to walk away from this, from him.

Yet how could she stay, when everything between them was so uncertain? One change of his mind and she'd lose her job, her accommodation, possibly her self-respect because who gives up their life on a hope and the whim of one man?

She'd also lose her heart, forever buried in Nantucket. Never to be seen again.

Liam watched as Jade filled the kettle with water and bent over the range cooker, pressing buttons until she found the way to ignite the gas.

Fuck, she looked exactly like he'd imagined she would. As

soon as the builder had confirmed it was completed, he'd needed to show her. He didn't know why, only that he'd wanted to see her standing in his home in her bikini top and tiny denim shorts.

But now he had, he knew the image would be forever imprinted on his mind. He wouldn't be able to walk in here and not see her. Even when she was thousands of miles away.

'Here.' He rummaged in the cooler and brought out a box of teabags. He'd arranged for all the essentials to be delivered; beds, bedlinen, towels in the bathrooms, a sprawling sofa, televisions, dishware, pans and utensils for the kitchen. The rest he'd add to in time. 'And you might want this.' He slid the teapot he'd bought onto the granite island, took out the pastries and bread rolls and then walked over to the fridge to dump the rest of the contents of the cooler; breaded chicken, cold meats, milk, beer, wine, salad boxes.

He heard a gasp, and turned to find her holding the teapot, a look of awe on her face. 'You bought me a teapot?'

He shrugged, like it was no big deal. Like he hadn't scoured the island to find one, before giving up and getting a local potter to make him one instead. 'Figured it might make that hot water more appealing.' She inhaled a shaky breath, and damn if she didn't look like she was about to cry.

'Holy cow, it's a worm.' She sniffed, her hand tracing the daft creature he'd asked the potter to incorporate into the design. 'A worm holding a book.' She lifted her eyes to his, and the blue glistened. 'You didn't just buy me a teapot, you had one made for me.'

'Teapots aren't in high demand here, apparently.'

She carefully placed the teapot back onto the granite island before leaping into his arms. 'Thank you. That is the most thoughtful thing anyone has ever given me.'

'Jesus, Jade.' He shifted them so his hands were under her perfect ass. 'You deserve more than a freaking teapot.'

I'd give you the world.

She was warm and curvy in his arms, her eyes bright with delight, lips curved with pleasure, but the words were stuck in his throat. For too long he'd had to protect himself, to live with the mantra of not letting anyone see how he felt, he wasn't sure he could live any other way.

Maybe he'd find his bravery before she left.

'Don't disrespect the teapot,' she admonished. 'It's perfect.'

And so was the day, he thought later as they sat on the beach together, remnants of their picnic shoved back into the cooler. They'd been for a swim, Jade had her bikini on. His hangover from Friday's Bachelor party had finally subsided. All was well with the world.

'What are you looking for?' he asked mildly as she started to pull everything out of the beach bag she'd brought with her. Towel, hat, sunscreen, some lightweight see-through thing he thought might be a sarong, bag of… 'Gummy bears?'

'Of course. Can't have a day trip without sweets… Ah, there they are.' With a triumphant yelp, she dug two books out of the bag and pushed one over at him. 'This is yours.'

He glanced at the front cover. 'I told you, I don't read.'

'But you also asked me to recommend a book to you.'

'That was when I was trying to win you over.' He looked down at the book again, and then at her face, the eyes that held a touch of disappointment. 'Sorry, that was rude.'

'It's okay. Books aren't for everyone.'

She reached to take the book away, but he held on, aware that if he was to have any chance of winning her over permanently, he needed to open up. 'I've always resented books. Grandma used to disappear into one for hours, and then she'd emerge, misty eyed, telling me about the lives of the people she was reading about, often involving travel, usually a romance.' He felt the familiar tightening of his throat as he tried to push past the memory. 'I grew to hate the reminder that I was cramping her style, stopping her from living the life she could have had if she hadn't had to bring me up.'

Compassion swamped her eyes. 'You know she adores you, don't you? That if you were to ask her to choose between travelling the world or being with you, she'd choose you every time.'

'Maybe.'

'Oh, my God, you ninny. *Definitely*. I've seen the pair of you together, remember.'

He suspected she was right so he let it go and focused back on the book. 'Why this one?'

'It's a thriller, which I figured was probably your genre as you like to work things out, but it's set in the world of finance.' She smirked. 'I know how interested you are in money.'

He studied the back cover, wasn't sure if it would be his thing or not, but that wasn't the point. 'You bothered to choose me a book.' *That* was the point. 'The least I can do is read it.'

And that was how they spent the next couple of hours, reading together, her lying on her back, using his chest as a pillow. They stayed until the sun set, filling the sky with a pallet of oranges, pinks and reds. There was nothing quite like a Nantucket sunset, as it was a 360 view.

'Today has been epic,' Jade told him as they headed back later that evening.

He held her gaze. 'It's not over yet.'

She laughed. 'I say yay to that, but before you turn my brain to mush again with your dirty sex talk, I wanted to thank you for sharing your new home with me. It was … I was…' She huffed. 'Okay, I'm going to sound cheesy, and maybe too much, but it was an honour to be let inside, to see that glimpse of you.'

She was honoured? 'I wanted to show it to you. Wanted to see you in it.' He took her hand and raised it to his mouth, dropping a kiss on her knuckles. 'Your opinion of it mattered to me. *You* matter.' It was as far as he could go, at least for now.

His bravery was rewarded when her eyes shone, the blue deepening as she tightened her hand around his. And just when he thought the day couldn't get any better, she whispered. 'You matter to me, too.'

Chapter Thirty-Four

Jade didn't think anything would be able to beat the sight of Jeremy and Leroy exchanging vows on the beach – correction: on the decking, on the beach – surrounded by flamingos and a wedding party who'd all been instructed to wear something pink.

As if it had been ordered to, the sun had set at the perfect time, creating a beautiful rose-pink hue to the sky and a deliciously romantic light for the photographs.

'It clashes with your hair,' Leroy had murmured dryly to an ecstatic Jeremy, who'd waxed lyrical about how he'd always planned for the pink theme so it would match the sunset. The besotted expression on Leroy's face had told their guests he wouldn't have his new husband any other way.

But then there had been Liam's best-man speech. As expected, it had been short and to the point, ending with him saying Jeremy and Leroy weren't just employees, they were friends.

'But I'm your best friend,' Jeremy had asserted, giving Liam a big wink.

To the surprise of everyone, Jeremy included, Liam hadn't just smiled, he'd nodded. 'You're my best friend.' Then he'd added, 'But remind me of this tomorrow, and I'll deny it.'

Now the night was in full swing and the heart-melting moments kept coming. Jeremy's expression when he saw the flamingo fairy lights strewn up across the bar. Jeremy and Leroy doing their first dance together. The whole happy vibe as all their friends and family joined in.

And a new highlight, she thought, a low sizzle beginning in her belly as Liam strode towards her, looking like he'd stepped out of a World's Hottest Men in a Tux photoshoot.

He drew her purposefully into his arms, lips brushing her ear. 'Did I tell you how gorgeous you look?'

Emotion clogging her throat, she smoothed her hands down his shirt. 'Did I tell you how much you rock a flamingo bow-tie?'

He smiled. 'I was going to say you can say what you like, I'm never wearing it again. But maybe I can give you a private viewing.'

She pictured Liam, wearing nothing but the bow-tie and a sexy smoulder and promptly tripped over her own feet. It earned her a low chuckle. Totally worth it.

It was times like this she forgot she'd be heading home in a week. In fact she'd spent the last few days forgetting a lot of things. Like the fact they'd both expressed feelings for each other, but neither had really showed their full hand. Maybe it was down to her to be the brave one. She was the one who had to decide whether or not to return. Whether to give up life in Twickenham, for life in Nantucket. A life close to her family, or a life with new friends. A publishing assistant or a bookshop manager. A single woman, or a woman dating an extraordinary yet complex man whose hard shell protected the vulnerable boy.

Suddenly, she felt Liam grow rigid. When she glanced up, she saw his expression had turned harsh, his jaw tight. 'What is it?'

'I didn't realise he was invited.'

She followed his gaze and frowned. 'Oh, you mean Henry. I'm not sure he was, because I don't think Jeremy likes him very much. Maybe one of the SOB team told him about it. I know his dad owns the Chase Resort, but have you two ever actually met? I can introduce you if you like.'

'No,' he replied curtly, all the warmth gone from his face, leaving hard lines and a wintry stare.

She flinched. 'I wasn't planning on telling him we were sleeping together, if that's what's got your boxers in a twist.'

He looked incredulous. 'Have I ever given you the impression I *don't* want people knowing?'

He'd introduced her to his grandma, held her hand at every opportunity, danced with her tonight in a way that made it clear they were intimate. 'Then what's wrong?'

She didn't have time to hear his answer, because Henry had spotted them. Holding the hand of a beautiful brunette in an elegant turquoise bias-cut silk dress, he marched towards them, a fixed smile on his face.

'Jade. Have you met my girlfriend, Sabrina?'

No, it couldn't be. Yet from the tension radiating off Liam, the way he'd reached for her hand and was gripping it like it was the only thing keeping him upright, she knew the name wasn't just a coincidence. 'Hi.' She smiled awkwardly at the other woman.

Henry turned to Liam. 'I believe the pair of you are already acquainted.'

Liam stared back, stony-faced and silent.

'I didn't know you were coming,' Jade ventured into the wildly uncomfortable silence. Holy shit, Liam's ex looked like a frigging supermodel, all long-limbed sophistication and unnerving confidence. One glance at her own dress and it suddenly felt too tight, too short. Too low cut. Too *tarty*.

'I heard from Philip that the SOB team were getting together, so I didn't want to miss out. Especially as we're celebrating.'

Henry glanced around him, spotting the DJ behind them. 'In fact, let's do this properly.'

Jade held her breath, an ominous feeling settling over her. 'I don't like this,' she whispered, but it was like Liam had left and a cold, marble statue taken his place.

'Excuse me one minute, everyone,' Henry announced into the microphone. 'I'd like to add my own personal congratulations to Jeremy and Leroy. I hope they'll forgive me hijacking their wedding for a moment to also recognise this lady,' he waved a hand over in Jade's direction. 'The blonde in the … charming pink dress.'

Ouch. Not just the words, but the way he said them. Anger burned in her stomach even as her eyes pricked with tears she was absolutely not going to shed.

'Jade is more than her hair colour.' Liam's voice cracked through the air. 'If you don't realise that, you're more ignorant than I thought.'

'I do realise it.' Henry smirked over at Liam. 'Because Jade has managed to do what many of us had feared was impossible.' He paused, checking he had the attention of the wedding party. 'She's forced Liam Haven to change his mind about knocking down our quaint, much loved bookstore.' A cheer went up around the group. 'According to my source, he's also scrapped his plans to expand the hotel onto the waterfront. Of course if he thinks this will change how many feel about him, we should remind him we have long memories. Who can forget how he bought up a beautiful part of our island only to ruin it by turning it into a flash modern resort? Or more recently, how he stopped us from mooring our boats on the wharf next door? But at least this action has shown he will buckle under pressure.' Henry's eyes found hers. 'So here's to you, Jade. Whatever womanly spell you put on the man, we all thank you for it.'

A murmur went through the group and suddenly she was

surrounded by people congratulating her and asking her about the shop. She wanted to escape, to run up to Henry and shove at him for being so frigging rude, so condescending. For making her feel like some cheap strumpet who'd used sex to get Liam to change his mind.

Yet whatever her humiliation, for Liam it was worse.

An arm slid around her waist, and she jerked around, only to find Jeremy. He took one look at her and swore colourfully. 'Excuse us everyone, I'm taking Jade away. Groom's prerogative.'

'I don't know what Henry's doing here,' he muttered as he led her away from the crowd and towards the relative quiet of the beach. 'I didn't invite him.'

'He said something about Philip mentioning the SOB group getting together.' Jade halted and stared back at the bar. 'Where's Liam? I can't see him.' Her heart began to race. 'I need to see him. This is all my fault. If I hadn't put together that group—'

'I was the reason Henry joined the SOB group,' Jeremy cut in. 'If Liam's throwing out blame, I'm ahead of you.'

'What did Henry mean about the waterfront?'

'I don't know. I don't think the boss has got the concept of besties yet. Still keeps everything to himself.'

'Henry made it sound like I slept with Liam to get him to change his mind. However awful and degrading that looks for me, it's a thousand times worse for Liam. Like he's weak enough, stupid enough, to have his head turned by me.'

Jeremy gave her an affectionate smile. 'His head *has* been turned by you, and he's neither weak nor stupid.' He laughed ruefully. 'I also imagine he's heard worse insults.'

Her heart twisted. 'That's exactly the point. He's going to take this so hard.'

'But this time he's not alone. He's got us to support him.'

Jade could only hope that would be enough. 'I think I know where he's gone.'

Jeremy kissed the top of her head. 'Then go to him.'

He'd been here before. Started to feel accepted, even loved, and it had all been a fucking illusion.

As he sat on the top deck of the yacht, his mind tortured him with flashbacks.

Elementary school on the island, classmates looking at him strangely. 'How come your mom left you? Can't have liked you much.'

Boarding school, and Henry and his friends laughing in his face when he asked to join in their card game. 'Like you can afford it. We don't play with Monopoly money, we play with the real stuff.'

April, when he'd overheard her laughing with her friends. 'The sex is great, but I'm dumping him soon. I mean, he doesn't even have a boat.'

Sabrina giving him that cruel smile he'd not realised she was capable of. 'Sorry, but Dad says I can do much better. And I think he's right.'

He tightened his fingers around the whisky glass. The fact Henry's slurs had hurt, was entirely his own fault. Sure, the way Henry had painted it was wrong, but the sentiment was the same. Jade *had* put a spell on him. Thanks to her, he'd changed plans that had been years in the making. Hell he'd even started to open up, let people in… His stomach clenched, acid burning at the lining.

He should have known better. The moment he lowered his defences, he got shafted.

'I thought I'd find you here.'

He forced his body to stay still and not leap up and cling to her, like it wanted to.

Jade walked slowly towards him, shapely legs shifting beneath the short pink dress that fitted her curves so perfectly. Gorgeous, stunning, sexy as fuck.

But going home next week.

She slid next to him on the sun pad, and memories of the first time they'd sat there crashed through his mind. Memories he couldn't afford, because it was time to pull up the drawbridge, to lock down his defences. Put himself into protect mode.

'That was … awkward.'

'Brutal,' he corrected, taking a moment to study her face, the lines of tension. The telltale red rim around her eyes. A reminder he hadn't been the only one humiliated tonight. 'Your dress isn't charming, it's perfect, shows off your killer body but also makes you look vibrant, confident. A woman embracing her sexuality. You're not a blonde, you're an inspiring, strong, magnetic, vivacious woman who happens to have blonde hair. You didn't put a spell on me, you showed me how to be a better man with courage, creativity and ingenuity.' He hung his head, disgusted with himself. 'I should have said all that out there. I'm sorry I didn't.'

'Don't be. You've said it now.' Her body leant against his and he inhaled her scent, feeling a brief moment of comfort, of rightness. 'Sabrina was your ex.'

It wasn't a question, but he answered anyway. 'Yes.' And because he knew Jade, he added. 'She's as shallow as she looks.'

He watched Jade fight not to smile. 'I thought she looked elegant. Willowy, like a model.'

'I thought she looked skinny. Cold. A good match for Henry.'

A huff of laughter left her and she reached for his hand. 'Now we've put my jealousy to bed, tell me why Henry hates you so much.'

He raised his head to look at her. 'You can probably guess.'

Her eyes searched his. 'He was part of the gang that Adam was in, the gang at boarding school?'

'He was the unofficial leader, yes.'

'But that doesn't explain why he hates you. It can't just be because you were poor.'

He'd told Jade so much already, it seemed petty not to tell her everything. Starting from tomorrow, he'd shore up his defences again. 'His father slept with my mother.'

'Oh … *oh*. You're half-brothers.'

'We share some DNA,' he corrected. 'Henry's father has never acknowledged me as his son. He paid my mother off and then washed his hands of both of us. I'm the reminder to Henry that his family isn't perfect. I'm also the reason his parents split up.'

She fell quiet, but her hand was still wrapped tight around his and between that, and the gentle sway of the boat, some of the bitterness began to recede.

'You're not the reason,' she said finally. 'His father being a cheating bastard is the reason.'

He let out a humourless laugh. 'Not the way Henry sees it.'

'So that's why you're so driven to make money. Not just to stick two fingers up at rich bullies, but to let Chase senior see what he'd missed out on. To make your resort bigger and better than his,' she added.

He could almost see the wheels turning in her mind as she pieced all these jagged parts of him together.

'I needed them all to see I was somebody. Not just a person they could ignore, walk away from. Reject.' As his voice choked on the last word, he wondered if it sounded as pathetic to her as he feared. 'This guy you've been seeing, the successful businessman who has his life together? It's a fucking illusion. Inside I'm an angry kid with a giant chip on my shoulder.'

'No.' She clasped his hands with both of hers and squeezed tight. 'You might be a man people have tried to ignore, to put down, but you're resilient. You didn't crumble under what they did to you, you became a winner, not a victim. A man who built a frigging company from nothing, using only his wit, his drive, his strength. Flipping heck, can't you see how bloody awesome you are?'

The words soothed, his wounds feeling less raw. Grateful, he bent to kiss the top of her head.

The buzz of her phone cut through the moment and she sighed, diving into her fluffy, pink candyfloss of a handbag. 'That will be the groom, wanting an update.' She tapped the screen and read out the message.

> Have you found him? Please tell me you have and he's not thrown himself off the wharf. FYI: we strong-armed Henry out of the resort. For 'we', read Leroy. I provided encouragement and a piece of my mind.

Despite his gloom, he managed a smile.

'Oh, wait, there's another one.' Jade's eyes scanned the screen.

> PS. Philip says Liam's revised plans are for affordable housing on the waterfront. I told this to Mary. Expect news to have filtered round the island by tomorrow lunchtime. Ditto the fact Henry was out of date and the resort wharf can be used for general mooring. Oh and I found out Haven Resorts is funding a library for the school. The boss tried to keep it anonymous but it's time island gossip was Haven positive. If he isn't happy, tough. I'm a boss too now.

She looked up at him. 'I'm going to have to reply. If I don't he'll continue to blow up the phone.'

'It's his wedding day. Surely he's got better things to do.'

Her phone buzzed again. 'Want to bet?' She glanced down at it.

If you've found him and are currently bumping uglies, tough. I'll keep interrupting until you reply.

'Christ.' It was embarrassing how touched he was. 'Put him out of his misery.'

Jade smiled and typed something into her phone before jamming it back into her handbag. When she met his eyes again, the affection he saw there nearly flattened him. 'Affordable-housing, donations to the school. You did good, Liam Haven.'

'A wise person once told me I was turning into a rich arrogant prick. Thought it was about time I did something to reverse it.'

Her expression softened, eyes shining with something that looked an awful lot like pride. 'So, what now?'

You go home and I get on with my shallow life and try, hopelessly, to forget you.

'Do you want to head back to the wedding,' Jade continued, watching him carefully, or—'

'Or.' He rose to his feet and gave her his hand. 'I choose or.'

Chapter Thirty-Five

S he knew all about the elephant in the room, but this was the airline reservation on the coffee table.

Jade watched as Liam's gaze slid over to it. She'd offered to cook him a meal tonight and, knowing he would see it, she'd printed out her reservation and placed it on the table, next to the bowl of nuts. Every time, over the last few days, when she'd raised the fact she was going home, he'd quickly changed the subject.

It was now Thursday. She was flying out on Saturday.

She needed to know if she'd be saying goodbye, or see you again soon.

Handing him his beer, she glanced pointedly at the reservation. 'I could cancel it.' There. She'd got hold of the elephant and dragged it right in front of their noses.

His jaw muscle twitched. 'No, you should go.'

'Okay.' She tried to keep her voice steady, but it was impossible when disappointment weighed so heavily inside her, her knees threatened to buckle. 'And what about coming back. Do you think I should do that?'

'I think you should do whatever you want to do.'

Frigging hell. She wanted to grab him by the shoulders and shake him. 'Okay, let's put it another way. Do you want me to come back?'

There was a flare of irritation in the eyes that briefly met hers. 'Of course I do. I've already told you that.'

In keeping with how he'd been the last few days, ever since Henry had taunted him with both his words and the perfectly gorgeous Sabrina on his arm, Liam had retreated behind an invisible gate, blocking her from getting close. 'Why?'

'Why do I want you to come back?'

'Yes.'

He exhaled sharply, leaning forward, arms on his knees. 'We've been through this. I care for you. I enjoy your company. Plus, you've made this big fuss of keeping the bookstore open.'

'Oh, my God, sod the bookstore, what about us?' Frustrated, fearful, she plonked herself down next to him. 'We promised to keep talking to each other, but these last few days you've closed up. How am I supposed to make a life-changing decision when you won't discuss how you feel?'

His eyes refused to meet hers. 'What I feel is that you need to go home, pick up your life and work out for certain what you want before you make any big plans.'

'Right, okay.' Calm, she told herself, and inhaled a deep breath. 'What I feel is that you're pushing me away.' She touched his cheek, forcing his eyes to meet hers. 'Is that what you're doing?'

'I don't know what the fuck I'm doing.' He exhaled harshly. 'You're asking for something I can't give you. Asking me to make myself vulnerable when I've spent the vast majority of my life trying to make sure of the opposite.' He jumped jerkily to his feet. 'Jeremy can find one of the resort staff to manage the bookstore while you think about what you want to do.'

This was not how she'd envisaged her last few days going. Not after the closeness of the previous weeks. 'I get that you're protecting yourself, but this shield you've put up, it's hurtful. You're acting like you're not bothered what I do, not bothered if you never see me again. Not bothered about *me*.' Emotion lodged in her throat like a boulder. 'And I swore not to let a man make me feel I wasn't good enough ever again.'

He slammed his eyes shut, cursed. 'You're more than good enough. That's not what this is about.'

'Then what is it about?'

His gaze flew to hers. 'It's about being realistic, Jade. You've been here three months, half of which you spent hating me. It's hardly a stable foundation for a life-changing decision.' He dragged a hand through his hair in a jerky movement. 'If you want to come back because of the island, because of the friends you've made, the bookstore, that's different.'

'So I can come back and work for you, but not come back *for* you?'

'Fuck, Jade, I can't let myself think about us.' His gaze, when it finally met hers, was a mixture of bleak and tortured. 'You think I'm not acutely aware how easy it's going to be for you to forget me the moment you get off that plane and return to your real life?'

She let out a strangled laugh. 'You are not a man anyone can easily forget.'

'Oh no?' His expression turned harsh. 'Ask my mother. Or my father.'

And there it was, the pain he hid. A pain that was going to prevent her from ever being allowed into his heart. 'You've named two people who never bothered to get to know you.' Her own heart felt impossibly heavy as she stood to face him. 'If they had, they would see what I see. A man it's so easy to love, it's ridiculous.' She reached for her courage. 'I'd be happy, no *ecstatic*, to stay if you asked me to. But you don't want to know that, do you? You'd rather hide behind your wall of hurt and tell yourself you're being sensible, protecting us both, when really all you're doing is condemning yourself to a life half lived. And me to a life of missing you.' Sadly, she bent to pick up his jacket and handed it to him. 'I hope one day you'll find someone worth ditching that hiding place for. Meanwhile, we should say goodbye.'

He looked stunned. '*Now?*'

'Yes, now. Let's not have a slow, drawn-out death.'

He took the jacket from her, hands gripping it so tight she could see his knuckles turning white. 'I'm not ready to say goodbye.'

'No? Then you need to work on giving out better signals because right now the only one I'm getting is that I don't matter enough for you to shift out of your comfort zone.' She stared him straight in the eye. 'I'm willing to come back, to fight for us. But I deserve a man who's willing to fight in return.' With that, she reached up and planted a gentle kiss on his mouth. 'Forgive me if I don't see you out. I'm trying not to break down and blubber in front of you but I can guarantee if I have to wave you off, it will end in a mess of snot and tears. I refuse to let that be the last image you have of me.'

He swallowed, gaze raking her face, his eyes a dark storm cloud. Then he sighed, and drew her into his arms. She felt his lips press the top of her head. 'This isn't what I want.'

'Then send me a clearer signal.' The tears were massing, burning her eyelids. She didn't want to listen to words of hope, when the last few days had only ever screamed hopeless. 'Now go, before I embarrass both of us.'

She turned round, squeezing her eyes shut as she listened to the sound of his footsteps down the stairs. It was only when she heard the click of the door that she opened them.

She was steady as she picked up the undrunk beer, the bowl of nuts. Steady as she turned off the oven and took out the lasagne. Steady right until she spotted the bookworm teapot sitting on top of the worktop. Then she crumbled to the floor and let the tears flow.

Liam told himself it wasn't being cowardly. Nantucket had taken his total focus for the last three months but now he had a resort manager in place – something he'd dragged his heels for far too long over when the solution had been obvious – it was time to check on his other two resorts.

So after a night of tossing and turning – the sleepless nights, absent while he'd been sharing a bed with Jade, had made a grim return – on Friday morning he headed the yacht in the direction of Cape Cod. There he met with his management team and for an hour he forgot all about Jade and the fact she was leaving tomorrow.

Her and her damn signals. What did she want from him? He'd been the one to ask her to stay in the first place, hadn't he? He might have told her to go home, but he'd also said he wanted her to come back.

'Liam?'

Fuck, he'd totally zoned out. 'Sorry, can you repeat the question?'

The resort manager, Hank, gave him a quizzical look. 'Is everything okay? You seem … distracted.'

'I'm fine,' he barked. Since when had he ever discussed anything other than work with these guys, anyway?

Hank nodded, repeated the question and as the meeting rolled on, he tried not to imagine Jade frowning at him in disappointment. He also refused to think of her when he apologised to Hank afterwards, telling him he was dealing with a personal issue.

He spent the afternoon at the Edgartown resort in Martha's

Vineyard, where the aforementioned lack of sleep and whisky overdose from the night before began to finally kick in.

By the time he dropped in on his grandma, his head was throbbing and he just wanted to crash. What he didn't want was a message from Jeremy.

> Jade changed her flight, she's going home today. Presume this is your doing?

Angry with him for the dig, and Jade for fucking *leaving*, he stabbed out a reply.

> She's a grown woman, capable of making her own decisions.

Jeremy's response didn't pull any punches.

> I hope, being a grown man, you let her make that decision with full knowledge of the facts? In other words, you didn't chicken out of telling her how you felt?

Liam turned off his phone in disgust. And wished he could turn off the replay of last night just as easily.

'Oh dear, what's happened?' His grandma gazed at him worriedly as she opened the door.

'Nothing's happened. I've spent the day either in meetings or travelling between meetings.'

She humphed. 'Something you've spent your working life doing. What else has happened?'

'Jeremy messaged to say Jade's gone home today, that's all. It leaves us scrambling to replace her.'

'I see.' The look she gave him told him she saw right through him.

He shifted awkwardly. 'Actually, you don't. She was always going home, so this put it forward a day, that's all.'

He tried not to flinch as she studied his face. 'Is she coming back?'

'I don't know. I doubt it.'

'Did you ask her to?'

'Of course.' Maybe he'd gone about it in a half-assed way, but he was done being rejected. Fucking done. Even if he'd dropped to his knees and pleaded with her to return, how long before their relationship fizzled out? Before she realised she could do a lot better than the emotionally stunted local pariah?

'Did you tell her you loved her?'

Oh, no. He wasn't doing this. Moving past her, he walked into the kitchen and threw open the fridge door. 'I don't.'

While he gazed, unseeing, at the jars of condiments – how many things did she need to spread on her bread? – he felt her come up behind and wrap her wiry arms around him. 'Time to stop being that angry young man, afraid to let people in.'

With a deep sigh, he closed the fridge door. 'I've tried. It's not that easy.'

She reached to clasp his face. 'You're my grandson and I know you. You're strong. You can do anything you put your mind to. Your father, mother, April, those boys at school, Sabrina … their rejection wasn't a reflection on you, it was a reflection on them. They were too ignorant, too selfish to realise what they lost by not including you in their lives. Jade is neither.'

'It was her choice to leave.'

Her expression turned sad. 'But you gave her nothing to stay for.'

'I gave her the bookstore she loves.'

She patted his cheek. 'I know you're smarter than that.'

Smart was one thing. Scared was another. So it was good it had ended on his terms, wasn't it? That he'd been in control this time. 'The house is ready,' he said, anxious to change the subject.

She smiled. 'When do you want to move in?'

'As soon as possible.' He paused, picturing himself back on the island, walking past the bookstore, sitting on Sconset beach. Having a drink at the resort bar. Jade would be everywhere. 'I think I'm going to find it very hard living in Nantucket without you.'

She patted his hand. 'Then I'll get packing tomorrow.'

'What about John? Will you be okay leaving him?'

'You don't need to worry about me. John's got a boat. I'm sure I'll be seeing him. But you won't be happy unless you persuade that lovely girl back. And if my senses haven't failed me, she won't need much persuading. Now, go and relax while I fix us both some supper.'

Head feeling heavy, his heart even more so, he dragged himself over to her sofa and slumped down on it. He wanted to rest, to forget everything, but his brain wouldn't let him. For the first time in his life, he didn't know what to do. He knew what he *wanted*, but he didn't know if he had the backbone, the resilience, to go after it. And even if he had, how did he get there?

Without conscious thought, he powered his phone back on and dialled the one person he thought could help him.

'Are you phoning as my boss?' Jeremy answered. 'Because if you are I need to tell you, respectfully, that you've majorly fucked up.'

He shut his eyes and leaned back against the sofa. 'And if I'm calling as your friend?'

'Then I'll take out the "respectfully".' There was a pause. 'You know nobody can replace her, don't you? And I'm not just talking about the bookstore, which I've asked Ramona to take care of, by the way. Temporarily, I hope.'

The thought of the store being managed by someone else tore at Liam's heart.

'Of course whether you can be replaced is up for discussion,' Jeremy added, an edge to his voice that Liam didn't appreciate.

'Jade will be hard-pressed to find someone else with your particular brand of broody, stubborn, closed off bloody-mindedness. Then again, she may prefer to go for a warm, sensitive, romantic sort—'

'I get the picture,' he gritted out, that tear in his heart now a full-blown rip. This is what he'd set himself up for? Not just life without her, but life without her in the knowledge he'd stood back and allowed it to happen. She'd said she wanted a man to fight for her, yet he'd been too scared of injury to risk going into battle. 'I can't believe I'm saying this, but are you around tomorrow? I need to pick your brains.'

Chapter Thirty-Six

She'd not even been back a week, but already Jade knew the answer to the question Liam had posed to her. *Go home, pick up your life and work out for certain what you want.*

Then again, she'd known before she'd come home that she'd wanted to go back to Nantucket, to live a life with him in it. Even if it meant flying back on that tiny Cape Air nine-seater Cessna, which had given her more than a few moments of *holy shit*, alongside the amazing views. What she couldn't do, was go back to Nantucket and live a life there without him. She loved the island, had grown closer to some of the people than she'd thought possible in such a short space of time. But it was Liam she was in love with.

'Daydreaming again, Sis?'

She shook herself and turned to face Lauren, who'd surprised them all by accepting the mid-week dinner invite. 'Maybe, a bit.'

Lauren handed her a glass of wine. 'Mum said she's got the kitchen covered. We've been instructed to sit and relax.'

'Better do as she says, then.' Jade accepted the glass and went to sit on the squishy cream sofa. 'How's Ned?'

Lauren smiled. 'Still younger than me.'

'Don't you mean still junior to you?'

'Ouch. Why don't you say what you really mean?'

'I just think, be honest with yourself. He doesn't fit the mould of the man you had in mind. It doesn't mean he's wrong for you,' Jade added. 'You can't choose who you fall for.' If you could, then Jade would've chosen someone way easier to love than a certain grouchy resort owner.

Lauren gave her a quiet appraisal. 'You're missing Liam, aren't you?'

'Yes.'

'Do you think you did the right thing, coming home rather than staying and trying to make a go of it?'

It was the question that kept her awake at night. She'd done exactly what Liam had predicted, and left him. Rejected him. Yet could she really jack in her job and fly back out there when she didn't know where she stood? He liked her, liked the sex, but was she content to bumble along, waiting for the day he realised she wasn't his type? That, actually, elegant brunettes with rich pedigrees were what he wanted all along. 'I think so, yes. I'm done with guys who want to get away with only giving part of themselves. I want a man prepared to go all in.' She gave her sister a sad smile. 'Only that way will I know if he meant everything he said up to that point, or if it was all just to keep me having sex with him.'

'Good for you.'

Except … why did she feel she'd let him down, like everyone else in his life had done, except his beloved grandma? 'Oh God.' She pressed a hand to her chest, the ache almost unbearable.

'It was obvious what you saw in him,' Lauren continued, oblivious to her meltdown. 'He was definitely drool-worthy, but too grumpy for you. I know a lot of women go for that taciturn, broody thing, but someone as warm and sunny as you really needs a man—'

'I need him,' Jade cut in, feeling panicked. 'Shit, I shouldn't have come home. I should have stayed and told him how much I loved him. Maybe that was all he needed, some reassurance from me. To feel loved when he's spent so much of life feeling the opposite.'

'Oh.' Lauren peered at her. 'So just to be clear, you like grumpy now? Because none of your previous boyfriends have been like that.'

'He isn't grumpy, he's reserved.'

'Sorry, but I definitely saw grumpy when I FaceTimed you the other week.'

'He was protecting me.' She levelled Lauren a look. 'You talked down to me, implied managing a bookstore wasn't a proper job.'

Lauren reared back. 'No, I didn't. Did I?' When Jade nodded, her sister's face fell. 'Shit, that's awful. I didn't mean it like that. You'd only been doing it a short while, and I just thought it was like a paid vacation.'

'And I was going to come home when it finished and get a proper job,' she finished for her.

Lauren winced. 'I suppose, yes.' Her face crumpled. 'God, I'm sorry. I guess I don't understand jobs that aren't involved with healthcare or science, but that's no excuse.' She leant forward. 'Tell me what you did managing the bookstore. What did it involve? Educate me so I can be a better sister from now on.'

Touched, Jade began to describe what she'd done on the island, not just getting to grips with the store, but the events she'd run to increase business and bring the shop into the centre of the community. The more she talked, the more she felt an acute sense of pride. And an even more acute yearning to be back there.

'Wow, Sis. That's incredible. No way could I have done what you did. I'm awful at making friends, at networking. And as for thinking creatively, like your speed dating for book lovers idea, forget it.' As Jade's phone buzzed, Lauren rose to her feet. 'You check on that. I'll check on Mum. Make sure she's not in danger of burning the dinner. Or the house, for that matter.'

Before she walked off, Jade reached out to stop her. 'Thank you, for what you just said. It means a great deal, coming from you.'

Lauren shook her head. 'Don't thank me. I should have said it ages ago. You've always been so supportive of me, yet looking back I never gave you the same respect. Too focused on me. From now on, I'm going to do better.'

Lauren's words, coming on top of her already sky-high emotions about Liam, brought a lump to her throat and Jade was glad of the distraction of the message from Jenny, one of the girls at work.

> Have you seen this??

Frowning, Jade clicked on the link and her eyes filled with tears as she read it. It was a job advert for Little Bay Book Shack. He was replacing her already, yet he'd told her the job was hers. Had he assumed she didn't want it. Or had he changed his mind?

Requirements: must be creative, smart, compassionate, light up any room with a smile, able to get on with anyone, including the surly resort owner. Be willing to build a life with said surly owner.

Her heart tripped. Holy cow.

Quickly, before she let the balloon of hope become untethered, she messaged Jeremy.

> Was this advert your doing?

A reply pinged straight back.

Joint effort with boss man. Are you going to apply? Pretty please??? He's back to being an asshole again.

He didn't know what the hell he was doing. The job ad was out there. He'd shown his hand. The safe option was to wait and leave the next move up to her.

But what if she didn't make a move?

It was the question that had sent him flying three thousand miles across the Atlantic. Fuck safe, he had to know if he had a chance of persuading her to come back.

The taxi came to a halt and Liam climbed out, eyeing the red-brick terraced house warily as he paid the driver. What if Jade wasn't in? She could be out on a date. Or she could be at home with a date. Or just at home and not want to see him.

Or...

Goddammit.

He squared his shoulders and, holding tight to the package he'd brought with him, strode up the steps, heart galloping a million miles an hour.

He wasn't expecting her sister to open the door.

'Oh, it's you.'

He took a moment to regret being so curt with Lauren the one and only time he'd talked to her. 'Is Jade home?'

A slow smile spread across Lauren's face. 'She is. But we're in the middle of dinner. I guess you can come and wait while we finish.'

'Who's that, dear?' A voice echoed from inside.

'Just someone trying to sell something.' Lauren raised a brow.

'I assume that's why you're here? To sell Jade on the idea of going back with you?'

His heart felt like it was about to explode, his emotions were on a knife edge. He wasn't in the mood for games. 'I'll wait outside.'

'Oh no, Mum would go mad.'

'Why would I go mad?'

Holy Mother of God. If he wasn't in the mood for games, he certainly wasn't in the right frame of mind for polite conversation. Even with this short, smiley-looking woman with eyes that reminded him of Jade's.

'You'd go mad if you knew Jade's boss, or should I say, ex-boss—'

'Boyfriend,' he interjected, feeling like a fucking fourteen-year-old.

Lauren smirked. 'If you knew Jade's ex-boyfriend was waiting outside for her while we finished dinner.'

'Oh, well.' Those blue eyes swept him up and down. 'If you've come here to upset her, I will be the first to throw you out. Then her father will try and rough you up, though he's got a bad back and is unlikely to make much of a mark, but you need to pretend that he's hurt you.'

'And don't forget me,' Lauren added. 'I've had self-defence training and I know exactly where to put my knee and my elbow to inflict maximum pain.'

'I get it,' he said. 'Upsetting Jade is the last thing I want to do.'

That elicited a smile from the mother. 'I'm glad we got that settled. Now, give me your jacket.' Her gaze dropped to the small parcel he carried. 'And whatever you've got there. I'll pop it in the cupboard under the stairs. Are you hungry? I made a stew so there's plenty left.'

Okay, he could do this, he thought as he followed her down the hallway. He could make polite conversation with Jade's family while she was in the room, close enough to look at but not touch. To see her face but not know how she felt about him being there until he was able to get her alone.

Fuck.

The moment he stepped into the large family kitchen, his eyes collided with Jade's. She gasped, and her knife and fork clattered to the table.

'We have a visitor.' Jade's mom turned to him. 'I'm Kathy, this is Donald,' she waved a hand towards the balding man at the head of the table. 'Lauren, you've clearly already met.'

'And me.' Jade cleared her throat, her gaze a mix of emotions too complex for him to decipher. 'You've already met me.'

'I daresay you're the reason he's here.' Donald gave him the sort of look any doting father would give a man he didn't trust with his daughter. 'But if he dares to upset you, he'll have me to answer to.'

'Dad.' Jade groaned, burying her head in her hands.

'What? My warm, big-hearted, spirited, champion of a daughter has been hurt enough by men not treating her right.'

Liam watched Jade blink back tears before turning his attention to her father. 'I have no intention of hurting your daughter. Ever.'

Donald gave him a steely glare, then nodded.

A beat of awkward silence followed, broken by Kathy. 'Someone go and fetch another chair for Liam while I get him some stew.'

He felt like he was in some alternate universe. One where he was meeting Jade's parents for the first time as a shy, awkward youngster. It had to be the reason he put up no objection and simply slid, meekly, onto the chair Donald set next to Jade.

Immediately he inhaled, registering her unique smell, his body stirring into life for the first time since she'd left him. He was desperate to touch her, just to reach out his hand and wrap it around hers, but he didn't know if she'd accept the gesture. Or smack him in the face.

'How long have you been in England?' Kathy asked as she set a plate of mashed potatoes with some unrecognisable brown meat in a brown gravy in front of him.

He glanced at his watch. 'Nearly two hours.'

'You came straight here from the airport?'

What the hell else was he going to do? Seeing Jade was his sole focus. Persuading her to come back with him, his sole purpose. 'Yes.'

Beside him, Jade let out a noise that sounded like a snigger. 'This is going to be interesting,' she whispered.

'What is?'

'Seeing you being interrogated by Mum. I'm warning you now, she's a master.'

'What are you two whispering about?' Kathy called over to them.

Jade gave him an innocent look. 'I was asking him why he was here.'

He baulked. 'Seriously? You want me to do this *now*?'

'Well, it would be good to know.' It was only then he saw the fine line of tension around her mouth. She wasn't nearly as collected, as assured, as she was letting on. 'Have you come to ask me about the bookstore? Because I saw you'd advertised the manager job already.'

Lauren gasped, but Liam ignored her. If he was going to have to do this in front of her family, so be it. 'Then you'll know I didn't come here for the shop. I've come for you.'

'Oh.' She swallowed, her gaze bouncing up to his.

'Yes, oh.' He glanced down at his plate. 'Do you want to keep talking, or should we finish eating and go somewhere more private?'

'I vote for the first,' Lauren stated. 'If you're interested in my view, that is.'

Jade's eyes searched his, and a small smile played around her mouth. 'Mum's cooking isn't the best, so eating fast is probably advisable.'

'Hey, I heard that.' Kathy looked over at her daughter. 'Five minutes. You finish your meals and we get to learn a bit more about this mysterious man who's landed on our doorstep. Then you can escape next door.'

Jade smiled. 'Deal.'

Liam looked down at his plate, shovelled a forkful of brown slop, and geared himself for five, painful minutes, knowing the time after that could be even more painful.

Chapter Thirty-Seven

Frigging hell, she couldn't believe Liam was here, in her house. Making stilted conversation with her family … okay, her mum, as she was the chatty one. She was also the one to blame for putting them all through the ordeal of the last twenty minutes. The fact Liam hadn't actually turned around and walked straight out again after being threatened by her five-foot-nine, sixty-year-old dad, was remarkable in itself.

Even more remarkable was the fact that Liam had engaged in the conversation. He wasn't Mr Chilled and Relaxed, never would be, it wasn't his style, but he was courteous, polite, respectful. In fact, if it was possible to love him any more, she would have done after he'd valiantly not only eaten the stew, but requested a second helping.

Lauren's eyes had nearly popped out, her dad had raised an eyebrow and her mum had giggled like a schoolgirl.

But enough was enough. *I've come for you.* Her heart crashed against her ribs. She was a mess of emotions; hope, longing, fear that she'd read the situation wrong.

She was making herself dizzy with all the scenarios playing out in her head.

Jerkily she jumped to her feet, the chair scraping across the tiles. 'Interrogation time is over. You asked for five minutes, you've had way more than that.'

Her mum smiled. 'That's because Liam knows a good stew when he sees one. But fine, yes, you two go off and have your talk. We'll clear up.'

As everyone stood and began to pick up the plates, Jade narrowed her eyes at her mother. 'Do I have your guarantee we won't find you camped outside the door with a glass to your ear?'

She chuckled. 'Promise.' Then she walked up to her and whispered. 'Nobody has ever forced two helpings of my stew down their neck. That man is completely in love with you. And I heartily approve.'

In love with you. The words rang in her ears. Was he? Or was he a man who'd had manners drilled into him by boarding school, and his grandma.

Heart in her mouth, Jade glanced at Liam, who stood stiffly by the door, watching her. He appeared taller than she remembered, his physique more impressive. His looks far too glamorous for a three-bed terrace in Twickenham.

Silently she walked past him and into the living room opposite, her heart hammering so hard she was sure he could hear it. The door shut with a loud click.

'What was worse, Mum's cooking or her questions?'

He slid his hands into his jeans pockets. Note to self, faded denim jeans were her new favourite clothing on him. 'Her questions. The stew was fine.'

Jade choked out a laugh. 'Said nobody about Mum's stew, ever.'

'Yet, you all sit down and eat it.'

'Only because she'd sulk for weeks if we didn't.

'Your family is very—'

'Crazy? Ridiculous?'

'Protective.'

She thought of her dad, the beautiful words he'd said. The fact he'd faced up to a man half a foot taller, twenty-five years younger and significantly fitter. 'I guess they are. That's what you do for the people you love.'

A pair of shimmering silver eyes burned into hers. 'Yes.'

Inside her chest, her heart tumbled. That's what he'd done for her, she realised, with Lauren, then with Henry at the wedding. He'd stuck up for her, protected her. Just like she had, him.

'You left early.'

'Only a day.' Oh shit, had she got this wrong? 'Is that why you're here? To sue me for breach of contract?'

He stared at her incredulously. 'You think that's why I travelled three thousand miles?'

'To be fair, I don't know because you're not telling me, so all I'm left with is guesswork.'

He was so formal, so rigid. She wanted to fling her arms around him but she still wasn't sure whether she was reading him wrong.

'You asked for a signal, Jade.'

You need to work on giving out better signals. 'You're my signal?'

His shoulders slumped. 'Fuck. I'm going to kill Jeremy.'

'What? Why?'

'He said I needed to make a grand gesture.'

That bubble of hope was rising again. 'You're my signal *and* my grand gesture?'

'Yes, sort of.' He looked rattled, she thought. Beautifully, adorably rattled. 'I brought something else, but now I'm thinking about it, that's more an icebreaker. An apology for being such a dick. My head was so far up my own ass I couldn't pull it out in time.'

She stared back at him, feeling as unsure as he looked. The signals were positive, but the message itself unclear. He'd come to ask her back, but in what capacity? For how long? 'Should we start with the icebreaker, then, it seems appropriate.'

He nodded and darted out, returning a few seconds later with a small box wrapped in silver paper and adorned with a beautiful pink bow. 'I had nothing to do with the wrapping. That was the lady who made it.'

'Made it?'

He huffed out a breath. 'Just open it.'

She'd never been one for delayed gratification so she tore at the packaging, gasping when she saw the keyring nestled inside. 'Holy shit, it's a bookworm. An actual bookworm,' she whispered, eyes travelling along the small furry body and over the bespectacled face before drifting down to the little arms that clutched at a soft furry book. 'Sparks is going to have his nose well and truly put out of joint. If caterpillars even have a nose, but you know what I mean...' She trailed off and looked up at him. He could have easily bought her something extravagant that required little effort. Yet he'd bought her *this*. 'Thank you.'

Again those silver eyes rested on hers, a soft sheen to them that sent a ball of emotion shooting into her throat.

'I should have told you I love you,' he said roughly, taking a few steps towards her until he was right there, the soft material of his shirt brushing against her fingers. His warmth, his smell, sending her hormones into meltdown. And that was before he trailed a finger down her face. 'Run the bookstore, if you want, but come back with me, please. Build a life with me.'

Her heart tumbled. Love, joy ... explosions of both detonated inside her until she felt she might burst with happiness. It was almost too much to take in. The fact he'd travelled all the way over to see her, endured meeting her parents, found someone to make her a bookworm key ring. God, she was going to cry. Not pretty tears but great hulking waterworks that would make a red blotchy mess of her face.

Liam was about to have a heart attack. There was no way his body could cope with the pace the organ was currently pumping.

'Say something,' he croaked out. 'You're killing me here. Oh fuck, not tears.' His heart plummeted. 'I don't know what tears mean. Please, Jade. Shit.' He wrapped his arms around her, crushing both her and the damn worm against his chest. 'Tell me you're okay.'

She sniffed. 'I'm not okay.' He reared back, only to find her giving him a watery smile. 'Okay is definitely not the right word for how I feel. Okay is a middle-of-the-road word. It's like "fine", and I'm not fine. I'm far from fine or okay.'

'Jade,' he warned. 'I'm on edge here.'

Her smile grew wider, though alarmingly the tears kept gushing down her cheeks. 'I'm not fine, you muppet, because I'm frigging *ecstatic*. Euphoric, elated, and probably a bunch of other e words I can't think of right now because I'm so *excited*.' The smile she shot him pulled the breath from his lungs. 'I'm utterly and completely in love with a man who loves me back. A man who's flown across the Atlantic to give me the most beautiful, thoughtful gift I've ever received. Aside from my teapot, obviously.' She looked down, fingers fondling the worm, and sniffed again. 'Your signal, your grand gesture to come here, it was amazing, but you had me at the icebreaker.'

'I did? I have?' He was too shocked to fully take it in. 'You don't need time to think about it?' What the fuck was he doing? 'Forget that. Don't think any more. I'm taking your first answer.' He rested his head against her forehead, his whole body settling, relaxing for the first time in a week. 'I love you, Jade Taylor. I have for a while now, ever since you gave me those audiobooks for Grandma. Probably before that. Even when you were fighting me, I was falling for you.' He touched his lips to hers, felt the tingle of it shoot down his spine. 'I'm sorry I was too much of a coward to tell you before.'

'We were both burned by the past, both wary of giving away our hearts.'

His mouth found hers again and this time he felt the urgency, the pulse of lust along with love. The need to claim her not just with words, but with action. 'Can we get away from here?'

'Um.' She kissed him back, her tongue tangling with his, her hands sliding down his chest before slipping open a few buttons. 'Where did you have in mind?'

Her fingers found his bare skin and he hissed out a breath. 'My hotel room.' He lifted her up, hands beneath her butt, and when she wrapped her legs around him, he walked them to the wall and thrust his hips against her, making them both moan. 'Need to get out of here now, before your parents burst in and I lose the brownie points I gained from two helpings of stew.'

She giggled, pushing her own hips against his and causing him to harden even further. He was in her parents' front room, and so close to losing it he should be ashamed, but he was too fucking happy to care.

For a few minutes they made out, his hands tangling in her hair, their hips doing a rhythmic dance. Finally, he drew back, groaning with frustration as she slid slowly down him and onto the floor.

'Let me just grab a few things.'

'Like?'

She rolled her eyes. 'PJs. Underwear.'

'Don't plan on you wearing any.'

'Toothbrush.'

'You can borrow mine.'

'Make-up.'

'You're fucking gorgeous enough without it.'

She beamed and patted her heart. 'Okay, then, Romeo, let's go. We might be able to sneak out—'

There was a tap on the door. 'Anyone in there want dessert?'

Goddamn it. Jade slid him an amused look, clearly struggling not to laugh. 'Her puddings are better than the stew.'

'You're what I want for dessert,' he almost growled.

'Um, thanks, Mum,' Jade shouted back, 'but we're heading out.'

She smoothed down her hair and he attempted to adjust himself into a position that didn't say *raging erection*.

She looked down at his fly, licked her lips and gave him a cheeky smile before opening the door.

It was an agonising few minutes while they waited for an Uber. When it finally arrived he almost bundled her into it. After confirming the hotel with the driver, he was about to put his phone back in his pocket when he saw the notification.

'Um, dare I ask what Operation Double BJ is?' Jade asked, reading the message.

'You can ask.'

Hastily he replied to Jeremy's question.

> Operation Double BJ a success. Over and Out.

Jeremy's reply was even quicker.

> Whoa, not over and out. I need details. Was she impressed with your grand gesture? How much grovelling did it take? When are you guys coming back? Did she like the key ring? If not, I told you it was a dumb idea. If she did, I agreed it was a fabulous one.

He rolled his eyes as an impatient Jeremy came back again.

Er, hello?

With a shake of his head, Liam powered off the phone.

When he turned to Jade, she was grinning. 'You really should reply, you know. He'll only sulk if you don't.'

'I'll message him. Later.'

She gave his side a gentle nudge. 'You really are besties, aren't you?'

'He's a friend. I'll admit to a good friend. And that's the last we're going to talk about him tonight.' He dropped a soft kiss on her mouth. 'From now on, the only man I want you thinking of, is me.'

'Deal.' She reached into her pocket and dropped the key ring with the brown furry worm onto his lap. 'You and Wormy. My two favourite men.'

He stared down at the four-eyed creature and sighed. Then again, if that was what had tipped the balance into her being in this taxi with him or not, he figured he had a lot to thank the thing for. 'As long as my name is first.'

She leant into him. 'You will always be my number one. So, when do we go home?'

The word curled around his heart. 'Whenever you want. I bought an open-ended ticket.' He wrapped an arm around her. 'I wasn't sure how long it would take to convince you.'

'Ye of little faith. You should have realised I was totally in love with you. I gave you enough hints before I left. *A man it's so easy to love, it's ridiculous,*' she quoted, settling further against him.

'I was too scared to believe it.'

She turned to him, her expression soft. 'Give me two days. One to resign, one to spend the day with my family.'

'Whatever you want.' His heart feeling deliciously full, he

kissed the top of her head. 'As long as you come back with me, you can take as long as you want.'

Acknowledgments

Writing this book cost me a fortune – and I have Bonnie from One More Chapter to blame for it! You see it was Bonnie's idea to set the story in a place I'd previously never heard of.

The plan had been for the book to be based in the Maldives, based on The Barefoot Bookseller concept, which was the idea of my fabulous agent, Hannah. I honeymooned in the Maldives and okay, it was thirty years ago but I was confident I could picture the islands so it didn't take a great leap to imagine Jade working her temporary bookseller stint in a cute thatched bookstore perched on the white crystal sands of the islands, with the Indian Ocean as a backdrop.

But Bonnie suggested we shift the book to a different island – Nantucket – to give it more of a small-town feel. After some feverish research (where the hell was Nantucket?), I was quickly sold on the idea. Totally different from the Maldives, but wow, the island off Cape Cod looked so quaint, so pretty, so different. And the more I read about it, the more I fell head over heels in love with it. By the time I'd written 'The End' on the first draft, I told my husband I had to go and check it out (for research purposes, obviously…). We combined it with a visit to Cape Cod and Martha's Vineyard, both wonderful in their own right, but the highlight was Nantucket, a little gem of a place in the Atlantic Ocean with a wealth of history that is beautifully preserved in the immaculate old colonial buildings, the cobbled streets and the wharfs lined with pretty grey shingle buildings. Although the Little Bay Book Shack and the Haven Resort come from my imagination, I hope I've managed to weave some of the magic of the real Nantucket into Jade and Liam's story.

So, when it comes to thanks, the two most important ones must go to my agent Hannah for the original idea of having my heroine go somewhere special to manage a bookstore for a few months, and to my editor Bonnie for suggesting that the somewhere special be Nantucket. Oh, and I guess I should thank my husbahd, too, for coming with me on what proved to be the holiday of a lifetime. 😊

Thanks also to Bonnie, Jennie, Charlotte, Emily and everyone behind the scenes at One More Chapter who helped turn my words, full of plot holes and misspellings, into the book that you are now reading. And for the beautiful cover.

Liam was a not-quite-billionaire, living on an island, so it made sense for him to have a yacht. But it's only when I started to write about the yacht, I realised how little I knew about them. What size was okay for one man to operate, how did you sail/drive (!) the thing? I'd like to thank my amazing Master Mariner cousin, Karley, who has herself (during her 16 years at sea) served on a super yacht, for her advice on all things nautical!

This is also my chance, as always, to thank the friends and family who continue to support my writing: my lovely mum-in-law Anne; my sis-in-law Jayne; nieces Maddi, Tiggi and Gracie; cousins Shelley, Kath, Kirsty and Hayley; Auntie Jan; and friends Charlotte, Sonia, Jane, Carol, Tara and Priti. You are superstars, every one of you, and I'm not sure I'd have made it to this stage if it hadn't been for you guys cheering me on.

Thanks also to the amazing book bloggers who have been kind enough to read and review my books, take part in blog tours and give me a shout out on social media. Your support is priceless.

Finally, the most important thanks of all go to YOU. I am so grateful that you chose one of my books to read and hope that you'll fall a little in love with Liam, Jade … and Nantucket.

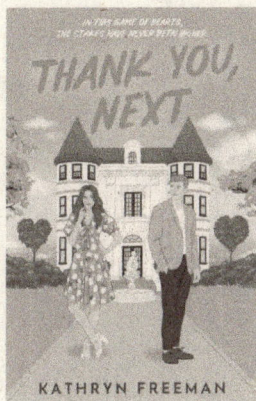

Molly Harris is the queen of rejection.

When her latest boyfriend, gym-fanatic Duncan, dumps her to go on reality dating show *The One*, she's determined not to let 'The One' get away. If Molly can prove that they're meant to be, she might just get the happily ever after of her dreams…

But on the first day of filming, another reminder of her painful history walks into Happily Ever After Towers: Ben Knight, her it's-not-you-it's-me heartbreaker. The one she loved before Duncan.

In four weeks' time, who will she meet at the altar? Duncan, the first person who ever made her feel loved, or Ben, the first person who made her *feel*?

Available in paperback and eBook!

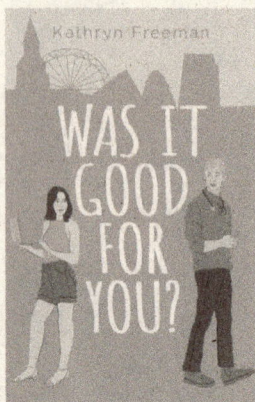

If you're not a ten on Sophie's spreadsheet, you're never getting her between the bedsheets…

No aspect of Sophie's life goes unrecorded in her Excel spreadsheets, so when she accidentally sends it to her entire contact list instead of just her best friend, Sophie has a lot of uncomfortable explaining to do.

First on the list? Dr Michael Adams. After a disastrous first date, Michael scored a '3' on Sophie's 'love life' tab, but when she shows up to apologise for sharing his result with the world, he issues an unexpected challenge: ten dates to prove that love can't be calculated by an equation or contained by boxes on a spreadsheet.

Sophie isn't someone who's used to thinking outside the digital box, but there's something about Michael that makes her want to take a chance…

Available in paperback and eBook!

NOBODY PUTS ROMCOMS IN THE CORNER

Kathryn Freeman

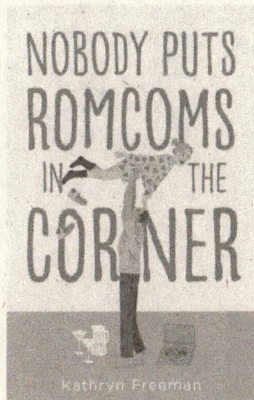

Not an expert, not even close, not in any of this. But nobody will try harder than me to make you happy.

Sally is a classic romantic and Harry is a classic cynic, but when a drunken bet leads the new flatmates to (badly) recreate 'the lift' from Dirty Dancing, and the video goes viral (#EpicRomcom-ReenactmentFailure), they both realise there's potential financial benefit in blundering their way through the romcom lexicon for their suddenly vast social media following.

Now, as Harry and Sally bring major romcom moments to new life – including recreating that classic diner scene – their faking it turns to making...out and suddenly they're living a real life romcom of their own!

But like all the greatest love stories, the road to happily ever after is paved with unexpected challenges for this hero and heroine...

Available in paperback, eBook, and audio!

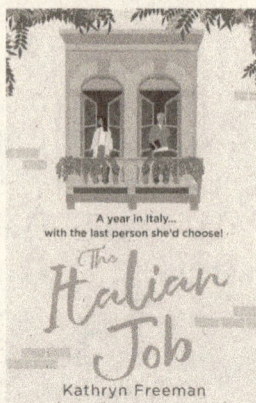

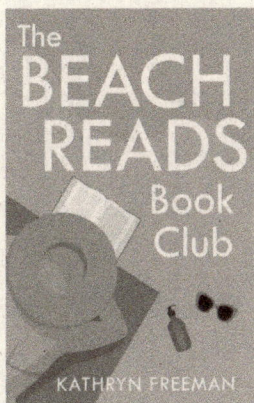

Welcome to the Beach Reads Book Club. Where love is just a page away…

When Lottie Watt is unceremoniously booted out of her uptight book club for not following the rules, she decides to throw the rulebook out the window and start her own club – one where conversation, gin and cake take precedent over actually having read the book!

The Beach Reads Book Club soon finds a home for its meetings at Books by the Bay, a charming bookshop and café owned by gorgeous, brooding Matthew Steele, and as the book club picks heat up, so too does the attraction between Matt and Lottie.

If there's anything Lottie has learned from the romances she's been reading, it's that the greatest loves are the ones hardest earned.

Available in paperback, eBook, and audio!

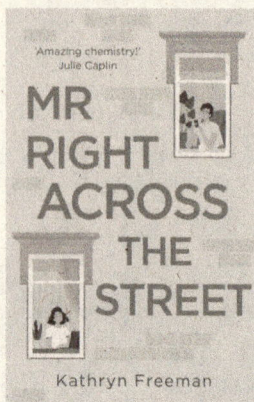

'Amazing chemistry!'
Julie Caplin

MR
RIGHT
ACROSS
THE
STREET

Kathryn Freeman

Mia Abbott's move to Manchester was supposed to give her time and space from all the disastrous romantic choices she's made in her past.

But then the hot guy who lives opposite – the one who works out every day at exactly 10 a.m., not that Mia has noticed thank-you-very-much – starts leaving notes in his window…for her.

Bar owner Luke Doyle has his own issues to deal with but as he shows Mia the sights of her new city he also shows her what real romance looks like for the first time.

When he cooks up a signature cocktail in her honour, she realises that the man behind the bar is even more enticing than any of his creations. And once she's had a taste she knows it will never be enough!

Available in paperback and eBook!

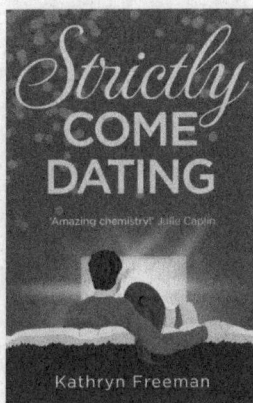

Strictly
COME
DATING

'Amazing chemistry!' Julie Caplin

Kathryn Freeman

Saturday nights are strictly for dancing…

As the glitter ball shimmers and sequins flash, forty-year-old Maggie remembers the pull of the dancefloor. But now, as a newly divorced mum of two, Maggie's certain her dancing days are over. Or are they…?

Encouraged by her friends, Maggie dusts off her silver stilettoes and enrols for dancing classes, all she needs now is the perfect partner.

Enter Seb. Young, carefree and hot as hell, Seb is definitely a perfect 10! Even though everything about him is outrageously inappropriate! But as Seb sweeps her across the dancefloor every week, Maggie begins to see a new side to him; kind, caring, funny, strong.

And Maggie realises that he's the only one she'd like to foxtrot with…perhaps even forever?

Available in paperback, eBook, and audio!

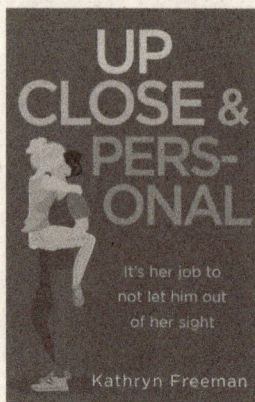

UP
CLOSE &
PERS-
ONAL

It's her job to
not let him out
of her sight

Kathryn Freeman

She can't let him out of her sight...

British actor Zac Edwards is the latest heartthrob to hit the red
carpets. Hot, talented and rich, he sends women wild...all
except one.

Close protection officer Kat Parker hasn't got time to play
celebrity games. She has one job: to protect Zac from the stalker
that seems to be dogging his every move.

Zac might get her hot under her very starched collar, but Kat's a
professional – and sleeping with Zac is no way part of her remit...

Available in paperback and eBook!

DAEDALUS
IS DEAD

DAEDALUS IS DEAD

SEAMUS SULLIVAN

TOR

First published in the US 2025 by Tom Doherty Associates / Tor Publishing Group

First published in the UK 2025 by Tor
an imprint of Pan Macmillan
The Smithson, 6 Briset Street, London EC1M 5NR
EU representative: Macmillan Publishers Ireland Ltd, 1st Floor,
The Liffey Trust Centre, 117–126 Sheriff Street Upper,
Dublin 1 D01 YC43
Associated companies throughout the world

ISBN 978-1-0350-8590-3

1 3 5 7 9 8 6 4 2

A CIP catalogue record for this book is available from the British Library.

Printed and bound in the UK using 100% Renewable Electricity
by CPI Group (UK) Ltd

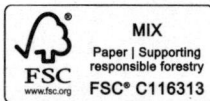

MIX
Paper | Supporting
responsible forestry
FSC
www.fsc.org **FSC® C116313**

Visit **www.panmacmillan.com** to read more about all our books
and to buy them.

For Mom, Dad, and Deirdre

DAEDALUS
IS DEAD

PRELUDE

WHERE I'LL BEGIN

The walls proceed in straight lines and meet at right angles. Corridors beckon toward other corridors; doorways frame empty rooms. The tops of the walls make a black ribbon of the sky, stars glimmering like silver coins in still water.

I turn corners and pass rooms. My legs ache, and the scars on my left arm burn with remembered pain. The moon is hidden by the walls, but its light paints the walls gray and black. I am not lost. I've been walking a long time. I am following, and I am followed.

The smell of the sea draws me right at the fork. A slash of moonlight shows me a faint, dark stain on the flagstones up ahead. I ignore my groaning knees and crouch, knowing what I'll find. The print of your foot, the left one, damp with salt water. The heel of your right footprint a stride away at the moonlight's edge. You're never far from me, here.

Then: a snort. Close by. Still air drawn into wet nostrils once, twice. A deep sigh as the air steams back out between sharp teeth. He's one turn behind me, maybe two. A long, slow scrape of horn against stone. He can move unnoticed here when he wants to, quick and quiet as thought. Sometimes he lets me hear him. Part of the game.

I may be dreaming, or dying. Or I'm awake now and all the rest was a dream, and we've always been here. You ahead, him behind.

And her, of course, somewhere none of us can follow. Among the stars, maybe, looking down.

He snorts, breathes in my scent again, and his hooves clop around the corner, but I'm already up and running, ignoring the wrong turns and the blind corridors, looking for the next puddle of seawater, the next broken feather, the edge of your tunic disappearing around the next bend, and I'm sprinting now, never mind the steady, clopping hooves I can barely hear over the blood pounding in my ears, pounding with joy because I've almost found you, can almost see your face and clasp you to me, and I have so many things to tell you after so long apart, I'm already thinking about what I'll say to you first, where I'll begin.

THERE CAN'T BE
ANYTHING WORSE

We push aside my workbench and tools to clear a space in the middle of the workshop. You help me fasten the wings to my shoulders and arms. Then you stand back as I extend my arms and flap once, twice, feeling the air resist as water resists an oar. A breeze rises, making my sketchbooks mutter. My diagrams and drawings rustle on the walls and scuttle across my drafting table. The stone floor is cool under my feet. Then it only touches the tips of my toes. Then it's gone, for with each flap, the wings crack like sails filling with wind, and I'm flying.

Pigments and paintbrushes rattle in their boxes, charcoals roll across the floor. My shoulders burn. The harness creaks but holds. Your hair flies back, like that of an oracle when the gods speak through her. You stare up at me, unguarded awe shining on your face. You haven't looked up at me in months, not since your voice changed and your body shot up like a vine and left you half a head taller than me.

"They work!" You shout to be heard over the rising wind. Laughter in your voice like I haven't heard since you were little. I've been locked in here with you for years, building and building. How long since I've startled you out of your studied blankness and your half smiles and simply built something that made you proud?

My sketches hurricane around us, the wall hangings billowing and whipcracking, and in the heart of this storm I think of the maker of storms who sits on high Olympus, and the ones who sit beside him, and their jealousy. An ingot of lead settles in my belly. There will be a price for this.

We're ready to fly before sunrise. We take nothing with us but our clothes and our wings. I climb onto the sill of the wide window by my drafting table. All your life, we've gazed through this window, over the palace walls, toward the shipyards and the sea. I extend my wings and jump.

Cool air murmurs in my ears and plucks at my tunic. Our tower and the rest of the palace grounds fall away until they're a half-finished sketch in the predawn. Stretches of wall lit by sentry fires, slivers of moonlight flashing from well bottoms. Once this was an assortment of fields, before I drew the majesty of Knossos on calfskin and promised it to a king. Your world entire.

You drop from the tower window, wings white as a dollop of spilled cream, and my stomach drops with you. Then you glide, wobble, arc up, shoot past me and into a somersault, laughing. I bark your name, thinking of sentries' arrows. But your laughter warms me as we spiral up past the top of our tower and see the wide country beyond the palace, farmland and city streets, sand and waves, the calfskin unfurling without end.

Minos has confined us to our rooms since the debacle with Theseus. He's doubled the palace guard and the archers on the seawall. To avoid them, we fly inland, over the Labyrinth.

Branching emptiness between the walls, shadows and silence.

In one of those pools of shadow, where the purple of dawn doesn't reach, the Minotaur's body lies still. I know he's there. His head struck off and carried out. His moon-pale fur fly-speckled, streaked with rivers of old blood. His thick, crushing hands nibbled by crows.

We soar over pasture and then over sea. Salt air stings my eyes. A lone fisherman leaps to his feet at the sight of us, almost capsizing his small boat. A high, strange voice whoops for joy, and I realize the voice is mine.

Knossos and Crete are behind us. Minos is behind us and cannot follow. We're free.

We fly north over waves that break the sunrise into rubies. As the day brightens, I begin to spot dolphins and sea turtles swimming below us. Larger shapes move in the depths. I feel a pang for the sketchbooks I left behind.

I call back to you with the names of fish and seabirds, but I don't know if you can hear me. You bob above the waves, keeping to the safe altitude we've discussed. You're sparing with your wingbeats now, gliding for long stretches with eyes closed, seeming to enjoy the wind on your face.

I designed Minos's warships myself and know how many leagues of ocean we must cross to escape them. We keep far enough from islands to be mistaken for birds. I take comfort in the even green lines of Samos's vineyards, the white orderly columns of Apollo's temple on Delos.

A cold downdraft plucks at my feathers and stiffens my arms and legs into gooseflesh. The sea jolts closer, does a nauseating little dance with the sky as I teeter and right myself. Again I see the tempest raging in our tower room, my tools and furnishings trembling in fear of the gods. Your face looks up from the heart of the storm, watching me with an expression I took for pride. But there's something else in your face, some deeper emotion I can't name.

The sky is too big and too open. The hairs on my neck and scalp prickle, awaiting the thunderbolt. I bank left, meaning to call back a warning, but you're nowhere in sight.

Your wings pummel the air to my right. Sea and sky dance again as the gust of your passing makes my wings bob and dip. Your face is an abstraction of shadow and sunlight, unreadable. You shout to me but the wind takes your words, and then you're soaring, climbing up and away from me, toward the noonday sun.

"Icarus!" I call. You don't hear me, or you don't listen. I call out again and give chase, but you're younger and stronger. You leave me behind. I feared this, fretted about it, and as I struggle into the sky after you, I'm also back in our tower room, in the gloom of early morning, warning you not to do anything blockheaded.

"Stay close to me once we're over the water," I say, fastening your wings. "Fly where I fly. Too near to the sea and the feathers become waterlogged. Too near to the sun and the wax that holds the feathers together will melt."

You swing your arm and flap the left wing. The sheet covering an unfinished statue billows to life, and dust plays in the corners of the room.

"Icarus. Do you hear me?"

"What'll we do?" you ask.

"We'll fly out of here and might even fetch up alive on dry land, if you'll only listen to me a moment."

"Afterward, I mean. If we get away. What then?"

"We'll need protection. I'll offer my services to another king."

"Like Minos."

"Nothing like him. I won't allow it."

You're staring out at the sea. I reach up to put my hands on your shoulders. How silly I must look to you. A potbellied, gray-bearded little tinkerer, cluttering up our tower lair like a magpie. This place has grown too small for you. Your suddenly-lanky skeleton seems ready to leap out of your skin. Your elbows upend sculpting tools and works in progress every time you turn around. It's past time we were gone from here.

"You don't have to work for any king if you don't want to," I say. "You don't have to build, or study. You can compose poetry, or count the stars for all it matters. You'll be a man soon, and can do whatever you want."

You nod but don't answer.

"Icarus," I cry, climbing still, the ocean a sickening distance below. You're high above me and shrinking. "Icarus!" I tell my arms to fly faster and they want to. They want to. But. The sun is hot on my face. Our wax will melt. Our feathers will come loose, flurrying toward the water. I curse myself for a coward, trying to keep the dot of you in sight.

The sun is too bright, and I lose you in the golden blaze of midday, which makes rings and disks of light play behind my eyelids.

When I catch sight of you again, you're falling, a shower of stray feathers trailing after you.

There is no breeze.

The sea is glassy and untroubled.

You fall in silence, as if the gods are waiting for the sound of impact.

I fold back my wings and dive. The wind shrieks in my ears. You're facing down, but in the smooth surface of the ocean I see you falling up from a cloudless sky, your mouth agape, your hand extended. I open my wings and swoop, reaching. Your image races toward you, your inverted self grasping for me from the water with simple need in his eyes. And then the two of you meet and shatter as you hit the ocean.

With a ring Minos gave me, I pay the fishermen to search for you, and on the second night of searching, you snag one of their nets. They tell me a lucky current dragged you into the shallows near the broad green coast where they fish.

You didn't drown. The impact broke your ribs and drove them inward. I tell myself that you died instantly. I tell myself that if I had been brave enough to strip off my wings and dive into the water, I couldn't have saved you.

Recalling what I can from the court physician, I clean your body. I dress the wounds left by the fall and by hungry fish. I anoint you in oil and clothe you in a fine tunic one of the fishermen wore on his wedding day.

I bathed and dressed you when you were small. You'd giggle and climb into the bucket, making it overflow, folding yourself up like a hermit crab to fit inside. This is nothing like that. You're cold and quiet, your limbs are long and strange and broken, and I can pretend that we don't know each other, that you're a traveler who met with ill luck and deserves a little kindness.

We build a pyre for you in the village square, and when the fire dies we pour wine over the ashes.

I cut and sand planks to make a chest to hold your bones, and I bury you in a cairn by the sea cliffs.

When Minos stops looking for me, I'll come back here. I'll raise a monument to you and a temple to Hephaestus. I prayed to him as I made our wings. I prayed for him to spare us Minos's sword and the Minotaur's jaws. And he did.

This makeshift ceremony and this rude monument will see you safely through the underworld, across the river, into the arms of the god we don't name, the god who waits below and receives many guests.

Why did you do it, Icarus?

You couldn't have known the lengths I went to, trying to keep you safe. The wings were the least of it.

Why wouldn't you let me keep you safe?

When I'm not mourning or building, I sleep, and when I sleep I have the first of the nightmares that will never leave me.

In the nightmares, I'm walking along the shore, watching the steady blue surface of the sea that killed you. Or I'm in my workshop, sketching broken white feathers. Then I turn a corner, I pass through an arch, and I find myself between high walls of smooth stone, in a long corridor that leads to more branching corridors, all of them open to the starry sky.

The most frightening part isn't finding myself back in the Labyrinth, or knowing who waits for me there. It's realizing that the places I was in before, perhaps all the places I've ever been—a festival day in the Athens of my youth, a spring afternoon when I held you cackling over my head—those places too were part of the Labyrinth, and always have been.

I wake up clawing at the blankets.

The worst has happened, I tell myself.

There can't be anything worse waiting for me.

Years after I bury you, Minos finds me in Sicily.

He comes alone, wearing an old traveler's cloak dusty from many roads. He carries a conch shell and claims to know a riddle that only the wisest king in the world can solve. The guards laugh but let him in with the day's petitioners.

Sicily is far enough from Crete that even Minos would have trouble mustering an invasion by sea. Even better, the king here is a forgettable, inoffensive king who requires no elaborate new ways to kill people. I make modest improvements to his ships and seawalls, redesign his palace's ventilation and plumbing, and he's content to leave me to my research and my grief.

My new workshop is larger than the one at Knossos, but because I no longer bother to clean it, it's messier and seems smaller. There are no guards. I'm free to come and go, although I don't.

I'm dissecting a gadfly when my forgettable king walks in, holding the conch shell. "There's a man come to court," he says. "He's traveled far. He dresses like a beggar, but he holds his walking stick like a spear-haft and talks like a man used to giving orders."

I don't move. I'm remembering Minos's proud mouth, the sneer that came after he chose the means of execution but before he gave the order. Of course he's found me. Who am I, to flee him?

My forgettable patron, seeing none of this, sits opposite me. With an eager air, he puts the conch shell on the workbench between us. He lays a length of thread next to it.

"The man poses a riddle," says my patron. "He has posed it to many kings and none has solved it. He who answers correctly is the wisest king alive."

I stare at the conch and the thread. "Surely the riddle's supposed to test you, not your advisors."

"A king's only as wise as his wisest advisor." My patron is a pragmatist.

Minos may as well have signed his name. The thread on the table is the same kind Ariadne gave to Theseus, who unspooled it behind him as he ventured into the heart of the Labyrinth.

Poor Ariadne. Of all the people who survived the ordeal at Knossos, she's the only one I miss.

"The challenge," says my patron, "is to guide this thread into the curling conch shell, and out the other end."

I can see Ariadne's brow furrowed in concentration, then the sly way her eyes would meet mine when she'd worked out the solution to a math problem.

"Daedalus," her memory says to me. "You've already gone and solved it, haven't you?"

"Daedalus," says Minos's memory, and as he speaks I'm back in my bed in Knossos, a month after your birth. My bones ache from weariness, and my thoughts are as slow and cloudy as honey. Your cries have awakened me, and someone is standing in the corner by the crib I've built, holding you close and soothing you. At first I think it's your mother, but as her name leaves my mouth I remember that she's gone. And I am here alone with you, and with Minos, who pats you on the back and smiles at me as you snuggle up to him.

"You're a brilliant craftsman," says Minos, as if he's continuing a conversation we've been having. "The best I've met. But you don't understand your limitations."

It's dark, and I don't hear the usual sounds of slaves tending the gardens and cleaning the palace. Only the crashing sea, and your faint little breaths. Knossos sleeps. How long has Minos been in here?

"You cannot grant life," says Minos. "You cannot end it with a word. That is the province of gods and kings." He strokes the curls on the back of your head. He draws close to the bed and stands over me. "You will never leave here. You will never build for another king. Tell me that you understand."

My tongue is fat and dry and sticks to my mouth. I nod.

"The words, Daedalus."

I clear my throat. You yawn and nuzzle your face against Minos's shoulder.

"I will never leave here," I say. "I will never build for another king."

Minos smiles. "We're going to make wonderful things together," he says, and hands you to me. You stir, beginning to cry as he leaves the room.

"Daedalus?" says my patron. "Can you solve it?" I stare at the conch and the thread in front of me.

"You don't have to," says Ariadne's memory.

"You will never leave me," says Minos's memory.

I pick up the conch and the thread. I say, "We'll need honeycomb and an anthill."

The solution is impossible to unsee, once I've worked it out. I tie the thread to an ant's leg and lure it through the conch with a drop of honey. I show my forgettable king. Then I wait in an antechamber as he presents the solution to Minos. I listen as Minos reveals himself. Only the ingenious architect Daedalus could have solved that riddle, Minos insists. Hand him over at once.

He threatens Sicily's shipping routes, but there's no heat to it. The possibility of defiance doesn't occur to him. He's swept away his enemies in wars like a man knocking over a game board. He's the son of a god. Great Zeus sired him, becoming a bull and forcing himself on Minos's mother. He's proud of this. I had to decorate the halls of Knossos with frescoes of the rape. I had to paint an expression of ecstasy on Queen Europa's face as the bull pinned her. White bulls in the tile patterns of entrance halls. Golden bull horns forking up behind Minos's throne. Storming up and demanding me is his entire plan, the only plan he's ever needed.

"He shall certainly be returned to you," says my patron.

My patron invites Minos to feast with him before taking me back to Crete. Minos must be weary from his long search. Perhaps he'd like to bathe, and have my patron's daughters bring him oils and fine clothes, before he sits at the head of the table and enjoys the honors that are due him from one king to another.

Minos accepts. Why refuse what is due him?

I've built a beautiful bathhouse for guests, one worthy of a king. The wall tiles have been shaped to resemble shells. Clamshells and oysters, the ever-shrinking spiral of the nautilus, and yes, the thorny conch. The jugs for scented oils are blown glass, shaped like water droplets. The smooth, heavy tub at the room's center is a single chiseled block of marble, with the flukes and tail and small, aged eyes of a leviathan.

I hope Minos notices these details as the princesses undress him and help him into the bath.

The greatest innovation is a long marble spigot jutting from one wall and overhanging the tub. It allows warm and cool water to flow out and cascade into the bath.

The water tanks are in the next room, two of them, huge metal basins. One sweating basin filled with cool water, and one blackened basin filled with hot water. I am standing by the second basin, stripped to the waist. I'm stoking the fire under the basin and listening to the water bubble and boil.

The princesses must be folding Minos's clothes now. They must be picking up his cracked leather sandals and gnarled walking stick and leaving the room. Leaving him naked and alone in the tub. I hear him barking after them. He's not used to being ignored.

I hope he appreciates all the trouble I've gone to. I hope he knows who is doing this to him. But it's not important if he doesn't. I'll live.

I open the sluices and the hissing, boiling water leaps into Minos's bath.

He screams, more in fury than in pain. Things like this don't happen to him. If he thought they could, he wouldn't have come alone.

I picture his skin bubbling and sagging as he tries to climb out of the deep, smooth tub I've carved for him. I'm picturing raw fingers like peeled pomegranate, sliding from the tub's rim as he falls back into the burbling bath. I picture red, steaming water spilling out of the tub and onto the tiles.

His screams are fainter, his splashing weaker. The steam filling the bathhouse is a hot cloth against my face. Minos falls still in a cloud of impenetrable white and a thickening smell of stew.

Icarus, no good thing has happened to me that I haven't wanted to share with you. An early snowfall makes me want to crunch through the white, chasing you. An urn in the city marketplace bears the likeness of Heracles, and I almost bring it home as a gift for you.

I wish you were standing with me now, hearing water drip on tile and waiting for the steam to clear.

We did it, Icarus. We fixed him. He's gone. We're finally, irrevocably free of him.

After Minos is buried in secret, my life becomes mercifully predictable. I make a return trip to your fishing village and erect a monument over your cairn, carving the story of our escape and your fall, of Pasiphaë and her encounter with Poseidon's bull, of the birth of the ravening Minotaur. I carve you as a boy, playing games in our tower rooms. I carve you laughing in flight. I do not carve the Labyrinth.

I build the temple to Hephaestus too, a grand one, though he's little-worshipped here and passersby look at me strangely.

After my return to Sicily, I eat better, and leave my workshop more to walk in the palace gardens or the city streets.

The high stone walls still appear to me every night. Fortunately I've never slept much.

No one asks what it was like on Crete, so I don't talk about it with anyone but you.

Ariadne would understand, but I can't find a trace of her, only rumors. She fled with Theseus, that's sure enough. But my forgettable king checks through diplomatic channels and finds that when Theseus returned to Athens and ascended the throne, Ariadne was no longer with him. There's a rumor that he left her on Naxos, but our envoys tell me that no one in the ports or towns of Naxos has heard of her. She might have walked off the surface of the earth altogether.

I content myself with rising early and going to bed late, with tinkering and writing, with beachcombing at dawn. One morning I'm hunting starfish in a tide pool when my heel skates on a rock slick with seaweed. I crash into the pool, breaking my ankle in the fall. By the time my screams draw help from the palace I'm delirious with pain from the break and from the salt water in my scrapes.

The king's physicians attend me, but the ankle turns green, then black. It sends tendrils of green and black toward my heart. After several nights spent sweating on my sickbed in the king's apartments, I see your face among the huddled doctors. As night falls I hear the *clip clop clip clop* of hooves on the floor above, and then, though no one else looks up, I hear the Minotaur, bellowing with hunger.

I'm feverish, and dying. Since it isn't sleep but death that waits for me, I'm able to close my eyes without fear. The Minotaur and the doctors have left me in peace, and the night enshrouds me in darkness and in silence.

Why did you do it, Icarus?

I'll ask you myself, down there in the dark.

TOUCHED BY
THE GODS

In the first days of your life, when we were prisoners on Crete, locked away together in our tower in Knossos, I made you gifts. The Acropolis of my native Athens, carved in miniature from an olive branch. A relief, in hammered silver, of the stars and planets in the sky the night you were born. Sketches of you in charcoal, portraits on terracotta cups and jars, statuettes adorned with vivid pigments made from seashells.

When you were a few months old, I realized that these weren't ideal gifts for a baby, and I refocused my efforts on toys you could throw or chew. An enamel seahorse that spat bathwater. A leather ball weighted to roll in loops and curlicues. Baked clay blocks with which you could build your own temples and battlements.

In your fifth year, you wanted toys of a military bent— black ships that belched fire, wooden soldiers with bronze armor and spears—but I was building enough of those for Minos and would build none for you.

The year you turned six, I gave you your own stylus and wax tablets, and I was up late one night sharpening the nibs when I heard the sandals of the guards tramping up the stairs of our tower. When our personal guards came up, their footsteps were lazy and meandering. These steps were double-timing, which meant a visit from Minos himself.

Catching his breath, the king of Crete and the conqueror of the sea lanes stared through me like a man trying to recall a dream. His tunic smelled sour. He fingered a fresh bandage on his sword hand.

"The child," he said.

"My king?" You were sleeping in the next room. I kept my voice low, hoping Minos would imitate me and keep from waking you.

"Asterion," said Minos, obliging me with a whisper.

"How is he?" I managed not to say "it." Half the palace heard the screams of the midwives and the lowing of the child. In the morning, the chambermaids who brought our food shared tales of the child's cloven feet, his calf's head and golden eyes, his fur as white as quicklime, his nubs of horns that grew to sharp points before he was a day old. His mouth already lined with gnashing teeth.

"You are to build his home," said Minos.

"Ah," I said, as if nothing could be more reasonable. Minos seldom knew exactly what he wanted from me, but he was clear about the penalty for failure.

"It is to be impregnable. Inescapable. And grand. He is of royal blood, and touched by the gods. He is not to be chained or confined."

I nodded, the safest way to end a conversation with Minos. I listened as the king and his guards tramped back down our stairs.

A little before dawn, you emerged from your room, roaring like a lion. You scampered toward me, snarling as I flung my hands up in mock horror. I caught you under the armpits and hoisted you up, ignoring the twinge in my back. You buried your head in my shoulder. We stayed like that, watching as gray morning took shape outside the window. Each of us feeling the solidity, the still-thereness of the other.

"No lessons today," I said. "I have to work."

You leaned back and beamed at me, hating lessons.

By noon, my sketchbook was crowded with underground galleries, temples on stilts, a statue of Poseidon Earthshaker holding Asterion's cage aloft in one hand. My biggest roll of calfskin parchment, propped by the wide window for royal audiences, was blank. The window framed the battlements and towers I'd already built for Minos, and the waves of the ocean turning to fire in the summer sun.

You had breakfasted, read, pretended to be a centaur, played with my chisels until I told you to stop, walked the ramparts with your nurse and a guard, raced around the gardens with the children of the palace slaves. Now you waved the handle of a paintbrush at me as I sketched.

"You have to slay me," you said.

"All right." I took the brush with my free hand, still sketching with the other.

"I'm a sea monster!"

"And who am I?"

"Perseus!" You sounded annoyed at having to explain so obvious a thing.

"And why are we fighting?"

"Raaaaaaaaaaaaarrrgh!" You gnashed your rows of teeth and waved your tentacles until I got up from my workbench and chased you several times around my drafting table. You reminded me that Perseus wore winged boots, insisted I bounce after you with the slow, floating steps befitting a man walking across the sky. When I stabbed you with the paintbrush you rolled about on the floor, your death screeches growing weaker as gouts of invisible blood shot from your chest to stain the walls and drawings.

After several such deaths, I picked up my sketchbook again. You came back to life and offered me the paintbrush once more. I shook my head.

"Still?" you asked.

I nodded.

"Why not that one?" you asked, pointing.

"The king wouldn't like it."

"And you'd go away."

"That's right."

"Like Mother?"

I didn't say anything. I sketched a prison ship shaped

like a winged heifer. "Here's our central problem," I said, after some thought. "Minos was cuckolded by a bull. The child has unmanned him. He'll never admit to this. He wants both a prison that hides his shame and a monument that shows off how manly and unbothered he is."

"What's unmanned?"

"An architectural term. We'll cover it later."

"How do you know when he's going to like it?"

"Usually I don't know for sure. But when I like it, when the idea feels right, that's the time to show him."

"How long, though?"

I shrugged. "The sooner I have it, the safer we are."

You went and kicked your ball around, stirring up sawdust from a half-finished rocking horse.

As the shadows lengthened and the screams of the prisoners wafted up from the dungeons, the tramping of sandaled feet sounded again from the stairwell, and I readied my excuses for Minos. But it was only Princess Ariadne.

In those days I tutored all the royal children. Ariadne was the only one to visit us outside of teaching hours. She would have been twelve. Typically she'd bound in with a question in place of a greeting. When I sketched animals, how did I get them to sit still? When building a temple to a god, how did I make it fancy enough to please the god but not fancy enough to anger the others? She brought drawings she'd made with borrowed charcoal. A mechanical horse, a self-propelled boat. Could such things be built? How would I go about it?

Today, she trudged in without a word. Her eyes and nose were red. You brightened up and said hello to her five or six times until I shushed you.

"How's your mother?" I asked her.

Ariadne took off one of her gold-and-coral bracelets, valuable enough to buy my old house in Athens, and threw it as hard as she could out the window. She dragged a stool across the stone floor and plunked it down by my work-bench, making as much scraping noise as possible. She glared at the chief guard, who opened his mouth, thought better of it, and shut it again. Then she sat down by me.

"My mother is alive," she said. For a moment her eyes turned wet and her jaw convulsed, a sob struggling to get out. But evidently she'd decided not to cry again in front of the guards. It passed. She wiped her eyes and stared at my parchment with a general hatred. "What are you making?"

"I don't know yet."

"Can I help?" Her voice had softened, making it more of a plea than a question. Anything, I supposed, to keep her mind off of that monstrous birth, and the monstrous coupling that led to the birth.

My parchment was a blizzard, a bleached bone. The white, rolling eye of an oracle having a fit. I threw a sheet over it and stood.

"You can help," I said.

Bats flew over the beach in the dusk. Slaves built the pyre and led out the sacrifices, a goat and a ram from the royal herds. I cut their throats myself and felt the hot blood sprinkling my toes, turning the sand to mud. Ariadne bit her lip. You covered your eyes. As the slaves poured out the libations and laid the bodies on the pyre, I raised a prayer to Hephaestus, beseeching him for a design worthy of my king.

We stood upwind of the puddled blood, and I hoisted you on my shoulders to watch the flames. Ariadne stood with us. After a time she said, "My mother lay with a white bull. That's what they're saying in the kitchens. Because my father offended the gods."

I said nothing.

"She wasn't in her right mind. The gods made her want the bull. Not even to get at her. To get at Father."

I shifted from foot to foot. You played with my hair, a habit when you were drowsy, ever since you were a baby. "That's what they're saying," I conceded.

"What kind of gods would do that?" she said. "Why ask them for anything?"

"Hush," I said, though if the gods wanted to take offense, it didn't matter how quiet she was. "You know why. I'm sorry you had to learn so early." She sniffled, and I put an arm around her.

We watched the smoke rise toward Olympus, blotting out the stars in a long black column that made the firmament resemble an immense door beginning to swing open.

That night I dreamed of high walls meeting at right angles, of wandering a narrow and infinitely branching path open to the heavens and to the cold eyes of the gods. I rose before the sun and set to work filling the blank parchment.

EVERYONE'S HERE

It's dark, darker than my sickroom in the palace. I wonder if I'm still in Sicily, dying, or if I've finished.

"The pain should be gone now," says a new voice. A woman's.

The doctors must have moved me. My soft bedding is gone, replaced with a long slab of cool stone.

"Give your eyes time to adjust," says the woman. She sounds familiar, like the parent of a childhood friend.

A strong arm encircles my shoulders and helps me to sit up.

I'm sitting among smooth stone blocks the size of cottages, by the edge of an old quarry filled with dark water, beneath sky the color of smoke from a funeral pyre.

Your mother is sitting next to me.

"Oh no," I say.

"Be kind to me," she says. "I've died."

She's older now. I suppose we both are.

"You got away, then," I say.

"For a time."

Naucrate grasps my hand and pulls me to my feet. Her hands are what I've missed the most. They're still strong from sewing and weaving, rough from the laundry and the dyeing vats. To feel those hands is to be held with care and purpose.

My broken ankle isn't broken anymore. It takes my weight.

I yank my hand out of hers. She looks at me like she's about to box my ears. I've seen her do it to enough chambermaids and cooks at Knossos.

Instead she says, "Thank you for burying Icarus."

"He's here?" I look for you in the gloom but we're alone.

"Everyone's here," she says. "Eventually."

"He's safe?"

She nods.

"Let me see him."

"Come," she says. "I've been sent to guide you."

She follows a gently sloping path downhill. She doesn't look back. Already she's fading from sight, her shape a patch of gray against a darker gray.

I hesitate. The prospect of a walk with your mother does not delight me. I didn't try to find her after you died, and she didn't come looking for me, and that was best.

The quarry echoes with a lonely *drip, drip, drip*. Nothing moves in the surrounding woods. There are no insects chirping, no sounds of birds or animals in the brush. I feel exposed, like the landscape itself is listening. I don't want to be here by myself.

And you're up ahead.

I hurry after her.

The path weaves down through gnarled pines, and then through the stumps of pines. The felled tree trunks have been stacked by the side of the path in log piles. The logs have been sitting out a long time, warping and sprouting toadstools. I quicken my pace, but your mother stays ahead of me, walking in slow, even strides.

After a time she calls back over her shoulder. "What did you tell him about me?"

"Nothing," I say. "I didn't talk about you at all. When he was old enough to ask, I let him think you were dead."

"I wasn't."

"You might have been."

Hurt silence from her.

"You left us," I say. "I could have told him worse."

I know, my dear one. I'll answer to you for this. But put yourself in my position. Imagine yourself alone, with a child to raise, in that slaughterhouse of a palace. Would you tell your child that his mother left him there? Would you tell him she was happy and alive somewhere, without him? Would that be kinder?

I'll tell you the truth of it when I see you, my Icarus, and I'll welcome your wrath in return.

The ground has leveled out and the tree line is behind us. We pass fields of plowed earth where nothing grows.

We pass the wooden frames of unfinished houses, where nothing crosses the threshold but blown dust. Ahead of us, low hills on the horizon and a sound of rushing water.

Tall rank grasses rise from murky puddles that squelch and fill our sandals with mud. Queer blue-green lights flare up and dissipate in the distance. The roar of the river draws near. The low hills, I see now, are beached ships, slimy from the sea bottom or burnt hollow. The ships have Athenian insignia, olive trees sewn into their sails or owls painted on their hulls.

A signal fire marks the river crossing. It's fueled by broken oars, torn rigging, ragged sails past repair. Other travelers huddle by the fire, casting hungry eyes toward the river and the place beyond the river.

Rhythmic splashing cuts through the sound of the rushing water, and a wide raft drifts into the firelight. It's piloted by a tall, gaunt man who seems to be all sinew, pushing the raft along with a pole. The travelers mill at the riverbank, many imploring him in languages I don't recognize. He says nothing, but points with his pole. The ones he chooses step out of the crowd and onto his raft. When he points at Naucrate and me, the hairs on my neck and shoulders rise. Again I feel exposed, seen more fully than I wish to be.

Naucrate takes my hand to help me aboard the raft. She steadies me as the ferryman pushes off for the opposite bank. I hate that her touch still calms me.

Better not to think about it. "How did you die?" I ask.

"Plague," she says. "They dug pits on the beach, and threw in my body and the bodies of my family, and burned us."

"Ah," I say.

"Before that I had twenty years. Twenty years of sweeping my own porch and stoking a fire in my own hearth, not anyone else's. I stocked my own larder and ate with my own husband and my daughters."

"I'm glad you saw Kythira again," I say, and I am glad, in spite of everything. "I'm glad you found your people alive."

She smiles. It's the first time I've seen her smile in this place. A small, secret smile, and well-worn, like a battered gold ring she's carried for years in a hidden pocket.

I don't ask for details, and she doesn't offer any. Better to think of it as a good omen. Every splash of the ferryman's pole brings us nearer to you.

The band of greater darkness marking the far bank resolves into a row of structures on the shore of Hell. Gates and custom houses, temples and markets, all built of pitted and crumbling stone. Less a city than a primeval ruin. The other travelers spill from the raft. They find their way to gates or buildings particular to them, as if called.

Naucrate leads me to a building resembling one of the public courts of Athens. Jurors' benches encircle the courtroom, and at the back of the room a raised platform awaits the judge.

"It doesn't make up for anything," says your mother,

"but I thanked the gods I had enough strength to hold him when he was born. I never forgot the little weight of him. Every day I remembered that."

"When can I see him?" I ask.

There are others in the court with us, roughs with a half-starved look, dressed in rags. In Athens, such men often served as paid jurors. They eye me and whisper to each other.

"I'll tell Icarus you love and miss him," she says.

"I mean to tell him myself." I try to sound firm, but my voice comes out shrill with panic. I'm searching for a way out, but the jurors have arrayed themselves in front of the exits.

"He'll be safe," says your mother. "Please understand. I'm being allowed to keep him safe. There's a price."

I reach for her, but guards of the court seize my arms. I yell at her retreating back. "Who sent you to fetch me?"

At which point the judge arrives, his footsteps a series of wet and ragged slaps on the stone floor. His robe of office drags behind him, heavy with water that puddles around the hem and sends up curls of steam. He surveys his courtroom, the flesh of his ruined face bubbling and sagging, and when his eyes find me, I see a hatred burning in them that will outlast the stars.

Because who else would preside as judge of the dead? Who but a legendary warrior king, a son of Zeus, and nephew to the god of Hell?

"Bring forward the accused," says Minos.

WALLS BUT NO ROOFTOPS, DOORWAYS BUT NO DOORS

The Labyrinth wanted to grow.

The first drawings were charcoal on calfskin. Asterion's nursery at the center, walls and pathways unfolding in all directions. Corridors turning, doubling back, branching, terminating in blank walls. Walls but no rooftops. Doorways but no doors. The whole structure could be thought of as a single, elaborately chambered room, open and impenetrable.

It was a public safety measure, a vessel to hold Minos's cruelty. It had an inside, where the danger was, and an outside, where we were.

The walls spread to the calfskin's edge like a bloodstain. I laid the skin on the workshop floor, placed more skins above and below and beside it, kept drawing.

We cleared the old parade grounds between the palace and the sea. We began digging the foundation, hauling away black soil, then red clay further down. We unearthed coins stamped with the faces of dead kings, a child's enamel ball, a dagger, a foal's skeleton. We hammered stakes into the ground to mark the walls, strung twine between the stakes, weaving the Labyrinth into being. We dug trenches for the heavy limestone blocks that would make up the walls.

Still the design grew. Minos grumbled but paid off the neighboring farmers. We tore down cowsheds and chopped down orchards, cut new stakes to mark new walls, dug the outlines of new junctions and dead ends. Men fainted in the heat, their palms torn bloody by the ropes they used to haul blocks. We cut so much limestone that the old quarries hollowed out the sea cliffs. Half a cliff face sank into the waves one day like a weary man falling into bed. It took eight men down with it, two of my best stonemasons among them. The waves were too fierce for divers, and Minos wouldn't hear of delaying work to bury slaves, so we left them to Poseidon.

That would not happen to me. I would come home to you. I would not be swallowed up by sea or stone, drowned or crushed, doomed to stalk the outskirts of the underworld without a proper burial, kept from you even in death. These men were slaves, whereas I was an architect of note who worked on pain of death and could never leave. We didn't speak of ourselves as slaves, not once. I would come home to you.

We built the walls from the center outward, reasoning that it was the best way to keep from losing men and supplies in the winding hallways. We hung stones from winches to hoist in teams. We wore wet rags on our heads to keep off the sun, and wet rags over our mouths to keep out the dust.

Early on, when the nursery was finished, the cistern dug, the drinking troughs and drains tested, the walls inlaid with mosaics of Minos and Europa and that wretched bull, we spread a thick layer of straw on the floor and set out a dish of milk and a few armfuls of your cast-off toys. Minos led an honor guard across the construction site. The column of soldiers looked small as it meandered through the Labyrinth-to-be, the armor of the soldiers flashing in the sun, their banners flapping in the gusts that swept the broad open space. The king's men held up the edges of his cloak as he climbed in and out of trenches. Minos held a bleating, wriggling form bundled in a purple blanket.

The king and his priests and the court poet all recited some grandiose nonsense about Asterion's miraculous birth, how it proved that Crete had the favor of the gods. Then they trudged back to the palace, leaving us with the child, some guards and nursemaids, and the afternoon's work to finish.

Ariadne lingered too. I'd been excused from teaching her brothers and sisters while the Labyrinth took shape. None of the others seemed to miss the lessons any more than I did. My troubles were legion, but at least I didn't have to worry about some future king of Crete taunting Princess Phaedra with a dead frog or a wooden mannequin.

Asterion was waist-high and walking already, at

scarcely six months. He toddled about naked, nipping at the hands of my laughing workmen, chasing them around the newly cut limestone blocks. His long horns struck sparks where they grazed the stone. When this happened he lowed in excitement and clapped his hands. He grabbed at our tools and begged food from our lunches, rocking from hoof to hoof until we took pity on him.

Ariadne watched as our foreman fed Asterion bits of bread and olive.

"How will he eat when you're finished?" she asked.

"We'll leave him food," I said. I hoped I sounded convincing. I hoped Minos had a plan for that.

"He'll have to find it, though."

"He'll know this place better than anyone," I said. "You're worried?"

She stared at her half brother, his cloven feet, his golden eyes. His fur was nearly the same ghostly shade as our local limestone. Already he looked at home here. He lifted his arms until the foreman picked him up and carried him around the nursery. As they walked, Asterion reached out and ran his plump fingers along the mosaic tiles. Pasiphaë, I'd heard, wouldn't pick her son up, or venture into the same room as him.

"He's only a little boy," said Ariadne. She called Asterion's name, and he wiggled out of the foreman's arms and ran to her.

One day, the rope frayed and split as we hoisted a stone block to the top of a wall. It fell and crushed a man, and his blood pooled on the newly laid flagstones. Before the dust of the stone's impact had settled, the foreman gave a whistle and men stepped forward to lift the block. Someone ran for the temple to arrange funeral rites. The noise had unnerved Asterion, and one of the stronger stonemasons held the squirming, lowing boy to keep him from seeing the blood.

"Stop." Minos only had to say it once. He'd been a battlefield commander of some repute, and his voice carried over the commotion. We all stopped, and looked to our king, standing in one unfinished corridor where the Labyrinth gave way to muddy fields.

Only the blood continued to move.

"He smells it," said Minos. And Asterion was whining, straining toward the blood. "Let him go."

The stonemason knelt and set the boy down. The little hooves clicked across the flags. Asterion leaned over, almost toppling, and splashed at the pooling blood with a chubby hand. He extended a long, pointed tongue and began to lap up the blood.

"Touched by the gods," said Minos.

We watched Asterion drinking, steady, patient, making a low quiet slurping sound, his throat throbbing, a faraway, contented expression on his face.

After that, Minos sent meat every day. Pale, silent guards brought the meat into the Labyrinth on platters of beaten gold. They didn't speak to us. They shooed flies from the meat, which was red and dripping. They set the meat down and waited for Asterion to come.

Often Minos came along to watch Asterion eat. He chuckled as the boy's sharp teeth tore meat from bone. He clapped his hands and remarked how big his Minotaur was growing. That was a word he'd coined, Minotaur. The bull of Minos.

We all knew where the meat came from, and why there weren't quite as many voices screaming from the dungeons now, and why the butchers drank themselves into a nightmare-addled sleep every night. But what good would it do to dwell on that?

What kind of monster would I have been, to tell you then what I'm telling you now?

We weren't as kind to Asterion anymore. When he tried to eat from our hands we pushed him away or slapped at him. No one wanted to bathe him, and his hands and mouth were crusted with days-old blood. He tottered after us, lowing and reaching up to us, smelling like a butcher's block. We kicked at him or ignored him. He was chest high now, and too big to pick up anyway.

"It's not his fault," said Ariadne, on one of her visits. She'd taken to smuggling greens and roots to him while Minos was elsewhere. Today Asterion was resting his head in her lap and crunching an apple. "He eats what's put in front of him. He doesn't know where it comes from."

I inclined my head in a solemn way, promising to keep my men under control.

Asterion bleated and tried to run after her when she

left. Her visits were growing shorter. She was learning to feed him without having to look at his face. His expression never changed when he ate. He kept that faraway, contented look, no matter what he was eating.

Now that the days were shorter, we worked by torchlight after sundown. Most of the palace was asleep when I shambled to the kitchens in the evenings, begged some warm water from the cook on duty, and went out to the herb garden to wash away the dust and blood in the dark. Then I could trudge up the steps to our tower rooms, still smelling blood, still seeing Asterion's throat throbbing.

Before I collapsed into my bed, I would check on you in your bed at the far end of the room. I think you pretended to be asleep most nights. I pretended not to notice that you waited up for me. I listened to your breathing and thanked the gods for it, wished you a whispered good night.

One night you whispered back to me. "I miss you."

"I miss you, my heart." I sat on the edge of the bed and stroked your hair.

"I heard a crash and shouting."

"A dropped stone. No one died today."

"When the wind blows this way I can hear *him*."

I knew who you meant.

"He cries out like a boy," you said.

"He's not like other children," I said. "Don't trouble yourself."

"He must be lonely."

"He's part god, part king, and part wild creature. Loneliness is his lot in life."

"Can I have another blanket?"

I brought you one and tucked it up to your chin. You shifted under the blankets, getting comfortable. The night air was cold and crisp.

"You're not staying away because you're angry with me?"

"No, my love. Never. The king demands it."

"I'm sorry I didn't let you work."

"What are you talking about?"

"I didn't let you draw. When you worked here. I used to steal your paintbrush so you'd chase me. It made you angry."

"Did it?" All I remembered was your laughter, your exaggerated death throes as Perseus overcame the monster. "I liked having you in my workshop. We looked at my designs together."

"I don't think so."

You had been unusually attentive at six. Hadn't you?

"You're kind to him, aren't you, Father?"

"Of course we are," I said. "Don't give it a moment's thought." I kissed you and went to my own bed. "How were your lessons with Lysandra?"

"Dull. We hated them."

Would you remember Lysandra now? She told marvelous stories. That seemed important. You turned seven, then eight while I built the Labyrinth. If we spoke of leaving, we'd be punished. If we spoke of the world beyond Crete, we'd be punished. But who could take offense at nursery stories, and the worlds they contained?

Nestled under the covers, I closed my eyes. Bloody hands reached up to me. Asterion whined to be picked up. I opened my eyes.

"She told you stories after your lessons?" I asked.

She had.

"Tell me."

And you spoke to me of princes and talking animals, of goddesses who lived under the earth and palaces that rose from the sea. When you had told all of Lysandra's stories, you returned to Perseus, your old favorite, defying the Medusa's grip of stone with his winged sandals and winged steed. At last I slept.

The ground froze, and we hacked at the frozen ground to build the Labyrinth. The ground turned to mud, sprouted weeds and mushrooms, and still we built the Labyrinth. It was a honeycomb of entrances now. We circled the growth, marked our starting and stopping points with flags. When we had to venture in, we marked our way with chalk, and kept the open ground in sight.

Asterion was by now chin-high to most of us. Minos sent him meat twice a day, and while the walls hid his meals from us, we often heard him chewing. He liked to steal around corners and watch us work. We'd look up to find him picking his teeth with a splintered bone, or filing down his long nails against a wall. It took a moment to spot him now, white fur against white stone. A glimpse of movement, the click of a hoof, and there he was, seeming to spring from the rock itself. An ageless fiend, hewn from the earth with the rest of the place. We threw fragments of stones to drive him off. When we pushed him or slapped at him now, he snorted with laughter and returned the blow. He cracked a man's skull that way, thinking it was a game. We needed to finish work. But the Labyrinth wanted to grow.

We rushed, and turned careless. Hammers shattered hands, saws slipped and bit into flesh. Men working double shifts grew faint and feverish. They spoke of Artemis walking atop the walls with her silver bow. When men died, we tried to smuggle them out with the rubbish and bury them in secret. If the guards spotted us, we were under orders to leave any casualties for Asterion.

One night as we worked by torchlight, a mason's chisel bit off his index finger at the first joint. As he screamed and his fellows looked for the fingertip in the shadows, Asterion appeared at a bend in the corridor. Nostrils flaring, he clopped toward us, making low, insistent grunts, reaching for the maimed man the same way he used to beg for olives.

The foreman ran to stop him, and with a lazy backhand, Asterion dashed his head open against a wall.

Asterion looked as surprised as any of us. This was a new way to play a familiar game. He was so strong now, all muscles and teeth and bloodied hands.

He stepped over the corpse, toward us, toward the place where the Labyrinth ended and Crete began.

We might have thrown down our tools then and fled for open ground. We were about to. But a stern, cold voice I recognized as my own shouted, "Drive him back!"

We raised hammers and pry bars, shovels and torches and stones. I swung a long measuring stick to rally the men, and we surged toward the boy who was touched by the gods, and as we charged we heard Asterion laugh with glee. We hadn't played with him in so long.

He gored men, trampled them down, tore faces to ribbons. He threw shattered men onto the tops of walls to die noisy, gurgling deaths. He crushed men in his arms. His teeth ripped chunks of meat from necks and shoulders, until our axe handles and putty knives turned slick with blood.

We could still hurt him. It only took more work now. A torch shoved against his snout. The blade of a shovel swung hard at his ribs. The expression in those golden eyes changed at last. Why were we doing this to him? The game wasn't supposed to hurt so much.

He bellowed, as if he'd like someone to pick him up. But there was no one to pick him up. So he turned, and swept up the foreman's body, and clopped back around the corner and into the Labyrinth, leaving a dripping red trail that no one followed.

He was careful after that. The ground baked in the sun, and the Labyrinth grew, and we no longer saw him. When a man went missing we didn't hear a sound, didn't notice until someone found his tools, hours later.

I carried out my work. I left the work behind when I came home to you.

As harvest time drew near and the farmers prepared to feast Demeter, I went looking for Ariadne. I found her foraging in the herb garden.

"We've missed your visits," I said. "Is there anything you'd like me to leave out for him?"

Ariadne shook her head. "Nothing," she said. "The Minotaur is nothing to do with me."

The first frost came, and the Labyrinth grew, and inside, seen only by the sun and the moon, the gods and the dying, the Minotaur walked in search of food.

IT WILL ALWAYS
BE BOTH

Once again, I wipe the blood from my eyes and look up at the statue. Thinking about the weight and durability of the stone keeps the pain at a distance. The burning and the bleeding are elsewhere. Hell is elsewhere, and I am here, contemplating stone.

It's a statue of Minos, of course. He's over a story tall. His muscles are exaggerated, his helmet tucked under one arm, his spear cocked back and ready to throw. He sneers down at me, triumphant.

The inscription at the statue's base reads, YOU WILL NEVER SEE YOUR SON AGAIN.

My prison in the underworld is a kind of bathhouse, a yawning cave filled with fiery water and burning white mist. The statue stands at the center of the cave. A scalding waterfall pours in through the only entrance, a man-sized hole near the ceiling, far too high for me to reach.

The water splashes and swirls around the hot rocks and sand that make up the cave's floor. It forms pools that bubble and fume, sending up columns of the noxious white steam that scours my skin and makes me sweat blood. It stings my eyes, makes a teary blur of my surroundings. An iron grate in one corner drains the water. The sand and rocks don't burn as badly if I keep moving, stepping from one dry place to another. I can keep clear of the boiling water but never the burning steam. None of this is the worst part.

They built this place under the fiery waters of the river Phlegethon, all for me. Minos bragged of it as the guards of the court, tired-faced men I remember from Knossos, stripped me. They threw me in through the hole in the wall. At times, the steam clears and, right above the waterfall, I can see moonlight streaming in through the hole. I hear the babble of voices and the laughter of women. I smell roasting lamb and hear wine sloshing into cups.

I'm not sure how long I've been down here. They may have forgotten me.

Hundreds of candles line the nooks and crevices in the walls, the better to show me the mocking statue and its inscription, the unguarded exit forever out of reach.

The mist in this place does something to my thoughts. I'm losing parts of you. The first little story you told me, when you were beginning to speak in sentences, one evening by our tower window while I was coaxing dinner into you. Those words are gone. The birds we catalogued on the battlements together—their colors and songs, your satisfaction at spotting and naming them, your favorites, your nicknames and questions—they're taking flight, one by one, leaving empty air. I may have lost more than I realize. That's the worst of it.

Once again I pick up a broad, flat rock I've found, wincing as it scorches my hands. I widen the trench I've been digging along one side of the statue's base, allowing the noxious water to flow in and make a deep, sizzling pool against the statue's foundation. It took a long time to dig the hole, and a longer time for the water to eat away at the stone. Slowly, slowly, the foundation has begun to crumble and sink. The statue has begun to list.

Cracks have formed in the statue's base on the opposite side, and I wedge hot rocks into the cracks to widen them.

This all takes a long time. I build in my head while I work and wait. I'm planning a house for us in the countryside outside Athens, have I told you? I know a place of rolling hills and shady groves near the seashore. My father took me hunting there when I was a boy. I never learned to love hunting, despite his best hopes. But the shape of the landscape stayed with me.

It's a way to hold you in my memory, to keep you in a place where the mist can't scour you away.

I've picked out a spot for us on a hillside with a view of the ocean. I'm imagining you helping me as we haul and lay foundation stones. I talk of southern exposure, how the angle of the roof will shade our front porch in the summer and allow the sun to warm us in the winter. It's summer now, and we shoo dragonflies away as we gather clay by the riverbank and fire it into bricks. At night we lay our bed-rolls in the grass by the building site and sleep under the stars. You tell me how Perseus earned his place in the night sky, and why Orion's constellation topples into the ocean when the sign of the Scorpion appears. And so the days and nights pass.

I wish I could remember the color of your hair.

At last, the statue falls, and Minos shatters on the smoking rocks.

I drag large pieces of the statue, or roll them end over end. I strain my arms and dig my feet into the burning sand. I line the pieces up at the foot of the waterfall. I take the smaller pieces and smash them into powder with rocks. I fill Minos's helmet with the powder, mixing it with sand and with my own sweat and blood to make mortar. I stir with a fragment of Minos's spear shaft. I murmur a prayer to Hephaestus as I mix, offering my blood as a sacrifice.

The biggest fragments of the statue form a row, as flush with the wall as I can make it. Shattered pectorals, fragments of regal forehead. I smear mortar along the top of the first row and add more fragments, calves and biceps and buttocks and shoulders, stacking and cementing the pieces to make a gruesome staircase.

The mortar dries slowly. It may take years. But our house outside of Athens grows and expands, our garden flourishes, the walls keep us warm in the winter, and in the evenings of my old age you read me your poems as I drowse by the hearth. Sometimes your voice is the musical chatter of a young child, sometimes it's the creaking, deepening voice of a young man, sometimes it's lost to me and I can't recall how you sounded.

I wedge my bloodied toes into Minos's sneer to make a foothold. Minos's cupped left hand is the capstone, the final stair. If I stand in his palm and stretch, my fingers can reach the edge of the hole in the wall, and I can climb out.

Icarus. I will be with you soon.

The mist is thick here. My raw hands slip twice on the hole's edge, and I almost fall. Drops of spray from the waterfall bite into my arms. I leap. My elbows and forearms scrape against the stone lip of the opening. I stub my toes kicking against wet rock. Blood-slick, mewling like a newborn, I scramble up through the hole.

The tunnel is dark and sweltering, filled with the roar of water. I keep a hand on the wall and walk to one side of the burning stream. Water splashes and babbles ahead of me; another waterfall fills a small pool at the tunnel's end. There's a circle of light overhead. My groping hand finds metal rungs set into the wall. I grasp them and climb, water falling past me, fire lapping at my back and shoulders. The circle of light grows and I clamber through.

An iron grate slams shut behind me. I stand.

I'm in a yawning cave filled with fiery water and burning white mist. The statue of Minos stands at the cave's center, upright and whole. The inscription on the base now reads, HE WILL FORGET YOUR FACE.

Icarus. How many times have I done this before?

I curse Minos. I smash my hands against the rock walls. I'm trying to remember the color of your eyes. I'm trying to hold on to the picture of our house outside of Athens. I'm reciting measurements and lists of building materials, long past the point where I can remember why.

Some time after that, I find a broad, flat rock, kneel by the statue, and begin to dig.

The sand burns my knees and feet. The steam scours my skin. Minos towers over me. I dig at the statue's base with a heavy rock in my blistered hands. None of this is out of the ordinary.

Then, for the first time in a long while, something unexpected happens. A woman clears her throat behind me. At the sound of her voice, I smell figs ripening on the branch. I had forgotten there were such things as figs. I pause in my digging. I turn from my work to see a woman, or something in the shape of a woman. Her dress is the color of corn husks in autumn. Her smile is kind, though I suppose the smile of the cowherd tending his cows is kind in a similar way. Looking at her for too long gives me vertigo. So I return to my digging, which is easier to understand.

"You're Daedalus," she says.

I glance at her again. "I'm . . . Daedalus?" The name sounds familiar.

"Formerly of Crete," she says. "Formerly of Athens."

Confused, I look at the statue to get my bearings. The

inscription on the base of the statue reads, YOU WILL FOR-
GET HIS NAME.

I don't know whose name I've forgotten, but I know
that I've forgotten someone, and the immensity of the loss
is like standing before an ocean on a moonless night, a
huge dark ocean heard and felt but not seen. Covering my
face, I crouch down and rock on my heels.

A rustling, and the woman is at my side without seeming to move. She touches my arm, and her touch is cold
dew on a hillside at daybreak. In this place it comes as a
cooling balm.

"Here," she says, offering her hand. I take it and we're
no longer in a cave but in a root cellar with walls of dark
earth. Carrots and radishes line the walls in stacks. She
scoops a handful of earth from the wall and holds it out,
inviting me to breathe it in.

The dirt smells pungent and rich. I breathe deep.

"I'm Daedalus," I say, the name beginning to feel right
in my mouth. "Father . . ." I wait, trembling, and then the
name bubbles up. "Father of Icarus."

Your name. Oh, Icarus, my Icarus. Gods deliver you
from the likes of Minos.

"They built your bathhouse at the confluence of the
Phlegethon and the Lethe," says the woman. "You burn,
yes, and you also forget. Minos has never hated anyone
so much."

I answer, "Neither have I," and she nods as if this is
only proper. She motions for me to follow her and I do. If

I keep my gaze on the earthen walls, I can watch her from the corner of my eye without feeling dizzy.

It should be impossible, but the root cellar, deep in the ground, is the antechamber to a sprawling throne room in a moldering palace on a hill. The throne room is open to the overcast sky. The front entrance is an empty archway, framing a fearful country lit by scattered fires and marsh-lights.

Facing the landscape is a tall black throne, glimmering and jagged. It's obsidian, built to huge proportions. A throne where the god whose name we fear to speak can sit and sur-vey his kingdom. There's a smaller throne next to it, a rude, wild-looking throne hammered together from logs of white poplar. The woman sits in it, and I prostrate myself on the ground before the throne. It seems the least one can do upon encountering Queen Persephone in the throne room of Hell.

"A woman came to me yesterday and clasped my knees," says Persephone. "She said she'd been seeking an audience with me for a long time. She told me that Daeda-lus, the father of her child and the greatest architect of his age, was unjustly bound in Tartarus, and if I freed him, he would build me wonders."

"I will," I say, still prone.

"I have little use for the works of men," she continues. "Can you build me the tracery of veins in a maple leaf? Or the many chambers of a pomegranate?"

It would be safest not to answer, I decide.

"Still," she says after a moment, "my winter palace is drafty and ill-maintained, and since I must live here for half of every year, you may as well see what you can do with it."

I raise my eyes to her. She sees the question in them.

"Your Naucrate is very brave," she says.

"Please, may I see my son?"

She bites her lip, and the creek beds of the world crust over with ice.

"There's only so much I can do for you," she says, with a glance at the obsidian throne that towers over hers. "I am queen here. I am also a prisoner here. Both things are true."

I wait. She sighs, and frost hardens the roads of the world.

"I've spoken with my husband," she says. "You can complete your sentence in my service. But you cannot see your son again. Minos was adamant, and my husband won't overrule him on this."

I consider the rough, marshy landscape below us, where the dead gather in camps and scattered dwellings. I recall the decaying structures on the riverbank.

I say to Persephone, "Do you care for your kingdom?"

She frowns, and in the orchards of the world olives and figs wither.

"You're a prisoner here," I say. "With respect, my queen, everyone is a prisoner here. And the gloom and disorder of this place is such that no one can forget it."

Jars of olive oil turn rancid. Carrots and turnips bloom with brown rot. I'd better arrive at my point quickly.

"What if your new palace had public gardens for your

subjects? What if the gardens were ringed by river walks and by dwellings, and roads linked the dwellings to the markets? What if there were art, and theaters, and dancing grounds, and the million little stages that let citizen and slave take part in the place where they live?

"My queen," I say, "might this entire kingdom become more a home than a prison?"

"It will always be both," says Persephone, sadness in her voice. A sadness fit more for mourning blighted harvests and burnt forests than the little lives of men.

Still, I know enough to wait as she considers my words.

"It would be the work of many lifetimes," she says at last.

"What do we have but time, my queen? My works are yours. And your husband's. If he'll meet my price."

"He dotes on me," says Persephone. "I'll speak with him again. Complete the work. Please us. And you may go to your son."

Buds struggle to life on frostbitten branches. Red-feathered and blue-feathered birds dot landscapes of gray and brown, tittering the opening notes of a song.

INTERLUDE

WHAT WOULD YOU LIKE TO SEE?

The half-built palace at Knossos smelled of quicklime and rang with the sound of hammers. Sea breezes wafted through unfinished walls. Outside, cookfire smoke made thin columns over Minos's tent city on the plain. I walked in the central courtyard, following the new head housekeeper.

"Fig trees here," said Naucrate. "Pears here. Then apples."

She led me through rows of invisible trees. She and the groundskeepers were going to plant an orchard. Right then there was only dirt and lumber.

"If you can dig two cisterns, we'll avoid many, many fights between the gardeners and the cooks."

We passed through the kitchens-in-progress. I consulted my notes and amended diagrams. Naucrate worked from memory, where she kept her purchase orders, her inventory, her daily tasks, her meal plans for the royals and the slaves.

"If you can put a ramp at the back entrance, that'll make it easier for the porters to roll the wine casks up from the docks."

Naucrate didn't have a Cretan accent any more than I did. She came from Kythira, where Aphrodite first rose from the sea. Pirates took her one morning as she haggled at the well in her village square. She'd come to hire a nursemaid and a housekeeper. The pirates sold her to Minos, who put her to work as a laundress.

"Come look at this," I said.

A long corridor linked the kitchens to the dining hall.

"We're building light wells and windows to let in sunshine and fresh air," I said. "Even here on the lower floors. Everyone working down here will have that. And they'll be able to see this." I stepped to one side, extending an arm to indicate the long, sunlit hallway.

"A wall," said Naucrate. "Lovely."

"These interiors will all be painted," I said, leading her along the blank wall. She was smiling a little, laughing at me a little, and this warmed me as much as the sunlight. It was work, to get her to look outward, away from her lists and orders. But I've always enjoyed my work. "We can paint gods, or birds, or cattle. Seascapes, maybe. Can you find me more of that blue pigment the Egyptians sell?"

"It's on the list."

"Footraces," I continued. "Boxing matches. Wars. Love stories. Us, even. All of us who work here, and the ones we serve. Whatever you like. The paintings will be beautiful, and we'll be the only ones, out of all the people of Crete, who get to walk past them every day." We stopped, and I put a hand on the wall. "What would you like to see?"

"Seascapes," she said. "We get a better price on blue if I order in bulk."

"All right. Seascapes, then."

Naucrate looked down the empty hall, down the length of the mural that wasn't there yet.

"This could be a good place," I said. "In spite of everything. We could make this a good place."

Naucrate went quiet. She took my hand, and her palm was hot and damp as she led me back the way we came. The promise of rain and lightning hung in the muggy air.

That night, she came to my room for the first time.

Athens was overbuilt and architecturally hidebound, no place for an artist to make his name. I'd followed stories of a new king on Crete, a conqueror in need of a grand palace. No design would be too ambitious for such a man. They'd talk about the palace, about whatever I built next, for generations.

"We'll buy your freedom and the baby's," I told your mother-to-be. "Once his palace is finished, he'll make me a wealthy man."

"You think he's going to let you go," said Naucrate. It was less of a question, more the diagnosis of a delusion.

It became harder to ignore the growing number of guards at the docks, at the edges of the construction site.

Tall, broad men, scarred from foreign wars, often bored, dicing or arm wrestling while we worked, not seeming to watch me but keeping a line of sight to me wherever I went.

❖

After your long and bloody birth, your mother said she heard horses. She said they were in the courtyard outside, stomping and snorting, a whole team of them impatient to be on their way. She said a charioteer was talking to the horses to calm them, whispering in their ears. His low voice like cold air seeping under a door in the night.

"There's no one out there," I said. It was late, and the midwives tended Naucrate by lamplight. Her skin had turned gray from loss of blood. "We're here with you. I'm here and the baby's here."

Holding you was disconcerting. Your eyes were sunken and your cheeks were chubby. I could feel your bones beneath the blankets and baby fat. How strange, I thought, to make a person.

She needed rest. The midwives ushered me out. You were asleep on my shoulder.

I walked the palace with you. Down the tower steps, along the battlements, through darkened halls, into the courtyards, and past the saplings of fig and pear and apple trees. The walking motion helped you sleep, and I could concentrate on each step and not think about your mother, or the horses, or what I would do if we lost her.

Days of this while the midwives tended her. We walked. I brought you to the wet nurse. We visited your mother when she was strong enough. I moved my bed and your basket into my workshop so she could sleep undisturbed. I carried around a mat of reeds, placed you on it in different rooms, watched your puffy eyes dart around while you chewed on your hands.

It was late again, the night we ascended the tower steps to find Naucrate gone, the midwives talking in low voices over her empty bed.

The stomping, snorting horses. The grim charioteer whose name we never speak. They'd taken her.

I was thinking about her grudging smiles and wondering what kind of funeral rites she'd want when one of the midwives took my arm and told me that Naucrate had not died. She'd climbed out of bed while her attendant slept, and she'd stolen away in the night. Some of her jewelry was missing, and a Phoenician merchant ship had sailed early from our docks.

Your mother hadn't spoken much of Kythira, but she'd often gone quiet with me, her thoughts in another place, with other people. The restless hooves of those terrible horses must have frightened her so, reminded her that she only had so much time, that she had to choose.

So she had chosen.

She didn't even try to convince me to escape with her.

Was she so certain I'd talk her out of it? Or betray her?

I placed you on the mat in the room that belonged to the two of us now. The midwife was saying something I couldn't understand. You stretched in your sleep, straining against your swaddle. I watched you breathe. I waited for you to wake up and cry out. We'd walk the palace, you and I. One room would open into the next. I'd feel your breathing against my chest. Your eyes, your mother's eyes, would dart around as we walked, drawn to light and motion.

Feedings would follow feedings. I would sing you half-remembered lullabies, coining new lyrics to replace what was lost. I would talk to you of landscapes and building materials so you'd hear a familiar voice, talking of things beloved.

A good father was a thing to build, a project like any other. One simply did what a good father might do, hour upon hour.

You stretched, blatted awake. I picked you up and propped you on my shoulder, putting a foot forward, then another.

"Hello, my love," I said, over your rumblings. "Here we are."

A STRUCTURE THAT SHOULDN'T EXIST

I set foot in the finished Labyrinth once, only once.

Gum-eyed, yawning, I crossed the square from the palace to the mouth of the Labyrinth. The outer wall bristled with ladders and scaffolding. The mortar dried in silence. It waited.

We'd laid the final stone late the night before, done the last of the weatherproofing, counted heads to make sure the Minotaur hadn't picked off anyone new, and left as fast as we could.

Tomorrow we'd tear down the scaffolding. Minos would speak fine words and send the first weeping prisoner into the Labyrinth at swordpoint.

Today, though, was a gift from the king. None of us were to work today. We were to celebrate with our families, celebrate our completion of the great monument. Life was short, after all.

The Labyrinth had no gates or doors, nothing that could be locked or closed. The high wall simply opened. I'd seen it that way in my dream. No children played in that square; slaves and supplicants took the long way around, to avoid passing in front of the opening in the wall. Silence filled that place, as wine fills a cup. As if it was haunted by what was going to happen there.

I crossed the square and entered the Labyrinth, following the chalk arrows we'd drawn on the flagstones to point the way back out. As was our practice in fair weather, we'd left our tools piled along one wall a few turns into the Labyrinth, planning to collect them after our holiday. When the weatherproofing was inspected and the scaffolding dismantled, we'd gather our tools, leave the way we came, and erase the chalk arrows, the last living men to walk out of that place.

But I'd forgotten your present in my bag, with my tools and wax tablets and stylus. It was a papyrus scroll, older than me, tucked into a sealskin bag and bought from an Assyrian pirate for a purse of gold. On the scroll was a poem. The adventures of a hero king of Uruk who withstood famine and flood, braved the houses of the dead to rescue a comrade. It made little sense to me, but you loved adventures and heroes, and gifts from distant places. It wouldn't replace the months and years that the Labyrinth took, days of yours I missed completely, nights I came home late to the sound of your slow, quiet breathing in the dark. But today I could sit with you on the grass near the sea, on a bright clear summer's day, and see your smile as you unrolled a new poem that was older than Athens.

My bag was propped against the wall where I left it, at the end of a long row of hammers and rope coils. The poem was still inside. I gathered my things and turned to go.

When I rounded the first corner, the chalk arrows were gone.

There was a damp patch on the rough flagstones where an arrow might have been scrubbed away with a wet rag. Or I'd made a mistake, turned the wrong corner. I tried to double back, but couldn't be sure which branching path I'd followed to get here.

The trick was not to panic. I closed my eyes, pressed my back against cool, solid stone until the spinning sensation stopped. I'd barely walked a hundred paces in. I'd turned no more than three corners. I was within shouting distance of a bustling palace on a bright summer morning, in a Labyrinth of my own design. I would find my way out.

Three or four corners. Was it three or four?

Outside, gulls were crying. An axe thudded into a stump, splitting wood for the kitchens.

Sit, I told myself. Don't run. Don't make blind turn after blind turn and travel further down the gullet of this place. Remember. See the schematic you drew. The entrance is here. The wrong turns start immediately, the obvious exits that glide deeper toward the Labyrinth's center. If the corridor where we keep the tools is straight back, then the turns leading out must be . . . here, here, here.

I got up and walked and made the final turn.

Blank walls, empty corridors. No exit.

Remembering the schematics wouldn't work if I couldn't tell where I was starting from.

The walls were high and smooth, the stones uniform in shape and color. They dulled the eye. They encouraged me to overlook openings, to forget turns and intersections as soon as I passed through them. Depth was hard to gauge. The sky was a narrow blue river without a wisp of cloud. I couldn't see the palace or the inland hills or even the angle of the sun, which seldom reached the floor of the Labyrinth. I'd been inside perhaps an hour.

I could still hear the axe chopping wood, sheep bleating in a neighboring field. But sound echoed here, and breezes carried voices over walls and around corners. The wood-cutter could be on the opposite end of the Labyrinth, or a few paces away, on the other side of a wall.

"Help!" I called up, cupping my hands. "I'm lost in here! Help me!" If my men had to scale the walls to get me out, the jokes would follow me for the rest of my life. But I'd be alive to hear them.

I shouted a while longer. No one shouted back. The axe *thunked* into the stump and rested there. The sheep took their bleating elsewhere. Faint on the wind, the sound of children screaming happily, the smell of pig roasting on the bluffs by the sea.

Everyone who knew me would be out celebrating to-day, by order of the king. You were one of those children running among the revelers on the grass. I'd left you there this morning, promising you that I was coming right back with something I'd forgotten. You'd be wondering what kept me. It must be almost midday by now. You'd ask after me. Someone would come looking.

Until then, though, a stranger screaming in the Labyrinth, well! That was like the crash of waves, part of the landscape.

"Please!" I screamed once more.

Around a corner, behind a wall, some other soul in the Labyrinth snickered.

Anyone might have seen me walking in, followed me, and scrubbed away the arrows. Anyone who'd lost a limb to the Labyrinth, or a friend or a lover, had reason enough to hate me. Maybe in their haste they'd trapped themselves, erasing the arrows as they came in and not as they left. They might have a blade.

Maybe I'd be lucky to meet them, before I met the Minotaur.

I didn't shout any more. I listened.

If my enemy had any accusations or declarations of revenge to make, they weren't ready to share yet.

No one's coming, I told myself. It's been hours and no one's called out for me. Poor Icarus doesn't know where I went. He's out there, kicking a ball, telling himself not to be such a worrywart. Sparing a nervous glance at the palace every minute or so, hoping to see me jogging across the grass. Ah, for Perseus's winged sandals! Or even one of the ladders propped outside. One was as unreachable as the other.

Get out of this, I told myself, or he'll never know what happened. He'll think I ran, like his mother.

Concentrate. See the Labyrinth from above. Here's the exit. Here are paths snaking away. Say I'm here. Turn here, then here, then straight for a long while. Two lefts, a right, and out.

Another twisting corridor, more silent hallways, clear blue sky overhead.

I could smell the Minotaur on the walls now, his reek of sweat and dung. I couldn't hear him, so he was either sleeping or stalking quietly after me. Milky fur veined with old blood the color of rust. I might not see him until he was on top of me.

Some objects in an empty room caught my eye as I passed. Little asymmetrical lumps in a corner, breaking the pattern of smooth stones at right angles. I went into the room, stooped to pick one of them up.

It was the palm-sized figure of a man, molded together from fur and dried manure. There were other figures littered about. A woman carved from bone, a little boy with horns. Birds. The moon. A white bull whittled from the wood of some discarded tool. A bundle of bloody, knotted-together rags that I finally recognized as a ball for kicking.

He'd made his own toys.

I couldn't stay here. I went out again, trying to retrace my steps, failing. The smell of him thickening.

A hissing sound, dead ahead, stopped me.

A blade unsheathed.

My betrayer. He was close now, and I could hear his raspy breathing, smell his sweat. He was as panicked as me.

"I'm going to cut your hands and feet off and leave you for *him* to find," said a voice from around the next corner.

He did have a blade. I had my stylus and your poem and my fists and feet.

"My brother died building this place for you. Not right away. A cave-in crushed his chest. He fought for days."

He was working himself up, summoning the nerve to turn the corner with his sword swinging.

"I'll spare you," said the voice, "if you can tell me his name."

I'd kept a list at first, truly, planned to commit it to memory. But the list grew too long, and would it do all that much good, make anyone any less dead?

"That's what I thought," said the voice. "Bastard."

I raised my stylus, waited for him to round the corner so I could blind him and run.

He didn't round the corner. He gurgled. Slowly, slowly, from around the corner, a dark red pool of blood spread into view.

I waited for the thud of a falling body but it never came. Only chewing, slurping. Big gulps of breath between swallows. That rank animal smell.

He must have crept up behind and opened my enemy's throat with a long nail. Easy as uncorking a jug of wine.

I hadn't seen the Minotaur in over a year. His every breath was a seismic rumble. He sounded much bigger.

I had until he finished his meal to find a way out. Either I would see you again, talk with you and hold you and marvel at the world with you again, or I wouldn't.

Strangely enough, it wasn't your voice I heard as I stared at the spreading blood. It was Ariadne's.

"You worry too much," she said.

Sleeplessness had driven me to the kitchens late one night, and I found the princess grinding herbs by lamplight.

"I can't help but worry," I said. "We've lost too many men. Maybe there's no helping it, and that's the price when you build a structure that shouldn't exist around a creature who shouldn't exist. What if my turn's coming? What becomes of Icarus then?"

Ariadne pushed aside her mortar and pestle, drew blood from her index finger with a pinprick, caught three drops in a bowl.

"Father takes all the credit, but it was Mother who helped him conquer the seas. She could summon a fair wind, call down storms on our enemies. She still can. But she needs help now."

Queen Pasiphaë was rarely seen outside of her rooms. Her windows burned with unearthly light at odd hours. Household slaves left food at her doorway, glimpsed a wan figure in a frayed, diaphanous tunic, indifferent to them, whispering charms and curses.

"I'm sorry," I said. "What happened to her wasn't fair."

Ariadne shook her head.

"Fairness doesn't enter into it. You always come back to

this in our lessons: There are rules. Father was meant to sacrifice the white bull to Poseidon, and he didn't. Mother could have talked to him, made him honor the gods. She's changed his mind on bigger matters. But she didn't. There was a lapse, a rule broken, and she paid. She was hardly at fault, barely out of step, but it wasn't about fairness. What happened next was simply what happened next."

"No one can live that way, never making a mistake, never missing a step. Not forever."

"No?" She wrote a word on a slip of papyrus in letters I couldn't read, touched the paper to her lamp's flame, and let it burn to nothing. "We're not like most people. We see the patterns most people don't. Because we have to. That's how we're going to do extraordinary things while others are eaten alive."

And before my eyes, a wind stirred in the closed room, and the wind blew the lamp's flame sideways, and Ariadne smiled a proud smile as our shadows danced across the walls.

Backing down the corridor, away from the widening pool of blood and the hulking, chewing mass around the corner, I took inventory. My stylus was the only sharp edge at hand. It would have to do.

I slashed at the skin of my left arm with the tip of the stylus, tearing open a vein and letting the blood gush out. Don't scream, I reminded myself. The Minotaur's teeth will hurt worse. I tried not to look at the wound, already feeling faint. I wet my fingers in the blood, and when I reached a

fork, I turned right. I stooped and drew an arrow on the
floor with my blood, so that when I looked back I'd see an
arrow pointing right.

At the next fork I did this again. I turned left. I looked
back and copied the first arrow. Next to my first arrow,
pointing right, I drew a second arrow, pointing left. I copied the two arrows at the next fork, then three, then four, so
that each turning point was marked in blood with a list of
the turns that had gotten me there.

Finding a path out wasn't the problem. I had dreamed
this place into being, stared down into maps of it every
day for years. Fixing my own position was harder. Not impossible. Not for someone who could record the pattern.

I had to tear open two more veins to keep the blood flowing. My breathing was fast and shallow. The floor was beginning to tilt, and my host would scent the blood and follow,
and night was coming soon. I still couldn't recall how far I'd
come, where I'd turned. But that was all right. The growing
list of turns was at my feet, telling me where I'd been.

Now, I told myself. See the maps. See the shape of the
path that led here, the identical lines arranged in a unique
shape, like the strokes of a stylus making letters. Find that
shape in the Labyrinth.

There.

There I was.

Behind me, breath through wet nostrils. A rough
tongue lapping blood from stone.

I wouldn't get another try.

See the drawings. See the way out. This is already part

of the path. Turn here, here. Straight on, past the parts of the Labyrinth that are not the path.

Behind me, hooves on stone.

Here. Another turn. Another.

Ahead, sunlight on the flagstones of the open square.

Hot breath on my neck.

The walls fell away. The stones of the square were warm against my cheek. I curled up, trying to make myself small now that there was too much sun, too much open space.

If he followed me out, killed me in the open, that wouldn't be as bad.

But no. There was a fullness in the shadows just inside the entrance to the Labyrinth, and then the fullness was gone. He'd gone back inside. Inside meant blue skies and bird-song, starlight, meat when he called for it. Outside meant cuffs and curses, spitting, an axe handle to the stomach.

I'd taught him that.

"That's right," I shouted at the gap in the wall. "I taught you!" I was shaking. I scrambled to my feet, grabbed a pry bar propped against a pile of boards, and smashed it against the Labyrinth's outer wall hard enough to draw sparks, again and again for as long as I had the strength, which wasn't very long. When I was done, when I was a panting, snot-dripping tangle of limbs at the foot of the wall, the Labyrinth stood. It might stand for a thousand years, blind, silent, swallowing lives and forgetting them at once.

Maybe I looked as if I had died in the Labyrinth, as I called to you on the grassy bluff overlooking the sea. Bloodied, staring, wailing your name. No wonder you paled, hesitated before leaving your games with the other children and running to meet me.

I clutched at you, looked at your teary face to make sure you were here, I was here, I wasn't still in there, never, never would I go anywhere near that place again, never once.

"I'm so sorry," I was babbling. "I tried and tried to come to you and I couldn't, hours I was in there, I'm sorry I was gone so long and you were waiting for me all day. Don't be frightened."

You were shaking your head now, your brimming eyes wide.

You saw it then, didn't you? You knew then that I'd built something terrible, truly terrible. You could see it in my face and hear it in my every shallow breath. You'd gotten a glimpse of the horror I'd tried to keep away from you.

How long until you saw it fully?

You took a step back from me. You wiped your nose with the back of your hand.

"You only just left," you said.

I nodded, understanding nothing.

"Father," you said, slowly, as if I might run. "It's still morning. You weren't gone all day."

Stares from the other children.

The tears spilled over now, and when you spoke you

sounded angry that I'd brought you to this in front of your friends. You grabbed my hands and shouted the words, as if to wake me up.

"You were only inside for half an hour."

THERE IS
A PATH OUT

The best part of being dead is that I can always work and never need to sleep. I don't have to dread closing my eyes and opening them again inside the Labyrinth. I don't carry the fear with me into the waking world. I don't find myself paralyzed for hours in one spot, wary of leaving my drafting table or my little garden of asphodel in the palace courtyard, for fear that corridors will unfold endlessly before me and I'll never find my way back. There is a path out, and I'm on it.

A team of dead cartographers and land surveyors is assigned to show me around Hell. They all have an unkemptness about them, the distant eyes and delayed responses of men going mad by degrees. This, one of them explains, is because Hell is as big as it needs to be, which renders the performance of their jobs technically impossible.

Still, they show me the deepest parts of Tartarus, where

the light fails and the air thickens. Where the Titans strain at their bonds with tectonic groans. Where Typhon vomits smoke and molten rock, his breath deepening the gloom, his rage singeing the hairs from my arms as we pass.

We traverse the chained body of Prometheus the Titan, who made the first men. We make base camp at his navel, and a day's hike gets us to his breastbone. Prometheus can see us by now, and, recognizing me, praises my work. He talks cheerfully of how his designs must have influenced mine, for what is the human body, with its branching veins and winding bowels and many-chambered heart, if not a Labyrinth? At this I grow faint and need to be guided back to camp. My scars throb where the stylus bit into my arm. Prometheus invites me to come see him anytime, for he has little company, excepting the eagle. As if summoned, the eagle descends with a screech and sinks its beak into his liver. Prometheus's invitations dissolve into screams, and the clammy flesh beneath our sandals quakes and pales.

At my request we double-time through Elysium, where rays of golden light pierce the clouds, where trees are heavy with fruit and singing birds, where streams babble, where heroes wrestle and spar and swap lies on flower-speckled riverbanks, where poets swoon over the bravery of the heroes, and where the women and slaves look as miserable as they are everywhere else.

I'm more interested in the wild places that border Elysium. Steep and ragged mountains that no one has crossed. Caverns that echo with the squeaks of bats and sparkle with jewels. Deserts where white toads emerge from burial mounds of black sand. A subterranean ocean where blue jellyfish glow in the deep.

Charon squeezes us aboard his ferry to survey the rivers, and it's on one of these trips that I hear voices calling my name, and see figures gesticulating on the far bank, which marks the dreadful empty country outside of Hell.

"No burial," says Charon, when I ask him. "No fare."

We're moving faster than the dead can follow, but more figures appear on the bank downriver, calling to me. Familiar faces spit at me. Familiar voices curse me. The drowned stonemasons, the crushed and missing men. There are so many unclaimed bones scattered in the Labyrinth, picked over by the Minotaur and by vermin, bleached by the sun but never touched by the hands of friends or kinsmen. Entombed but unburied.

The dead are shouting louder now, but not at me. They scatter, fleeing upriver and down. I'm about to ask about this until I smell dung and blood, and see his long, sharp horns and then his white body rising and rising over the riverbank.

Oh, but he's grown big. His hugeness is obscene on the open ground, his milky fur indecent in our perpetual midnight. He needs stones and mortar to clothe his nakedness. His breath makes fog in the night air. He snorts and snuffs at the river's edge, perplexed, once again, by a barrier beyond his understanding. I imagine his heavy bones discarded at the center of the Labyrinth, the skull cleaved off. His wide headless trunk looking, without the bull's head, like the lost remains of a most formidable hero. Songs and stories his only epitaph.

"Him," I whisper.

"No burial," says Charon again, unimpressed.

The Minotaur bellows, more in fear and sorrow, I think, than in hunger. The Labyrinth was all he knew. Haunting the open country must be unbearable. I watch him grow smaller until a bend in the river hides him from sight.

The design stage takes longer than the construction stage, for Persephone and her king can shape the underworld with a thought. But working out the height and shape of the doorways, the light source of each room, the composition of the frescoes, the statues in the cornices, all that takes time. I finish the schematics and the new palace appears, sure and steady as a moonrise. I design the public gardens, the plazas, the streets, the docks, building outward in rings.

Persephone won't tell me, but I feel that you're close by. I'll walk through a newly built agora or along a canal. I'll find a nice spot to sit and listen to the nightingales and smell the narcissi. I'll wonder if you ever sit here, and whether the spot brings you happiness.

I wonder about Ariadne too. I send my surveyors and

apprentice draftsmen out to the taverns I've built, and there they talk of the ingenuity and beauty of the legendary princess of Crete. Once in a while a drowned sailor or starved musician will share a story of their own. Theseus abandoned her, the stories agree. After they fled Crete together, he left her on Naxos and sailed back to Athens alone. From there, the stories grow wild and unreliable. Travelers claim they've seen her dancing in the woods, ringed by bloody-handed maenads, a handsome young man crowned with vines dancing beside her. These travelers admit to being in their cups at the time. That's as much as I'm able to learn. She seems never to die.

I find subtler and stronger ways to bind the monsters and unfortunates in Tartarus. I content myself with gilding the edges of Elysium, since it's filled with preservationist cranks who like things as they are. I settle for a statue here, a temple there.

In the world above, mountains are worn down. Kingdoms rise and fracture and are subsumed by other kingdoms. Hell becomes prettier, but it's still Hell.

On the day my work is finished, Persephone declares a festival, shortens the roads and byways, and throws open the gates of Elysium to the common dead.

Hundreds of thousands tramp into paradise, gray shadows marveling at the green grass and golden light. They carry pale beans and wheat watered from the Styx and grown in darkness. They carry kindling and coal. They lead black rams and pigs, reared in sunless pastures and fattened on mushrooms. The dead build fires and spread blankets on the grass. They cut the throats of the animals and roast the best cuts of meat over the fires, offerings to Persephone and her king, whose name we fear to speak. They pour wine into mixing bowls and share meat on skewers. Someone strikes up a lyre. The heroes of Elysium, hungry for a new audience, are holding games in Persephone's honor, racing chariots, boxing, feeding on the cheers of the assembled dead.

My work's an afterthought here. I've built a marble pavilion by a duck pond. I like to think of you standing in the pavilion, finding inspiration in the green hills and soaring mountains, reciting one of your epics, coaxing gasps and laughter from the crowd. I'm an afterthought, too. I haunt the festivities, stepping over the blankets of the dead with a skewer of meat I can't identify or taste, impatient to take my leave. A widow laughs as the four husbands she collected in life jostle each other to refill her cup. A deserter, released from Tartarus for the day, shifts position with a rattle of leg irons. His armored back is a pincushion of arrows. He's chained to a heavy stone, and sits upon it. He balances a boy on his lap, tells war stories in an antiquated dialect to children or grandchildren sitting cross-legged on the grass.

Finally, I see Persephone sitting on a rock by the pond, feeding the ducks. Her garments are bright red and gold; it must be autumn in the world above. No one else looks at her or talks to her. I have leave to approach. I join her at the pond's edge, watching ducks the color of midwinter sunlight fight for bits of bread.

"Satisfied with it?" she asks, meaning Hell entire.

"That's less important than what you think, my queen. But yes. I'm happy with it."

"Enjoy this," she says. "The anticipation of reward can be sweeter than the thing itself."

I stand respectfully straight. I don't grasp her knees and beg to see you. I watch her reflection in the pond and say, "Please. Is it time?"

Persephone sighs, and in the world above bonfires release the last of their smoke. "It's time," she says. "I'll tell you where Icarus can be found."

She names a place and I nod, grateful, but the goose-flesh is already spreading on my neck and arms.

I swallow.

"Say it again. My queen."

She names the place again.

And again, it's snatched from my mind as soon as the words leave her lips.

I stare at the ducks, to keep from seeing Minos's statue towering over me, wreathed in scouring mist.

"Something's wrong," I say.

Persephone's face in the pond shows no surprise.

"It's better if she shows you," says the queen.

I follow her gaze across the pond. Your mother is there. She's wearing fine clothes and a small diamond brooch in the shape of a forked scepter, marking her as a household servant of Persephone's.

The queen herself is gone by the time I've run along the pond's edge to Naucrate.

"What is this?" I ask her. "What's happened to him?"

"Come and see," she says.

We walk out of Elysium, over plains of dry and brittle grass, until the ground turns marshy, then rocky, beneath a blanket of ankle-deep fog. A roar ahead of us like the approach of thousands of ironclad feet. The horizon resolves into a river and a wall of black cliffs, a single white tower rising from the foot of the cliffs. Tower and cliffs climb farther than I can see, into the murk that is our sky. Then I begin to understand what I'm seeing.

A waterfall, crashing down from the world above. A river of forgetting, running through the cave of Hypnos, then tumbling fathom after fathom into the depths of Hell, to flow through the sunless places. The river that is a goddess, the river that brings oblivion. The Lethe.

Naucrate says, "After I handed you over, Minos freed me and his men took me here. To see what became of our son."

I'm running now, toward the white curtain of water, the mist thickening. Your mother calling after me. She's sorry. Her words already half-drowned by the crash of water.

My mouth is shaping your name, but the din of the water drowns all words. The mist shrouds everything but the cliffs and the falls, the river roaring past, the slippery rocks cupping pools of water.

Two white goose feathers float in one of the pools at the river's edge.

You were here.

You stood right here.

My mouth is moving again but the roar of the falls has scoured your name from my memory. No. No no no no no, I won't forget you again, not again. I clamber back over rocks and through pools until the mist lessens and I can hear my own voice rasping, "Icarus, Icarus."

Staring back at the white curtain of water, I see the blinding rays of the sun, the glassy face of the sea. One more place where I can't follow you.

"Why did you do it?" I shout. I mean your flight into the sun, your disappearance into the river, all of it.

Something seems to move through the mist, emptiness in the shape of a woman. Something interrupts the crash of the falls, little absences of sound, a string of silences that could be the high, cruel laughter of the river goddess whose touch is forgetfulness.

"You see now," says Naucrate, behind me. "He could be some anonymous shade, cleansed of his memories and wandering the paths of the dead. He could be a breeze now, or a bird, or a tree, or a rock. He didn't want us to follow. And *she* won't let us remember."

No wonder Persephone agreed to take me on so easily. She'd made a little show of reluctance, that was all. How else would I think it was my idea?

I peer into the falls, but the unseeable goddess in the mist is gone now, if she was ever there to begin with. "Why would he leave us like this?"

Naucrate offers me her hand and says, "You're the visionary, Daedalus. You tell me."

We follow the riverbank away from the falls until the white waters grow smoother, dark with silt. The rocks give way to soft pungent soil, and willows with bone-white blossoms thicken along the banks. Ravens croak at us from the branches. Maybe they feed on memories that wash up on the shore. I don't want to think of you living as a tree or a rock or a spring in a clearing, some life that's simpler and happier without us.

After some time I let the question out, the one that's bubbled at my lips since I awakened to your mother's touch in the darkness.

"Why didn't you ask us to flee with you?"

"My Daedalus. You were a beautiful man, but not a brave one."

"I built wings. I killed Minos."

"When it was too late. Icarus spent thirteen years in that terrible place. Because of us."

Knossos hadn't always been a terrible place. It wasn't preordained. The willows scattering their petals in the river remind me of the unplanted orchard where Naucrate and I walked together. The potential she saw there.

"It wasn't all bad," I say. "That afternoon when you showed me the fruit trees and I showed you the mural. That's a good memory."

"What do you mean?" There's something heavy and dangerous in her voice.

I remind her. I tell her about the sunlight on the blank wall, the seascape we decided to paint there. I tell her about the heat of her hand in mine.

Naucrate says, "That's not how it happened."

"Of course it is."

She stops. She speaks slowly. "Minos was there."

"No. We were alone."

Your mother makes a withering face, a who-do-you-think-you're-fooling face. She's used it on merchants to great effect.

"He was going hunting. He had the master of the hunt with him, and he was carrying his javelin and tapping it against the wall as he walked. Talking the whole time about a wild boar he wanted to flush out. You don't remember?"

All I remember is Naucrate looking down the length of the blank wall, the length of the empty corridor.

"He was coming down the hall toward us. We saw him a long way off, and I took your hand to lead us away before he could speak to us."

She'd taken my hand because she wanted me. Hadn't she? It was desire making her palms sweat. Not fear.

I say, "It was such a long time ago."

"He was there." Branches break under her feet as she draws close to me. Her eyes are wet and angry. "I had to make sure I was never alone with him because I remember exactly what would have happened if I was."

"All right. What difference does it make now?"

"Why did I come to your room that night? You're clever, Daedalus. You'd have me believe you're brave. Tell me why I chose you."

"Enough."

"Minos wanted me. He wanted me and he wouldn't have asked. You were kind enough, and once it looked like you had a claim on me, he left me alone. He probably knew it would be easier to make you build for him if you had a family."

Minos is standing over my bed, holding your little body. He's saying, "You cannot grant life." He's saying, "You will never leave me."

I close my eyes and lean back against the trunk of a willow. The bark is rough against my skin. Something many-legged slithers along my shoulder but I can't be bothered to brush it away. "This certainly appears to be Hell."

"He was there."

"He was there," I admit. "I didn't know that was why you came to me."

"You saw enough. You'd have known, if you wanted to."

"I suppose. I'm sorry."

"Doesn't matter. I'm rid of him now." She tramps forward, the matter settled.

I huff after her, through the thinning trees.

"Eternal torture, I can understand," I say. "Eternal reward, fine. But if the only thing waiting for us down here is more of what we were doing up there—another murderous autocrat to work for, more silence from our little boy—I can't face that. I might go back to my cave and my statue."

The willows shudder in the breeze as we pass from under them, as if the trees themselves are inconsolable.

"I came back for you," says your mother.

"Eventually," I say. "Why is that?"

She thinks and says, "It doesn't change what I did, to him or to you. But I don't want to go on doing the same thing I did before."

We say our goodbyes, and I walk until I see the city walls. Without realizing it, I've trekked back toward the palace, toward my workshop. Where else would I go?

Why did you do it, Icarus?

And how did I ever think I could keep you safe?

I walled up a boy in a maze so his stepfather could feed him people. Who could blame you for wanting to wash away every last trace of your life in Knossos?

So. If I'm ever to see you again, I have to change the river's mind, and yours.

Whatever I do next, it can't be more of what I've done before.

There's an unspoiled valley in Hell that I've corralled off with fences and warning signs. It's far from any roads the dead walk. There are caves in the cliffsides and black, swift-footed deer in the valleys, and cold water in burbling creeks. Asterion could be happy there, away from the barren fields of that in-between country on the wrong side of the river, away from the fleeing ghosts calling him monster. I like to think of him free in the wild places of Hell, the narrow hidden places, among things that crawl and fly and leap from shadowed rock to shadowed rock. I could bring him there, do the poor boy one good turn at last.

As risks go, I'm contemplating a small one. I've been frightened for so long, and I'm tired of it. And he can hardly do much harm now.

I'm paid for my work in gold and silver coins, with Persephone's face on one side and the other side blank in tribute to the king of this place, whose face we fear to see. I fill my purse with coins and walk alone to a little-used pier hidden by reeds. Charon waits for me at the appointed time, leaning on his barge pole. I hold up the purse heavy with coins.

"This should be fare enough for everyone whose bones rest in the Labyrinth," I say. "You can count it to be sure."

I hesitate, then add, "You'll find a little extra for yourself. Everyone, you understand? And not a word to the king and queen about Asterion."

With that, I pour the gold and silver into the ferryman's outstretched hands.

When Charon doesn't report back I go looking for him, until one of my surveyors spots him by the side of the Acheron, pinned to the muddy bank with his own broken pole. His eyelids flutter as four of us together pull the pole from his shoulder, and his ancient pitiless eyes glisten with tears of pain.

"Something's wrong," he whispers, in case that's unclear.

I wave the surveyors away.

"Where's the Minotaur?" I ask, doing my best to keep my voice low, to keep the panic out of it. We're nowhere near the valley I intended for him.

Charon only points to the scattered logs of his raft bobbing in the current, and to the trail of cloven hoofprints climbing the muddy riverbank, pointing inland, toward Elysium.

YOU CAN WIN
IN A POEM

The wind swept the Labyrinth clean and the rain washed it. No one who ventured inside ever came out. Already it seemed older than me, as if all we did was unearth it.

On winter nights the Minotaur bellowed from cold and hunger, and on one such night I tied half a brick to the thickest blanket I could find and threw them both over the Labyrinth's outer wall. He was four years old.

In the summer, carrion birds clustered along the Labyrinth's walls in particular places. You could see them from a high enough window, and mark where the Minotaur caught his latest offering.

We were at war again, this time with Athens. Minos was growing older, and wanted everyone to see he had the bloodlust of a man half his age. Death was in the walls, in the food we ate.

"You've served me well, Daedalus," said Minos one day, misty-eyed and smiling at me over a map of Athenian sea-lanes.

I smiled back, and began estimating how much time we had. Minos grew sentimental when he was planning to feed someone to the Minotaur. We'd seen this with the treasurer, the head groundskeeper, the personal chef, the master of the hunt, the court sculptor, and countless messengers. The dungeons were empty, and Minos was too proud of his Labyrinth and his stepson to stop sending them bodies. He assessed one's usefulness against one's flavor at every summons. Low-ranking functionaries and slaves had a measure of safety because he was bad with names.

"I hope to serve you a long time yet, my king." I moved wooden ships across the map to intercept the Athenians. I'd improved upon Cretan shipbuilding techniques until our navy cut through the seas like arrows in flight.

"The war favors us," said Minos, moving ships of his own and catching the Athenian navy in a pincer formation. "You've brought me security here, and you'll bring me victory when Athens bows. No man has done more for Crete."

The implication was clear. When Athens surrendered, Crete would be the undisputed ruler of the seas. No need for new coastal defenses or siege engines. No need for Daedalus. Then all that remained was to wait until one of my designs displeased him, or until you jostled the king's cupbearer on a narrow stairway. And the Minotaur would enjoy two meals.

"As in all things, my king, I serve at your pleasure."

That afternoon I met Ariadne at the construction site for her new dancing ground near the amphitheater. My men had leveled the ground and were now laying tile. We often talked at construction sites. The tap of chisels and the shouts of workers meant the guards, always a respectful distance away, couldn't hear what we talked about.

"He's going to kill us," I said.

"He's considering it," said Ariadne. "You know how variable his moods are."

My breathing had gotten fast again. The scars on my arm felt hot and alive. I put my head in my hands.

When I lift my head, I promised myself, I will not see limestone walls on every side. I will not hear Icarus calling for help behind a wall, around a corner, where I can't see his face or take his hand.

I am not in the Labyrinth. Not yet.

"I hate him, Ariadne. I can't draw when I'm like this."

She squeezed my shoulder. The air smelled of sweat and dirt and I breathed that in, imagined straight lines on parchment becoming rows of bricks becoming palace walls. My breathing slowed and deepened. A songbird trilled. It would have companions soon, as the days lengthened.

"He's testing you," she said. "He wants to see what you'll do."

"So do I."

"He took Catreus to the siege of Megara—do you remember this? Took him right to the front. He was as old as Icarus is now."

I nodded weakly. Stories of Ariadne's home life seldom made me feel better.

"Father put him in command. Wouldn't help him. He said a future king of Crete should know what it's like to send men to their deaths."

"The poor boy."

"He lost almost an entire battalion. A thousand men died before the walls of Megara, cursing his name. The smoke from the funeral fires blotted out the sun, and night came hours early." Her tone was matter-of-fact. She might have been describing a family dinner. "He did better on the second day."

The afternoon had turned hot and dusty, and the men stopped to rest and ladle out cool water. We accepted a few sips, which tasted of the mint and barley they'd mixed in.

"I can talk with him after the feast," said Ariadne, when work started again. "If I act regal enough in front of the princes, he should be in good spirits."

Remembering her etiquette lessons, she sat up straight and cast a haughty look at the waves on the horizon.

The feast with our allies and tributaries was to fall at the month's end. We were safe until then, provided Athens didn't surrender early.

"How many princes are we expecting?" I asked.

"Thebes, Sparta . . . Argos if they don't cancel."

"Plan on marrying any of them?"

Ariadne stuck her tongue out at me. "If I don't like a suitor, I tell him that old story about Mother."

"Not the one about the creatures."

"Mmmm hmmm."

Minos was famous for infidelity in his younger days. A rumor had sprung up that Queen Pasiphaë, daughter of the sun and no stranger to sorcery, had cursed Minos's manhood so that any time he slept with another woman he would ejaculate millipedes and scorpions.

"That whey-faced little princeling from Lemnos? First I told him the story, and then I told him I've been studying herbs and rituals and magic myself, and suddenly he remembered all his obligations back home and set sail."

I laughed, and forgot the crush of limestone walls for a moment. She was good at that.

"Thank you for talking with your father."

"Only to put your mind at ease."

"Do you suppose he'll listen?" I said, gently.

She hissed an arcane word at a passing fly. It dropped out of the air, bounced once, and lay dead. She scowled at it. "I can tell him where the enemy's ships are," she said. "I can send them ill wind. He couldn't have built this kingdom without Mother and he won't keep it in his old age without me. He'll learn to listen."

"He'd be wise to," I said, in a neutral tone.

"Besides," she said, brightening again, "you've escaped

worse than this. You'll escape this time, whether I can help you or not. It's like you've always said: There are rules to everything."

With her brothers at war, her sisters married off or making themselves marriageable, Ariadne alone continued her lessons with me. I ground lenses so we could magnify and draw the scales of fish, the wings of dragonflies. We dissected flowers from the gardens, diagraming the pistil, the anther, the filament. We charted the phases of the moon, the tides and currents, the migratory paths of birds. But the things her mother taught her were beyond even me.

"Rules keep birds in the air," she went on. "They appease gods and the children of gods. We study the rules, we live in safety."

"Once in a great while I like to imagine there's more to life than safety. Do you think you'll never marry?"

She kept her eyes on the sea, where the ships of the princes would appear and where, one day, a ship might carry her off.

"I don't suppose I will. Not until I meet someone as interesting to talk with as you."

Gravel crunched behind us, and a man cleared his throat. It was a guard I knew. I'd made him a honeybee pendant to give to a swineherd he was wooing. In exchange, he was to bring me bad news before it reached Minos.

"It's Icarus, sir. I'd hurry."

You were nine, so I don't know how well you remember your performance that afternoon. You drew a respectable crowd to the hillside in the shadow of the smithy. The smith's soot-covered boys were there, and your friends from the palace and stables and fields. You were standing on an overturned water trough, holding wax tablets in one hand and an invisible club in the other. You were swinging the club and shouting poetry at the top of your voice to be heard over the blacksmith's hammer. Showers of sparks in the smithy behind you cast your shadow, tall and unbowed, over the children on the grass.

"As the hammers of the Cyclopes crash upon the thunderbolts of Zeus," you read, "until each is sharp and strong enough to rend the earth, so the club of Heracles kissed the raging Minotaur!"

When the cheers died down, I said, "In spite of all, I believe most of you are intelligent young people who don't want your loved ones eaten." Everyone turned to gape at me. "So after leaving, right now, I know you won't tell another soul of this."

They scattered as I drew near to you. I yanked the tablets from your hand. You'd engraved the title of the poem into the wax at the top of one tablet: *Heracles Slays the Minotaur.*

Ignoring your shouts, I ducked into the din of the smithy, crossed to the furnace, and threw the tablets in. The smith made a show of absorption in the shield he was hammering. You swatted at my hip with closed fists until I hauled you out of the smithy by your ear.

"Why'd you do that!" You were red-faced and crying.

"Lower your voice."

"I spent all week writing it."

"When we get home, all your tablets and all your styluses are going right into the rubbish heap." I wiped your face with my tunic. "I don't need you to develop a sudden proficiency in mathematics. I do need you to keep yourself safe. No more poems."

You squirmed out of my grasp. "We were careful."

"All it takes is one person talking to Minos. Never give him a reason."

"He doesn't need a reason."

I finished cleaning your face and stood back to check my handiwork. It was past time I cut your hair. "True enough."

I'd left you too long with Lysandra and her nursery tales, plied you with too many old stories scrawled onto crumbling scrolls or carved into clay tablets. Somewhere along the way you'd started taking it all too seriously. It was one thing to look to Olympians and Argonauts for some harmless amusement. It was another thing to go to them for answers. And now you'd moved on to live performance—topical live performance, no less. I blamed the court poet, with all his caterwauling about heroes. I wouldn't have minded seeing him fed to the Minotaur, but unfortunately he had a knack for making up flattering songs about Minos and his ancestors.

"Why Heracles?" I asked.

"He's the strongest."

"Didn't he kill his own family?"

"He was driven mad, Father."

"Even so."

"I just like the stories, Father."

We started home, trudging across the palace grounds in silence, our tower looming ahead, our guards walking far enough behind that they could deny overhearing anything of import. You kicked at the ground as we walked.

I cleared my throat, and when you were glaring up at me and I had your attention I said, "I sought Minos out, did I ever tell you that? I left the safety of Athens and came here of my own free will because they were making up poems about Minos's courage in battle, and I thought if I came and built a palace for him, there'd be poems about me too." I shook my head. "A young man's idiocy. Still, they led me to you, so I can't say I'm sorry I ever listened to poets."

"Their loved ones were eaten," you said.

"What?"

"You told my friends not to get their loved ones eaten," you said. "Most of them already lost someone."

That stood to reason. Everyone had lost someone.

"The poem was meant to cheer them up, was it?"

You nodded. "You can win in a poem."

I wonder now if that's why you flew too high. If it was that simple. Lightness, escape on the winged sandals of Perseus. I was already toying with the idea of building wings, some part of your favorite story made real, though the problem of getting them aloft would vex me for years.

The literal in aid of the figurative. Knossos and the Labyrinth and the Minotaur's bloody hands falling away from
you. Allowing you to ignore your father's tiresome voice
and forget, for once, to be on guard. To forget yourself. Is
that what happened as we flew across the sea? Simple joy,
simple forgetting, lightness and freedom at last, no warning heavy enough to pull you down to earth in time?

But that lay far ahead.

"You worked on it all week?" I asked.

You nodded again.

"I wondered why you were so quiet. Here I thought you
were doing your sums."

You shook your head.

"Happy with it?"

You shrugged.

"Could you show me your next poem before you perform it?"

This elicited speech. "I can keep my tablets?"

"Let's say you can. Assuming you stay away from current events. And anything I read, and deem unsafe, goes
into the fire. Could you accept that?"

Another nod.

"Being a hero isn't the same as being a good man," I
said.

"Why not?"

"The second one's much harder."

We neared our tower. One of our guards lagged behind
to shake a stone out of his sandal, then jogged to catch up.

"That's all I need you to do, Icarus. Stay safe and grow up a good man. Remember that for me?"

An emphatic nod. "But I can keep my tablets?"

"You can keep your tablets."

You ran the rest of the way home. As I climbed the stairs after you, I felt the first tickling of an idea. Nothing I could put into words or drawings yet. Experience had taught me to leave this idea alone for now. Give it room to grow. This I did, until the orchards were in bloom and the final tiles were laid on Ariadne's dancing ground.

On the night of the feast I maneuvered a seat across from Minos. Laughing and talking with Ariadne and the princes, I brought up the great heroes, until everyone spoke of their favorites. Mighty Heracles, dauntless Jason, swift Perseus. At each pause in each story I called for our cups to be refilled.

"May our lives echo across the centuries like those men," I said, raising my cup in a toast.

Minos's cheeks were flushed and his eyes dreamy.

The night air was cool and the insects were singing as we processed to the dancing ground. Minos grabbed me by the elbow.

"Loyal Daedalus," he said, "I know they'll sing of you for years hence, for your genius and your Labyrinth."

"I'm not so sure, my king."

Minos's mouth was a thin line. If I didn't sway him I might face the Minotaur tonight.

"Right now," I said, "your Labyrinth and your Minotaur are curiosities for travelers, and little-known outside of Crete. No great story has happened there. Not yet."

Minos drew himself up taller. "What do you mean?"

"There is a way to ensure the Labyrinth's fame endures, and Crete has a place in songs."

We crowded around the dancing ground in the torchlight. Ariadne, flowers in her hair, led out the retinues of the princes. The tiles at the edge of the dancing ground depicted the red and gold rays of the sun, and all they nourished: grapes, barley, olive trees, youths with their hands clasped in courtship. At the heart of the dancing ground, a unicursal path coiled and twisted. As complicated as this version of the Labyrinth looked, the path led inevitably from the center out. There were no wrong turns, no ways to get lost. It was a wish, I suppose. For her as much as for me and you.

"If the Labyrinth is only feared on Crete, its fame will die in Crete," I continued. "If it's feared throughout the world it will pass into legend, along with the king who built it."

The dancers formed a ring as the musicians played. As Ariadne danced, laughter flashed in her eyes. Her bare feet fell just so on the tiles, awake to the pattern of the dance and the beauty of the pattern. I'd carved and painted each tile by hand for her.

None of them deserved her.

"Daedalus," said Minos. "Explain."

"It's simple, my king. When Athens surrenders—which they will—demand a tribute from them to keep the peace."

The dance turned wilder. The tunics of the dancers were dark with sweat. Ariadne's steps grew frenzied, her hair came undone, and she thrashed like one communing with the gods.

"Athens," I said, "must send their sons and daughters to feed the Labyrinth."

JUST ANOTHER DEAD MAN

By the black waters of the Lethe, where white, eyeless fish nibble the memories of the dead, I've built a museum. The dead gather on the front steps to meet friends, or to watch the jugglers and fire-eaters perform on the riverfront. If they venture inside, into the cool blue glow of will-o'-the-wisps under glass, they can see a small part of the history of Hell.

Here, behind an iron guardrail, is the broken chain that once bound Cerberus. It's thick as a man's arm, but the middle link was ripped open long ago by Heracles, and twenty strong men couldn't bend it back now. Over here is a rough-hewn seat of stone, knee high, where our king, he who receives many guests, once trapped the hero Theseus. Leaning over the rail, I can see a faint dark stain that might once have been the hot blood of a living man.

I wait, tapping my sketchbook against my thigh. He'll

come. If anyone can help me track Asterion and recapture him quietly, it's the man I'm here to meet. The sweat from my hand is wrinkling the calfskin pages. Persephone needn't find out. Our king, whose name we fear to speak, needn't find out.

A big fellow in simple dress sidles up and looks at the stain with me for a time. Eventually he says, "I left half a buttock stuck to this thing."

"Not so loud," I say, and he grins.

It's Theseus, all right. Slayer of the Minotaur, hero king of Athens. We met once on Crete, back when we were alive. I barely spoke to him, but he talked at length about his own deeds.

The graying warrior beside me looks older and bears more scars than the sword-thrusting young maniac who feasted at Minos's table. But even though he moves like an old veteran now, keeping his back to the corners and a line of sight to all the exits, he's still got the same cocksure tone, the same habit of standing like he's posing for a statue.

"Daedalus," he says, patting me on the back and nearly toppling me headfirst over the iron rail. "You've come up in the world."

"So have you," I say. "King of Athens and all that."

"Just another dead man now."

"Still," I say, "I would have loved to see Athens again."

"If you did come back I'd have had to kill you."

"Well, yes, obviously." The weapons I built for Minos sent too many Athenian ships to the sea bottom, and the Labyrinth swallowed up too many Athenian youths.

"That's all done with, anyway," he says, with more than a little sadness. He nods at the stain. "Gods on high, did *that* hurt. And I've felt the edge of a sword more than once."

You've told me the story often enough. How Theseus and his best friend descended to the underworld, still living, to carry off Persephone.

"I don't know why you were in such a hurry to come down here," I say. "All you had to do was wait like the rest of us."

"The danger was the point," says Theseus, wistfully. "Feeling the blood jet out of me, clawing my way back up to clean air and sunshine . . . what I'd give to feel that once more!"

I'm on the verge of feeling sorry for him when he opens his mouth again. "Has she asked about me?"

There's the Theseus I remember.

"No. The queen of Hell has not asked about you."

He grunts. I picture Ariadne on the beach at Naxos, screaming at the stern of Theseus's ship until the sails are a black dot on the horizon. I remind myself that punching him would only hurt my hand.

"Elysium," I say. "The disappearances. The god of Hell, he who receives many guests, has asked me to resolve the matter and to do it discreetly. Tell me."

"It's funny that they sent you," says Theseus. "I've been thinking of the Minotaur."

Someone coughs on their way out. The museum is nearly empty. I can walk out too, I remind myself. Whenever I'm ready, I can walk right out. There's no open sky above, no warren of wrong turns and dead ends waiting ahead of me.

"Many men I've killed," says Theseus. "None died like him."

"There were no men like him," I say, softly.

"He fought me for a long time," says Theseus, "and at the end, right before I got my hands around his throat and squeezed, his nostrils flared and he snorted in one last breath. Taking in my scent. And he smiled. Damnedest thing! Even after I struck his head off to take back to Athens with me, the smile stayed. I kept his skull mounted outside my throne room, and every day that grin reminded me there were worse things than wars and treaties!" He laughs, but too hard. An I'm-not-scared laugh.

"The disappearances," I prompt.

Theseus leads me over to a statue of hundred-handed Briareus. "So far it's only minor heroes. Elpenor. Palinurus. Little men, no offense. I had to find Homer and his poet friends to be reminded what they did. Something came to Elysium to hunt."

Only minor heroes. I can still fix it.

There's time to make things right. Plead my case to the Lethe. Ask her to send you back to me. Soon, Icarus. Give me a little time.

"Something came to Elysium," I say, doing my best to sound incredulous. "And, what, it's killing them? Again?"

"Not killing. Ending."

I have no idea what to say to that, so instead I say, "Who?" Pretending I don't know full well who it is.

"I've been telling you. We found Elpenor's tent kicked in. His sword broken. Drag marks ending at the river. And right there, at the water's edge, left for me like a love token . . ."

"What?"

"A cloven hoofprint."

I don't have to fake the shudder.

"What say you to a hunting party?" says Theseus.

Finally. Let him think it was his idea. "You don't suppose . . ."

"It's him," says Theseus. "I'm sure of it."

The roof is not open to the stars. The doorways don't lead to empty rooms. We are not in the Labyrinth.

"He's been down here all this time," says Theseus. "How hungry he must have grown."

Slippery rock and wailing wind. Fog below us. Snow the color of moth wings blowing through skeletal pines. The path winds up toward a cotton-colored sky and a mountaintop that never draws closer. I wonder again if we've wandered into the wrong place, but then Theseus calls back to us, boisterous as a host bellowing for more wine, and I remind myself that yes, this is Elysium.

"Another hoofprint," he says when I've scrambled up the mountainside to join him. It's big, and cleaner around the edges than the other prints. "The snow's hardly begun to fill this one," says Theseus, licking his lips. "He tires."

"Splendid," I say. Not having a sword, I touch the manacles on my belt. The metal's cold enough to burn my hand.

"Not long now," Theseus says to his men. The hunting party is mostly minor heroes in sword-bitten armor. They've spent the ascent telling interminable stories about favorite stabbings from their glory days. "Fight bravely," says Theseus, "and when we're back in the green fields you'll have your pick of girls and boys!"

Laughter and the glint of blades unsheathed. I grimace. Theseus claps me on the back hard enough to knock a dusting of snow from my cloak. "My friend," he says, "you'll be back in Hell's heart soon enough. You needn't carry the gloom of Tartarus in your face."

I push past him up the path. This forces him to jog ahead of me in order to look fearless, so that's a small pleasure.

"Daedalus, what's your quarrel? You can't still be cross that I solved your famous Labyrinth."

"Ariadne solved it," I say.

"You're thinking about her, maybe?"

Well, why not? Most of his friends are brutes and camp followers who keep his cup filled and praise his muscles. He could do with a little honesty. "I'm thinking of how you abandoned her."

"I didn't abandon her."

"It must have been some other Theseus who left her on Naxos."

He squints back at me. "When was the last time you spoke with Ariadne?"

"Not since Crete. I had to hear it all from dead poets and maenads."

"They told it wrong."

"Tell it to me the right way, then."

He scratches his beard. Spits. If I didn't know him better I'd guess he was trying to spare my feelings.

"It's good to be out here with you," he says at last. "Let's not spoil it."

I start to tell him that it's impossible to spoil an activity with a person you hate, but he rambles on.

"You have to understand, I've been here for such a long time. Mostly it's orchards and meadows and endless feasts and pretty people who let you have your way with them and you don't even need to carry them off. Everything's easy and nothing's risky. I was beginning to doubt. But facing real danger again, walking out to meet it with a blade again after so long . . ." He grins. "You must give my compliments to the king and queen of Hell, Daedalus, for this is truly paradise."

I'm about to insist he talk sense, but my mouth hangs open as I see movement on the path above us. At first I think a boulder or a mass of snow is falling toward us, only the boulder has long, cruel horns and long, thick arms that wrap around Theseus as it lands on his back. Theseus is a strong man. His back doesn't break. He keeps his footing. He whirls, trying to break the hold, and as he turns, the Minotaur's golden eye looks into mine.

Theseus fights bravely. His arms are pinned. He slams the Minotaur against the mountainside hard enough to make thunder and knock down snowdrifts that sweep handfuls of men from the trail. He takes a lurching step toward his sword, which has landed in the slush at my feet. I'm watching the Minotaur's muscles working beneath the sleek fur of those massive arms as they lock together and tighten. Far away, Theseus's men are screaming for me to pick up the sword or clear the path. Then several parts of Theseus crack at once, and I think of fat popping in a sacrificial fire. Theseus is screaming now too, as the Minotaur lays him down, and there's a tenderness to it, a look of concentration in those golden eyes, as the Minotaur strips off Theseus's breastplate and, with a long, curved thumbnail, slices him open from throat to groin.

I hear the men vomiting and cursing the gods, and Theseus is still awake and screaming, and the Minotaur is concentrating, concentrating, as his red and steaming hands rummage through Theseus's insides. He pushes aside lungs and heart, widens the hole, then leans forward and plunges his right arm into Theseus up to the shoulder. It's impossible, a conjurer's illusion. The Minotaur's arm should burst out of Theseus's back, but instead it reaches through Theseus as if his body is a curtain hiding some deeper recess. Then the Minotaur grunts with satisfaction. His arm emerges, holding a lump of matter that shines and oozes like molten gold. In mid-scream, Theseus vanishes. He leaves bloodstains on the snow and a fading echo. He ends.

The Minotaur takes a lick of the golden, dripping mess bathing his forearm. Another. He sighs like a builder enjoying his first gulp of cool water on a hot afternoon.

Then he turns to me. He sniffs the air. He smiles, scenting another old friend.

I run down the mountain after the retreating men, only now seeing the familiar pattern of branching paths in the cloud-shrouded valleys below.

Pebbles skitter down from the trail above me as I descend the mountain. Theseus's men scream in the mist, growing fewer and fainter, until I'm alone. When I reach the river I shout at the boatman to push off and the rowers to heave-ho. I jump from the wharf into the moving boat as it pulls away. The willows at the water's edge rustle. There's a splash behind us as we row upriver and away from Elysium.

I watch from the stern of the boat until at last we round a riverbend and pass the warehouses and pastures marking the outskirts of the capital. The white towers of the palace come into view, jutting from the hill at the center of town like a bone from a broken leg.

It's a long way from Elysium to the palace. The river twists and the roads double back on themselves and the landscape changes when no one is looking.

He'd never follow me over such a distance. Not the boy touched by the gods. He was too scared to claim me when I lay a few paces from the mouth of the Labyrinth, easy prey. He'll follow his old patterns, staying in the hunting ground he knows, stalking the heroes he craves. We studied him, Ariadne and I. We know how he behaves. There's not a whit of heroism in me. It would make no sense for him to follow me, no sense at all.

In my mind, Ariadne lies on her back, gazes up at the painted constellations, and says, "The gods don't have to make sense."

Statues of Persephone and her husband watch us from the city walls as we tie up at the docks. I pay the crew and tell them to forget they saw me.

Walking inland, I find a little wooded park with stone benches and tables, and I lie down and curl up under one of the tables. For a long time I shelter there, listening to the sounds of the park, watching the sandals of people going for walks. I'm affronted on Theseus's behalf, that in my hiding place lovers are still meeting for assignations, children are playing, cypresses are continuing to grow, blackbirds are singing.

THE GODS DON'T
HAVE TO MAKE SENSE

The heroes came from Corinth and from Megara, from Tiryns and from Troezen, from Athens itself and from as far as Lemnos. They carried shields embossed with harvest scenes, palm-sized statuettes of local gods. They wore armor blessed by river nymphs and carried swords with names that no one but them bothered to remember. For all I know, these prizes still wait in the Labyrinth for anyone brave enough to claim them.

Some of the heroes snuck into the Labyrinth at night, and we didn't know about them until their screams and the roars of the Minotaur woke us. Other times they marched at midday to the Labyrinth's entrance, stood in the public square separating that place from the palace, and declared that they were here to kill the Minotaur and end the bloody tribute of Athenian youths. Minos indulged them, watching from his balcony with the court poet and the captain of the guard. Sometimes, for dramatic effect, he'd have the guards fire a few arrows wide of the latest hero as he disappeared into the Labyrinth.

The Labyrinth, remember, had no gates or doors. The gap in the high wall simply waited, and the men who charged into the gap did not return. One man, a Spartan, wandered for five days, delirious with hunger and drinking pooled rainwater. Shouting over the walls, he cursed us, then mocked us, then sang songs of worship, having come to believe that the Labyrinth was the universe entire and the Minotaur his god. It was a relief when his god finally ate him.

The court poet catalogued them all, making them sound more magnificent than they were. No one seemed to mind. It was more pleasant to believe that heroes were marching past us to die courageously, even if we saw with our own eyes a train of shiftless brigands committing a noisy and prolonged form of suicide.

You watched the heroes die and listened to the songs of their deaths. You visited the armory and took sparring lessons from the captain of the guard. You knew better than to speak about it out loud, but I began to worry that once you were grown, you were planning to kill the Minotaur yourself.

"It's all such a waste," I said one night, as we both lay awake in our tower, listening to the Minotaur lowing for food. "They're not accomplishing anything. Why is this the sort of person we celebrate?" Discouraging you directly wouldn't work. I had to ask the right questions, make you reconsider.

"They're not helping anyone," you admitted. Some of the weight left my chest. To be alive in Knossos was to go about wearing armor of heavy dread, so constant we didn't notice it until it lightened.

Then you said, "Eventually everyone's in a situation where there's no longer any hope. Maybe we admire people who face that because we wonder what we'll do."

Your voice was changing and you grew taller by the day. You spoke rarely enough now that it startled me every time. You were spinning complex thoughts I couldn't guess at.

I missed the days when you'd greet the clop of horses' hooves or the flight of a bird with a little boy's laugh. When we did talk, you sounded strange and sad.

In my gentlest voice, I said, "I'm sorry, Icarus, but what do you know about no hope? You're still a boy."

"I'll be a man soon." You didn't sound excited about it.

"Not for a little longer," I said. Gods grant us a little longer, I thought.

"He fed Evander's father to the Minotaur. And Dion's. And Niko's mother. And everyone accepts that because what else can we do?"

I wonder now if some heartsickness had its teeth in you by then. If you had no hope of defeating the Minotaur, only hope of release. Is that why you twirled and laughed in your wings? Is that why you flew too high? Not lightness, but heartsickness, an end to pain?

I worried about it then. I'm not such a fool. We woke

and washed and dressed, all of us, in full knowledge of terrible deaths we never saw and barely spoke about.

All I could offer you was the recitation I used to fall asleep. I whispered some version of it to myself every night, since the day the Labyrinth enfolded me.

"There are things he doesn't control. Rules set for us by the gods. How much a stone weighs and where a wall casts a shadow. Even a king can't defy such rules. Understanding those rules, seeing their beauty, that's where I find hope. Maybe you'll find it in rhyme and meter. You'll outlive him. You'll find what's beyond him. Even if it doesn't seem like that now."

You were quiet for so long I thought you'd fallen asleep. Then, your voice soft, with the strangeness and dread gone from it for a moment, you said, "Thanks, Father." And a few minutes after that, yawning, in sleep's doorway, you added, "You're a good man."

Then you slept, and I lay awake thinking about how to get us far away from there.

One morning soon after, the breeze through our window carried the familiar tang of blood and the cawing of rooks. If the latest tribute had screamed in the night, I'd slept through it. They weren't screaming now. I unfurled the scroll I used to chart the Minotaur's feedings. The scroll was lined with spaces indicating hours and days. When each hunt was over and the Minotaur settled down to feed, I marked the time with an X, and noted some details about the person in question. It all looked orderly and sensible this way, the charcoal making neat, straight lines, days becoming boxes, sacrifices becoming letters and patterns.

I drew the latest X, then went to Ariadne's room.

She had an ocean view and several rows of wooden shelves I'd built myself. The shelves were heavy with rock and leaf specimens, and stranger trophies. Drawings and models of birds and fish. A wooden cow's heart one could take apart and reassemble like a puzzle. Books of pressed flowers. Herbs to bring sleep and healing, herbs to settle the stomach or sicken an enemy. A sacrificial knife with the rays of the sun stamped on the handle. Whenever a suitor was too interested, she showed him these things until he made his excuses and withdrew.

Ariadne was examining her own scroll by the window when I arrived. We compared.

She said, "Last week's feeding was one of the heroes, no?"

"Yes, the little one from Pylos, with the bow."

"And before that?"

"One of the Athenian tributes."

"Two days before that?"

"The same."

We rolled up our charts. I let her say it first.

"When he eats a hero it takes him, on average, three times as long to hunt down the next meal. He's slower to hunger."

I nodded. It was freeing to be with someone who could see the answers on their own. I didn't need to talk as much.

"It's too great a difference for the usual explanations,"

she went on. "They're not three times as big. They can hardly be three times as filling. And yet."

"He's acquired a taste for them," I said. "Some element they bring to his diet, something we can't measure or see. I don't like it. It doesn't make sense."

Ariadne flopped backward onto her bed. She stared up at a vault of constellations I'd painted when she was little. "The gods don't have to make sense," she said, without rancor.

"I hardly know what it means," I said.

"We will," she said, with a faint smile. "I wonder if he has any idea how celebrated he is." She meant the Minotaur. "I wonder if he's contented in there, or if he knows there's a world out here." She fell into a pensive silence, watching the painted stars as if begrudging them their place in the painted sky.

The guards outside were placing bets on how long the next sacrifice would last. No one was listening to us. I drew closer to Ariadne.

"There's something you should know," I said.

At this point the wings only existed as sketches in my head. I hadn't dared draw them. I was working out the aerodynamics, calculating lift and drag, weight and wind speed, caging my panic with numbers and proofs.

You spoke the truth, Icarus. You were going to be a man soon, and already you were having the strange thoughts of a man. Once you were brave enough, or hopeless enough, to try your sword against the Minotaur, I wouldn't be able to keep you safe any longer.

Safety meant escape. It meant flight.

"There's a way for us to get free of this place," I said, believing the words as I allowed myself to say them, to think them, for the first time.

I reached for Ariadne's hand.

"Come with us," I said.

I asked again later, as we walked along the beach collecting shells. The crash of the surf hid our words from the guards.

"I told you," said Ariadne, "two can fly more easily than three. I'm in no danger here, not like you and Icarus. Take him and let the wind speed you."

"How could we leave you?" I asked, at a state dinner. Minos was making two guards fight each other for the amusement of the Egyptian trade delegates, who watched with queasy faces. We spoke under the clash of blades, the hoots as Minos and his courtiers threw bits of food at their favorites.

"You're like a sister to Icarus and a daughter to me," I continued. "We love you too much to abandon you here."

"Can you take Phaedra with us?" she asked, between careful, courtly bites of food. "And Catreus, Acalle, and the rest? If I'm like a sister to Icarus, my sisters and brothers are his siblings too. Can you take my mother? We've stayed together through Father's wars and affairs and rages, and I won't leave them now."

"We can send for them," I promised. We were walking along the outer wall of the Labyrinth together. The Minotaur was eating a hero from Samos, and the hero was not entirely dead yet, so his screams gave us some privacy.

"I can build warships for a new king wherever our wings take us," I went on. "We can come back here with a conquering navy. We can teach your family ciphers in the meantime and send them messages on the legs of birds."

"Father would use warships," she said. We were in her room, charting the Minotaur's feedings again. The guards were playing dice in the hall. "Warships would put my family in danger. We've learned how to keep ourselves safe here, Daedalus. We charm, we deflect, we win wars and build kingdoms. We say no to kings and princes without seeming to say no. When I meet a prince who can make me happy, I might even say yes. This could all be mine someday. I step where the rules say I can step, and I do it well."

We had been at this for weeks. There was no reasoning her into it. And I had the strangest sense that her answers were not truly her answers. There was another answer beneath them, an obstacle she kept hidden from me.

I sat beside her on the bed.

"You don't belong here anymore," I said. "You're meant for better things. We both are. Icarus too."

I put my hand on hers.

"We've waited and waited," I said. "What sense is there in waiting any longer?"

Ariadne slid off the bed and went to the window. Mist hid the horizon. No ships bearing suitors had come for nearly a year.

"No, Daedalus," she said. "Save your son. The less I know about how you'll go, and when, the better."

When she didn't say anything else, I said, "All right."

Ariadne stayed at the window, waiting for me to go. "You were the one safe place in all the world," she said, without turning.

RUN AND I
WILL FOLLOW

Teetering, arms extended for balance, I clamber over wet rocks toward the roar of the falls. I don't dare look behind me. I have to fight, this close to the Lethe's headwaters, to hold on to your name. Icarus, I say under my breath, marking every precarious step, every exhalation. Icarus, Icarus, Icarus.

The white column of the waterfall emerges from the mist. I think again of an infinitely tall door beginning to swing wide. I bellow your name and the sound is swallowed up by the immensity of the gap in the door.

"Icarus! I paid everyone's passage across the river. All the unburied in the Labyrinth. The Athenians, the heroes, our friends, everyone! I paid *his* way. Do you understand?"

My throat is raw. The falls rage on.

"He has my scent now."

He followed me back to the capital. I don't know why.

Revenge is outside of his vocabulary. He'd just as soon seek revenge on the sky, the rain, the stone walls that hemmed him in. He preys on heroes, and I am no such thing. It makes no sense at all.

But then, it made no sense for a child to spring from the union of bull and queen. It made no sense for him to eat human flesh. The boy touched by the gods has defied reason all his life. Why would death put a stop to that?

So he followed me. Patient, quiet, he let me catch glimpses of him. One figure too many among the marble statues silhouetted in the agora. Breath curling in an alleyway, horns moving by torchlight. He was in no rush. Where could I go?

Remember the plan. I kneel, cold river water dragging at the hem of my tunic. "Hear me, goddess."

The falls rage on. The river won't hear me without a suitable gift. Before I can think better of it, my clammy fingers fumble for the sketchbook in the damp folds of my tunic.

The calfskin pages are warped and curled from the mist and the clenching of my fists. They're fat with my sketches and ideas. I have many sketchbooks like this one, but the book itself is not the sacrifice.

I plunge the book into the foaming waters of the Lethe, wetting my arm up to the elbow. The pages thrash in the current as the book tries to swim out of my grasp and downstream. The sketches of temples and libraries and statues and flying machines are fading from the pages, I know. But they aren't the sacrifice.

One last time, I think about the weight and malleability of sandstone, of limestone and marble. How to carve and paint a statue, what pigments to use, how to make them and from what. Landscape, light. Cornices, columns. Load-bearing walls. Airspeed and lift. Your toys. Her dancing ground. Asterion's nursery. I think of the techniques and tools, the numbers and rules I've mastered over many lifetimes.

For all the good any of it did.

It's all going now, the charcoal fading from the calfskin. My gift to the river. All my knowledge, all my skill. I'll never build again, not so much as one stone atop another.

One memory lingers when everything else is gone. My first building in Athens, a little brick-and-timber temple in the shadow of the agora. The week construction ended, I enlisted my father on some errand so we'd have an excuse to walk past it. Making a show of nonchalance, I pointed it out to him. My father was not given to praise, or architecture, or much of anything apart from hunting. But he spared a glance at the bright reds and blues of my temple, the statues in their finery on the pediment. He squeezed my shoulder absently, hard enough to hurt, though I never minded since his touch was rare. "A good, strong temple," he said.

Tears run down my face as that too fades.

I lift the blank, bedraggled pages from the river, and stand, wondering why my cheeks are wet.

Remember the plan.

"Hear me, goddess," I say again.

And I can hear my own voice now. The din of the falls seems to recede. She's listening.

"Please tell Icarus what I've done. He needn't stay. He needn't remember. All I ask is to see him and talk to him. I want to explain myself, and ask why he flew too high. Then he can go back to whatever he's chosen. Will you tell him?"

Downriver, a flock of ravens erupts from the willows. He's close.

Remember the message.

"I can't stay. I love my son more than anything. Will you tell him?"

And then I am dismissed. My petition is under consideration. The din of the falls rises to pound again at my ears.

But not before I hear his grunt, the clicking of his hooves on wet stone.

I turn from the falls. I clamber down the rocks, away from the river. Keeping my eyes ahead of me.

He won't run me down on open ground.

He'll wait until I'm walking a tangled forest trail, or a narrow street in the capital. The path back to my workshop in the palace is long and twisting, marked by dark corners and dead ends. He couldn't ask for a finer hunting ground.

It's the only path left to me.

If I'm quick and clever. If I don't hesitate or look behind me. It's my path out.

⚎

I can't find the rutting palace.

I can see it easily enough, white and luminous on its

hill at the heart of the capital, a stalk of asphodel rising from a burial mound. The road I'm following through the agora points straight to it, past the stalls of dead potters and fishmongers hawking their wares. Then a canal intercedes and the road bends. The dwellings turn smaller and meaner, the torches spaced farther apart, until I'm following a lean and weedy walkway overlooking rubbish heaps and a slow, malodorous river of sludge.

The city is strange now, stranger for its familiarity. Like finding my own severed arm in the gutter. I know I built all of this, even if I can't remember how, or why I built it this way and not that. I walk among towering heaps of stone that have nothing more to say to me.

High above me, a marble causeway, blazing with black iron lanterns shaped like three-headed watchdogs, links the agora and the palace gardens. It's right there. I simply can't reach it.

This is something more than forgetting, something more expansive, older, and dreadfully patient.

My path ends at the head of a crumbling brick staircase, which leads down into stench and marsh grass and, huge and half-hidden in the causeway's shadow, a high, gaping tunnel mouth from which the city's refuse burbles in a slow, steady stream. It has a waiting look, the tunnel mouth, like it has always been here, knowing I'd come eventually.

The skin of my left arm tingles, my hot blood pulsing under the scars.

From the depths of the tunnel, unhurried steps splash toward me.

I scurry back the way I came. I find a broad plaza, catch sight of the palace between the courthouse and a bank. Closer now. Remembering the quickest way from here, I follow staircases that switchback up through a rock-strewn park, up a wall of coarse uneven stones, through an archway, and into a well-to-do neighborhood. My parents, patriotic Athenians who no longer speak to me, live near here in a drafty house of many rooms. I hear the echo of my father's voice, feel his strong fingers squeezing my shoulder. My breath catches in my throat, though I couldn't say why. The palace gardens lie beyond these mansions.

But no, once the high walls of the wealthy are out of sight, the path dips, and I pass under the shadow of an aqueduct, keeping pace with the windblown trash as it bustles past warehouses and seedy taverns, finally dead-ending on some ramshackle pier by a slow-moving bend in the river.

"Say!" I shout this to a trio of passing sailors. "Who's the idiot who designed this town?" They walk faster to get away from me, their feet *clunk clunk clunking* along the wooden pier.

I follow the slow current of the black river a while, trying to get the palace in sight again. *Clunk clunk clunk crunch crunch.*

I stop. No one is behind me. I walk a little farther.
Clunk clunk crunch.

I look down at the splintered boards of the pier.

Quickly I walk back up the pier, back toward high ground.

Beneath my feet, beneath the pier, other footsteps shadow mine, crunching in the wet sand by the riverside, gathering speed as I begin to run.

I try again, and again. I pass the same evil-smelling brewery four times. I glimpse the palace over walls or across seas of rooftops. Always it's above me, beyond me. I ask for directions, but the dead shake their heads and hurry on their way.

And always, below or behind or ahead of me, the unhurried click of hooves on stone.

I used to know what every building was made of, the blueprints, the measurements. No more. It's not important now. But was the capital always this nonsensical? Were the streets so convoluted, so cheerless and dark? The statues and walls and gardens and bridges at the city's center—were they so lofty, so mocking, all this time? Was my design always so cruel?

What did I really build down here?

"Help!" I cry. Down the length of a tree-lined boulevard, mothers scoop up children. Dead men sleeping under hedges wrap their blankets tighter. "I need to get to the palace!" It's amazing how quickly people can walk the other way, vanishing into shadow.

My head swimming, I lean over a low wall and glimpse, finally, a human face looking into mine. A vagrant peers up at me from the foot of the wall below. I'm glad of any help, though he's a startling sight, a ragged old man with tangled white hair and a stained cloak, his faced as lined as a dried apricot, his eyes crazed, so bloodshot and raw they look like burnt flesh.

"Do you know the way to the palace?" I ask, and the vagrant moves his lips with mine, mocking me. "If you don't know you needn't make a game of it," I say, and again he imitates me. Incensed, I spit in his face, and his face breaks into ripples spreading outward along the dark still waters of the canal below. I flee, understanding now, barking with laughter. I wouldn't talk to me either.

The clicking hooves follow. *Clip clop clip clop.*

I hear them on the other side of a long hedge in a park, in the alleyway behind a bakery.

Clip clop clip clop clip clop.

Come, they seem to say. *Run and I will follow. If you're careless, if you're slow, I'll hug you to me. I'll open your ribs and eat until you're all gone. Don't be careless. Don't be slow. Run, and play with me always.*

The rooftop domes and high colonnades of the temple district sprawl before me. There's no use pretending I can escape by my wits alone. I climb the steps of the largest temple, where statues stand before the sacred fire, Persephone and her king, his face hidden beneath a hood. The priest tries to turn me away but relents when I throw my heavy purse at his feet. His acolytes lead in the fattest black ram from the pens out back. I can hear the rams kicking and bleating out there, smelling something monstrous nearby.

I whisper my plea into the trembling ram's ear. The

priest hands me the dagger, and I draw it across the beast's throat. Sacrifices are becoming a habit today. Maybe I can become a priest myself, now that I'm not an architect any-more.

The priest and his acolytes butcher the victim and lay the fat on the fire, carrying the smoke and my prayer up past the stone faces of our dread king and queen. I'm hur-rying back down the temple steps before the first curls of smoke blacken the ceiling. Past the edge of the square, be-yond the light of the torches, something snorts once, tast-ing the night air. I double my pace, leaving the square in the opposite direction.

Clip clop clip clop clip clop.

Soon. The answer to my prayer will come soon, or not at all.

Clip clop clip clop.

There, nestled into the wall behind the temple of Arte-mis, is a doorway, square and unassuming. Through the door, lit by pale will-o'-the-wisps that mimic the moon, I see the white birches of the palace gardens. The call of a screech owl welcomes me home.

Clip clop clip.

I'm not an athlete, but once I'm within yards of the door, my feet don't touch the ground. I vault through, and the back of my cloak snags for a moment, and then my feet hit the rich black loam of the gardens, and behind me there is no doorway, no monster, only a blank stone wall.

My prayer's been answered. I sink to my hands and knees, burying them in the good earth.

When I collect myself and shed my cloak, I find four ragged tears in the cloak's hem, the kind a clawed hand might leave.

Don't go, they seem to say.

I brush myself off and trudge toward the palace. Now to learn whether I've escaped one punishment by bringing down another.

⚎

The Athenian war dead have gathered again in the outer gardens. They're in their usual spot, visible from my workshop window, chanting for me to be sent back to Tartarus. Those who burned with their ships shake charred fists within coronas of flame, superheated air rippling over their heads. Those who drowned bob in place, their feet never touching the ground, faces swollen and framed by wafting hair. The dead press their hands against spear wounds, pull arrows from their throats to gurgle insults. The Minotaur's victims are the new arrivals. They're the ones who huddle close to the others, clutching a neighbor's arm or elbow for comfort. They're the ones who keep looking behind them.

I close the gap in my curtain, then step back from the window into the gloom of my workshop. The smells of copper and brine and cooking meat will linger at the edge of the gardens for days, but I'm glad they're here. It's a bad time to be alone.

My workshop in the heart of Hell is filled with shadows

and hiding places. It's crammed with scale models and half-built prototypes. A faster boat for Charon, long and narrow-keeled, made from hollow bones. Manacles the height of a man for Prometheus. Things I'll never finish now.

What a relief, I realize, to be done with all this, to be surrounded by stone and wood that will remain stone and wood, with no obligation to become anything else.

I haven't heard his hooves in the hallway yet.

I sit and drum my fingers on my drafting table by the window. The shouts of hatred from outside often kept me company while I worked here. The king of Hell left notes on my table. I rarely saw him. He'd steal into my workshop wearing his cap of shadows. The notes would say *Make the cages smaller*, or *Don't scratch yourself so much*, and the purpose of such notes was to remind me that he watched me work, and could be watching at any time.

Such lightness, to have a head empty of designs. Whatever happens next, I'll never see this place again. At last, at last, I have nothing more to give these people.

There's no note on the table now. If the Lethe brings you my plea, I may yet outpace the Minotaur and watch you walk out of that wall of water. If the king doesn't know. If he hasn't seen.

A wooden stool rises from a nearby corner, where the shadows are thickest. Invisible hands carry the stool toward me and set it down by my chair. It creaks with the weight of a sitting body.

I stare ahead at nothing, waiting for the god to appear and pass judgment.

Persephone flickers into view and rests her husband's cap on my table. She's several months into her stay now, and her skin is the pallid color of something that lives at the bottom of a deep dark pool. She smells of mulch. "So," she says in a voice like wind through bare branches. "You've gone and broken Hell."

I keep her in the corner of my eye. "He doesn't know?"

"Not yet."

She heard my prayer in the temple. Not him.

I relax. Persephone frowns, and agony blooms in my head and chest. I fall to the floor and curl into a ball. In my mind's eye, mushrooms push up through a carpet of rotting leaves.

"Would you like to try again?" she asks.

"Yes, my queen." I uncurl slightly, touch my forehead to the floor in an approximation of a bow. "Hello, my queen."

"Better," says Persephone.

"We can fix this before he finds out."

"I would love to believe that. Perhaps I would believe that, if you'd come to me *before* the most celebrated hero in Elysium was torn apart and eaten. We'll never know. You're going to tell me how this happened."

"I can tell you a theory." I grab ahold of my drafting table and pull myself to my feet. The cap of shadows is still on the table, a fine silver mesh woven by Hephaestus himself. It's as old as the world, and untarnished. This is the first time I've seen it up close. The beauty of it gives me courage.

"A theory," says Persephone. The stones of a burial mound turn green and gold with lichen. "I'll miss building with you. Not many people see the potential in this place."

"We're not finished." I'm not an architect anymore, but I can bother her with those details later.

"I vouched for you and you lost Theseus. You bribed our ferryman and your pet monster ran him through. You are finished. I'll be lucky to keep my throne."

"I've asked the Lethe to bring Icarus back to me. Do what you will with me. But let me see him first."

Persephone shakes her head. A dead tree roils with termites and wood lice. She asks, "Where's the Minotaur now?"

"Not far. He has my scent."

"We'll wait for him here." Her lips part to show teeth, small and white as maggots in a wound.

"There's another way," I say. I'm steady enough to cross the floor of my workshop, to gesture at empty surfaces and let her imagine possibilities. I've proposed many buildings and inventions to the king and queen of Hell, and the buildings and inventions came to pass, and I'm not in Tartarus yet.

"The Minotaur's been killing heroes who are already dead. It should be impossible. If we can understand how he feeds and why, he might be useful to our king. Another Cerberus. Bring your husband that, and you may find him quicker to forgive." And like that, I've imprisoned Asterion once again. I'm sorry, poor boy. I wish I could say it was difficult.

"You spoke of a theory." Persephone is suddenly in

front of me without seeming to move. I hop back. I clear my throat in what I hope is a dignified manner.

"Ariadne and I studied the Minotaur," I say. "We believe he learned to eat heroism."

"What does that mean?"

I shrug. "We worked out how he behaves but not why."

"You would describe yourself as heroic?"

"I would not, my queen."

"Then what does he want with you?"

"I don't know. I'm missing something. But fear not, my queen. I'm quite prepared to seek out Ariadne and ask her."

"She's not in Hell."

"I know. With your leave, I'll go to Olympus to see her."

This is all plausible-sounding, but if I'm honest—and I should try to be honest with you, of all people—I have other reasons to seek out Ariadne. I want to learn what Theseus was about to say, and what kind of life she lived after he left her on Naxos. I want to talk with her about what happened near the end of your short life on Crete. Was it joy that killed you, or sorrow, or something else? Maybe she noticed something I didn't. She can help me work out what to say, when you come back to me.

"No." The word falls like grave dirt onto a body.

"Please, my queen. Let me make this right."

Persephone says nothing. I'm told that in the spring, when she rejoins her mother in the world above, she's a colorful and gay goddess. I've never seen her that way, though I'd like to.

I return to my drafting table and sit. The Athenian dead have dispersed. The gardens and palace are quiet. Hell could be empty of everyone but us.

"You let me build for you over lifetimes," I said. "'You may go to your son.' You could have warned me."

"I kept our bargain."

"Like your husband kept his, I suppose."

For an instant I am a jumble of bones crammed into an urn, with dirt and stones heaped onto my head, and I can feel the drip of rain and the mouths of insects tearing away my last morsels of flesh and hair.

I lean on the drafting table to steady myself. I say, "All that your mother endures, kept from you during the many days of winter, I endure. I can set things right with Icarus. I can set them right with the Minotaur. All I ask is time."

"You will not go to Olympus," she says. "You will not see your son. After a thousand years in Tartarus, perhaps we'll let you out to try again."

"Thank you," I say, "truly," and with one motion I sweep up the cap of shadows, put it on, and vanish.

INTERLUDE

FAWN SKINS AND CROWNS OF IVY

I heard the next part of Ariadne's story in Hell, from a dead maenad. She was there for most of it, and heard the rest from the princess herself.

Ariadne did flee Crete in the end, with Theseus. She helped him kill the Minotaur, her own half brother, who once rested his head in her lap and ate apples from her hand. She led the killer Theseus safely out of the Labyrinth with a length of thread. She conjured a strong wind to speed him back to Athens. For her trouble, he abandoned her on Naxos.

Whether she wept, or cursed the faithless prince, or stood in the surf staring after the ship with regal dignity, eventually night fell and it came time to seek shelter. A fugitive from her father, she would have avoided the low, mud-brick houses of the seaport. Instead she struck inland, through brush and forest, searching for a cave where she could pass the night in safety.

What must the maenads have looked like, when she saw the flames of their torches through the pines? What must she have made of the wild women, clad in fawn skins and crowns of ivy? What could she have thought of the snakes in their hair and the fresh blood that fell from their hands to sprinkle the grass as they danced around the red carcass of their kill?

Foremost in my mind: What compelled her to emerge from the woods in the morning, as the maenads nursed hangovers around the dying fire and empty wineskins? Why did she ask to join them?

"Something about how all the rules in the world won't protect you," the dead maenad told me. "How there's men who'll trip you up no matter where you step."

It must have been freeing, no longer being a princess or a marriage prospect. When she danced with the maenads, the dance was her own, born of drink and divine ecstasy. She stepped where she wanted now. She ran through the woods at night. Given strength by their god, she tore pines up at the roots, and milk and honey sprang from the torn earth. With her new sisters, she wrestled wild pigs in the underbrush, ripped fistfuls of meat from their flanks, ate them red and bloody.

No one came looking for her. No one bothered her. In the village, remembering what became of men who disturbed the maenads, they ignored the fires and music in the woods, and locked their doors at night.

Years passed. She made friends and talked of plants and animals and divinity, though she wouldn't say much about Crete. She knew where to find the best herbs for cooking, for medicine, for communing with the god, and for seasoning wine. She served as a healer and later as a helper to the high priestess. She worked in the vineyards of the maenads, and with her knowledge of plants and soil she improved their crop yields and the potency of their wine.

One day, as Ariadne tended to the grapes, a stranger stepped out of the rows of vines and greeted her. He appeared to be a young man with kind eyes and ruddy cheeks. His cloak was threadbare and his sandals nearly worn through with walking. He was the first man she had seen in years who wasn't running for his life.

"How does a princess and the granddaughter of the sun come to be here, paying tribute to a god?" he asked.

"I'm here for myself and for my friends," she replied in a grave voice, which was spoiled by the faint smile beginning to steal across her face. "There's no escaping the gods, but I don't seek their company."

The stranger laughed long and loud at this, and as he laughed the grapes grew fat and ripe on the vines around them.

"I feel the exact same way," he said.

YOUR
INNERMOST
HEART

The steeds harnessed to the chariot are the same ones that carried off Persephone when she was a girl, the ones Naucrate heard champing in the courtyard the night you were born. They're as swift as death, and the groom I bribed showed me how to feed the horses sugar and what to whisper in their ears. Still, our ascent seems to take days, until at last the chariot rises from a fissure in the ground, and I smell grass and see the stars.

A window glows in a distant house, and a dog unleashes a torrent of barking, but already the house and the dog and the fissure in the field are sinking away with the rest of the earth. The black horses gallop into the night air without slowing. Cold wind plucks at my cloak and numbs my hands. I can barely keep a grip on the reins, but the horses seem to know the way. Through gaps in the clouds I can see the churn of dark oceans and the blaze of cities.

We're higher now than even you dared to fly, my brave boy.

I touch the cap of shadows to make sure it hasn't fallen off. The woven metal is warm to the touch, in spite of the cold. I wonder how far behind me Persephone is, how much time I'll have when I reach Olympus. I pull the cloak closer about me.

A wedge of deeper night splits the horizon, blotting out the stars. A crown of lights at the distant summit. The horses rear and climb. The winds wail against the face of the mountain. I clutch at the rail of the chariot to keep from sliding out, grateful to be mostly blind as the face of Mount Olympus falls past us in the dark.

Colonnades and rooftops of white marble adorn the peak, and shadows dance by firelight between the marble columns. The heat of the torches warms my face. I can hear the music of the flute and lyre, and voices of unearthly beauty singing a drinking song.

We pass through a dark archway, toward a sudden beam of sunlight. An incongruous thing to find buried in a mountaintop at night. Then the hooves of the horses clatter on stone and we're at rest in the palace of the gods. It smells of manure and straw, and these familiar things give me encouragement enough to hobble out of the chariot. I pat the necks of the horses, and they snort and stamp without gratitude or fear. They seem to feel that I'm at the appointed place at the appointed time.

Horse stalls extend further into the mountain than I can see, and from the stalls I hear the whinnying and the stamping of many beasts. One white horse tosses its mane, then flaps a pair of brilliant feathered wings like those of a swan.

My heart skips. I'm picturing the delight spreading across your face when I tell you I've seen Perseus's winged steed. And I will tell you, my love. I've stolen from gods and stormed the heavens. I've called down my own doom. But I won't go back to Tartarus without seeing you, hearing your voice. I've come too far to lose you again.

The beam of sunlight is shining from a nearby stall. I stop there a moment to warm myself in the sun, for it is the sun. Squinting through my fingers, peering at the edges of the blinding glare, I glimpse manes of fire. It can only be the team that pulls Helios, Ariadne's grandfather, from east to west across the sky.

Someone clears his throat, and I notice a pair of preternaturally beautiful young men waiting beneath one of the archways leading out. One young man holds a mucking rake and the other holds feed bags. Minor gods, or mortal princes kidnapped for their good looks. I realize I'm still invisible. They think I'm the god of Hell and are waiting for me to leave. They stand aside without a word as I walk past them, toward the laughter and the music.

The corridor winds. The music and light wax and wane. Echoes lead me astray. The skin of my back feels as thin and brittle as onionskin. I glance down at my left arm. That's sweat making it slick, not trickling blood, only sweat. In a moment I'll see the right path and continue on my way. My arm is not bleeding. I am not back there.

A beautiful boy carrying a tray of empty goblets and dishes almost runs into me. I dodge, then retrace his steps, passing more servers. Walking by the doorway of a washroom, I hear a young woman weeping. Then the corridor opens.

The great hall throbs with talk and music. The lyre player and the flautist stand on a stage at the near end of the hall, faces flushed, firelight gleaming on their skin. Columns the size of oak trees hold up the high roof, leaving the hall open to the moon and stars. Lovers in expensive clothes recline on couches or fondle each other against pillars. Tired servers sneak out into the cold of creation to gobble bites of scavenged food. The center of the hall is a high-burning bonfire, ringed by a crush of dancing bodies.

A laugh like thunder booms out from the party's center. It vibrates through me, making me feel as if I'm made of glass. I must tread carefully now, for I'm in the presence of gods, and uninvited. I stalk the fringes of the party, listening for Ariadne's voice among the revelers.

Careful as I am, I can't avoid glimpses.

The air pressure drops and sand and salt water splash over my sandaled feet as something shaped like a man trundles past me, humming a sea chantey. He carries a trident and a white bull's head on a plate.

Gray eyes flash from one corner, where a tall woman with an owl on her shoulder describes the slaughter at Troy, with such flair and ferocity that the whole bloody mess sounds like a grand adventure.

The thunderous voice by the fire booms out again.

"Home?" it says. "I won't hear of it. We've barely begun!"

As he speaks, he seems lit by flashes of lightning. I see shoulders broad like hillsides. I see Minos's nose. Or, to be accurate, I see that Minos had the nose of his father, Zeus, Lord of Creation.

An exhausted guest pleads the lateness of the hour.

"Nonsense!" thunders Zeus. "There are cups unquaffed and maidenheads intact!"

Forced laughter from the guests.

"Hephaestus!" he calls.

The heat of the forge singes my beard as the smith of the gods passes by. Hephaestus is a volcano of a man, bulky, sweating through his tunic. He leans on a cane of dark wood with a handle of gold. His ruined legs make every step a wobbling dance, and he hisses like a bellows from the effort and the pain. Zeus, his own father, once threw him from Olympus.

I risk annihilation. For a moment, I look straight at his hands. They're so big and so worn that the calluses form mountains and valleys. As the crippled god shuffles toward the fire, I find I'm weeping, because everything I've built, everything I've imagined and made real, he has given me.

Zeus slaps a palm against Hephaestus's back, making a thunderclap that stings my ears. A prolonged hiss of the bellows as the smith struggles not to fall.

"What took you so long?" demands Zeus, jovial. A merry father jesting with his son. More forced laughter from the guests. "Give us more night."

The bellows hiss quickly now, and the teeth of gears clatter and rattle at the center of the hall, and then all around us.

At first it looks like Olympus is falling into the sky, and I wrap my arms around a pillar for balance.

Outside, the stars and planets are moving backward.

I want to wake up. I don't want to know what I now know. The stars and planets, the earth and the moon, all follow their own long and twisting paths built by the hands of one god at the whim of another. They swoop and circle and wear intersecting tracks in the sky. Ever in motion, ever in service to those terrible pathways.

I knock over the tray of a server, and golden liquid pours out and drenches a guest. She swears at him, but I'm moving past them toward the stars, which are still spinning backward and seem to be below me, ready for me to fall in.

"You're my just and loving god," says a familiar voice.

I don't fall. I turn to see Ariadne not ten paces away. The years have made her more beautiful. She wears pale purple garments fit for a queen and a diadem fit for a goddess. Her hair is longer, held in place by silver pins shaped like snakes. Her back still has that regal straightness she practiced at Knossos, but she smiles easily, and is talking with her mouth half-full of food. I've never seen her so relaxed, even when we were alone.

"I'll say our goodbyes and we'll go," says her companion, a ruddy, handsome man in a dark purple tunic and a crown of vines. I can look right at him without pain, for

Dionysus, god of wine, was born to a mortal mother, and raised on earth.

"Thank you," says Ariadne. "You're a good husband, and I'm going to devour you once we're home."

She gives him a soft, slow kiss.

They're about to leave. No time to be clever. I take off the cap of shadows. The guests before me jump back.

"Ariadne," I say. "It's me."

She turns and sees me. She studies my face, her mouth working silently.

"Don't touch me," she says.

Dionysus twists my arm behind my back and marches me away from her. He's stronger than anyone I've met. It feels like a hold he's practiced on drunken celebrants.

"Who is this?" he says, calling back to Ariadne.

"Daedalus," I say.

His grip tightens. I groan.

"Don't hurt him," Ariadne says, circling to look at me. Her face is ashen. It's understandable. I am dead. I haven't washed in some time. Anyone would be frightened.

"I didn't mean to scare you," I say. "I need your help."

Her expression doesn't change.

"I can have him torn apart, my love," says Dionysus. "If you change your mind."

A circle of revelers have gathered to watch us as if we're a play. They all look to Ariadne, who has the next line.

"Why do you need my help?" she asks.

"Icarus is lost. And Theseus is gone."

"Gone."

"The Minotaur ate him. Now he's after me."

She mutters an oath. "It's all right," she says to Dionysus. He releases my arm but leaves a firm hand on my shoulder.

Our audience loses interest, and Ariadne leads us away from the heat of the bonfire, to a chilly corner by an ice sculpture of satyrs chasing nymphs. She takes an empty goblet from a server, then hands it to Dionysus, who taps it with his finger and hands it back filled with dark red wine. She takes a long drink. She wipes her mouth.

"Tell me what happened," she says.

I tell her about you, and about my botched attempt to make amends. I tell her what befell Theseus, in as much detail as I can. I try to frame it in technical terms, but her eyes still brim with tears. Even after the way he treated her.

"The lump Asterion pulled out of him. Like flowing gold, yes?"

She's using her half brother's name again. I haven't heard her say that name since she was a young girl.

I nod.

"Ichor," she says. "It flows in the veins of the gods, but everyone has a little, even mortals. Heroes can have a great deal. That's what Asterion likes."

"He shouldn't be after me, then!"

Dionysus pulls me a step back. I mop my brow.

"I'm neither strong nor brave," I say. "You know that as well as anyone."

Ariadne examines me the way she would a pressed flower that got damaged. "Heroism isn't strength or bravery, Daedalus. It's the conviction, in your innermost heart, that the entire story is about you."

"That isn't how I think of myself."

Her voice is cold. "Then I don't suppose you have anything to be afraid of."

A guest in the crowd lets out a nervous giggle. The ice sculpture drips. I am deeply afraid.

"Ariadne, it's been such a long time," I say. "I've loved you and I've missed you since the day you left. I don't know if I've done something to wrong or offend you, but if I have, tell me and I'll make it right."

"Do you not remember?" She sounds more astounded than angry. "The last morning we spoke. In my room. You must remember."

"I asked you to flee with me and Icarus."

"You asked for more than that. I said no in every way a person can say no."

Again I feel that teetering sensation, that feeling of an imminent fall from dizzying heights.

I shake my head. "You forgot how to say 'no' quickly enough when Theseus came along."

"That's enough," says Dionysus.

"We would have cared for you," I say, ignoring him. "Why you wanted to run away with that walking bicep when he abandoned you the first chance he got—"

"I asked him to leave me on Naxos," says Ariadne.

"Listen," says Dionysus, and his voice warms me like a cup of hot wine on a winter's evening, until I relax into his arms. "It's important that you listen."

"You climbed onto my bed that morning," says Ariadne, looking me in the eye. "You grabbed my hand. You said, 'We've waited and waited. What sense is there in waiting any longer?' And you tried to kiss me. I had to push you away and cross the room and wait there until you left."

It sounds familiar, like a story Ariadne once told me about some cad. Not me.

"How long until you tried again? How long until you whispered in Father's ear and forced me into marriage?"

"Shhhhh," says Dionysus, as I thrash weakly.

Ariadne says, "I left Crete because of you."

At first I think the roaring is in my head, until I hear the screams, and see the musicians throwing down their instruments and running. I can't see Asterion clearly through the forest of thrashing limbs. Only a horn-tip here, a gold-spattered claw there. Flashes of white fur and golden eyes between running bodies. He throws a server from his path and roars again, spotting me now. An eager, hungry roar.

Finally, someone is happy to see me.

NO WAY OUT

The last time I saw Ariadne, she ascended to our tower in the middle of the night. Her guards didn't come with her, and ours never stirred. She simply appeared, her features hidden under a hooded cloak, like a goddess in an old story, sent to test the hospitality of mortals.

We'd held a feast earlier that day for the latest Athenian tributes, and from what you told me, she'd taken wine-skins from the kitchens and shared them with the guards. Compliments of Minos, she'd said, and they drank deep.

When she came in, I was sorting goose feathers by lamp-light. The senior chambermaid normally used the feathers for stuffing pillows, and when I wanted to use her surplus, she asked no questions, being fond of you. First I checked each feather to see if it was bent or damaged. Then I sorted the feathers by size and shape. They had to fit onto the harness in an overlapping pattern or the wings wouldn't fly.

I paused in my work.

"I have a question," she said at last.

We hadn't spoken since the conversation in her room. I'd been waking up hours before dawn to construct and test our wings, which left me so tired during the day that I could barely speak to anyone. And Ariadne had said that the less she knew of our escape plans, the better.

That's not the whole truth, though.

I've been telling things a certain way, because I want to remember them that way. But my search is ending soon. Why seek you out, if I can't give you the truth?

I was angry with her for saying no. For not seeing the logic of taking me for a husband no matter how many times I pressed my case. I hated her for crossing the room to get away from me, making me feel foul and lonesome.

"Is there a way to enter the Labyrinth and find your way out again?" she asked.

There was a young prince among the Athenians at the feast, a muscle-bound loudmouth named Theseus. Impossible to ignore, he kept Minos and the rest of the table in an uproar with stories about slaying bandits along the road to Athens. The Labyrinth and the Minotaur awaited, but he didn't appear to mind. He would prove braver, stronger. He was special, like all of them.

Ariadne wasn't immune. Theseus talked of slaughtering Sinis, the strong man who liked to bend two pine trees until their tips touched the earth. He would tie his victims to the bent trunks, then let the pines snap upright again. Theseus overcame Sinis and gave him the same treatment.

Ariadne clapped a hand over her mouth at the grotesquerie
of it. Then she laughed, and there was horror in the laugh
but mirth too. Like he'd shocked awake some bloodlust in
her. She studied his massive arms, his eyes that stayed un-
smiling and alert even as he joked with Minos.

She wasn't asking me about the Labyrinth for her own
sake. If there was a way out, if she could find it, the Minotaur
would lie dead by morning. Theseus and his fellow tributes
would escape back to Athens. And so would Ariadne.

Him, she would leave with.

"He's your brother," I said, still thinking of Asterion.

"We were children. I left him there, yes. I can undo that.
That much, I can do for him."

Poor Asterion. He had one means of escape. The fists of
a brutish prince. Deliverance into Hell, and legend.

"There is one way out," I might have said. There was
a large spool of thread on my workbench. I was using
it to weave the feathers together before sealing them in
place with wax. Handing it to her would have been easy
enough. "Anchor one end of this by the entrance. Unspool
it as you go. Then follow the thread back out."

Only that's not what I said.

Princess or no. Who was she, to leave with him?

I shook my head, careful not to glance at the spool, and
said, "No. There's no way out."

Let her stay here. With her father who would never see
or hear her the way she wished to be seen and heard. Her
sisters married off, her brothers gone abroad to become
corpses or kings. Asterion bellowing through the years,

bellowing for the sister who never came to see him. Let her practice her spells for no one, gazing out her window at a still sea. Unseen. Unsought. More rumor than person. Growing older, slighter, until she fluttered through her darkened rooms like a restless spirit. Like her mother. Let her stay here and rot.

Ariadne nodded once. It was as she thought.

Then she reached past me and grabbed the thread from my workbench.

There was nothing else to say. She kept one eye on me as she went to the stairs. I expected tears from her, or hatred. But she watched me the way a person watches terrain, wary for a rabbit hole or a hidden creek bed that might trip them. Then she descended without a sound.

A moment later you stepped into the light. You had outgrown me by now, and when you spoke your voice sounded like gravel in a shaken jar.

"Ariadne?"

I nodded.

"She all right?"

I shrugged.

"Why did you say that to her?" you asked, looking at the floor.

My cheeks burned. "You should sleep," I said. "We'll need to be ready soon."

As you shuffled off to bed, or to sit up composing poems, or to reflect on the discovery that your father was not a good man, I called to you.

"Goodnight, Icarus. I love you."
You didn't answer.

The blazing sun hid you from me, but still I could hear the thump of your wings, steady and determined as you climbed.

Why did you do it?

What if you saw an entire life ahead of you, strumming a lyre at inns and parties, singing for coins, open sky and open country? Hedges for your bed in the summer, a warm spot by someone's hearth in the winter. A life spent avoiding kings and warriors and too much time indoors. Refusing to be hemmed in by walls. Trapping Minos, and the Minotaur, and your father in rhyme and meter where they couldn't hurt anyone.

What if it wasn't lightness or heartsickness, but simply your leaving me? What if you meant to live? What if you flew so high because you knew I was too cowardly to follow you?

I can't go on wondering. When the Lethe gives you back to me, I'll ask you. It won't be long. Each of us has so much to forgive, so many questions.

What did you see, Icarus, before you died?

Your father below you, growing smaller?

Or did you peer up at the noonday sun shining like daylight through an exit?

MY PLACE
IN THE SONGS

Dionysus steps between us and the Minotaur, pulling an ivy-festooned staff from thin air.

Ariadne turns and pushes through the fleeing guests.

I elbow my way after her.

She must understand that I didn't mean it. I didn't know. And even if I did. Given the things men and gods do all around us. What's my crime, next to theirs?

"Ariadne," I say, and she glances back long enough for a wood nymph to crash into her, spinning her around. I catch her, help her to stay upright. We find an overturned table and crouch behind it, sheltering from the trampling feet of the partygoers.

Behind us, Asterion roars loudly enough to be heard over the screams of the crowd. Dionysus grunts with effort. Zeus is laughing a madman's laugh, calling for his thunderbolts.

"You could have stopped me," I say. "I'm not a satyr. I'm not your father-in-law, forcing myself on young girls. I made a fool of myself for weeks. How was I to know?"

She wipes a trickle of blood from her nose. "You're clever enough to work for kings and gods. You knew."

"Why invite me to your room? Why let me believe you cared for me?"

She shakes her head. "No. I'm not going to do this again."

She climbs to her feet and stands over me.

"I don't think you're a satyr, or a monster," she says. "You're not anything that can't be faced. You were someone I loved, and I miss you."

Ariadne leaves the shelter of the table. She steps back into the crowd.

I rise to go after her, but she's gone. Olympus is gone.

The twin thrones of Hell tower before me. The doors of the throne room hang open and the rooftops of Hell sprawl below.

I can still hear the guests on Olympus screaming, Asterion lowing, faint and far away. I'm not really here. A part of me has been summoned for a royal audience, and there's no ignoring the summons of a god.

"I made a goodwill tour of Tartarus," says Persephone, behind me. "When I first became queen. I spoke with Sisyphus, pushing his boulder. Tantalus, forever trying to reach food and drink. I offered them release. Nothingness, you understand? I thought I'd introduce an element of mercy to this place. Do you know what they said to me?"

I shake my head.

"They preferred torture to nothingness. They could still imagine. They could still rage. I let them be."

A hand the texture of earthworms touches my wrist, moves down my hand, and yanks the cap of shadows from my grasp.

"They were unusually stubborn men," says Persephone. "Not everyone feels the way they felt. Now. What do you suppose is going to happen to you?"

"Icarus is coming back to me. Soon. All I ask is time to speak to him." I try to kneel before her, so that I can grasp her knees in supplication. She steps back with a laugh and I collapse onto the floor. Black beetles scurry over my hands.

"Don't offend me by begging."

"It wouldn't take long."

"You've had all the time you're going to get."

The rooftops of Hell proceed in straight lines and meet at right angles. The streets tangle and turn back on themselves, promising a way through. Alleyways beckon toward other alleyways; archways frame empty squares. I watch the distant lights of the city I've built, until they begin to blur. I wipe my eyes. "You sent Asterion after me."

"Of course I did. I can't leave this place until spring. But I can open a door, and the Minotaur can walk through."

"Will you spare Ariadne?"

"He's only there for you."

"If you do this to me, it will harm you too. You'll become a crueler goddess than you are."

She laughs again, a soft, sad laugh, and I see ravens feasting on a fallen army.

"I had to ask my father-uncle for permission before I could open the way to Olympus." She means Zeus. She wrinkles her nose at the thought of him. "Why, he said. So I could feed you to the Minotaur, I said. Do you know what he said then? 'We'll make a god of you yet.'"

She shrugs. Grass grows over the bodies of the soldiers. "This is who I have to become, Daedalus. Be thankful you can only do so much harm in one lifetime."

"His real name's Asterion," I say. "'Minotaur' is something Minos made up."

"You pick the oddest times to feel sorry for him."

"He's still a little boy. You should treat him kindly."

Persephone sniffs. "*Asterion* is overjoyed with his new hunting ground. They may keep him up there and feed him wayward heroes."

I brush a long white centipede from my clothes. "Is this what I deserve?"

She sighs, and a breeze stirs the dry grass of the battlefield.

"I don't know what 'deserve' means. You're a man who trifled with gods. This is what happens next. No more."

"Let me see my son," I say, but I'm back on Olympus, speaking to an empty hall with a dying bonfire at its center.

From a nearby darkened doorway, Asterion growls.

By starlight, I flee through the empty chambers of Olympus, and Asterion follows. I'm trying to reach the stables, moving as quickly as I dare. I walk through familiar doorways and pass reassuring landmarks. A fresco of centaurs being massacred at a wedding. A row of urns shaped like faces of unbearable beauty, overflowing with flowers.

Then I find a right turn where I remember a left turn, or I come through the final doorway and end up back in the hall with the dying bonfire. The stables are always around the corner. I can hear faint whinnying ahead of me and the *clip clop* of cloven hooves behind me.

Rooms and corridors feel as though people were there moments ago. I find meals half-eaten on tables, scrolls propped open, written upon in languages I don't recognize.

I don't run yet, because I have a terrible suspicion that as soon as I do I'll hear the *clip clop clip clop clip clop* of Asterion breaking into a run behind me. Then hot breath on my neck, claws parting the muscles of my back.

The gods are still here. Ariadne is still here, I'm sure of it. But like the stables, they always seem to be a room away, murmurs of conversation half-heard through a wall. When I press my ear to the walls, I can almost understand what they're saying. Zeus's laugh is thunder beyond the horizon. Ariadne is talking about her ordeal, saying my name as if I'm dead. I suppose I am.

I'm remembering how you toddled around our tower when you were barely a year old. Peeking through doorways, scattering my drawings, picking up a putty knife and parading it from one room to another. Everything you found delighted you.

They won't let me walk out of here.

Whenever Asterion is close, one room behind me, one bend in the corridor away from catching sight of me, he lets out a little sigh of satisfaction, and this too reminds me of you when you were small, pleased at having maneuvered over to my lap and sat down for a story or a bite of dried fruit.

I don't want this ending. I could learn to build again. What do I have but time? I can picture flying machines whizzing around the stalactites of Hell, terraced gardens on the hills of Elysium. I don't know if I deserve to go on, but I want to go on.

And I want to make things right with you. I want to understand why you did it, and answer your questions, the way I used to. Maybe there are words you needed to hear me say when you were alive. Words that let you believe you could be whatever kind of man you decided to be. You still can, Icarus. It's still true. What do you need me to say?

Asterion has been following me for hours, or days, or weeks. The sun doesn't rise. This will last as long as the gods want it to. Panic is a storm brewing in my chest. Soon I won't be able to keep from running.

He'll eat me, like he's eaten so many heroes before me. He'll break my bones and lick my golden ichor from his hands. And I'll have my place in the songs, oh yes. Centuries hence they'll sing of the ingenuity of Daedalus. As they sing of wise Odysseus, who hanged his house slaves, and brave Achilles, who dragged Hector's corpse through the dust before his mother and father, and dauntless Jason, who spurned his wife and doomed his children. As they sing of gallant Theseus and just Minos.

I pass into the great hall again, and this time I walk out between two columns and sit down on the building's edge, with the night above me and the curve of the earth far below my dangling feet, and there, small under the stars, I wait for Asterion to find me.

I did it. I hurt Ariadne in the way she said I hurt her. When she rejected me, I lied to her and tried to trap her on Crete. I didn't do it to survive. I did it because I wanted to and because I could.

Ariadne, I did it and I'm sorry. I say the words aloud.

Dead of Athens, dead of Crete.

Naucrate, Asterion.

Forgive me.

Icarus, my heart, my only one. I failed you worst of all. There are things I'd pay any price to share with you, things I'd pay any price to understand. I'm sorry. I love you, my brave boy.

From the entryway behind me, at the near end of the hall, I hear Asterion's little sigh of satisfaction.

I'll feel his teeth first, I think, sinking into my shoulder. Then his claws, lifting me over his head and opening me in the starlight. I'll feel a faint breeze on my face, a cold wind from between the stars that I have never felt before.

He'll peel layers of self aside to find a thing like molten gold at the heart of me. His golden eyes will look into mine in that final moment, as if to say, *You poor brute. You've been lost in here for so long.*

But wait.

I startle, feeling a gust, turning my head toward motion.

A stir of wings at the far end of the hall, a glimpse of white vanishing between columns.

Icarus?

Has the river brought you back to me?

Courage strengthens my limbs. I jump to my feet.

Persephone whispers in my ear.

"Mercy. A chance. You can still catch him. You're the hero, after all."

The gods are raising cups to me, eyes flashing, great calloused hands pounding tabletops, chanting my name. "Run," they cry. "You can make it!"

Minos watches, feasting and drinking with his uncle the god of Hell, wagering on how far I'll get.

Don't go, my love. I'm only a turn or two behind you. I have so much to tell you.

A gleeful snort behind me, his *clip clop clip clop* gathering speed, but I'm faster than him, the thought of you gives me wings, shows me the path, a waterlogged feather here, a puddle of brine here, and in a moment I'll see you, touch your shoulder, hug you to me, I'll tell you what's in my heart, my brave boy, I'll finally know why you did it.

I love you. I forgive you. I'm almost there.

ACKNOWLEDGMENTS

Here's how great an agent Cameron McClure is: She didn't overpromise, she told me straight that it might be tough to sell a debut novella, and then she went out and sold it. Eli Goldman at Tor bought the book and suggested a diabolically gorgeous shape for it. Matt Rusin at Tor made the home stretch of the editorial process as fun and exciting as I dared hope. David Seidman painted a Labyrinth scarier and more beguiling than the one in my head; gods help us if he ever decides to build a real one. Russell Trakhtenberg's design gave the cover depth you could get lost in. Sam Friedlander and Cassidy Sattler patiently answered questions about my first book tour. Mary Louise Mooney and Jeff LaSala saved me from a deeply embarrassing *Aeneid* typo.

Ian Fahey and Aviva Pressman helped me out as beta readers, Emma Benintende gave me real-life architecture pointers, Emily Plumb shared ideas that became two of my favorite chapters, and Josh Sippie helped me get the book in front of folks at every stage of its development. Robert Repino helped me write and sell my first story, and has shared writing advice and encouragement ever since. Reid, Ola, and Danielle at PGWG were the best writing group, and friend group, anyone could ask for.

Madhuri Shekar and the kiddos continue to enlarge my life, and the scale of the ideas and emotions I want to write about, in ways I never dreamed possible. I love you all so much. I could not have written this book without you; thanks for letting me hide from you sometimes to go work on it. Our nanny, Maltie Singh, took care of all of us and gave me time to write.

Chris Hamsher, my eighth-grade English teacher, was the first person to teach me Homer, and he also performed the entirety of "The Tell-Tale Heart" for us by candlelight one Halloween without a word of preamble or explanation, which is a big part of why I write fiction now. He passed away far too soon; check out his novel *Alan's First Labor* (which also draws on Greek mythology) for a sense of the kindness and generosity he showed me and all his students.

My beloved parents, James and Eden Sullivan, teachers themselves, kept me safe, read to me, took me to the library, and have always given me their unflinching love and support even in the face of foolhardy decisions like becoming a writer. My sister Deirdre, often the more creative sibling and usually more willing than me to demand a better world, challenges and inspires me constantly. This book is for you three, with my thanks.

ABOUT THE AUTHOR

Lisa Damico Portraits

Seamus Sullivan grew up in the Philadelphia area, went to college in Washington, DC and lives in Jersey City with his family. His fiction has appeared in *Terraform* and his book reviews have appeared in *Strange Horizons*. He writes about parenthood, mythology, superheroes, Americana, memory, loneliness and mortality. *Daedalus Is Dead* is his first book.